BRITTANY ELISE

The Calling of the Trinity

Black Rose Writing | Texas

First printing

This is a work of fiction. Names, characters, businesses, places, events, and
incidents are either the products of the author's imagination or used in a
fictitious manner. Any resemblance to actual persons, living or dead, or
actual events is purely coincidental.

ISBN: 978-1-68433-532-9
PUBLISHED BY BLACK ROSE WRITING
www.blackrosewriting.com

Printed in the United States of America
Suggested Retail Price (SRP) $19.95

The Calling of the Trinity is printed in Plantagenet Cherokee

*As a planet-friendly publisher, Black Rose Writing does its best to eliminate
unnecessary waste to reduce paper usage and energy costs, while never
compromising the reading experience. As a result, the final word count vs. page count
may not meet common expectations.

Acknowledgements

For my sister, Ashley – thank you for being my voice of reason and for having the grace to tolerate the thousands of questions I tormented you with. You have encouraged me more than you know, and for that I am grateful.

And for Cristy – thank you for your insight and kindness. You challenged me to see things from a different perspective and supported me along the way. I'm so lucky to have the two of you in my corner. This book wouldn't have been possible without your help.

The Calling of
the Trinity

Chapter One
A Long Time Traveler

"He wouldn't have wanted this," Wren said, jaw clenching as he gazed at the rectangular hole carved into the earth below our feet. Niall's casket sat beneath a towering oak tree; the golden sunlight filtering through what was left of the autumn canopy and glinting off the casket's gloss-black finish. Rows of empty aluminum chairs were placed neatly in the grass behind us, soon to be occupied by the entire community of Silver Mountain.

"I know he wouldn't, but what choice did we have?" I spoke softly, squeezing Wren's hand. My dad, Emmett Callaghan, was standing in front of the little white church speaking with the pastor. He was dressed in the only suit he had–same shoes and tie he'd worn to my mother's funeral; my tear stains still visible against the deep shade of blue.

Somewhere nearby, a car door was shutting. The muted sound of footsteps shuffling through the grass followed, and then Blaire was sliding her arm across the middle of my back. She didn't say anything. She didn't have to. We were all thinking the same thing–all lost in the same silence as we gazed at Niall's casket.

Niall was dead because of us–because of what we were. If it hadn't been for the Trinity's awakening, then maybe he would still be here.

My stomach lurched at the memory that was forever seared into the darkest corners of my mind. Every time I closed my eyes, I saw the flash of the silver blade in the moonlight, the arc coming down to split Niall's throat in an ugly red smile.

I glanced up as a shadow passed over the casket and spotted my father. He cleared his throat, fiddling with the buttons on his sleeve cuff. "Uh, Wren, Pastor Ellington wants to know if you'd like to do a receiving line before or after the service."

Wren's whole body tensed. He glanced down at me, eyebrows contorting over his tawny colored eyes.

I thought I knew heartbreak, but the way he was looking at me caused my chest to tighten and ache in a way that I didn't know I could hurt. I felt so helpless because there was nothing I could do to take his pain away. "After would probably be best," I suggested.

Wren nodded once and glanced up as the sound of another car door shutting caught his attention. "Okay," Dad said, "I'll let the pastor know."

"Thank you." I gently tugged on Wren's hand. "Let's go sit down before everyone starts filing in." Blaire followed, lowering herself into the chair next to mine while melancholy music began to play from inside the church.

Annabelle and her family arrived next. They slid into the row behind us, and I turned to offer a small smile to my best friend while her father gave Wren's shoulder a brief squeeze. The town's very own gossip queen arrived soon after in her old Lincoln Towne Coupe, hubcaps scraping the curb as she rolled to a stop.

Margaret Lynn was the reason we'd been forced to have a public service to begin with. Over the years, Margaret Lynn had developed a bit of a reputation for sticking her narrow nose where it didn't belong. She lived in one of the oldest houses in town, wedged between the Village Salon and the Baptist church–supposed prime real-estate for rumor and scandal. After Niall's death had been released to the public, the media crew had chosen to interview Margaret on live television.

"*Bit of a hermit if you ask me,*" Margaret Lynn had told them. "*He was a nice enough man, but he'd been holed up in that cabin ever since his brother was killed back in the early nineties. Folks said it was a hunting accident that got him, but nothing like that has happened in Silver Mountain since.*" On screen, Margaret twisted a flower embroidered handkerchief in her meaty hands. She looked over her shoulder, almost as if she feared being overheard, (hello contradiction) and lowered her voice as she leaned into the camera. "*Some local folk believe the Whelan family is cursed, but that's just silly superstition.*"

"*Could you elaborate on that Miss Rhodes?*" the reporter asked, and the cameraman zoomed in on Margaret's papery complexion.

"*It ain't very proper to speak of the dead,*" Margaret Lynn said. Her pale eyebrows furrowed, adding another wrinkle to her already wrinkled forehead. "*But some folk around here think it might not be so coincidental that the only murders to happen in Silver Mountain have been in the Whelan family.*"

I'd turned the television off after that. The only thing Margaret Lynn had succeeded in doing with that interview was causing the townspeople to be even more suspicious of Niall's death than we needed. Niall wouldn't have wanted such a public service–Wren was right about that, but we were hoping this would prove we didn't have anything to hide.

When word of Niall's murder hit the front page of our local paper and blasted every television screen, the whole town came together in an adhesive ball of anxiety and fear. As much as I hated to admit, Margaret Lynn was right. The townspeople were right to be scared. Silver Mountain didn't have criminals–*period.* They wanted answers and justice, but they could never learn the truth about what happened on that horrific day...

I swallowed over a lump that was lodged in the back of my throat and focused on the weight of Wren's hand. It was like a solid block of granite, moored beneath my fingertips. Though I could feel the warmth of taut tendons against my palm, I had to keep stealing glances up at his face to make sure he was still breathing. He sat like a statue, eyes fixed on the casket. I slipped my index finger to the inside of his wrist, letting it rest on the artery. Seconds passed before his pulse leapt against my fingertip, and I closed my eyes in brief solace. It was strange to me, how a single heartbeat could make all the nerve endings in my hand spring full of life and strength in the midst of such darkness.

Pastor Ellington was reading a passage from the bible, closing out the service. When he finished, he welcomed people to pay their final respects while the men from the cemetery lowered Niall's coffin into the ground. The townsfolk lined up to shake Wren's hand and offer their condolences. I stood beside him, just a slight step behind, and watched the sorrow and sympathy coloring the expressions of our community members' faces. Wren's beautiful face was a mask of forced appreciation. I could see the pain behind his eyes and watched it pull the corners of his mouth into an unnatural tight line. I squeezed his hand with mine, hoping it would convey the reassurance he needed.

Blaire was staring at me; her unblinking dark eyes fixed on mine. I didn't have to guess what she was thinking. I clenched my jaw, shaking my head stiffly to let her know that now was not a good time for her to use her gift. As an empath, Blaire has the ability to read auras and influence moods and emotions by a simple touch. It's a handy little gift, but Wren wasn't the kind of person that liked synthetic anything. Werewolves are highly emotional beings–fueled by things that don't necessarily influence a human. It's better to just let them go through the motions.

Wren's hand tightened around my fingers; his body turning as rigid as a steel beam. The joints in my knuckles began to crack as his grip constricted. "Wren," I breathed, "you're hurting me." He let go of my hand in an instant, his features shifting in remorse when he realized what he'd done. A second passed before his gaze cut to the back row of the cemetery, right around the same time the back of my neck started tingling... I turned my head to see a woman standing beside an oak tree. Chestnut hair framed the razor-sharp bones of her face and fell below her shoulders in sleek waves. The elegant way in which she composed herself was no match for the keen look in her predatory dark gaze.

"Werewolf," Blaire breathed the warning against my ear, flashing her glowing moonstone ring in my peripheral.

"Wren's mother." I knew her by gut instinct. I'd heard that Gabriella had the sort of presence that filled a room. I saw Wren in her features–the sculpted facial structure, the full lips, long lashes and amber eyes.

"I take it that's not a good thing?" Blaire assessed, glancing back and forth between our faces.

I opened my mouth to speak but quickly clamped it shut, frowning when my father entered the scene. Gabriella smiled like the Cheshire cat and welcomed my dad's embrace.

I cringed. "Why is she here?"

"I don't know," Wren answered through a tight jaw.

"Who's the chick your dad's talking to?" Annabelle asked me. She'd popped in front of us, pointing a thumb over her shoulder. "She's a total hottie."

"Wren's mother," Blaire answered this time, crossing her arms over her chest.

Anabelle's eyebrows lifted to her hairline, dark eyes expanding. "*Oh.*"

Mr. and Mrs. Carter were walking up to us now, their mouths drawn into downcast lines. Mrs. Carter placed her small palm on Wren's shoulder. "Let us know if you need anything, you know where to find us."

"I appreciate you coming, thank you," Wren said.

"Sorry for your loss." Mr. Carter shook Wren's hand. "Annabelle, you ready to go?"

"I think I'm going to stick around for a little while," she said to her parents, "I'll be home before dark."

Worry clouded Akari's features as she said, "Have someone drive you home please, and be home by five."

We'd gone from a town where nothing exciting ever happened, to a town put on lockdown over night. Annabelle's parents had given her a strict curfew. She had to be home right after cross-country practice ended and wasn't allowed out of the house after dark during the weeknights. Even my dad had tightened up my rules a bit–requesting that I not walk through town alone and was constantly asking about my plans and making sure that someone was going to accompany me if I was. I needed to tell him the truth about what I–about what *we*–were, but I was scared to involve him any more than necessary.

My dad would never admit it out loud, but he was afraid of what I could do… not afraid *of* me, per se, but afraid *for* me. When we'd lost my mother years ago to cancer, her death drove him to the brink of a great depression. It was because of that fact alone that I wanted to protect my dad from any further pain. If he knew about the Trinity, I was afraid he would try to get involved and I wasn't willing to risk losing him, too.

Wren was watching our parents with a fixed gaze. Gabriella seemed impervious to the fact that we were all staring at her. After a minute I decided to look around, checking to see if anyone else I didn't know was lurking in the midst of the crowd.

"She's alone," Wren said, confirming my silent suspicions. "She wouldn't risk bringing the others."

"Do you want to leave?" I asked him.

"Well I for one want to see what this wagon's about," Blaire said, Irish accent thicker than usual. She reached up, sweeping the curtain of raven-black hair back from her face. The wind and sunlight were playing within the strands, revealing hidden shades of twinkling ruby.

"Translation?" Annabelle raised her eyebrows.

"It's an insult," Blaire said. "You don't want to be called a wagon, trust me. And don't you be sayin' it to no one, either."

Wren smirked, crossing his arms over his chest. My dad turned and pointed in our general direction, but it was me that Gabriella's predatory gaze swept over. Her red lips pursed together, jaw muscle flexing. My dad started walking in our direction and Gabriella followed.

"Look who I found." My dad needlessly gestured to Gabriella.

She'd stopped about two feet in front of us, and her mouth twitched into something that resembled a half smile. "Son," she spoke in a soft tone as if to test the waters.

Wren said nothing. He just met her eyes with a hard glare.

"So this is the infamous womb donor we've all heard so much about," Annabelle said flatly, looking the woman up and down.

Blaire choked on an involuntary giggle, and my Dad's face went ashen with horror at Annabelle's outburst. Gabriella, however, seemed entirely unfazed. In fact, the corner of her mouth rose upward in amusement.

My dad's gaze shifted to me, and I pursed my lips in a tight line. "We're going back to the cabin," I uttered. "Catch up with you later?"

"Uh, sure, kiddo. Just give me a call if I need to come and pick anyone up." He looked at Annabelle and then turned his attention back to Gabriella. "Are you in town for a while?"

"A couple of days at most," she replied. "I'm staying with some friends outside of town."

"Let me take you to Josephine's for some lunch."

"Thank you, I'd like that. It would be nice to catch up with an old friend." She smiled and added emphasis on the word *friend* like it meant something more than that. I all but rolled my eyes, looping my arm through the crook of Wren's elbow, and led the way out of the cemetery. The further we walked away from Gabriella, the easier the air was to breathe.

Chapter Two
The Harbinger

Niall's cabin sat atop the mountain, tucked within a quaint meadow that was surrounded by a grove of towering pines. A wisp of smoke rose from the chimney, coiling through the atmosphere before joining the clouds. Inside, I shrugged out of my jacket, draping it over the back of a kitchen chair as my lungs filled with the scent of sweet grass and sage. Niall may have been gone, but so much of his spirit still remained, nestled in the shell of his home. A dull ache throbbed behind my breastbone, and I reached up to massage the hurt with the heel of my hand.

Blaire helped herself to the fridge, shuffling through its scarce contents until she came up with a few beer bottles that were tucked in the back. "Anyone care for a drink?"

"I think I'll pass," Annabelle commented. "My parents will smell it on me and I'll be grounded until I'm thirty."

"Suit yourself." Blaire twisted the cap off and took a long pull from the bottle before setting in on the table. A beat later her phone buzzed and she fished the mechanical device from her pocket, studying the message. "It's from my sister. Her flight arrives tomorrow night."

I nodded. Bryna, Blaire's sister, was in the process of making her way to the States from Ireland, and she was traveling with singularly dangerous cargo.

When Rionach the Dark was vanquished in the Battle of the Dark Ages, she left behind her talisman. Nothing on earth could destroy such magic, so the White Witch placed the powerful trinket under the protection of the Aurora Coven. It's said that the amulet possesses the power to return the Dark Witch to her physical form.

There were Dark forces at work trying to achieve just that, and it was up to the Trinity to stop it from happening. We were recently led to believe that Blaire's aunt was a part of that force, and though neither of us wanted to think she was capable of convening with the Darkness, we thought it best to get the talisman on the move.

"Has anyone from the Coven seen Penny?" I asked.

Blaire shook her head. "No, not yet, but that doesn't mean she isn't there."

"Do you really think she would have fled to Ireland?" Annabelle asked.

"If she truly is trying to get her hands on the talisman, that would be the only logical move," Blaire answered. "She's tapped out her resources here. Perhaps she hoped to intercept Bryna, or perhaps she's gone into hiding. There's no way of knowing for certain what her intentions are." Blaire's voice cracked as she scratched at the label on her beer bottle. Tiny beads of paper were collecting on the counter beside her trembling hand.

"Blaire," I spoke softly, "we can't be sure that those rogue werewolves were telling the truth about her. There's still a chance Penny could be innocent."

Blaire openly scoffed. "I appreciate you trying to make me feel better, but all evidence points to the contrary, I'm afraid. If she were innocent, she wouldn't have run."

"I just don't understand what would make her do it," Annabelle commented. "You have to be mentally warped if you want to bring the ultimate mistress of evil back to the land of the living."

No one had a reply for that.

I mashed my lips in a tight line. The night we had invoked the Trinity bond, we learned that the Dark Witch's spirit could only be summoned by her own bloodline. A werewolf by the name of Garrett informed us that Penny—and therefore Blaire—just happened to share Rionach's DNA, which is how Penny's role supposedly came into play. Someone or *something* knew how to find her and coerced her into the shadows. We just didn't know why.

My head was beginning to pound from the tangled web of information we still couldn't piece together. I dragged my hand across my face, pulling at my eyelid as if that alone could tear away the weariness from all the sleepless nights my mind refused to shut out the chaos.

"So," Annabelle cleared her throat, fingers drumming against the counter, "what exactly are you planning to do with the amulet once you have it?"

No one spoke right away. Annabelle had asked the golden question, and between fighting the werewolves in the Hollow, fabricating the scene of Niall's death and planning his funeral, we hadn't had much time to formulate a solid plan.

"We'll think of something," Blaire said. She picked up her beer bottle, and took another long pull as a knock at the door drew our attention. "Expecting company?"

Wren shook his head, nostrils flaring as he scented the air. "I hope you're hungry."

I frowned as he walked to the door and opened it. Torrance was standing on the porch with a forlorn-looking Huck and a disheveled-looking Jamie behind her. She stepped through the doorway and crashed into Wren's frame with an impressive bear-hug. "I'm so sorry about your dad, Wren." Her voice was muffled against his shirt. "We weren't sure if you wanted any company, but I know I wouldn't want to be alone on a day like today."

"Thanks, Tor." Wren patted her back and shared a look of surprise with Huck.

"Okay, Tor, let the man breathe." Huck pried Torrance away from Wren with one hand while he stepped into the kitchen with a large box of pizza in his other.

"Sorry for your loss, man," Jamie said, following the others inside. "We come bearing gifts." He opened his jacket and pulled out a bottle of whiskey.

I fought the urge to roll my eyes as I closed the door behind them.

"Hey, I saw that look," Jamie said, pointing an accusing finger at me when I turned back around.

"What look?"

"The *I'm-disappointed-in-Jamie-for-bringing-alcohol* look," he clarified.

"Oh, right," I said, "that look."

Jamie narrowed his eyes. "I just thought it would be a nice gesture, you know, to numb the senses or whathaveyou."

"I'll drink to that," Blaire said, snatching the bottle out of his hands. "The legal drinking age in Ireland is eighteen so technically, I'm not breaking any laws."

Annabelle snorted. "Pretty sure it doesn't work that way but we'll go with it." She opened the pizza box and inhaled the scent of melted cheese until her eyes rolled back with delight. "Wren," she turned to him, "where are your plates?"

A few moments later, the seven of us were nestled in the living room, crowded around the coffee table with the box of half-eaten pizza and the drinks that Torrance had managed to whip up in the kitchen. I didn't ask what was in the concoction, but the amber liquid burned going down and warmed the pit of my stomach in drowsy contentment. Perhaps 'numbing the senses' could be forgiven after everything we'd gone through.

"What's that on the mantel there?" Torrance pointed to a blue porcelain jar above the fireplace as Wren added a log to the fire.

He glanced up, hand brushing bits of bark from his pant leg. "My grandma," he replied with a glib tone. A hint of a smirk tugged at the outer corner of his mouth.

"Oh god, Wren, I didn't mean–" She flattened her palm to the side of her cheek that was now turning a bright shade of pink.

"Way to go, Tor." Huck laughed as he picked up his drink.

"Well, I didn't know! It's just very… pretty," she said, eyebrows contorting. "I thought it was a decoration."

"It's okay Torrance." Wren was smiling. "I never met her."

"Still…"

"Well, I think I need another drink," Blaire announced. "Refill anyone?"

"I'll take a refill," Jamie slurred.

"Looks to me as you're langered enough," Blaire told him.

"And what is that supposed to mean?"

"It means she thinks you've had too much to drink," Huck said. "Right?"

"Precisely."

"Have not. You want to hear the alphabet backwards?" Jamie volunteered. "Z, Y, X, W–"

"–Please, spare us the torture," Annabelle interrupted, holding up a hand. "We all know you won't make it past 'W' anyway."

"Hey, I take offence to that."

Beside me, Wren stiffened. He turned his head a fraction, listening to something the rest of us couldn't hear. A moment passed before there was a knock on the front door, and Wren was on his feet before anyone could blink.

"What's that about?" Torrance asked.

Blaire and I exchanged a look before I pushed myself upright. "I'm just going to go check on him, I'll be right back."

I found him in the kitchen with his hand on the doorknob. "Cops," he mouthed, nodding toward the opened bottles of alcohol on the kitchen counter. Adrenaline snapped through my veins, chasing lingering toxins from my bloodstream, and sobered me.

I opened the closest cupboard and stashed the evidence inside. The last thing anyone needed was to be busted for underage drinking. I hung back a few steps, just enough so that I could still see and hear what was going on when Wren opened the door.

"Sorry to bother you son. Could I come in for a minute?" Officer Stevenson asked. Silver Mountain had a small force, and Officer Stevenson had been the cop on duty when Wren and I went to the station to report Niall missing. His name was Carl, and his father, Martin, was the sheriff. Carl wasn't much older than us, and his loose use of the word 'son' didn't sit well in my gut.

"It's not a good time. I have company," Wren answered flatly.

"This won't take long. I just have a few questions about your father." Officer Stevenson took a step closer, reaching up to put his large, meaty palm on the door. Wren squared his shoulders and gripped the handle to barricade the entrance. I could see the skin stretching across the back of his hand–tendons popping.

"I already told you everything I know," Wren said.

"I'm just trying to cover all my bases." Officer Stevenson smiled, revealing his perfectly straight white teeth. This might have come off friendly if I hadn't been able to detect the testosterone fueled charge pulsing behind his dark eyes. The two stood at equal height, but where Wren was lean-muscled, Stevenson was bulky.

Wren didn't budge.

"You see," Officer Stevenson continued. He pulled his sunglasses from the top of his head and wiped the lenses on a white cloth he'd pulled from his pocket, cleaning invisible blemishes. "Your father didn't exactly have a clean record. I've been doing some digging, and I happened to stumble upon an old court case of his from the nineties... Does the name Clyde Sheridan mean anything to you, son?"

A bolt of panic shot through my chest and the little vein in the side of my neck began to throb in time with the beat of my heart.

"Sorry," Wren said, "but what does that name have to do with my father's murder case?"

Officer Stevenson's mouth twisted into a smirk. "Well, it could mean nothing, or… it could mean everything."

"I don't really have time for games, Officer," Wren snapped. "If you're trying to imply that my father had something to do with the case involving my uncle, you should double-check your records. My father was found innocent."

Officer Stevenson nodded slowly before he spoke. "Even so, when a man is on trial for a murder case and is murdered several years later–innocent or not, it's worth looking into. I just want to know if Niall had any enemies… perhaps someone was looking to settle an old score."

"What are you suggesting?" Wren's low tone grated on my nerves, prickling the tiny hairs on the back of my neck. Officer Stevenson stepped back; a natural human reaction when a more dangerous predator lunges in their path. He didn't have to know what Wren was to sense the hidden threat. He recovered in an instant, puffing out his chest before leaning closer to Wren in the doorway.

"I don't think Niall killed your uncle," Officer Stevenson paused, "but I do think he's responsible for killing the man that did."

My breath caught.

Remy had been shot by a hunter–Clyde Sheridan–when Remy was in wolf form. But when a werewolf dies, he returns to his human skin. Clyde saw Remy Change back, and pack law demanded that Niall cover up their tracks in order to keep the pack's secret safe. Niall had killed Sheridan in cold blood, fabricating the scene to make it look like Clyde had taken his own life.

Waves of nausea rolled through my stomach, but I swallowed hard, forcing myself to hold composure. There was a line, I reminded myself; a line between doing the right thing and the wrong thing when it came to protecting those you love. Niall had crossed that line. But as I stood there–staring at Officer Stevenson–I knew that I would have done the same thing to protect my own family. A hero wouldn't. A hero would see the moral line between good and evil and choose to give up something they loved for the greater good. But I was selfish. All of those gray areas blurred around me, smudging that line even more.

"That's an interesting theory Officer, but you'll need hard evidence to back it up," Wren spoke in an even tone.

Officer Stevenson snickered. "Well that may be, but like I said, I'm just trying to cover all my bases. Perhaps someone close to Sheridan found out the truth and decided to take matters of revenge into their own hands…"

Wren's right arm was braced on the back of the door, and I watched as the muscles and tendons bunched tightly beneath his skin. I stepped up to the door, sliding my hand across Wren's lower back in an attempt to calm him. He was so close to the Change. His muscle and skin felt as solid as steel beneath my palm. "Officer," I said, sliding beneath Wren's arm in the doorway, "we just put Niall's body in the ground; please give us the respect of this one day."

Officer Stevenson's eyes fixed on Wren's before slowly moving his gaze to mine. He tipped his head in false courtesy. "Miss," he said, slowly backing away from the door. When he reached his cruiser, he called over his shoulder, "Oh, and if you can think of anyone who might have a grudge against Niall… just give me a call."

Wren waited until the cruiser had pulled out of the drive before closing the kitchen door. He dropped his hand, rolling it into a tight fist at his side.

"Are you okay?" I wrapped my hand around his wrist and squeezed.

Wren nodded as he closed his eyes, making a concentrated effort to keep the Change from taking over. Blaire stepped into the doorway, mouth pressed in a thin line. "Maybe we should call it a night, yeah?"

"I think that's probably a good idea," I said.

"I'll go round up the others."

Annabelle poked her head into the kitchen as Blaire departed. "Everything okay in here?" she asked. "We heard voices."

"The cops came by," I told her. "I think we're going to call it a night."

Sensing the tension still hanging in the air, Annabelle chewed her lip in concern, but she chose not to ask any questions. "Yeah, it's almost five. My parents will have my head if I don't get home before the sun sets."

"Sorry about all of this, Cat," Wren said to her.

"Don't apologize. This isn't your fault."

He made a small sound, like the start of a laugh that fell short, catching in the back of his throat. None of this would be happening if it weren't for our direct lineage. Granted, we didn't cause the Dark Witch's spirit to return, but our powers had been awakened because of her very existence. This was still our town, and while we remained, our community was at risk and that *was* our fault.

The others filed into the kitchen. "I guess the party is over, huh?" Torrance asked, sweeping her long, wavy blonde hair back from her shoulder.

"Yeah, I think we're all just a little tired," I said, pressing my lips together. "Thanks for coming over though."

"Let us know if you need anything." She wrapped her arms around my shoulders and then gave Wren a hug. "We'll see you guys on Monday."

We said our goodbyes and watched from the window as our friends rolled out of the drive. I turned to Wren, wishing that I'd had the ability to read minds. He'd always been quiet, but the last couple of weeks were starting to take a toll. He wasn't shutting me out, but I could tell he was shielding me from his grief.

"I suppose I ought to ask for the sake of formality," Blaire's voice punctured the silence, "is it all right if my sister stays here with me until we figure out what we're going to do about the amulet?"

"Of course," Wren said.

Blaire had moved out of Penny's house just to be on the safe side. Wren had offered her Niall's bedroom, and she'd made herself at home. I'd be lying if I said I was entirely comfortable with the fact that another female was staying under the same roof as my boyfriend–and a gorgeous female at that. Blaire was of similar height and build as me with a slender, heart-shaped face. I trusted her, in spite of my own insecurities, and tried to take comfort in the notion that Wren and I were bound to one another by something ancient that stretched beyond basic attraction.

"We won't be of much trouble, I promise," Blaire assured him.

"I'm not worried about it." He cupped the back of his neck and rolled his shoulders. The muscles in his neck began to ripple, the tendons protruding just under his skin. He was hurting, I realized. He needed the Change.

"You should go," I told him.

He shook his head, fighting against the ache. "I'll be all right. Just give me a minute."

"Go," I repeated, reaching for his shoulder. "I'll see you tonight."

He covered my hand with his before sliding out the door. Blaire pressed her lips together, giving me a sympathetic look. "He's going to be all right," she told me.

"I know," I replied, but the statement sounded more like I was trying to convince myself.

Chapter Three
Calling on Stars

"You're home kind of early. Where's Wren?" Dad asked as I came through the front door. I shrugged out of my coat and draped it over the handmade wooden rack in the corner of the room. Dad was holding a large red bowl, stirring its unknown contents with a wooden spoon rather vigorously.

"Officer Stevenson stopped by and brought up the touchy subject of Remy's murder case; it pressed a few of Wren's buttons so he just needed a little alone time to process," I answered. "What do you have there?"

"Oh, this?" Dad tipped the bowl so I could see the golden colored batter. "Pancake mix. I thought it seemed like a breakfast-for-dinner kind of day."

"You'll hear no complaints from me."

"So what did Stevenson have to say?"

"Well," I said, sucking in a breath. "He thinks Niall might be responsible for killing Clyde Sheridan."

Dad stopped stirring. He sat the bowl on the counter and turned to face me. "And what would make him think that? Sheridan's death was ruled a suicide."

"I don't know exactly... He's under the impression that Niall killed Sheridan to get revenge for Remy's death, and that someone close to

Sheridan found out and all these years later came back to retaliate." The worst part was that his suspicions weren't so far from the truth.

"That's ludicrous," Dad decided at once. "Stevenson doesn't have any business digging up old skeletons on the day Wren had to bury his father. Can you believe the nerve of that guy? I'll have to talk with Martin about this. I've never liked his boy. There's something off about his character." Dad pointed the dripping spoon in my direction for emphasis.

I cracked a half smile. "He's twenty-four, Dad. Not really a boy."

"Well he acts like one, regardless. They must not have any real leads if they're starting to look twenty-some years in the past for suspects." Dad frowned into the pancake batter. "Probably all thanks to Margaret Lynn and her big mouth for talking about the case on public television."

He was so obviously worked up about this. It was easy to see how much he cared for Wren, which only made the lie so much harder. I could tell him the truth, I thought. At least, *part* of the truth... He didn't have to know about the Trinity, but I could tell him that Wren was a werewolf and explain that Niall had been murdered by another werewolf... Of course, he'd want to know why, and again, all roads led back to the Trinity and the Dark Witch.

"You okay there, kiddo?" Dad was watching me.

"Hmm? Oh, yeah, I'm fine. Just exhausted, I guess."

"It's been a rough week," Dad agreed. He adjusted the temperature on the stove and poured the first helping of batter into the frying pan.

While he worked, I took down a couple of plates from the cupboard and two drinking glasses and placed them on the counter. "So," I paused, "how was your lunch with Gabriella?" I'd almost forgotten all about her uncanny appearance at Niall's funeral.

Dad stiffened. "It was nice." He didn't elaborate, so I let the silence hold steady for a moment. I wanted him to ask why we had all been so cold toward her. I would've come out and said it straight, but gossiping had never been my style. The silence lasted longer than I liked. "Annabelle was a little harsh, don't ya' think?"

And there it was. "No," I answered, "I don't."

Dad shot me a pointed look. "Okay then, what don't I know?" He scooped out the pancakes and loaded them onto our plates. I followed him to the kitchen table with the butter and syrup.

"Have you ever noticed the scar on the back of Wren's right hand?" I asked. It was kind of hard not to. It stretched from the knuckle of his smallest finger, curving to the knuckle of his thumb in the shape of a jagged crescent moon.

"Yeah." He severed a pancake with his fork, sloshing it through a puddle of syrup and shoveled it into his mouth.

"Gabriella did that to him. She stabbed him with a serrated kitchen knife because he was trying to defend her from the monster of a man she's married to. She pinned his hand to the table, Dad, and then she kicked him out. That's why he moved back here to live with Niall."

Dad met my eyes briefly before looking away. "She admitted that she'd been in a bad place mentally," Dad said a moment later. "She told me that she'd done some shameful things in the recent past, and didn't expect that Wren would ever forgive her... I didn't ask what those things were, seeing as how it wasn't my place. I'd just never imagined it would be something like that."

That's because she's an evil werewolf bitch, I thought. "Did she say what she was doing here–other than sticking her nose where it doesn't belong?"

"She wanted to pay her respects and be there for Wren." Dad shrugged. "She's visiting with some friends for a couple of days before heading back to Washington. She wanted me to tell Wren, in case he changed his mind and wanted to see her. I'm guessing he won't."

"I wouldn't count on it," I paused. "It just sucks the only family that really ever cared about him is buried now."

"He still has us," Dad said. "He's a good kid."

"Not really a kid anymore." I grinned.

"Eighteen may be the legal age for an adult, but you're still young, and you still have a lot to learn about the world." Dad winked and took his plate to the kitchen sink. I wondered if he'd feel differently if he knew about the very real and very evil Darkness we'd been fighting against. I chewed the inside of my cheek, deciding to let him linger in denial a while longer. It was safer that way.

The gray light of day faded into an onyx canvas and a smattering of silver stars broke through. I busied myself around the house, cleaning the kitchen and putting the dishes away. Dad had retired to the living room, watching whatever college sports teams were playing Saturday night football. I showered, spending more time than necessary standing beneath the hot water and letting it soothe the tension from my aching muscles. After, I checked my phone for messages but the only person who'd sent me a text had been Annabelle. I replied and stared at the numbers on the clock. Five minutes passed before I decided to call Wren's phone. It went to voicemail. I tried Blaire.

"Dia dhuit!" she answered.

I pulled the phone from my ear and stared at the receiver like the thing was from a different planet before tentatively putting it back to my ear. "I'm sorry, were you just speaking actual words there?"

Blaire chuckled. "It means hello. I thought I taught you that one already?"

She had, but my brain was just operating on a different wavelength tonight. "It sounded more throaty than usual." I blew out a sigh. "I was just checking to see if Wren made it back to the cabin yet? He hasn't called and I'm starting to worry."

"No, he's been gone since this afternoon. I'm sure he's fine though."

"I just don't like the idea of him being out there for so long when we still don't know where the rogue werewolves are hiding." They'd been hiding under the protection of the Dark Witch's cloaking spell–the Chameleon Shield–which meant they could be anywhere at any given time without us knowing. Every minute that Wren was gone was pure mental torture.

"He's smart and fast, and I highly doubt the other Weres will dare show their faces around here until the Dark Witch has returned to power, but we're not going to let that happen either," she added. "We're shielded too, ya' know."

"Yeah, okay. Just... call if he comes back to the cabin, please?"

"Of course," she paused. "How are you holding up with everything?"

I thought about that for a moment. Since Niall's death, my focus had been on Wren and how he was coping. But when I stopped to shine the spotlight on my own feelings, guilt had been ever so present, eating me from the inside out like a slow infestation of insects in a wound. "I don't know, Blaire. I still feel like I could have stopped Niall's death if I would have paid more attention to the vision I'd been sent before we performed the bonding spell."

Static lapsed between us. "I don't think that vision was sent to you because you were supposed to stop Niall's death from happening," Blaire said.

I'd had three visions leading up to Niall's death. The first was just a glimpse of the Hollow and the blood that coated the needle-covered forest floor. The second vision was the same, only there was a body of a werewolf lying there with a slit throat. At the time, my only concern had been for Wren, and I knew the werewolf's body wasn't his. The third vision, however, happened right before Niall was murdered–just mere seconds–and it showed his human body in place of the werewolf's. By the time I'd learned the truth it was too late. I'd snapped out of the vision in time to see the female werewolf cutting Niall's throat.

"If you were meant to stop it, the Earth Mother would have revealed Niall's human body to you sooner–not his wolf form."

"Then why show me at all?"

Another pause, and then, "I don't know, lass. Perhaps she was showing you that a sacrifice had to be made."

I snorted.

"I know that isn't comforting, Quinn, but it's all the truth I have right now. If anything, you should cling to the knowledge that there was nothing more you could have done to stop it from happening. Believe that." Her tone was adamant.

"It's hard." A lump was rising in the back of my throat, threatening to bring a wave of tears with it.

"Wren doesn't blame you," she said softly.

"I know. But that doesn't mean I don't blame myself."

"You'll get through this. Stay strong."

I sniffled, forcing back tears and swallowed over the lump in my throat. I'd have to force that guilt into something useful, because the sorrow I felt was a useless tool that wouldn't get us anywhere. I could break down after it was all over, but I still had to keep myself and my mind battle-ready. "Okay."

"I'll see you tomorrow, Quinny."

"Tomorrow," I agreed, and sat my phone down on the nightstand.

Since Niall's death, Wren had gone out every night to run. He didn't have to tell me why. I knew it was his way of dealing–or rather, *not* dealing with the loss of his father. As a wolf, he was able turn off the grief–disconnect the mental wire that linked him to human emotion. He could behave like an animal; like a predator where the only thing that mattered was his own survival. There was a part of me that envied that. How nice it must be, to just turn it all off–even for a small while. When he was gone, a hollow ache expanded through my chest; like a part of my own self was just... *missing*. I didn't know if he could feel that absence, but he always found his way back to me.

I knew what it was like to lose a parent, to feel like the world was ending because their light burned out before it should have. A day didn't pass that I didn't think of my mother or hear her laughter somewhere in my mind. Sometimes I'd wake in the middle of the night from a dream that I'd forgotten the sound of her voice, and the thought caused waves of fear to ripple through my chest. I didn't want to forget her, or anything about her.

I reached up, wrapping my fingers around the pendant that was nestled in the curve of my breasts. The arc of the crescent had become so familiar to me, like a security blanket I was always reaching for on some subconscious level.

As I lay there, fingertips pressed to the pendant, a sort of restless energy seemed to pulse through the air–reminding me of what had happened with my amulet before Niall's funeral. I recalled that spark of blue light, and the way the wall seemed to come alive with a hidden energy that beckoned to me…

When my mother died, the secret of what I was to become was buried with her. For so long I had been looking for answers–longing for the truth about my destiny. I had a feeling that whatever was hidden behind that wall would somehow provide the answers I was looking for. Part of me hoped that had been my mother's intention all along.

I'd wanted those answers. I had even gone so far as to speak the old Gaelic words to break the spell and watched as an outline of a door appeared from blue flame within the wall. My heart was pounding in my ears when I reached for the golden knob–and that's when my dad called up the stairs that it was time to go.

All of the eagerness that had welled up beneath the surface of my skin ran cold. A seed of doubt burrowed in, and I wasn't sure I was ready for whatever was waiting for me on the other side of that door.

Of only one thing I was sure… My pendant hadn't rolled into the wall by accident. That room wanted to be found. Power was calling power, and it wanted me to know that it had awakened. I sensed it right this very second, humming through the walls in my bedroom.

But I was afraid.

Ignoring it, I leaned back against my pillows. An hour passed as I lay staring at the ceiling. Dad had gone to bed for the night, and though my body was wracked with exhaustion, my mind just wouldn't shut down. I shuffled to my feet and grabbed my cross-country hoodie from my desk chair before heading down the stairs. I grabbed the afghan blanket from the back of the couch and slipped out the back door and wrapped myself up in one of the wooden lounge chairs.

The cool night breeze kicked up scents of the raw earth; dirt, pine, and crisp autumn leaves filled my lungs as I inhaled deeply. I used them to center my focus; concentrating on recharging my senses until nature was clinging to my fingertips, and Spirit's warmth was circling me. I tilted my head back, gazing at the onyx arc of the night sky above the silhouetted pine trees, and began counting constellations out of habit.

My mother had told me stories about the stars and all the secrets written within the constellations. They were like a map of my childhood; twinkling reminders of the bedtime stories she'd told me to get me to fall asleep. Remembering them kept her close to me–like another secret I could call to me whenever I looked up at the midnight sky.

"What are you looking at?"

Though Wren's voice was a welcoming sound breaking through the din of silence, I jumped a little. He had a knack for appearing out of thin air without a single sound. He was the perfect predator; dangerous, but I relaxed in his presence. "Pegasus," I told him.

Wren made his way up the staircase, dressed in a pair of jeans and a long-sleeved thermal that clung to the contours of his frame. He'd been keeping a backpack of extra clothing stashed beneath the deck for his Change. As he approached, I smelled the scents of the forest clinging to his skin; the pine still fused within the strands of his dark hair.

"Show me." He scooped me up in an effortless motion and sat down so that I was cradled against his chest with my legs dangling over the wooden chair arms.

I took his hand in mine, leading his index finger to the constellation above us. I pointed out each of the stars and landed on the brightest of Pegasus' stars. "That's Enif," I pointed out, "the orange supergiant."

"Enif," he repeated. "What's it mean?"

"It's Arabic for nose," I answered. "Enif is nearly six hundred and ninety light years away from us, and five thousand times brighter than the sun."

I sensed his gaze drift from the constellation and felt the bridge of his nose pressing against my jaw. His lips brushed against my throat, teeth nipping the tender skin. My head tilted on a sigh and I wanted to melt into him.

"Where have you been?"

"Patrolling," he answered, kisses punctuating his words. "Not far from here."

"I wish I could come with you." I pushed up on my elbow so I could see his face in the moonlight. The Moon had magic of her own, and it cloaked the creatures of the night in blue shadow. The lunar glow, I called it. It colored him impossibly radiant.

He didn't reply. Instead, he brushed a lock of hair back from my face; thumb tracing the outline of my cheekbone as he pulled me closer. When he kissed me, the rest of the world disintegrated, and I was out there drifting among the Pegasus constellation; close enough to touch Enif with my fingertips.

For a moment, I wished I could forget about the rest of the world and all of our impending responsibilities. Each brush or slide of his hands called to the fire within me–as if every inch of my body was made of sulfur and gunpowder, and his fingertips were made from fire. When his hands drifted beneath the hem of my sweater and pressed into the small of my back, I'd like to have forgotten my own name.

"Let's run away," I whispered against his lips.

"Don't tempt me."

"We could you know?" I rested my forehead against his. "It would be safer for everyone else if we were gone."

Wren shook his head. "This town won't be safe so long as the rouge werewolves are out there and the Dark Witch is a threat."

"Yeah, but she can't return to physical form without the amulet. We can take it some place far away… somewhere no one will be able to find us."

Wren was quiet for a moment. With my hand braced on his chest, I felt him draw a deep breath and release it slowly. "We'll be hunted."

"I know," I said.

"That won't keep those we care about safe." He reached for my hands, gathering them in his. He held them in the small space between us, gently squeezing as if to accentuate his point. I bit my bottom lip, brows furrowing because I knew he was right. Running away wouldn't fix anything. "It's late. You need to sleep," he told me. I started to protest, but he tightened his grip around my shoulders, picking me up as if I weighed no more than a bag of apples, and sat me upright on the deck. "Bed," he demanded, hands steering me toward the door. I rolled my eyes.

"You're impossible," I muttered, wrapping my fingers around the door handle.

He chuckled at that, the deep sound catching in the back of his throat. "I think I've definitely met my match."

"Just make sure you don't forget it," I teased. He nodded, giving me the okay to open the door. With his super-hearing abilities, he could hear a mole scurrying underground from a mile away. Handy little gift, I thought to myself as we headed up the stairs. I discarded the throw blanket on the back of my desk chair before climbing into bed. I slipped the silver pendant from my neck and hung it from my bedpost. Wren climbed in beside me and wrapped his arms around my waist. My heart thrummed beneath my rib cage, and I hoped I'd never grow acclimated to the sensation of his body so close to mine. He reached for my hand, lacing his fingers with mine.

"Are you okay?" I asked him.

"I'm fine." He pressed his lips to the back of my neck, the warmth of the kiss absorbing into my skin. "Better now."

"Do you want to talk about your mom?" I felt his body stiffen behind me, but his thumb continued to stroke my inner wrist. "You were surprised to see her."

"I was," he agreed, "but her coming here doesn't change the way I feel about what happened."

"Do you want to see her?"

"No. I've closed that chapter in my life and don't plan on revisiting it anytime soon. She'll be gone in a couple of days and that will be the end of it."

I nodded into my pillow. "I wonder where she's staying."

"It doesn't matter. Just get some rest."

A breeze ruffled the curtains in my window, and outside, the night creatures sang their melancholy songs. I closed my eyes but there was one last thing on my mind I needed to address. "Wren?"

"Hmm?"

"Niall wanted you to know that he loved you... that he was proud of who you are. Those were his last words." I didn't know why I hadn't told him before now. Perhaps I had been waiting for the right moment. I wasn't sure if now was right or not, but with the finality of today, it seemed like a good time to share.

"Thank you." He kissed my shoulder and gave my hand a gentle squeeze. With his arms around me, I managed to drift off to sleep. But even in my dreams I could feel the power humming through the walls. Through my delirious state, I swore I heard my mother's voice in my dreams.

"*Come find me,*" she said.

Chapter Four
The Demons Within

The smell of burnt eggs woke me from my sleep. I blinked a couple of times, trying to clear the cobwebs from my brain. I was alone, and with a quick touch of my hand, I could tell that the sheets had been cool for quite some time. The neon numerals of my alarm clock informed me that it was almost ten thirty–which was the longest I'd slept in weeks. I'd needed it, but the residual fog rolling around my brain indicated that a serious amount of caffeine would be needed to jumpstart my day.

The fire alarm began beeping from down below and just like that the clouds parted. I flung myself out of bed, dashing for the stairs. "Dad!" I called over the obnoxious high-pitched clamoring. I skipped down the steps, taking them two at a time and rounded the corner into the kitchen. Smoke was thick in the air and Dad was hoisting the kitchen window upward and fanning smoke out of the window with a tin baking sheet. "What happened?"

"I forgot I was cooking." A look of bewilderment contorted his features and widened his dark eyes. I grabbed a kitchen chair from the table and placed it underneath the smoke detector and climbed up; eardrums ringing painfully. I twisted with all my strength but the darn thing just wouldn't budge. "Twist it to the left," Dad called over the racket.

"I *am* twisting to the left."

"Come on Quinny, righty tighty, lefty loosey–I taught you that."

I rolled my eyes and dug my fingernails into the contraption. I was not about to get into it with my father before I'd had coffee.

A bright light bled across the floor as Wren opened up the front door and swept inside. He was wearing his beat-up leather jacket and carrying a tray of coffee; he deposited the tray on the table before reaching up and dexterously plucked the contraption from the ceiling. It took him less than two seconds to disconnect the battery and the awful buzzing stopped. I stood there, gazing down at him with a grateful expression. He extended his arms up to me and helped me down from the chair.

"What are we burning breakfast this morning?" Wren asked. He lifted his trademark eyebrow as the corner of his mouth twitched into something of a grin.

"Dad apparently forgot he was cooking," I said.

"I was distracted," he admitted, continuing to waft smoke out the screen window above the sink. The frying pan was pushed to the back of the stove, containing the remnants of charred scrambled eggs and bacon.

"With what?" I placed my hands on my hips.

"I thought I heard something in the walls," he said. "It's probably nothing, just mice coming in from the cold I bet. I'll have to stop at the Mill's and grab some traps next time I'm in town."

"Where did you hear the noise?" My heart picked up pace, and I sensed Wren watching me. He heard the change in my heartbeat, and I knew his eyebrows were furrowing into a frown without having to look.

"I couldn't pinpoint it," Dad said. "Behind the living room wall, maybe up toward the ceiling? I don't know." He waved this off with both hands.

My heart stopped beating all together.

"Maybe we can go to Jo's for breakfast," Wren suggested, "and in the meantime, I brought coffee." He picked up the tray he'd been holding when he walked in, offering us each a cup from the Silver Mountain Coffee House.

"Thanks Wren, that was very thoughtful." Dad reached over and took a cup from the cardboard carrying tray. "I'll just head upstairs and get changed."

After Dad had disappeared from our view, Wren turned his penetrating gaze on me. "Something you want to share with the class, Quinn?"

My heart skipped at the sound of my name. He'd used it so infrequently, but when he did, it sounded as though it belonged to him. "I was going to tell you," I said, shifting my weight. Wren took a half step forward, fingertips sliding around my upper arm. I started from the beginning, explaining what had happened before Niall's funeral when my pendant smacked into the wall. "I know she left it for me to find," I said softly as I finished reiterating the tale, "but I'm not ready to open that door."

"She's not afraid to fight an army of rogue werewolves, but a hidden door on the other hand…" He tilted his head, grinning.

"You think I'm being ridiculous?"

"No, I don't." He stepped forward, closing the small distance between us and pulled me closer. "It's personal to you."

"It makes me weak."

Wren shook his head. "Whether you open the door or not is your choice. But," he altered his tone, "I think your mom would want you to."

"And now he plays the guilt card." I sighed.

"It's just my opinion." He reached up, smoothing a strand of hair back from my eyes. My thick waves were especially unruly in the morning. "And when you do decide to open the door, I'll be right there with you."

"How do you know I'll open it?" I narrowed my eyes at him.

"Because I know you, Quinn Callaghan. You're curious by nature."

He wasn't wrong… I chewed at the inside corner of my lip and looked up at him with an apprehensive glance. "I'm afraid I'll be disappointed." *There.* I'd admitted it out loud.

"Okay, what's the worst possible thing you can imagine?"

I snorted. "I don't know... that there's nothing in the room, or like a note, telling me she doesn't want me to practice my gifts. I don't know," I repeated, shaking my head.

"I don't think that's what you're afraid of." His tone, combined with the look he was giving, was omniscient.

"Enlighten me, then." I welcomed his perspective.

"It might be the last thing your mother left for you, which makes it so much more sentimental. You miss her, and that room is holding something that will change the last memory you have of her and that, I think, is what scares you."

His declaration was delivered with tact, but it hit me with a force of raw, weighted truth. I let his words wash through until they had taken root and I felt brave enough to meet his tawny colored eyes. There was so much strength and warmth there. I wanted to tell him that he was right—that he'd hit the nail on the head, but I couldn't find the words.

"Breakfast?" He opted for a subject change, countering my silence.

"Right. I'll go get dressed." I turned for the steps, but as my foot hit the second step, I turned to face him. "What time did you leave this morning?"

"It was early. You were sleeping so well and I didn't want to wake you."

"Still having nightmares?"

"It's nothing I can't handle," he said, leaning against the wall. He didn't quite meet my gaze as I looked at him—really looked at him and saw the dark circles underscoring his eyes. I knew what monsters plagued his sleep.

"Wren, you know there was nothing you could have done..." He did meet my eyes then, and the look he gave me shattered a piece of my heart. Apparently neither of us could accept that we couldn't have stopped Niall's death from happening. "We were standing too far away. We wouldn't have reached him in time."

"Yeah, I know," he said. He lifted his hand to the nape of my neck, gently pulling me forward as he pressed his lips to my forehead. "I still should have tried."

C.

Jo's was crowded with finely dressed patrons. It was Sunday morning, and the regular church crowd was shuffling in after their services had ended. I spotted Torrance and her family in the front corner and waved as Nadine whirled by with a loaded serving tray. "Take a seat anywhere you can find one and I'll be right with you," she said.

We eased our way through the maze of crowded tables and found a booth that had recently been vacated. Salt and ketchup smears stained the surface of the table, but we grabbed a couple of napkins from the dispenser and helped clean up the mess. It looked as though it had been left by someone with a small child; I was wiping up something sticky that suspiciously resembled spittle.

"Really busy this morning," Dad commented, glancing around the room.

"At least it smells better than your kitchen," Wren teased. Dad shot him a look that only caused Wren and I to chuckle. A few minutes passed before Nadine strolled up to fill our coffee mugs and take our orders.

"Sorry about the wait," she said, dropping a couple of creamers and extra sugar packets in the middle of the table.

"No need to apologize," Dad told her.

Nadine always had a smile plastered to her face, but as she glanced up and really looked at who she was speaking to, her features shifted. Her blue eyes swept over Wren and churned with sympathy. I didn't have to be a mind reader to guess what she was thinking. It was the day after his father's funeral, how was he even functioning? She placed a hand on his shoulder, her painted fingertips squeezing. "I'm real sorry for your loss, Wren."

"Thank you," he replied. "I appreciate that."

"Well if you need anything, there's a whole community of people ready to help. You just say the word." She started to turn, halted, and pivoted on her right foot as if she'd just remembered something. She reached into her apron and unloaded an extra handful of creamers, patted Wren on the back and then strolled off toward the double-sided swinging doors of the kitchen.

"How long before I'm officially off everyone's radar?" Wren asked, reaching for a spoon to stir his coffee.

"She means well. We all do." Dad offered a small half smile.

I wanted to tell him that someone like him would never be off the radar. Anywhere he'd go, people would always notice. He just had that sort of discernable, commanding presence. And of course it didn't help that he was also jaw-dropping good-looking, either.

Beside me, Wren tensed; the spoon he was holding beginning to bend. I reached out and wrapped my palm around his hand, squeezing with force to get his attention. The little bell above the door chimed and I looked up to see the sheriff and his son walking in. Carl had his thumbs tucked through the belt loops of his slacks, his wide shoulders squared, and his beady little eyes scanned the room. The atmosphere chilled in the pulse of a second.

Wren let go of the spoon around the same time the restaurant resumed the steady buzz of chatter. I swept it off the table and placed it in my purse when my dad wasn't looking. He'd bent it in half without thinking.

The sheriff and his son started for the bar, but Carl had spotted us. His expression stayed neutral before very boldly shooting me a wink. He sat up on the barstool next to Margaret Lynn, tucking his sunglasses in the collar of his shirt. I wondered what sort of seedy information she was spilling this time.

Josephine bustled out of the kitchen to greet them; I watched as she handed them each a menu and filled their coffee mugs. I could see the tendons in Wren's forearms shifting. My dad was looking out the window, studying the work he'd done on the outdoor dining patio. I closed my eyes and called on the Spirit element, asking it to calm Wren before he burst out of his clothing and unleashed the werewolf version of the Incredible Hulk.

"Good morning!" Blaire appeared from the side with a bright smile pulling the corners of her mouth upward. She placed her hand on Wren's shoulder, and I felt his body slacken beside me. I deflated in an exhale.

"Well hi, Blaire." Dad turned and smiled at her. "What a nice surprise. Why don't you join us?" He scooted over to the window and patted the bench beside him.

"Why thank you Mr. Callaghan, that's very kind of you." She let her hand fall from Wren's shoulder and sank down in the space across from him. "I certainly hope I'm not imposing."

"Not at all," I told her. "I'm glad you're here." That was my subtle way of thanking her for showing up in the nick of time. Wren acknowledged her by a slight nod as he reached for his coffee mug.

"Have you eaten yet?" Dad asked, "We just ordered, but I can flag Nadine down and get something placed for you." He glanced behind the booth, searching the café for our waitress.

"Thanks, but I've already eaten. I won't pass on a mug'o scald, however."

"Scald?"

"Hot tea," I told him. Some of Blaire's Irish slang was starting to stick in my memory bank now–yet to be determined if that was a good thing.

"Of course," Dad said. "So how are things faring at the Magic Shoppe without Penny around?" We'd told him that Penny was vacationing in Ireland and Blaire was here running the shop in her absence. The lies were piling so high now, I was beginning to lose track of all the fabrications we'd created.

"Oh it's fantastic," Blaire said. "I'm having loads of fun."

"That's great, we're happy to have you here." Dad grinned. "Plus, we all like your accent."

"Oh Mr. Callaghan, you're the ones with the accent." Blaire playfully nudged his shoulder and giggled.

"So what time is your sister getting in?" I asked.

"Her flight is to arrive around seven. Thought I'd leave around six to give myself plenty of time to find parking and meet her at the gates."

"Be careful on the mountain pass, it gets pretty foggy up there in the evenings," Dad told her. He glanced at me, and I knew he was thinking of the accident I had foreseen years before involving one of my classmates. My stomach still tightened at the memory. I hadn't been able to stop it.

"I've got Penny's truck, not to worry."

A moment later, Nadine returned with our breakfast and filled Blaire's cup with hot tea. Wren stayed quiet beside me, eyes fixed on the back of Officer Stevenson's uniform. His silence could've been mistaken for grief, but I knew he was making a concentrated effort to keep the wolf at bay.

Nadine brought our check by, and Dad excused himself to pay the bill at the counter. Jo was there, smiling at my dad as he made his way up to the register. She leaned in, shaking the wooden bangles down around her wrist.

"She likes him," Blaire purred.

"I know. Everyone knows." I sighed.

"Does he?"

"I've pointed it out several times," I said. "I don't think he knows what to do, ya' know? With my mom being gone, I mean."

"You can't put a time stamp on the healing process. It's different for everyone," Blaire said. I nodded, shifting my gaze to Wren. He held himself so still, but there were moments when that granite mask cracked just a little, revealing a small glimpse of pain behind his eyes. I hated knowing that there was nothing I could do to fix it.

At the pulse of a second, the tiny hairs on the back of my neck prickled as though I'd been electrocuted. My chest constricted and I looked up, catching Blaire's expression across the table and knew she felt it too. Wren lifted his face, his eyes scanning the room until they settled on the far window that had a view of the parking lot.

"What is it?" I asked.

"Werewolf," Blaire whispered, showing me her hand and the magic ring on her finger that was glowing bright aqua.

"Stay here." Wren rose from the table in one fluid motion and eased his way to the front door before I could even blink.

I stood up. Blaire caught my wrist, eyes flashing up to mine. "You heard him, Quinn. He said to stay here."

"Yeah, small chance of that happening," I retorted as I yanked my arm free from her grip and started for the exit. I heard her sigh and knew she must have been right behind me as I opened the door. I scanned the lot and spotted Wren and another man near the dumpster next to the mouth of the alley. He was too far away for me to make out the details of his face, but I wondered if he was one of the werewolves we'd fought in the Hollow. If so, why had he chosen now to show his face in Silver Mountain?

"You don't know what yer doin'," Blaire scolded me as I started towards them. "It might be dangerous."

"Blaire," I spun to face her, "*we* are dangerous."

Her lips pulled together in defeat, her scowl softening. "I know that," she said. "But you still don't know what you're walking into."

"I've been cautious my whole life and it's never gotten me anywhere. I'm not sitting back and waiting to see what happens anymore." I shook my head.

She held my gaze hard, and though I sensed her opposing thoughts, she chose to keep them to herself. "Fine, but I'm going with you." She stepped in front of me and led the way around the side of the building to the mouth of the alley. The red bricks between the two buildings were crumbling at the base, weeds and grasses had sprouted through the cracks in the pavement, fanning over a stack of wooden crates.

The man standing next to Wren was straddling a big motorcycle. The chrome plates were gleaming in the morning sunlight, and the metal smelled hot mixing with the scent of exhaust fumes and leathers. He looked to be in his twenties with short spiky black hair, high cheekbones, and a square jaw. He was tall and sturdy-boned. Shards of glass from a broken bottle crunched beneath my boot, and the man turned his attention on me. His predatory black gaze dragged over every inch of my body, as if he were committing me to memory. The weight of his look caused a shiver to chase the length of my spine, but I stood my ground, raising my chin in the air.

"Friends of yours?" The man rumbled in a gruff tone.

Wren was looking at me hard, his mouth drawn in a tight line. I almost felt the heat rolling from his skin–saw the tension building in his shoulders. "Yes," he replied evenly, not once breaking eye-contact with me.

The man swung his long leg over the bike and deliberately made his way over to where I was standing. I heard nothing aside from his heavy boots falling on the pavement. He towered over me, extended his hand, and leveled his eyes with mine. "I'm Ryker Donovan," he informed me. He was handsome by male standards, but there was something cold about his gaze; I sensed he had an unforgiving nature.

"Quinn," I replied, taking his hand firmly. "What brings you to Silver Mountain?"

His jaw tightened. A flash of surprise turned into amusement as his lips parted. He was staring at me like he couldn't believe I'd had the audacity to speak to him. "I'm here on official business," he decided to answer. A moment passed before he let go of my hand and reached for Blaire's. Blaire, I noticed, was keeping her eyes averted from his face. "Now if you'll excuse me, I have other matters that require my attendance." Ryker walked over to his bike, swung his leg over and kicked the stand back. "Remember what I said about tonight, Wren." His mouth twisted into a leer as he pulled sunglasses out of his jacket pocket and slipped them over his cold, merciless eyes. "Bring your friends."

Wren nodded once, and Ryker started his motorcycle. The engine roared, echoing down the alley. He swung the bike around and zoomed out of the parking lot. The air was too still. I glanced at Wren and saw that his hands were rolled into tight fists, mouth curling in anger.

"I told her to stay inside," Blaire said. I twisted my gaze on her, scowling.

"You make it incredibly difficult to keep you safe." His voice was controlled, but his irises were swirling with an electric current.

"Who was he?" I took a step forward, matching his tone.

"He's the new Alpha Master of Thornwood," Wren said, inching closer and closing the distance between us. I felt the heat radiating from his limbs, watched as his muscles rippled and twitched across his forearms.

Thornwood was at least an hour's drive from here. It wasn't exactly a reputable town. I'd passed through a few times, (on my way to somewhere else because no one visited Thornwood on purpose) taking note of the rusted chain-link fences and trash that littered the overgrown yards. Storefronts and houses bore the mark of teenage rebellion with tagged graffiti all over the walls. Thornwood had once been nice–one of the oldest towns in the mountains–but now its name was truly emblematic of its prickly atmosphere.

"Thornwood has a pack?" My eyes narrowed. This was news to me.

"Yes."

"What did he want?"

"There's not much that happens around these parts without Thornwood knowing. Ryker heard about Niall's passing and wants to extend his condolences on behalf of the Thornwood pack. They're holding a tribute service in his name at their Were bar this evening."

My frown deepened. "*Wait*–how did Niall know these guys?"

"When I was a kid, the Thornwood pack and the Silver Mountain pack used to run together," Wren explained. "The previous Alpha Master and my dad were friends."

I heard what he was saying, but my brain was working in overtime; my thoughts bouncing around like an out-of-control racquetball. "Wren," I breathed, "why haven't you told me about them? I mean, what if Thornwood is in league with the Dark Witch?" I looked up at him, searching his eyes for an answer. "The wolves we fought in the Hollow—could they belong to Thornwood's pack?"

"I don't think so. The Thornwood pack hasn't been involved with Silver Mountain in years," he said. "They had an alliance with Niall when he was Alpha."

"So what happened when your mom left with your whole pack?"

"Niall claimed Silver Mountain as his territory. That's why my mother left and we found unclaimed territory in Washington. There's a lot you don't understand about my kind, Quinn. You don't have to be an Alpha Master to claim a territory, but you *can* be challenged for it. Ryker is the son of Thomas Donovan. Thomas was the Alpha Master when Niall held this territory. Thomas made sure the alliance held after what happened with my mother and Reese," Wren explained.

"But he's gone now," Blaire said in a quiet voice. She was looking at him in a way that made it clear I was missing something. "Which means…"

"That Silver Mountain is an unclaimed territory again," Wren finished. The muscles in his forearms rippled over the bones.

I squeezed my eyes shut, shaking my head. None of this was making sense.

"Do you think Thornwood wants to claim Silver Mountain?" Blaire asked.

"Maybe," Wren said.

"We can't let that happen. The park warden is already on high alert. If other Weres move into the area, they could be killed," I said. "We can't risk exposure."

"I know that. That's why I'm going to speak with him tonight and figure out exactly what he wants."

"And I'm going with you," I said defiantly.

Wren clamped his jaw shut, the tendons bulging in agitation. "It's not safe," he snapped. His midsummer night eyes bore down on mine with pious intensity. His irises were enlarging, swirling with the colors of the harvest moon. The Change was coming on fast and I knew he'd Change right there in the lot if we didn't stop him.

"Blaire—could you?"

"No," Wren growled, balling his hands into fists as he fought it. "I appreciate what you did for me in the café, but don't do it again."

Stubborn assed werewolf, I thought.

"He marked her," Blaire pointed out, eyes fixed on the ground. The wind was playing with her long spirals of hair, sweeping them back from her face. "You'll just give him a reason to track her if you don't bring her."

A low growl bubbled up Wren's throat, and when his lips parted, his canine teeth were extended.

"I'll make sure she's ready," Blaire said. "You should go, now, before someone sees you." Blaire wrapped her arm through the crook of my elbow.

Wren nodded, his summer eyes filled with a lightning charge. He turned for the mouth of the alley and slipped into the shade and melted into the shadows. I knew the forest was just on the other side. I saw the tops of the pine trees hovering over the building and knew he had slipped into the safety of the forest. I hated that he wasn't in control–wished that it hadn't been my fault this time.

"What do you mean Ryker marked me?"

"The way you postured," Blaire said, "he thinks you're a threat."

"But I'm not a werewolf." I looked up into her coal colored eyes.

"I don't think that matters, lass. You've sure made a fine mess now." There was no malice laced within her voice. Only sadness. I let her turn me away from the alley and back to the restaurant. I expected to feel fear, or anxiety, or a mixture of the two swirling through my gut, but I didn't. I didn't regret what I'd done. I was tired of hiding who I was and waiting in the shadows. I wasn't some damsel in distress that needed saving. No… I was more than that. I was a force to be reckoned with.

Chapter Five
Thornwood

"What has Wren told you about his previous pack?" Blaire asked. She was sifting through the stack of CD's Annabelle had on her desk (just about piled to the ceiling in height) next to her stereo. We were listening to a Kings of Leon soundtrack while Annabelle sprawled across her bedroom floor with trigonometry homework. I was lying on my back on top of her bed, holding the bent spoon I'd smuggled out of the restaurant up in the air, examining. I tried with both hands to get it to bend back to its regular shape, but the metal was not so malleable in my hands.

"Honestly not that much." I sighed, rolling on my side. I'd tried broaching the subject of his pack on several occasions, but it was far too much of a tender topic and Wren had a tendency to shift the conversation elsewhere. The truth was that Wren was the first werewolf I'd ever met, and I didn't know anything about them other than what I learned from Wren or heard in stories and legends. "He doesn't like to talk about them," I added, "or himself, really."

Annabelle snorted. I peered over the edge of the bed and shot her a pointed look. "What?" she croaked innocently.

"Werewolves are pack-oriented creatures by nature," Blaire chimed in. "It's encoded in their DNA. You'll experience that for yourself this evening. It's best if you mind your own, though I know that appears to be a struggle for you."

Annabelle snorted again.

"You really think I should have just stayed in the restaurant?" I propped myself up on an elbow. "What if Ryker had been one of the werewolves we'd fought against in the Hollow? Suppose there had been more than one. I couldn't just let him walk out there and risk his life," I told her, flopping back onto the pillows.

"He's just trying to keep you safe," Blaire said pointedly. She placed the CD she was holding back on the desk and crossed her arms over her chest.

"But I'm not some helpless being that can't take care of herself," I countered. "I told you. I'm not willing to sit back and just let things happen when I know there's something I can do to make a difference."

Blaire narrowed her eyes. "Did it ever occur to you that perhaps *your* presence was putting Wren in danger?"

"No." I frowned. "How could it?"

"Because you don't know anything about werewolves!" Her eyes bulged from their sockets. "They're not programmed like humans, Quinn. I don't know if you realize this or not, but Wren doesn't belong to a pack which means he is in danger. Out there–" she pointed out the window with a long, sharp fingernail "–he's the lone wolf, and lone wolves don't last very long when they're living in such close quarters to another established pack."

My brows furrowed and my lips parted. Even Annabelle looked up from her homework and listened intently. "But he's just one wolf," I said in a small voice.

"One wolf that belongs to no one," Blaire pointed out. "The wolves that are part of the Thornwood pack have already established their loyalty to the Alpha Master. He knows he can control them, and loyalty, as I said before, is predominant. It's already in their DNA. If one of the wolves goes rogue, the Alpha Master banishes it or kills it for breaking an oath. And since Wren belongs to no one, he has no allegiance to the Alpha Master, which means–"

"–That he is a threat," I finished for her, "because he could challenge the Alpha Master for his position."

"Exactly," Blaire said, tossing her hands up.

"But he wouldn't do that," Annabelle said. "Would he?"

"Of course not," I answered.

"That's not the point," Blaire said. "Wren needs to be on his game and if he's worried about you, then he's not staying focused. Like it or not lass, this is a matter of life and death. He needs to stay sharp." She leveled her eyes with mine.

I remembered the fight in the forest. It had taken the three of us to conquer the six werewolves that were working for the Dark Witch. I didn't know how many Weres were in the Thornwood pack, but I knew the odds–even with our supernatural abilities–weren't exactly in our favor. I squeezed my eyes shut, exhaling sharply as I pinched the bridge of my nose.

"Finally realizing the mess you've made, eh?"

"Blaire," Annabelle snapped, "*so* not helping."

"She's right," I said. "I screwed up." *Big time*. I'd let my anger fuel my resolve and cloud my judgement. I was so tired of watching the people I loved get hurt, so tired of sitting back and just letting it happen. Just because I was powerful, didn't mean that I was All-Powerful–and certainly not without the help of Blaire and Wren backing the force behind the Trinity. "So what happens now?" I breathed out.

"We need to work on your appearance for one thing," Blaire said. "You need to blend in and keep your head down."

I nodded.

An hour later I was dressed in a pair of black slim-fitted jeans, a low-cut white tank, and a sleeveless black vest–we'd borrowed from Caitlyn's closet. Lucky for me, she'd already left for SMU so as long as I got it back in one piece, she'd never know it was missing. I kept my black military boots on, and Annabelle applied a thick coat of black mascara and eyeliner.

"You should keep your hair down," Blaire said. "It gives you a strong look." She fluffed my dark ringlets below my shoulders.

"What about this?" Annabelle, who was enjoying playing dress-up with me, held up a tube of red lipstick and waved it like a magic wand.

"I draw the line there," I said firmly, pushing her hand back from my face. "I don't even recognize myself with all this heavy eye makeup; the least you can do is spare me the torture of lipstick."

"How about a compromise instead?" Blaire held up an alternative tube of matte lipstick that was a more earthy-mauve color.

I sighed.

"Tuck in your amulet," Blaire instructed. "It's paramount they don't find out you're a witch. There. Now you're ready."

"And let's go over the plan one more time, just to be clear," Annabelle said. "If your dad calls, I'll tell him you went to the airport with Blaire to pick up her sister, and then you're staying the night with me to finish a biology assignment."

"Right." I nodded.

"And if my parents ask, you're staying over at Blaire's to help get her sister settled."

"But really, I'll be in Thornwood with a pack of werewolves because I can't keep my big mouth shut," I added.

"Precisely." Blaire snickered and squeezed my shoulders. She was looking at me in the reflection of the mirror on Annabelle's dresser. "Only speak when spoken to, and keep your head down. Being around a pack is like being in an alternate universe."

"How do you know all this?"

"Because," she said, "I once had a Were for a lover."

My eyebrows shot to my hairline. "What happened?" Annabelle asked.

"The short version—witches and werewolves don't mix—unless of course you're the descendants of Luiseach and Conan." She winked at me.

"Long version?" I dared to ask.

"That's a tale best kept for another time. Come on, I'll walk you out so we can keep up our part of the story."

"Do you have your phone on you?" Annabelle asked. I patted my pocket, nodding. "Good. Call me later to check in."

"I will," I told her.

My stomach coiled in anxious knots when Blaire pulled into Wren's drive. The Pontiac was parked beneath the big pine tree, the screen door propped open on the porch. "Do you think he's still mad at me?" I asked when Blaire cut the engine. I gazed out the window, fingers poised on the seatbelt release button.

"I'm sure he's gotten over it by now," Blaire offered.

"I should have listened to you," I admitted.

"Don't be so hard on yourself. You've a lot to learn, but that's not a fault to you. Your instincts are sharp, despite how I reacted earlier. You've a lot of Luiseach's spirit in you. She too was a bit impulsive, but her heart was pure."

"And you?" I turned to look at her. "Are you like Aine?"

She smiled. "Aine was grounded, rooted in firm beliefs and sensible."

Now it was my turn to grin. I saw those traits in Blaire, knew that she was the foundation for which the Trinity was built on–even if the White Witch had been at the front line. The Trinity needed someone like Aine–someone like Blaire. Without her they wouldn't exist. "What about Conan?"

"He was a fierce and loyal warrior. He was brave, almost to a fault, but he loved Luiseach for all of hers." Blaire reached over and cupped the back of my hand with her palm. "This is a hard time for Wren," Blaire said softly, "just try to be his strength." She nodded and pressed her lips into a small smile.

"Thanks Blaire." I clicked out of my seatbelt and gave the door a shove. When my feet hit the gravel, I turned back to face her. "Listen,

Blaire, I know we haven't had much of a chance to talk since the whole Garrett thing. I just wanted you to know that if you want to talk about Penny, and…" I let my voice trail off. "Well, I'm here for you."

"I'll keep that in mind, yeah."

I pressed my lips together, lifting one of my shoulders. "Yeah. See ya' later."

"I'll call you after I get Bryna. We can meet up at the cabin."

"Be safe," I told her before closing the door. I crossed my arms over my chest to fight off the evening chill. In the distance, birds and other insects were filling the forest with their melancholy sounds. The sun was setting just on the other side of the trees, and the blue arc of the sky was slipping into shades of rose and gold. I reached for the door handle but Wren was already pulling it open. The pit of my stomach tightened and then warmed, like maybe I'd swallowed a lump of coal and looking at Wren ignited the burn.

He was toweling off his damp hair and wearing a long-sleeved black shirt with the buttons undone at the collar. He smelled like soap and other woodsy aromas that tangled in my nostrils. Surprise colored his eyes as they took in my unusual appearance, but there was something else there I recognized: hunger.

My heart leapt. "I'm sorry," I blurted before he had the chance to say anything. "I shouldn't have followed you out into the parking lot. I was angry and worried, and I wasn't thinking rationally. When I'm near you, my mental wires cross and I go into this crazy hyperactive mode to try and be super-Quinn because I feel like it's my fault you're in this predicament. I feel like I need to fix things, and in doing so, I only manage to screw things up worse–" He held his index finger against my lips.

His hands circled my waist and pulled me against his chest. I pressed my fingertips into his back, feeling the straight bones of his spine. *Goddess*, it felt so good to be in his arms–to have him touching me.

"It's okay," he said, fingertips sliding through the strands of my hair. His thumb found the curve of my jawbone, traced the length of it. He was looking at me now, studying my face with softness in his eyes.

"I'll be on my best behavior."

He gave a light-hearted laugh, the action parting his lips. "You'll have to be–dressed like that. Every eye in the room will be on you."

"Blaire said I would blend in."

"Impossible." He shook his head and pressed his lips to my forehead. When he pulled away, I saw the sadness in his eyes. "We should get a move on if we're going to get there on time. Do you need anything from the cabin?"

"No, I'm fine," I assured him.

He placed his arm around me as if it were the most natural thing in the world and led the way off the porch. He opened my car door and I slid in. When he hopped in the driver's seat, I jokingly said, "Maybe we could just pretend that we're on a date."

Wren glanced in my direction, throwing the car in reverse and began backing out of the drive. "I'm sorry we haven't had a chance to go on an official date."

"Not your fault. I don't much care for traditional-style dating anyway." I cracked a smile, but I was sure he heard the mild disappointment in my tone. While it was true that I was mostly happy to skip the whole awkward first date and forced conversation over a bland dinner, part of me kind of liked the idea of getting to experience something so human and *normal*.

"If this were a date," Wren said, deciding to play along, "where would I be taking you?" He glanced at me from the side, his trademark eyebrow shooting upwards.

"I don't know. Maybe to a movie, so we could share popcorn and hold hands in the dark," I mused. "And after, we'd stop for ice cream. We'd talk about hobbies, and interests, and music and life. But the whole time I'd just be wondering when you were going to kiss me." I laughed.

"You wouldn't have to wonder," he said. "I'd already have done it."

"*Werewolves.*" I rolled my eyes and grinned.

He reached for my hand, lacing his fingers through mine. "Distract me, Quinn. Let's pretend we're on a real date. What do you want to know?"

I thought for a moment, turning my head as I watched the forest blur in shades of green on either side of us. "I want to know how many girlfriends you've had."

He rolled his eyes. "Next."

"There's no evading the question Wren," I scolded him. "You have to answer."

"But none of them matter now that I have you."

"Them?" My eyebrows shifted upward. I wasn't naïve. I knew that there was no way a guy as good-looking as Wren with his testosterone-fueled werewolf genetics could claim to be entirely innocent. I saw the way girls looked at him–*hell*, I was one of them. It wasn't like he could help it.

"How many boyfriends have you had?" he countered.

"None really." I shrugged.

Wren made a face, like he was really supposed to believe that. "Come on, Quinn, tell the truth."

"I am telling the truth. I've gone out a few times, kissed a couple of guys, but that's it, really. None of them stuck."

"Hmph," he mumbled.

"Now you answer," I prompted.

"By those standards, I've never really had a girlfriend either." He flexed his left hand over the steering wheel, eyes gazing at the winding road in front of us.

"You are a very difficult person to communicate with," I said, not bothering to hide the irritation lining my voice.

He laughed. "I've been told that a time or two. It's probably the reason why I've never really had a girlfriend." He looked over at me and winked. He relaxed into his seat, looking much more at ease than he had earlier. It was like Wren was two sides of a coin, two entirely different emotional beings. I wanted a life that would bring out that happiness—make it permanent. "Look," he sighed, "I've had my share of fun, but I was younger and dumber, and things are different now."

"Do I need to be worried about STD's?" I lifted an eyebrow.

"Of course not," he said. "I wasn't talking about sex."

"Oh." I'd be lying if I said I didn't feel a wave of relief wash over me then. "I guess I just assumed that with you being…" I lifted a hand, waving it as I struggled to come up with the word I was looking for.

"You assumed wrong." He lifted my hand to his mouth, brushing my knuckles with his lips. "I'm only yours in that way."

"Good," I said, clearing my throat.

He grinned. "Can I assume the same for you?"

"Yes," I said, "only you." *Always you*, I wanted to add… We were leaving Silver Mountain now, passing through the town limits and crossing over on the highway that would take us south to Thornwood. I looked over at Wren, watching the way the last of the evening light played over his features. I stared at the hollow place beneath his throat, watching the muscles of his chest expand as he breathed. Part of me wanted him to just keep driving. We could go until the gas and the money ran out, and then just live off the land. If we made it to the beach, maybe I could open a little shop and sell herbs and potions like my mother had done. I wanted to know what Wren looked like standing in front of the sea—two powerful bodies, both full of wonder and mystery. But then I thought of my dad, and my mood dampened. I could never leave him. Not without knowing he would be looked after.

"Stay with me," Wren said, watching me from the side, "we're supposed to be on a date, remember?" He pressed his lips into a small smile.

"Sorry," I said. "I derail easily."

"I've noticed." He gave my hand a gentle squeeze. We kept chatting about life before we'd come to find one another, but the closer we grew to Thornwood, the quicker my heart thrummed in my chest. Wren, for his part, was pretending not to notice. It was my fault he'd been forced to bring me.

Minutes later we were approaching Thornwood, and the streets and sidewalks were worse than I remembered. We were stopped at the traffic light in the center of town and a group of teenagers dressed in baggy clothes, draped in chains, and covered in tattoos were standing on the corner. They weren't Supernaturals, but they piqued my alert system anyway. One guy, a teen no older than me, pulled out a switch blade and flicked it open. He was staring at Wren through the windshield, and the others surrounding him dissolved into crude cat-calling noises. The muscles in Wren's forearms began to ripple with the Change. Black hair sprouted across his wrist as he stared back. The boy started to walk in our direction.

"Wren," I breathed, covering his hand with mine. "Drive." The light turned green, and Wren floored the gas pedal, burning rubber through the intersection. The group of delinquents just laughed as we shot through.

"I hate this town," he muttered, shifting the gears with more gusto than necessary. "It's overrun by criminals and teenage junkies looking for their next fix."

"Why don't the cops do anything?" I asked.

"They're paid to keep their mouths shut."

"They support the junkies?" I frowned.

"It's all about control. If they turn a blind eye, they get a cut of the profits." A beat later we were pulling down a side street lined by a long wooden red fence. The paint had faded and was tagged with spray cans. Someone had painted a large wolf head with glistening white fangs in plain view.

"So much for keeping a stealthy cover," I said.

Wren didn't reply. We were slowing now, pulling into a gravel lot that was packed with motorcycles and big trucks covered in mud. Wren pulled the Pontiac in a spot closest to the exit. I wondered if he thought we were going to need to make a quick getaway. He squeezed my hand

and I released the air I must have been holding in my lungs. "Ready?" he asked.

"Yeah," I lied. A few hours ago I had been ready to kick some ass, and now I was just praying that my knees wouldn't buckle. Wren held my hand as we walked up the sidewalk. I heard music spilling from the bar and as I glanced up at the neon sign, my Supernatural senses kicked into high gear. My spine went rigid and my ears began to ring. Ribbons of pressure strangled my ribs, forcing the air from my lungs. I'd never been around so many Weres at once.

"Are you okay?" Wren was watching me, supporting most of my weight.

I nodded. "My senses are in overdrive. I just need to make contact and then I'll be fine," I said.

"Use the elements," he reminded me.

I called on Spirit and Fire to strengthen me and immediately felt the warmth of the elements circling me. I nodded again and Wren twisted the doorknob. At once, the overwhelming sensation crawling over my skin settled. The atmosphere was dark, shrouded by thick clouds of smoke. The putrid odors of cigarettes, urine, and alcohol burned my nostrils. I made a quick sweep of the room, scanning the bar and the pool tables in the far corner, making a note of all the exits, just in case.

"How can I help you, sugar?" A barmaid dressed in cutoff jean shorts and a black T-shirt bearing the bar's insignia appeared in front of us. She had short, choppy red hair that looked to have been fried one too many times with a flat-iron. Eyeliner had congealed in the corner of her eyes, but she pushed her shoulders back, sticking out her ample bosom—which was apparently her best feature.

"We're here to see Ryker," Wren said.

"Really?" she purred as if this were the most interesting thing she'd heard all day. She cocked her head to the side, placing a hand on her hip. I noticed we'd attracted more attention from the pool tables. A couple of big men stood twisting their cues between their large, meaty hands—watching with dry expressions.

"That's right," Wren said, standing his ground.

"I'm sorry hon, but no one gets in to see Ryker without an invitation... even if they are a sight for sore eyes."

"Let them pass Sal, I invited them." Ryker materialized from the shadows, dressed in a low-cut white V-neck and ripped blue jeans. A thick platinum chain adorned his left wrist, while a leather band covered his right. The bar went completely still. The woman named Sal stepped away from Wren but kept smiling in a rather coquettish manner. "This is Niall's boy, Wren Whelan," Ryker said.

"I know who he is. Caught his scent before the door opened. Sure have grown since I last seen you," Sal purred. "Got Niall's look, all right."

Ryker stepped in front of Sal and offered his hand to Wren. The men shook, and I did my best to keep my eyes from traveling up to his. I reminded myself that we were in Thornwood now and in a bar packed with Weres—more Weres than I expected. I noticed that the others in the bar had lowered themselves, tilting their head in a way that exposed the curve of their neck when Ryker walked in. They were all back to minding their own now, but a few were keeping close watch from the shadows. I scanned the room, wondering if those who were still watching were in the chain of command.

Ryker's gaze traveled in my direction. I could sense his eyes on me now, knew he was appraising me from head to toe. Wren stiffened, straightening to his full height beside me. Ryker grinned. "What's the matter love? You're not afraid are you?"

Blood rushed through my veins and arteries, humming in my ears. I couldn't help myself; I looked up and met his eyes, holding his gaze as if that alone would answer his question.

"She's a pretty little play thing," Ryker commented.

"She's my *mate*," Wren growled in a low voice. Sal chuckled and Ryker smiled, revealing large, glistening white teeth and deep-set dimples.

"I meant no offense." Ryker held up his hands. "I just assumed with her being human and all that she was only around for a bit of fun."

A sound mimicking a chortle whistled through my nostrils in disbelief.

Ryker's attention snapped to my face. "Have something to say?" he prompted.

"It's funny," I said, "you're talking about me as if I weren't standing here."

Wren moved his hand to my lower back and shot me a look, reminding me to keep a level head. Heat pooled in my chest and flamed in my face.

"There's that fire I was telling you about Sal. She's got more bite than most wolves." Ryker laughed, rocking back on his heels.

"That's bold behavior for a human. The young ones are all reckless and spirited." Sal chuckled and gave her head a half shake. She turned on her heel toward the bar. "What do y'all want to drink?"

Chapter Six
Magic Eight Ball

"It's on the house, in honor of Niall," Ryker said. He put his arm around Wren's shoulder and turned to face the crowd. "Listen up; this here is Wren Whelan and his mate, Quinn. They're guests in Thornwood and are to be treated as such in honor of the old alliance with Silver Mountain. Tonight, we drink to Niall's memory."

The bar erupted in howls that sent a shiver whisking down my spine. All around me, eyes were glowing yellow. I looked up at Wren and saw that his eyes had begun to churn with the pulsing current as well. Blaire's warning about werewolves belonging to a different universe began to take meaning. It was apparent that in a pack, the Weres were more wolf than human. The feather-light pressure of Wren's fingertips on my elbow reminded me not to gawk as he led me to the bar. A man dressed in full riding leathers got up from the stool and offered me his seat.

"There are no humans here," I murmured.

"The bar is spelled," Sal explained. "Humans just see an old locked-up warehouse with broken windows. The delinquents try to bust in every now and then but Appalachia over there does a pretty good job of keeping them out." She nodded toward the biggest mountain of a man I had ever seen sitting at the end of the bar.

"What do you mean the bar is spelled?" I asked Sal.

"By a witch of course," Sal said. "Thornwood is teeming with all kinds of Supernaturals. Now, what can I get you both to drink?" Her long fingernails, yellowed and galvanized from years of smoking, trailed over the draft beer tabs. Clearly, being legal age was not of importance in the Were community.

"Beer is fine," I said, propping my elbows on the table. Wren lifted his customary brow and nodded when Sal's gaze fell on him. I scanned the room again, taking special care to keep track of Ryker. He was currently leaning up against the wall just beneath a mounted deer head, talking with a couple of girls that looked to be closer to our age. The bar was larger than I expected. Neon beer signs lit up the walls and low hanging glass lamps hovered over at least twenty filled tables.

"Sorry about the intense greeting," Sal said, sliding me a tall glass of beer. The amber liquid sloshed over the side, dripping onto the bar top. "Ryker likes to be a little theatrical. He has a strong personality, but he means well."

"I probably should have stayed quiet," I said, picking up my drink. "I didn't mean to sound disrespectful."

Sal laughed. "Ryker likes a woman with a fiery temper."

Wren bristled beside me. "How long has Ryker been in charge?"

"Thomas stepped down last year," Sal answered. "He's an Elder now; he keeps a close watch over everything, but Ryker is a good leader. The kind of leader a pack like Thornwood needs. He makes the tough decisions with the pack's best interests at heart." Sal leaned over the counter in front of us, resting her chin in the palm of her hand. "Sure was sorry to hear about Niall's passing. Your father was a good man."

"Thank you," Wren said.

"They got any idea who murdered him?"

A lump rose in the back of my throat then. I gripped my glass, feeling the condensation dripping over my fingers.

"None," Wren said.

"That's a damn shame." Sal was studying Wren with an unwavering gaze–an expression that showed me she was practiced in the art of keeping her face neutral. I was sensing that perhaps she knew more about Niall's murderer than she was leading us to believe. Was it possible that his murderer had had any affiliation with the Thornwood pack?

I saw the girl in my mind, pictured her wild mane of hair blowing in the wind. I saw the color of her caramel eyes, and the way her lips seemed to curl in a naturally cruel sneer. Her image was seared into my brain, another face that haunted my nightmares.

"I wasn't sure what to expect when Ryker invited us out," Wren said a moment later. "It was... noble... of him to recognize my father." Wren was fishing.

"Ryker is a noble man," Sal said simply.

"So," I piped up, "is it normal to have a witch working for the pack?"

A small twitch lifted the corner of Sal's lip. "And why would you want to know, honey?"

"I'm just curious."

Sal's grin widened. I realized she knew that I was in fact a Supernatural of some kind. I wouldn't have been able to get into the bar otherwise, and her telling me about the spell had been a test. They knew I wasn't a werewolf because I didn't smell like one, but that didn't mean I had any intention of telling them what I was.

"I know some witches," I offered instead. "They're standoffish. I never see them hanging around any other Supes."

"Witches are a shady bunch," Sal said. "I'd never trust one myself. Never can be too sure what they're up to."

"I couldn't agree more," I said, raising my glass in a toast. Sal tipped her whisky glass against mine and tossed back the contents.

A young man walked up to the bar; he stood about six-foot-three with long black hair he kept tied in a ponytail at the nape of his neck. His face was narrow, the bones sloping to the sharp point of his chin. Kind, almond-brown eyes softened the harsh lines of his bone structure. "Well," he drawled, "just look what the cat dragged in, I don't believe it. Wren, it's good to see you man."

Wren stood up and clapped the guy on the shoulder. "What have you been up to Roy? It's been a long time."

"Nothing much man, same old same around here. Heard you were back in Silver Mountain. Are you planning to stick around this time?"

"I go where she goes." Wren looked at me, smiled.

Roy turned, as if noticing me for the first time. "Ah, I see." Roy extended his hand to me. "Nice to meet you, miss."

"Likewise," I said.

"So Wren found a girl worth settling down for, huh?" Roy laughed and shook his head. "Took you long enough to pick one." Roy turned back to me and leaned down so that his mouth was at my ear. "Our boy was a bit of a charmer back in the day. His methods were more catch and release though. Fun and done."

"*Wow*," I said, stretching out the syllable. I looked at Wren, tilting my head and raising my eyebrows.

"Don't listen to him," Wren said. "Roy likes to instigate."

"Guilty as charged." Roy laughed. I made a mental note to ask Wren about his previous experiences in Thornwood. I knew if I asked now, I'd be overheard by intrusive super-hearing werewolf ears. A few others came up to the bar after that, offering their condolences and sharing stories about the good times the two packs had when they ran together. As I watched them one by one, I couldn't help but get the feeling that this was all just a ploy to get Wren re-introduced to the pack–to show him what he was missing.

"By the way, how long is your mom in town?" Roy asked. "My mom loves the woman to death but I think she's ready for her to go back to Washington. I haven't been home much, but apparently all she's been doing is complaining and moping around about how much she misses Silver Mountain. It's driving my mom nuts."

"She's staying with Nelly?" Wren furrowed his brows.

"Well, yeah, you didn't know?"

"I don't make a habit of keeping tabs on her whereabouts. Gabriella and I aren't on the best of terms anymore." Wren flexed his scarred hand across his thigh, but Roy was oblivious. "So she's been hanging out in Thornwood, huh?"

"Yeah. That's how Ryker found out about Niall's passing."

"Hmph," Wren grumbled.

Ryker was making his way over to the bar now, his arms draped over the girls' shoulders. One was a vivacious brunette with curves in all the right places, the other a busty blonde with sky-blue eyes she couldn't seem to keep off Wren.

"Sal taking care of you I hope?" Ryker asked.

Wren held up his beer.

"Hi, Summer Boy," the blonde said. "Been a long time hasn't it?"

"Hailey," Wren greeted her.

Her eyes cut to me, a smug smile tilting the corner of her rose petal lips. She'd used a special nickname for Wren and she wanted to make sure I'd gotten the message. I had. *Loud and clear.* I kept my expression neutral. I wasn't giving her the satisfaction of reacting.

"You guys up for a round of eight-ball?" Ryker asked. "Sal, bring over a pitcher of the good stuff, would ya'?"

"You got it darlin'," she said, hopping to her feet.

Wren offered me his hand, helping me down from the barstool before meeting the others at the pool table. There were other Weres standing close by, their figures only half visible from the smoky shadows. Wren shifted me in front of him, drawing my back against his chest as his fingertips skated down the sides of my arms. This, I saw, did not go unnoticed by the blonde girl–Hailey? Her baby blues were pools of liquid envy.

Wren leaned down, his breath warm against my ear. "You okay?" he whispered so low I had to second guess what he'd said before nodding.

Ryker handed Wren a cue and offered one to me. "Three against three, guest breaks," he said, pointing his cue at me. I took a deep breath and walked over to the table, leaned over and carefully lined up the cue ball. On an exhale, I took the shot and the balls dispersed around the table with a loud clatter. The dark red ball, my lucky number seven, slid into the far right-hand pocket.

"Solids," I claimed. I moved around the table, searching for my next target. I focused on the purple ball, number four, and leaned over the table. "Side pocket," I called, pointing toward it. I lined up my shot and took it. The cue ball smacked into the purple ball, banking off the side rail and landing in the side pocket as predicted.

"If I'd known you were good, I might not have let you go first," Ryker sounded amused, casually leaning against the wall.

"Yellow ball, left pocket." I arched my back as I leaned across the table, grateful I was positioned in front of Wren. Tension hummed through the airwaves with an electrical pulse. The cue ball clinked against the yellow ball, but fell short of the pocket by half an inch at most. "Damn," I muttered.

"That was a good run," Wren complimented. He reached for me, and his fingers seemed to sear through the fabric of my clothes. I couldn't tell if he was keeping me close for his benefit or for mine.

"Hailey, you're up," Ryker barked. "Where'd you learn to play, Quinn?"

"Pool hall in Silver Mountain," I said. "My friends and I are extremely competitive. I don't like to lose."

"I'd say not," Ryker said, studying me and watching the way Wren's arms tightened around my waist.

I wanted to leave. I wished Ryker would get to the point already, but I knew he was enjoying the slow-torture of keeping us here. He might have been a respected, revered leader to his pack, but his predatory gaze made my stomach twist. Hailey missed her shot and released a rather canine sounding growl of annoyance.

"You'll get it next time, doll. Roy, it's your turn."

"How's Thomas?" Wren asked. "My father often spoke of their friendship. I was hoping to see him tonight."

"He's out of town on business I'm afraid," Ryker said. "There's a couple of Weres in the Asheville area that have been hunting in our territory."

"Can't have that," Wren said.

"No, no we can't. They just needed a friendly reminder about who the boss is around here." Ryker twisted the cue in his hands, keeping his eyes on me. "Which brings me to my next point of interest..."

"Silver Mountain," Wren guessed.

Ryker's lips spread in a slow, unforgiving smile. "Niall was a gracious man, allowing our pack to settle in such close quarters to Silver Mountain when we established our territory years ago. I think we can both agree that my father returned the favor tenfold when your mother left with the new Alpha Master and took your old pack with her. Now, that's a whole lot of land for one werewolf... He didn't challenge Niall for the territory and allowed him to remain in control even though he was a lone wolf." Ryker paused, reaching up to rub the stubble along his jaw. "Now that Niall has passed, it appears that Silver Mountain is back on the market. I'd like the Thornwood pack to lay claim."

And there it was. My eyelids flashed up, and I stared into Ryker's cold, ebony eyes. He was looking at Wren and otherwise oblivious to my gaze.

Wren snickered but there was no humor behind it. "I'm sure you're aware that the park wardens are patrolling Silver Mountain. It must have caught your attention that a rogue pack of wolves moved into the area recently, swearing their allegiance to the return of the Dark Witch. It's dangerous to be a wolf in Silver Mountain."

At the table, Roy missed his shot. Ryker pushed his massive frame away from the wall and ambled over to the table. "I have heard that, yes." He leaned over the table and the cue ball sliced across the table with lightning speed. The balls cracked together, ricocheting across the table before one sank into the right-hand pocket. "My interests are with the territory. I'm not concerning myself with witches and Dark magic. That doesn't have anything to do with my pack."

"So you're positive that no one in your pack could have gone rogue?" I asked before I could stop myself.

Ryker's cold electric gaze flashed up to mine. "The penalty of treason in my pack is death," Ryker growled. "No one would dare cross me. In fact, if Thornwood had claim to Silver Mountain, you wouldn't be having a rogue werewolf problem."

A sheet of ice caressed my shoulders, slinking down my back as his words echoed in the bar. The room fell silent. Ryker tore his lethal gaze away from me and shifted his attention back to the table. The next ball he called sank in the side pocket. I swallowed hard, forcing my attention on Ryker's face.

"I want you to consider joining our pack, Wren," Ryker said a moment later. "If you're planning to stay in Silver Mountain, you understand what not belonging to a pack could mean for you, right?"

"I don't suppose you'd consider honoring the old alliance?" Wren offered.

Ryker sneered. "I've had my eye on Silver Mountain for years. My pack would benefit from the natural resources the forest offers. Fresh hunting grounds, new business opportunities… The pack is growing, Wren, Thornwood needs to advance. The simple fact is this: we're taking over Silver Mountain and there's nothing you can do to stop it. It's because of the relationship our fathers cultivated that I'm even giving you the opportunity to join our pack. I'm sure you can see how generous I'm being with this offer. I sincerely hope you're smart enough to make the right decision." Ryker leaned over the table, sinking the last striped ball into the corner pocket. "Eight ball, right corner," he called.

I couldn't help myself. I called on Air silently and beckoned the element to blow the eight ball just enough to miss the pocket without it being obvious that I'd conjured it to move. A sharp pain shot through my temples but I bit the inside of my lip, clamping down on the pain. This was nature's way of punishing me for using the element to aid in my own personal gain. It was worth it. The eight ball banked off the side rail and spun like a top in the middle of the table.

Ryker clamped his jaw shut, and I watched with satisfaction as his muscle bulged over the bone in annoyance. "Wren," he growled, "you're up."

Wren straightened and made his way over to the pool table. I saw Hailey suck in her lower lip, watching the way Wren's shirt fell away from his chest as he leaned across the table. "Eight ball, side pocket," Wren called. The cue ball cracked into the eight ball with a loud clamor, rocketed off the rail and shot into the side pocket with ease. A smirk tugged the corners of my mouth, but I kept my eyes glued to the table. I sensed Ryker looking at me, knew that lethal gaze was burning holes into my face. I didn't care.

"Great shot, Wren," Hailey complimented.

Ryker shot her a stern look.

"It's been nice catching up, Ryker, but it's getting late." Wren straightened and met Ryker's gaze.

Ryker snickered. "I forgot you were still in high school."

"Not for much longer," Wren reminded him, "I'm eighteen." *Old enough to challenge him for the Alpha Master position.*

"You have three days, Wren. I'm counting on you to make the right decision."

Wren nodded, backing us towards the door. I knew it would be a mistake to turn our backs on Ryker–knew somehow he'd see that as conceding. Sal was at the door when we finally reached it.

"Take care, sugar." She gave us a hopeful smile.

The night air was cold and welcoming on my face. I sucked in a deep breath, letting it fill my lungs. Wren laced his fingers through mine and tugged me along; neither of us said a word until we were safe behind the doors of the Pontiac and on the road heading home. I watched the way the dashboard lights cast a soft glow across Wren's features– watched the way the air expanded in his chest in a rush.

"With the eight ball in there," Wren finally spoke, "was that you?"

"Yep," I said. "Pain burned like hell but it was totally worth it to watch him lose."

Wren chuckled. "You didn't have anything to do with my shot, right?"

"Of course not!"

"Just checking." He looked both ways before blowing through the red light at the center of town. The group of teens had moved on, but both of us were anxious to get the hell out of there. Wren kept casting glances in the rearview mirror, checking to make sure we wouldn't pick up a tail.

"What are we going to do?" I breathed, tipping my head back into the seat. "You can't honestly be considering joining their pack, right?"

"Not a chance."

"We can't let the Thornwood pack move into our territory either." I shook my head. "For one, it's too risky with the park wardens on the lookout for wolves in particular. Maybe you could talk to Ryker's father. Maybe he'd listen to you," I suggested. "He honored the alliance with Niall, I'm sure he'd honor it for you."

"Maybe if he were still the Alpha Master," Wren said. "Ryker has other plans; he's not the persuading kind."

"So the choices really boil down to join or...?" I swallowed hard, rubbing my clammy palms against my pant legs.

"Die," Wren finished the sentence. He reached over, taking my hand and holding it in his lap. His thumb rubbed soothing circles on the back of my hand but my lungs constricted as though all the air had been sucked out of the car. "We'll come up with something," Wren said, turning to look at me, "we've got a little time."

I snorted. "Three days might as well be three seconds."

"Hey, where's my fearless force of White Light?"

"She's shaking in her bones," I admitted none too proudly. I squeezed my eyes shut and saw the facts of my muddy future laid out before me: Bryna was on her way with an amulet that could mean the Trinity's destruction if we couldn't find a way to destroy it. Penny was still missing and for all I knew, trying to get her hands on the amulet to awaken the Dark Witch. There was a hidden room in my house that my mother left for me that I couldn't bring myself to open. A pack of werewolves were threatening to make Silver Mountain their stomping grounds and forcing Wren to join them. Niall had been in the ground for one day and his murderer was still out there on the loose. My head began to spin in dizzying swells.

Wren squeezed my hand. "There's nothing we can't conquer together."

I nodded and forced myself to smile.

But the thought of running away was growing in appeal, pulsing in the back of my mind with a sense of urgency. It wasn't the answer, but I was beginning to wonder if we'd have any other option.

Chapter Seven
When Calls the Light

Bryna was sitting at the kitchen table when we walked in. A lion's mane of thick red curls framed her face and spiraled around her shoulders. Her face was pale and lovely, dotted by freckles and accentuated by arctic eyes. I blinked against the diversity between the two sisters, wondering how they were blood related.

"This is Bryna," Blaire announced, squeezing her sister's shoulder. "These are Quinn Callaghan, and Wren Whelan."

Wren reached across the table and offered his hand.

"It's nice to meet you," I said when it was my turn. "We really appreciate you making the trip. You must be exhausted."

Bryna's eyes narrowed. She seemed to be scrutinizing my appearance with unspoken judgement burning behind her eyes. A moment passed before she spoke, choosing her words with care. "As a proud member of the Aurora Coven, making sure the amulet is safe at all times is part of my duty and highest honor. In any case, three witches are better than two in a situation such as this." She forced a smile. "Especially when one of us is the White Witch incarnate," she said as though she could taste the bitterness of resentment on her tongue.

I didn't know how to respond and was grateful when Blaire broke the newfound awkward silence. "So, how did the meeting go with Thornwood?

I glanced at Wren, sucking in a breath that ballooned in my chest while I sank into a kitchen chair. Wren joined me, and together we explained what happened in Thornwood. When we finished, a deep crease had formed between Blaire's dark eyes, but it was Bryna who spoke first.

"I'm never surprised by the foolish behavior of werewolves," Bryna said. "Too much arrogance in their blood if you ask me. No offense," she added as an afterthought, gaze sweeping up to Wren.

His eyebrow would have disappeared in his hairline if it were possible. "None taken."

"Thornwood has at least fifty Weres in their pack, and goddess knows how many other Supernaturals in their back pocket. Our odds of going up against them are obviously not good, but we need to think of something fast. Wren joining is out of the question," I said.

Blaire reached across the table and covered my wrist with her palm. "We're not going to let that happen. Perhaps we can regroup in the morning after we've all had a good night's rest. It's been a long day and I'm racked."

"But what about the amulet," Bryna said. "Don't you want to see it?" She was looking at me, eyes wide and expectant.

I'd been waiting for her to ask–sensed the amulet's presence calling to me the closer we'd gotten to the cabin. The old things always possessed energy, but this was different somehow. Instead of a gentle hum, it was almost as if the amulet was... *thinking.* "Tomorrow," I said, agreeing with Blaire. "It's been a long day."

"Very well," Bryna said. "We've a great deal to discuss about the amulet and the Aurora Coven. It's probably best if we all have fresh minds." She glanced at her sister and smiled in agreement. Her sky-blue eyes met Wren's once again. "Thank you for opening your home to me in a time of need. The Aurora Coven is very grateful for your hospitality."

"Make yourself at home," he replied.

I was finishing up at the bathroom sink, putting the toothpaste back in the drawer when Wren slipped in without a sound. His left hand skated across my hip as he kissed my brow and then reached for his toothbrush. It was such an ordinary moment–a boy and a girl standing next to one another, going through their nighttime routine as if the nightmarish world outside wasn't clobbering away at their door. These were all the moments that I wanted–that now seemed sweeter because of how few and far between they'd come. Every moment of normalcy was precious if only because I'd never know when the next would arrive.

After he finished, he plopped his toothbrush back in the holder (that now contained four toothbrushes) and met my gaze in the mirror. He tried to rest his hands on the counter, but found that any unoccupied space was now covered with makeup and various hair styling tools. A low sound rumbled from the back of his throat as he knocked a tube of mascara off the sink and caught it before it hit the floor.

"I'm sorry." I reached out, palm rolling over his warm bare shoulder.

"Why? You're not the reason I'm drowning in a sea of estrogen in my own bathroom. What even is this stuff?" He sat the tube on top of a half-opened makeup bag and looked at it as though it might unsheathe a set of fangs and bite him.

"That is magic for the modern-day witch," I said with a chuckle. Confusion furrowed his brow rather adorably as I looped my arms around his neck. "It's called mascara and goes on your eyelashes to make them longer, darker, and fuller. Some of us weren't gifted with perfect lashes like you, *Wolf Boy.*"

The corner of his mouth twitched. "You think my eyelashes are perfect?"

I nodded, tracing the tips of them as they fanned against my thumb. His hands circled my waist, pulling me close enough so we were breathing the same air. "Well in that case, I suppose I'll try to tolerate our new house guests," he said.

"It won't be forever," I paused, drawing away from his gaze. "Bryna seems about as cozy as a rose bush."

Wren cracked a smile that revealed his teeth. "Witches of the Aurora Coven spend their whole life protecting the amulet and hoping for the off chance they might be the revered heir of Aine Alderdice. I'm guessing she's probably a little sour that she didn't get chosen and her sister did."

"Maybe," I agreed.

"Come on." Wren took me by the hand and led me across the hall to his bedroom. The lights were off, so I let him guide me through the darkness with his adept night vision. Then he was pulling me onto the mattress. I adjusted myself to the curve of his body and began tracing the contours of his sternum with my fingertips. This was the first night he'd stayed in the house since Niall's passing. The air was clinging to fibers of sweet grass and sage, making it near impossible not to feel Niall's presence surrounding us.

I lay there for a moment, trying to lose myself to the relaxing sensation of Wren's fingers sliding through the strands of my hair. But every time I closed my eyes I saw Thornwood in my mind; the conditions Ryker set for Wren ringing in my ear like battle drums. I shifted on my side, propping up on my elbow as my eyes began adjusting to the lighting. I didn't have super-vision like Wren, but I could at least make out the lines of his body, the contours of his bare chest and the subtle glow from his eyes.

"What's on your mind?" he asked.

"Just thinking about Thornwood," I admitted. "What's the hierarchy like in a pack that size? Who's the Beta?"

Wren drew a breath. "Traditional wolf packs have around seven to fifteen members and the average werewolf packs have adopted a similar lifestyle. It's unusual for Were packs to be as big as Thornwood because of how difficult it is to keep the Subordinates in line. To be successful, a pack the size of Thornwood typically requires an established council made from their previous Alpha Masters. When a new Alpha is chosen, the old one will step down and become an Elder on the council. The Alpha Master still rules over the pack, but the council helps enforce the laws."

"What's a Subordinate?"

"They represent the rest of the pack population," Wren explained. "The Beta is the Alpha Master's second–a chosen member that would take over for the Alpha should something happen to him. The Subordinates have to answer to the Beta and the Alpha, but the Beta only has to answer to the Alpha."

"So Thornwood is pretty powerful," I deduced.

"The larger the pack, the more territory they can claim. The chance of another pack threatening them is rare and unwise."

I nodded, having a better understanding of where we stood in all this. "You didn't tell me you had friends there…"

I felt him shrug. "Niall and Thomas were close. Sometimes he'd take me with him when I visited in the summer. I ran with Roy and some of the younger Weres on a full moon. We just didn't keep in touch after I left." Another shrug.

I tried picturing him in wolf form, his brilliant onyx coat shimmering as he ran through the moonlit forest with the others. "Do you miss it?"

"Running with a pack?" I felt his chest expand as he drew a breath. "Sometimes," he admitted. "Wolves were meant to thrive in packs."

"And you're sure you don't want that again?" Though every ounce of my being was objecting the idea, I had to ask.

"No. Not on Ryker's terms. I don't know if you've noticed this about me, but I'm not the submissive kind." His timbre was a low vibration, sending welcome shivers across my skin.

"Oh I've noticed," I said, giggling.

"I'm sorry, was that a *slight*?" He moved with the speed of sound, gathering my wrists in his hands and pinning them above my head. I laughed as his teeth grazed the soft skin on my neck. His knees pressed into either side of my hips, trapping me beneath him. In the pitch-dark, I saw the yellow of his eyes glowing with a touch of the Change.

Weeks ago, he'd been scared to show me what he really was, and now it was like he couldn't hide it. I didn't want him to. "I happen to like who you are," I told him. He'd released my wrists, and I ran my palms up his arms, fingers dipping over the hard impressions of his muscles.

He moved behind me, drawing my back against his chest. I tried to focus on the rhythm of his breathing–the slight push against my spine as he exhaled. The heat radiating from his body was warm enough that I didn't need blankets, but it was also waking the embers in my core. I wanted him. But the last time we were together like that, I set every candle in my room on fire. I didn't know how to control it, and since we weren't alone I decided to concentrate on keeping my heart beating at a regular rhythm. The walls were thin, and the last thing I wanted was to put on a show for his new house guests.

"Who were those girls Ryker was with? They looked a little young for him…"

Wren's body tensed. "They're nobody," he said.

"You expect me to believe that?" I wasn't *that* naïve. "*Summer Boy.*"

Wren sighed. "Hailey and I have history and Ryker knows it," he admitted drily–like it bored him to speak of it. "Hailey's older brother, Maddox, is in Ryker's inner circle. For all I know he might be the Beta, and Maddox and Hailey are kind of a package deal. If I had to guess, I'd say Ryker was probably trying to use her in hopes that she would appeal to my senses and help persuade me to join the pack."

Now I stiffened. A peculiar, foreign feeling raked my stomach. The jealousy monster was clawing her way out of my gut.

"Quinn," he breathed–the beautiful sound of his voice and the way he said my name caught in the space between us.

"Yes?"

"I can't feel you breathing."

"What kind of history?"

He gave a flat sort of snicker and rested his forehead on my shoulder, shaking it. "It doesn't matter, okay? I'm yours and only yours." He ran his palm down my arm until he caught my hand in his and pressed a kiss to my shoulder blade. The feel of his mouth lingered there, an invisible tattoo on my skin.

"I'm sorry," I sighed, "I should probably get used to this, huh?"

"Get used to what?" he asked. I didn't have to see it to know he was raising his signature eyebrow. I could hear it in his voice now.

"You're an incredible... *force*," I decided on the word, "and people notice." I shrugged beneath his arms.

He laughed and it was a musical sound. "So you think I'm a force, huh?"

"Don't you know it?" I said meekly.

"Maybe," he answered a beat later, his thumb finding the curve of my bottom lip. "But I like hearing you say it now and then anyway."

"You're a force, Wren Whelan."

"So are you." He kissed me.

The room was still dark when my eyelids fluttered open. A string of whispers had pulled me from my dreams and forced me from an otherwise peaceful slumber. I pushed up on my elbows, squinting through the dark as I struggled to make out the shape of Wren's body resting beside me. His breathing was steady and even, nothing that would indicate he was awake and trying to talk to me. Perhaps I'd only been dreaming... I started to slide down against the mattress, closing my eyes as I settled into the pillow, and then the whispers tangled through my ears again.

I bolted upright.

An icy chill crawled down my spine, raising goosebumps on the back of my neck. A quick glance at Wren confirmed that he was still sleeping, and if he couldn't hear the whispers–that meant it was all in my head...

My fingers clutched at the bedsheets as I briefly considered that I'd lost my mind. Yet, there was something familiar about the energy in the house and it reminded me of the same energy that had been nagging me to open the hidden door inside of my own house. The indecipherable words hummed with it, beckoning me to answer the call. Tentatively, I slipped out of bed, toes brushing the cool hardwood as I sidled out of the bedroom.

Wren never budged.

The house fell silent as I padded down the hall, pausing outside of Niall's old bedroom. The door was cracked just a fraction; I pushed it open a little wider and the hinges squealed in protest. "Blaire?" I whispered. I waited for her to respond but silence was all that greeted me.

An indistinguishable string of words tangled through my head, this time sounding as if they were coming from the living room. I swallowed hard; my feet began to move without consent as the whispering grew louder still. I was being pulled, like an invisible tether had attached itself to my core and was towing me along. My fingertips trailed along the ridges and grooves in the plaster wall in a halfhearted attempt to stop myself from going. It was as if the spell had entranced me, stripping me of my own free will until the need of discovery was the only thing that possessed my consciousness.

A lamp remained lit in the far corner of the living room next to the bookcase. It cast a soft, orange glow that stretched along the floor and chased the shadows into the corners. But it was the unfamiliar wooden box resting in the center of the coffee table that held my attention. Beautifully intricate knot-work framed the box's surface, the Trinity symbol engraved on the lid.

"*I know what you are.*" I heard in my mind. The voice was feminine and elegant; a velvet caress. "*I know you want answers, White One. This is the only way.*"

A bright, radiating light shone through the seam of the lid as I reached for the box. My breath hitched as I peeled back the lid and peered down at the pendant that once belonged to Rionach the Dark. The amulet was breathtaking. It was exactly how I'd remembered it from my vision. The oval moonstone was colorless but its surface sparkled with an iridescent blue sheen. It was framed by ornamental silver filigree, forming the shape of a teardrop.

"*Touch it and know,*" the voice suggested.

I hesitated, hovering over the box as my subconscious rang with the signal of warning bells. The old power swelled through the center of the stone, twisting like clouds in a hurricane. The light was too bright–too powerful for me to resist any longer. I plunged my fingers into the box and wrapped my hand around the stone.

Light flooded through me, conjuring an invisible wind that swept my body backwards and lifted my chin high in the air. The tremulous current pulled me under and the floor slipped out from beneath me.

My vision swam over the rolling hills, soaring as though I were being carried on the wings of a majestic bird. We passed over the mountains, skimming over the tops of the pines as we fled for the eastern shores. It was there, tucked beneath the protection of the maritime forests, perched on a rocky cove that I saw a cabin. The structure rippled, showing me tiny sparks of neon green within a meadow.

"*I know what you are,*" the silken voice repeated. "*Your world is not safe, White One, not while the Dark spirit remains. Seek me. Seek the sun when day takes up the false cloak of night.*"

I gasped for air, sputtering and coughing as I came back to my body. Wren was holding me, gripping both my wrists firmly in his hands. Blaire and Bryna were gaping at me wide eyed and horror-stricken.

"You're okay, you're okay," Wren's voice was at my ear. I stopped fighting, collapsing instead against his chest. The amulet, I realized, was clenched in my fist. My breaths were coming in shallow, uneven gasps.

"What happened?" Blaire croaked.

"She was calling to me," I managed, half choking on air.

"Was it Rionach?" A deep crease formed between Bryna's eyebrows. She moved closer, studying my face.

"No," I said. Sweat dampened my brow. "It was someone else."

"*Who*, lass?" Blaire asked.

"I don't know," I said a little harsher than I meant.

"Take it easy," Wren's voice was at my ear again. He lowered me back onto the couch, and pulled me against his side, smoothing strands of mussed hair back from my face. "How'd you get the amulet?"

"It was on the coffee table."

"Impossible," Bryna retorted. "I put the box on the nightstand before I went to bed." She looked to her sister for affirmation and Blaire nodded.

"I heard whispering," I said. "I came to find you but everyone was asleep. It called to me, Blaire. I found it here on the coffee table, I swear."

A shadow of fear passed over her face then, darkening her features. "Are you absolutely certain that it wasn't the voice of the Dark Witch?"

"I know her voice." I remembered the feel of it, weighted with sharpness and poison. There was no allure to this voice–no pull of dark seduction. "I had a vision," I said, recalling it now that my heart began to settle. I explained to them what I had seen and what the voice had told me. "It was the same riddle the White Witch gave me the night we became the Trinity. Do you remember?"

Blaire pursed her lips in thought. "Seek the sun when day takes up the false cloak of night," she repeated.

"It's an allegory," Wren said a beat later.

"Right, I've got that part." Blaire began to pace across the living room. "But for what?" She tapped her bottom lip, continuing to pace.

"If those were words spoken of the White Witch," Bryna said, "then whoever is trying to contact you must be in league with the White Light."

"Unless it's a trap," Wren said. "I'm not putting trust in anything that comes from an heirloom of pure evil."

"You," Blaire spun on her heel and pointed an accusing finger in Wren's direction, "should maybe consider putting some actual clothes on, yeah?"

Wren lifted his eyebrow. I had been so caught up in what happened with the amulet that I didn't even realize he'd been wearing nothing but boxers. My face heated and Wren stood up slowly, snickering as he headed for the hallway.

"He *is* rather distracting," Bryna said.

"Yes, he is," Blaire agreed.

I lifted my eyebrows, glancing off to the side. "What time is it anyway?"

"Just after four," Bryna said. "I suspect none of us will be able to get back to sleep after this." She sighed and crossed her arms.

Wren returned dressed in a T-shirt and a pair of track sweats.

"We can't put the amulet back in the box," Bryna decided. "If it's moved on its own, or by whatever force, that means its power has awakened. We can't risk it being stolen from us or manipulated by another force. I'm afraid you're going to have to wear it." Bryna looked at me hard, her glacial eyes seeming to penetrate my skull.

"Why should she wear it?" Wren demanded.

"Because it didn't call to any of the rest of us," she answered in a sharp tone.

"All the more reason for her not to wear it," Wren snapped. His irises began to churn with the electric current of the harvest moon.

"Don't make me get a muzzle for your pretty face."

"Stop!" I held out both my hands and the amulet swung free from my grasp, curving down like a pendulum from my wrist. Everyone looked at me. "I feel confident in saying that the voice who called out to me wasn't evil. Whoever she was or *is*–I believe that she's trying to help.

I think the White Witch wants me to find that cabin." Even as I said it aloud, the belief seemed to take root in my core.

"It is possible," Blaire said after a long pause, "that a talisman can be used as a sort of communication device."

"How?" I asked, frowning.

"That's very old magic," Bryna said. "Talisman communication is an ancient form of scrying. A witch would have to be very powerful to find you–let alone use it to send you a message. That's assuming the being is even a witch."

"Can we track her somehow–find out where she's located?"

Blaire chewed the inside of her cheek in thought. "I'm not sure. There's a spell we can try but I'm not sure what good it will do. This form of communication is a lost form of ancient magic."

"Of course it is." I sighed.

"We might as well get started now. We've a lot to discuss," Bryna said.

"Right then, I'll go start the coffee." Blaire rose and headed for the kitchen as Bryna disappeared down the hallway.

Wren was looking at me. I could sense the weight of his gaze–been sensing it since he'd pulled me back from my vision. I shifted my head, finding his eyes and the deep concern that spread through his features. He didn't need to say anything. I knew what he was thinking. *This is too dangerous.* In silent response, I slipped the silver chain over my head.

"I don't like this," Wren said low enough so that only I could hear.

"We don't have any other choice."

Chapter Eight
Crash Course Lessons

A plume of dust lifted in the air as Bryna dropped a large leather-bound grimoire on the table in front of me with a bang. I coughed, batting the dust away from my nose as she stood at the head of the table. "As you must be aware," Bryna began in a tone that would rival an esteemed college professor, "the Aurora Coven has the greatest collection of grimoires and texts that have been passed down through Supernatural history. All the knowledge you wish to acquire is now a mere fingertip's length away. Blaire and I were fortunate to grow up in such an educational environment, and she's brought it to my attention that you weren't gifted with quite the equal opportunity."

My narrowed gaze slid to Blaire who sat beside me. Her shoulder twitched in an apologetic shrug.

"No matter," Bryna continued. "The witches of the Aurora Coven are the most privileged in all the world. Even if you had been raised among a coven, you still wouldn't be on our level. We'll help you as best we can, but I think it would be quite beneficial for you to start studying up on some of the material I've brought with me. Luiseach's heir needs to be sharp of mind." She beamed bright enough to cover up the patronizing implication of her words and plopped down into the chair beside me.

Wren had his back to the table, filling his mug at the counter, but I saw that his shoulders were shaking in silent laughter. I pursed my lips together to keep myself from retorting something I might later regret and met Bryna's gaze. "So," I cleared my throat, "what exactly do we need to do to cast this spell?"

Bryna reached for the grimoire and slid it in her direction, flipping through a couple of pages until she settled on a spell with a title written in bold, metallic ink in neat script hand: *The Tracing Spell.* "All magic leaves an imprint unique unto the one whom cast the spell," Bryna said. "It's sort of like a fingerprint–none two are alike. If we can figure out the origin of the magic that was used to bring you the message, then in theory we should be able to trace the magic to its owner."

I nodded slowly, hoping my expression wouldn't betray my total lack of comprehending.

"Take off the necklace," Bryna instructed, "and place it in the bowl, here."

I did as I was told and dropped the amulet down into the wooden pit at the center of the table. Bryna followed along with the spell's ingredients, adding dried herbs and spices to the mixture. She then uncapped a vial of clear liquid and poured its contents into the bowl; tendrils of purple vapor pooled over the edges, fanning across the table.

"Cool," I breathed, watching the hypnotic smoke curl off the edge of the table.

"It's not been tampered by Darkness," Bryna said, studying the coils as a frown creased her brow. "Odd though... I'm not sensing any particular pattern that would help us–"

Just then the bowl cracked in half as though it had been made with the durability of an egg shell, and the liquid, as well as the amulet, spilled out onto the table as the three of us jumped. "Was that supposed to happen?" I asked.

"No," Blaire said, jumping up to retrieve a towel. "It means it's untraceable."

"So now what?" Wren asked. He'd been watching in silence from the counter, arms cradled over his chest while we worked.

"I'm not quite sure," Bryna answered him, brows still knitted. "I suppose we'll have to do a bit more research on spells that can penetrate Old Magic." She reached for the amulet as Blaire finished mopping up the mess and extended it to me. "Keep this on you at all times. It's the only way to ensure its safety."

I slid the amulet back over my head and tried to ignore Wren's glower as he worked his jaw. "And in the meantime?"

"It's probably best if you go about your day as you would normally. It's important that we don't draw any unwanted attention to our quest. As forces of the Light, it's paramount that protecting the innocent always remains our first priority."

I nodded and failed to stifle a yawn. Between the four of us, we'd already gone through a pot of coffee and were working on a second. It was starting to become clear that no amount of caffeine was going to improve my energy level.

Bryna leaned over and pulled a smaller textbook from her messenger bag. "I'd like you to go through this book and see if you can find anything useful related to scrying," she said to me before turning to Wren. "If it's all right with you, I'd really like to amplify the safety measures around your cabin. The last thing we need is for the rogue werewolves to track us here."

"Blaire and I cast a protection spell after the Trinity's bonding," I informed her, "it's similar to the Chameleon Shield so the Weres shouldn't be able to locate us."

"That's all fine and well, but the cabin still needs adequate protective wards."

I opened my mouth to reply and felt the words die in my mouth before I could come up with a retort.

"Wren?" She blinked up at him, still waiting on his permission.

"Knock yourself out," he insisted.

"Excellent!" she said. *Goddess this witch was annoying.* "We've all work to do, so we best get to it. Call if you should need us," Bryna said, strutting off down the hall. After I heard the door to Niall's bedroom close, I fixed my glower on Blaire.

"What?" She feigned an innocent tone.

"Oh, I don't know Blaire, maybe you could have warned us that your sister was going to ride in on her high horse of superiority *before* she got here."

"She has a strong personality, but she means well," Blaire said, carrying her coffee mug to the sink. "Just give her some time."

"Time is something we don't have in abundance at the moment," I reminded her.

"And speaking of time," Wren said, glancing down at his watch, "we're going to be late for school if we don't get a move on."

I grumbled into my empty mug and scooped my new 'extra-curricular' magical study book off the table and stuffed it into my bag. Wren was already at the door, spinning his keys around his index finger as a smile of amusement flirted with his lips.

"Call if you should need anything," Blaire mocked as Wren and I exited the house. I couldn't be sure, but the echo of her laughter seemed to follow.

Her white-blonde hair looked silver under the fluorescent lighting of the classroom. I could scarcely believe what I was seeing. Hailey, the werewolf from Thornwood, was standing in front of Mrs. Combs' desk, holding a purple glittery binder against her chest. She'd handed Mrs. Combs a slip of paper and was waiting for instruction. The bell rang and Annabelle flopped down into the seat beside me.

"Who's the blonde goddess?" she whispered, leaning over her bag as she pulled out her French book. I couldn't answer. Instead, I watched Mrs. Combs rise from her desk chair and face the classroom.

"Bienvenue, Miss Reynolds," Mrs. Combs greeted her. "Everyone, this is Hailey. She's a transfer from Thornwood. Tell us, what brings you to Silver Mountain?" Mrs. Combs beamed.

"Well," Hailey said in a painfully cheerful tone, "my aunt recently accepted the new secretary position and couldn't stop talking about how wonderful the school was. I'm looking forward to the academic challenge and joining a sports team or two."

"Oh that's most excellent! Your aunt is just lovely. We're so lucky to have her join our faculty." Mrs. Combs turned and faced the rest of us. "I hope you all will do your part in welcoming Miss. Reynolds to our school. Go Foxes!" She giggled emphatically, raising a fist in the air in a "go-get-'em" display that made my stomach roll with nausea. "Hailey dear, go ahead and sit by Courtney." She pointed to the open seat closest to the shelves on the far wall.

Courtney, having spotted a kindred spirit, waved her over with a smile. I watched Hailey glide across the room with confidence that only a Were could pull off.

"Is that–" Annabelle started to speak, but I jammed the corner of my book into her forearm. Thanks to Mrs. Combs partnering program, all our desks were pushed together in twos to make it easier to work on group assignments.

I took out my notebook and scrawled: *Superhearing*. I tilted the page so she could read that it wasn't safe to talk right now.

Wren and I had picked Annabelle up for school that morning and told her what happened while we were in Thornwood. She understood the threat of what Hailey's presence meant for us, and I watched as goosebumps prickled her forearms. *So much for three days*, I thought disdainfully. Thornwood was already encroaching on our territory and I had a feeling Hailey was here on a reconnaissance mission.

I needed to talk to Wren.

When the dismissal bell finally rang, I jumped up from my seat and packed away my belongings with haste. Annabelle and I had lunch together, but I knew Wren had AP physics next period and if I hurried, I could catch him before class started.

"Save me a seat?" I asked Annabelle.

"Sure," she said.

I darted out of the classroom and took the stair steps two at a time as I jogged to the main level and passed through the lobby. I turned the corner and almost smacked into Wren's chest as he strolled out of his government class. He looked down at me and grinned. He knew I'd be there. His superior senses alerted him of my presence long before I arrived, but when he really looked at my face, his smile turned into a frown.

"We have a problem," I said.

"What is it?"

"Hailey," I said. "She was in my French class. I think she's transferred."

The muscle in Wren's jaw worked over the bone. He stayed quiet, his eyes fixed distantly as he worked over the issue in his mind. The tendons in his forearm began to twitch. I reached out, covering his arm with my palm.

"Look at me." I reached up with my other hand and cupped the side of his face. The rough stubble on his jawline scraped against my thumb. A beat later, his eyes blinked down to meet mine, but I saw the indignation flickering across the surface.

"All right," Wren's voice was rough and quiet, "just be on guard. We can't afford any slip-ups as far as the Trinity is concerned. We knew Thornwood meant business, so we're just going to have to play this smart."

"Do you think Ryker sent her here as bait?"

"Probably, but his intentions are futile. It's not going to work on me." Wren cupped my chin, fingertips lifting so that my gaze was locked on his. "I need you to be careful, okay?"

"I know," I said. "I'll be careful."

The bell rang and the hallway thinned as students scurried into their classrooms. "Talk later?"

I nodded and watched him slip out of view. The smell of food drifted from the cafeteria and my stomach twisted in a way that turned hunger into sickness. I couldn't even think about eating. I turned back for the lobby and excused myself to the ladies' room. I was overcome by the powerful scent of bleach but at least it was quiet there–save for the sound of running pipes. I turned on the hot water, which only ever reached a lukewarm temperature and held my hands under the running faucet.

The Dark Witch's amulet caught the light and gleamed in the reflection of the mirror. The stone was about two inches in length; solid, but I barely felt the weight of it against my skin. It was strange–wearing something that belonged to the ultimate mistress of evil and knowing what it had been used for. I reached up, grasping the stone between my thumb and index finger, turning it until the milky blue sheen caught the light.

'*Its power has awakened*,' Bryna had said. I wondered, leaning closer to the mirror, what that meant… The sound of distant musical laughter filled my head and I blinked, stepping back from the mirror as something caught my peripheral. Hailey was standing in the doorway.

"I thought I smelled vanilla," she said, slipping in behind me. A smile spread on her glossy lips as she stepped up to the sink, fluffing her hair. She slid her purse from her shoulder and took out a tube of lip gloss and began reapplying a thicker layer. "Strawberry," she told me, "used to be Wren's favorite."

I clamped my jaw and chose not to give her the satisfaction of commenting. I turned off the faucet and tore a couple of sheets from the paper towel dispenser to dry my trembling hands. I prayed she was too caught up in her own reflection to notice.

"How long have you two been together?" she asked, dropping her cosmetics back into her bag.

"That's really none of your business," I replied in a flat tone.

She giggled, and the sound made the hair on the back of my neck rise. "I'm happy for him, really," she said. "Clearly you have something the rest of us didn't." She shrugged as if it didn't matter, but I knew she was baiting me. "Still, I wouldn't get too used to it lasting, it never does with Wren."

I snickered, shaking my head as I started for the doorway. She sidestepped and blocked the exit. Was she really trying to play this game with me?

My eyes narrowed. "What do you want, Hailey?"

"I think that answer is pretty obvious."

"*Wren*?" I scoffed.

"He'll get tired of you," she added, reaching out and wrapping her palm around my upper arm and squeezing.

"You don't know anything about us," I snapped, peeling her fingers off my arm. Blood was building in my eardrums, ringing with ferocity. I knew she would be able to hear the change in my heartbeat–knew that reaction was what she wanted.

"I know that you can't produce an heir," she said with a malicious grin. "You see, Quinn, you're just a temporary distraction and Wren is still very young and let's face it–*male*. He has needs, and your soft human shell won't be able to handle the physical destruction that happens when a Were loses control to their desires. He'll get tired of being careful with you, and when he does, I'll be waiting. He needs to be with his own kind–with someone who knows how to handle him the right way. Call it animal magnetism honey, but you don't have what he needs."

"I hope you have an eternity's worth of patience, because I can promise that's how long you'll be waiting." I snatched my arm back and shoved into her shoulder hard as I exited the bathroom. Heat exploded beneath my skin as if my very own blood was boiling, and I wondered if this was how Wren must feel when the Change takes over. I wanted nothing more than to rip out of my skin and take off running through the forest. The element of Fire began tingling in my fingertips and knew that if I wasn't careful, I could lose control over my abilities.

Get a grip, Quinn, this isn't like you!

Still, there was something about Hailey's words that stung with brutal force. We were much too young to be thinking about it now, but I knew because of our differences that we could never have children together. But up until recently, that had been the last thing on my mind. We were two souls linked together, bound to one another by an ancient thread of reincarnation. He was as much a part of me as I was a part of him. Our bond was encoded in our DNA. Not being able to produce an heir wouldn't stand in the way of that… There were other options if we ever chose to have a family.

He has needs, and your soft human shell won't be able to handle the physical destruction that happens when a Were loses control to their desires. He'll get tired of being careful with you. Her cruel words echoed in my ears. I fled across the school building and pushed through the exit doors that led to the baseball field. Outside, the cool air rushed against my face, cooling the heat that had suffused my cheeks. I collapsed against the brick, the skin on my back scraping over the rough granules as I slid down the length of the wall. The physical pain was almost a welcome release. I raked my hands through my hair until my fingers settled on the pendent instead.

Something placid fanned through my being then, spreading slow like melting honey. It warmed my core, and my ragged breaths grew even. Now, I could hear the autumn birds chirping in the trees, and watched the dying leaves sweeping across the ground. The sound I'd heard in the bathroom–that dark, musical laughter filled my mind. *You can control them, White One. You harness the key.*

"That's an interesting necklace, Quinny," Dad commented. I was sitting at the kitchen table attempting to do homework. *Attempting*–because the walls were buzzing with awakened energy and the pulsating sound was vibrating in my eardrums. I was fidgeting, rolling the pendent between my knuckles and struggling to concentrate.

"Oh, yeah, I got it from the Magic Shoppe. Blaire special ordered it from Ireland." *Only half a lie*, I thought.

"Does it do anything?" Dad asked in a casual tone.

I stopped fidgeting. This was the first time since my mother passed that my dad spoke of magic–outside of my visions–that is. But those, he understood, couldn't necessarily be helped. His warm brown eyes were fixed on mine, patiently waiting for me to reply. I studied his face, searching for any sign that he might just be asking to be polite when in fact he didn't actually want to know.

"It's a moonstone," I answered. I waited a beat, gauging his reaction before I continued. "It has a lot of versatile properties, but it's known as a protective talisman that can unlock secrets and magnify emotions. It's also thought to harness the energy of the moon," I said. *This is probably why the Dark Witch was using it.* If I had to guess–that was how she managed to control a whole army of werewolves.

Dad nodded. "So, Blaire," Dad began somewhat awkwardly, "she's like you, isn't she?"

"U-uh," I stammered, thinking that perhaps my dad was a little more perceptive than I'd given him credit for.

"It's okay," he rushed. "You should have someone that you can talk to about–well–you know, magical things." He pressed his lips into a smile, and I saw something in his eyes I hadn't seen in a very long time: light. *Hope.*

"How did you know?"

"I just had a feeling." He shrugged. "Quinn, you don't have to hide who you are from me. I accepted your mother for who she was, and I accept you, too. Magic is a huge part of who you are as a person. I wouldn't want you to stop being you."

A sort of weightlessness consumed my entire being then. I felt lighter than I had in years–not realizing how important it was to hear my dad say those words. "I just thought… when magic couldn't save her that–"

"–No," Dad said, "It was never about what magic couldn't do. It was about what *I* couldn't do–as a man, as a father." He paused, and the energy pulsing in the walls seemed to lay still–listening, waiting. "I know it hasn't been easy for us to talk about since she's been gone, but, she would want us to."

I shoved out from the table and made my way over to where my father was standing at the sink and wrapped my arms around his waist. His arms tightened around my shoulders and I breathed in the familiar smell of him–the sawdust that always seemed to be clinging to the fibers of his clothing.

My heart swelled, chest contracting. For a minute, everything that was crushing down on me lifted away. The fact that my mother had hidden what I was destined to become in an effort to keep me safe didn't seem to matter anymore. I didn't have to know why, or understand her reasons for doing what she did. I could just accept it; like my dad had accepted me.

"Your mother loved being a witch," Dad said. "She was so excited to teach you about nature and help you use your gifts. I'm sorry that she couldn't be here to help you with your visions, Quinn. I always wished there was something I could do, but I never knew how to help. I hope you know I've always done what I thought was right."

"You've been great," I told him, tightening my hold. I felt his lips brush the top of my hair and then he was letting me go.

He looked down at his watch, eyes widening. "I've got to get ready," he said.

"For what?"

"Well," his cheeks flamed ever so slightly, "I sort of have a date."

"Shut up!" A huge grin expanded across my face as I jabbed his shoulder with a little punch. "Please tell me it's finally Josephine."

"What do you mean *finally*?" he said, turning for the stairs.

"Where are you taking her?" I followed him up the stairs and into his bedroom where his closet doors were spread wide open. Work boots, old shoe boxes, and his old bowling bag littered the bottom of the closet floor.

"Dinner," he said, sifting through the hangers, "and dancing."

"Dancing?" I lifted an eyebrow and pushed him out of the way. Emmett Callaghan was not known for dressing up. His preference to flannels and old, holey-jeans bearing the stains of various wood finishes was his signature look. But I happened to know there was a nice blue button-up tucked somewhere within the dusty, threadbare crypt he called a closet. "Since when can you dance?"

"Since prom of nineteen ninety-four if you must know."

I snorted and pulled the button-up from the back corner of his closet. "It needs ironed, but this will be perfect," I told him.

"I am capable of dressing myself, you know." He took the shirt I was holding and headed for the laundry room.

"Judging by your current appearance, I'd say that's questionable," I teased him on the way back down the steps.

When he reached the landing at the bottom of the floor, he turned and faced me. I was still a couple of steps behind him, so we were standing face to face in height. "You're okay with this, right?"

"It's been almost five years, Dad," I said. "Jo is crazy about you and you deserve to be happy."

He grinned—the right corner of his mouth pulling just a little higher than the left. "Well, as long as my daughter approves." He shrugged.

"She does," I said, spinning him around and giving him a little nudge toward the laundry room. "You get started and I'll go find you a matching tie."

He rolled his eyes but decided a verbal protest was not in his best interest. I headed back up the stairs and began combing through his closet for the small rack of ties he'd kept on the top shelf. I stood on the tips of my toes, grabbing hold of the shelf to give myself an extra boost when the wall's surface began to ripple.

I stumbled back, nearly tripping over my feet. The energy was getting stronger and the humming resumed to a loud roar in my ears. Without thinking, I reached up and squeezed the moonstone at my throat. *Just stop*, I beckoned. Just as sudden as the rippling had started, it ended. I stared at the wall for a moment longer, wondering why the pull of the hidden room seemed to be growing desperate for my attention. And why, also, that I had such a firm aversion to it.

The crease deepened between my eyes as the moonstone warmed beneath my fingertips. I didn't know what, but something didn't *feel* right. I grabbed the first necktie I could get my hands on and left the room.

Chapter Nine
A Night Within A Day

Annabelle was the first to arrive after Dad left for his date. She was looking at me in a way that made it clear she was waiting for me to snap, and she'd been looking at me that way ever since I told her what happened in the ladies' room with Hailey.

"I'm fine," I stressed, rolling my eyes.

"Does Wren know what Hailey said to you?" she countered.

"No. And I plan to keep it that way."

"Why on earth would you do that? I mean, the audacity of that chick is astounding."

"Because," I said, "Wren hasn't been handling stress very well lately and the last thing I want to do is add more drama to his already overflowing plate. I can handle Hailey. She's just trying to push my buttons. Ryker is using her to get to Wren and me."

"Yeah and his plan seems to be working," Annabelle blatantly pointed out.

I shot her a look, warning her to drop it. I was beginning to think the moonstone pendant had quite a bit to do with how I'd reacted earlier; the whole heightened emotions side effect- thing was not working in my favor.

"Fine," she breathed. "Where is my favorite werewolf, anyway?"

"Where do you think?"

"Still running patrol?"

"Yep." I dropped down on the cushion beside her. "He told me he'd be back by seven. He knows Bryna and Blaire are coming over to keep digging for a way to contact the person responsible for making me wear this thing." I lifted Rionach's amulet, watching as the milky stone caught the afternoon light filtering through the window. The blue sheen looked brighter now–a veil, for things hidden underneath.

"I still can't believe you're wearing it. It's creepy." Annabelle shivered.

"I don't have another choice. Bryna says its power has awakened, so we can't risk losing track of it. If the Dark forces find out we have it, they'll do whatever it takes to try and get it back for the Dark Witch–or Penny, or whoever is summoning her spirit's return. If we can't find a way to destroy this thing…" I let my words trail off, unable to finish the sentence.

"Blaire cast the Chameleon Shield spell, right?" Annabelle covered her hand with mine, squeezing. "They won't be able to find you."

"It's not permanent; it won't hold forever."

"We just need it to hold long enough," said a voice at the front door. We looked up, watching as Blaire and Bryna appeared in front of the screen door.

"It's open," I called.

"You should be more careful about speaking of magical things so freely when there are open screens and windows," Bryna told me. Her curly lion's mane of copper hair was pulled into a French braid with a single ringlet falling loose at her temple. "That's exactly why your home should be protected with wards. And for heaven's sake, you should keep your door locked." She reached back, twisting the brass knob below the handle after they'd stepped inside.

"A locked door won't stop a werewolf attack," I said, pushing myself upright.

Bryna pressed her lips together, but I could see the little tick in her brow. A beat later, Wren showed up in front of the door and yanked on the handle. A sharp, metallic screech sounded as his hand came away–still attached to the now broken brass arc. He muttered a curse under his breath, holding up the evidence.

"Case and point," I said, jumping up from the couch to let him in.

Bryna's alabaster cheeks burned a shade of strawberry and Annabelle burst out in laughter.

"Sorry," Wren said, dropping the broken handle in my palm. "I'll replace it."

"No worries," I said. "It had a rusty screw and needed replaced anyway."

He bent to kiss my cheek and then stepped around me as the group spread into the living room. Bryna opened a large bag that looked like it had been made from ugly utility carpet and began pulling spell books and candles to the surface. "These," she began, placing the contents on the coffee table, "are tools that should help us learn what the witch was trying to communicate with you this morning."

"Did you find a way to track her?" I asked.

"Not exactly," she replied, "but I found a spell that will allow us to recall your vision. I thought with all of us involved, maybe one of us might recognize a landmark or something useful. It's an old spell, so it requires a blood offering."

"A blood offering?" Annabelle piped up.

"Just a wee prick of the finger, nothing more," Blaire said.

"Right." Annabelle nodded.

"We should cast in the Nexus," Bryna said. "We'll need the aid of all the elements for this one."

My gaze cut to Wren. None of us had been back to the Hollow since Niall's death. The Hollow had once been my sacred ground–my safe haven, and now I didn't think I could ever look at it again and not feel and see the awful things that happened there. Wren caught my expression, eyes hardening with anguish.

"Does it need to be the Nexus?" My tone barely registered above a whisper. I glanced at Blaire, watching as the muscle in her jaw flexed.

"It is a bit of a trek," she added. "I think it's best if we don't venture too far into the forest while the rogue Weres are still out there."

"Fine. We'll just go far enough in to cast a protection circle in case a passing human should stumble in uninvited," Bryna said. She stuffed the candles back into her magic carpet bag and hauled the load over her shoulder. "Quinn, lead the way."

I straightened myself and led the others out the back door, down the steps and across the backyard until it met the tree line. Wren took my hand, wordlessly taking the lead as we stepped under the autumn canopy. He lifted his face to the wind, cataloguing the smells of the forest as we walked. I tried to mirror his steps so I wouldn't make too much noise–not that it mattered. Annabelle sloshed through the dead leaves like a hulking giant instead of the scant five-foot-one (still in junior-sized clothing) being that she was.

We were about four hundred meters into the forest when Bryna announced the location was good enough. I looked around, taking inventory of the big oaks, maples, and pines that surrounded us. The earth hummed with energy, flowing in the ground beneath us and up through the roots that were the life force of the prodigious trees. I took a deep breath, relaxing into the familiarity of the rich smells of my forest, letting it soothe the tension in my limbs.

Bryna dropped her bag, bending to retrieve the colored candle pillars, ceremonial athame, and a thick leather-bound book. "For this to work properly, each of us should stand with the element we have the strongest affinity for."

"Quinn should stand with Fire," Blaire stated. "Though I'm closely allied with Earth, I think Wren should represent the element." She pointed to the green candle. "I'll stand in for Spirit since Bryna is Air."

"What about me?" Annabelle asked.

"You can stand in for Water." Blaire smiled at her. "I have a feeling that you'd be a good match with the element."

"And I get to go on this little vision quest with everyone?"

"That's right," Bryna said, thrusting the blue candle into her hands. "Everyone needs to form up with the shape of a pentagram. Spirit candle at the apex," she said, ushering Blaire to the tip. "Put the candles at your feet."

"You okay with this Anna?" Judging by her expression I wasn't so sure; she looked as though she might throw up.

"I'm good," she said.

I looked up at Blaire and wondered if she saw the apprehension clouding my aura. Annabelle had seen me perform spells before and helped me practice honing my skill of Blood Magic–but she'd never participated in a spell as big as this. Was it safe?

Blaire nodded, almost as if she were reading my mind.

Bryna took the ceremonial athame and placed it in the center of the pentagram next to her spell book. I looked down at my palms and saw the faint pink lines that had healed from the night the three of us had linked ourselves as the Trinity; scars to mark our permanent bond.

In front of the yellow candle, Bryna lifted her hands, motioning for Blaire and I to do the same. The flame of Fire bubbled at the surface, and I flexed my fingers as my palms ignited with violet-orange flame. The brilliant display of light rolled obediently, waiting for the cue.

"*Solas*," the three of us commanded in unison, and the Fire jumped from our palms and lit the candlewicks. Bryna walked to the center of the pentagram and picked up the athame, pricking the flesh of her thumb. Fluidly, she moved to the Spirit candle in front of Blaire, squeezing a few drops of her blood into the flame.

"Accept my blood as payment for this Spirit quest." She bowed her head and passed the blade to Blaire who repeated the process. Then it was my turn. I barely felt the blade pierce my skin but the crimson bead bloomed at the surface, and I squeezed my blood into the flame before passing the knife to Wren. When he finished, he sat the blade back at the center of the pentagram, and returned to the Earth candle.

Annabelle was next. She didn't hesitate, only wincing a little as she pricked her thumb and then glanced up at Blaire for affirmation before squeezing her blood into the flame.

"Link hands," Blaire instructed.

Bryna's book was facing her as she read aloud the words of the ancient text. "Hear my voice Great Mother, with blood and Spirit link us now." The candle flames shot into the air, rising to Bryna's call. "We ask that you grant us third sight into Quinn's vision, allowing us to see what she has seen this day. Let the power of the witches soar, grant us sight beneath the starlit veil, so what is lost let it be no more. Lig sé a bheith níos mó."

At once, a great wind burst forth, spiraling upwards toward the sky with a vortex of dead leaves. My head snapped back and my eyelids clamped shut. The silken words the witch spoke to me echoed in the air, and again I was drifting on the wings of a large bird. The evergreen pines rushed by in a blur as the bird soared high over the mountains. The scenery shifted as clouds of varying shape and color rolled across the sky, but the bird never wavered from its eastern direction. The violet light of dusk became the backdrop of the maritime forest, and I could hear the ocean swells breaking over the rocky cove. The bird circled the old cabin, settling on the red brick chimney. The vision rippled, showing us a glimpse of a meadow with tiny, green sparks. A current sizzled through my temples like static electricity, and we all snapped back into our conscious bodies, gasping and sputtering for air.

Annabelle was on the ground with her eyes closed.

A bolt of dread-fueled energy snapped through my limbs as I flung myself to Annabelle's side. Wren beat me there, his arm scooping her shoulders up from the ground. Her eyes fluttered rapidly beneath closed lids. "I thought you said the spell was safe?" My gaze cut to Blaire who was kneeling beside me.

"It is," Blaire said. "I don't know what happened."

"Your powers are amped now that the Trinity has been awoken," Bryna explained. "I felt it too. If I weren't a Supernatural that spell would have knocked me flat out."

Annabelle groaned, her eyebrows scrunching.

"Annabelle?" I grabbed her hand as she blinked up at me.

"Ow," she groaned again, reaching up and pressing the heel of her hand against the side of her head.

"Are you all right?"

"Peachy." Her gaze drifted up to the left. Wren was supporting most of her weight, cradling her against his side. Her eyes widened, cheeks flushing. "Hey, paws off Wolf Boy."

"Oh yeah, she's fine." I giggled with relief as Wren helped her into a sitting position.

"What happened?"

"Sorry about that. The spell must have knocked you out," Blaire said. "Did you see anything?"

"Just a bright light and then… nothing." She shook her head. "What did you guys see?"

"More than that," Bryna said, resting her hands on her hips. She turned to me. "Did you recognize anything the second time through?"

I shook my head. "No."

Bryna crossed her arms and began pacing the forest in thought. Blaire studied her sister, eyes narrowing. "I know that look," she said, "you think you know something."

"There was a reason the vision quest was being led by an owl," Bryna said. *Oh, so that's what that was*, I thought. "I think we're dealing with an enchantress," she added.

I'd heard this term before but it had been years and the details blurred like the soft edges of a watercolor painting. "What's an enchantress?" Wren asked.

"A female witch with the ability to influence an animal's mind and possess its cerebral awareness. I believe that's what she was doing with the owl, she was using its mind in an attempt to lead us to her," Bryna answered.

"Too bad she can't just come to you guys," Annabelle said, pushing herself into a standing position. She wobbled, reaching out to steady herself on the nearest tree trunk. Wren shifted closer to her side, but she held out her hand, waving him away.

"It would make things easier, but there must be a reason she needs us to come to her," Blaire said. "It must have something do with the allegory."

"Seek me. Seek the sun when day takes up the false cloak of night," I repeated.

"Any idea when that might be?" Annabelle asked.

I shuffled my feet, staring at the brown leaves that coated the forest floor. Science was my thing—my brain didn't exactly compute hidden messages within a riddle. I was missing something so obvious. Rionach's amulet began to grow warm against my skin. I reached up, running my thumb over the glossy surface. The weight of it finally registered as it swelled. *Strange.*

"A false cloak of night is a play on words," Wren said. "To me, it sounds like we're supposed to look to the sun during a fake form of night."

"Well now that clears things up. Thanks for that brilliant deduction, Wolf Boy." Annabelle snorted.

"No, that's actually a good translation," Blaire said, holding up a finger as her gaze slipped to the side in thought. "The words are old so we'd have to rearrange them in order for them to make sense in present time. Like, a false night within a day."

"Why does everything magic related have to be a riddle?" Annabelle crossed her arms. "I mean why can't there be a straightforward answer like, 'show up at Mountainside Pizzeria at eight o'clock on Monday the 10th of October?'"

Wren lifted his trademark eyebrow.

"What? I'm hungry."

I grinned.

"Back to the allegory," Blaire said. "We need to be thinking of events that might take place when there's a false night within a day."

"So what... we're dealing with like a really cloudy day that blots out the sun, maybe?" I shrugged. "How else would there be a night within a day?"

Wren's gaze snapped to my face, his tawny eyes lighting up as if I'd said something exceptionally clever. "It's a solar eclipse."

"That's it!" Blaire said, snapping her fingers.

"Well done, Wren," Bryna complimented. "I think you're right."

I was nodding. "A solar eclipse can only occur when the moon passes between the sun and the earth and blocks out the sun's light." *Yes*, that seemed right. A spark of excitement shot through my insides.

"And thus creating a night within a day," Annabelle said, grinning. "Damn, Wolf Boy, you actually solved the puzzle."

"Don't act so surprised. You can thank me by buying the pizza." He grinned.

"I've seen the way you eat–no way do I want that bill."

"This is great guys, really, but we still need to know when the next solar eclipse is," I said.

Blaire held up her cellphone. "It's this Sunday."

My temporary high plummeted to the bottom of my gut. "So we have five days to figure out where that cottage from my vision is–assuming that's where we need to be for the eclipse, and only two more days to figure out the Thornwood problem."

"Mood killer," Annabelle said under her breath.

"I'm sorry. We're just working with limited resources here, and I'm worried. We need to figure out how to find this enchantress person." The amulet was pulsing now, like the slow beat of a heart. "I hate waiting around."

Blaire was biting her bottom lip, dragging her foot in an arc across the dried leaves. "It is a bit odd we've only been given a few pieces of information at a time."

"There must be an explanation," Bryna added. "You're sure there was nothing in that vision you recognized?" She was studying me with a pinched expression, as if she doubted I was telling the truth.

"No, Bryna, there wasn't," I replied with more snap in my tone than I intended.

"In the meantime, any ideas about what you're going to do about Thornwood now that Ryker is already moving his people into the school?" Annabelle asked us.

"Find a way to stall," Bryna said. "The enchantress has to be our first priority."

Steam was building in my ears but I chose to bite my tongue. I hated that Bryna could so easily push Thornwood's threats to the back burner because they didn't align with what she deemed "priority." If it were Blaire's life being threatened by the Weres, would she feel differently; or would the arrow-straight line she walked start to look a little smudged, I wondered?

"It won't matter anyway," Wren said. "Ryker won't back down now that he's made a decision. Even if we try to negotiate, that will make him look weak to his pack if he so much as considers another option. He won't risk losing respect. They're coming whether we like it or not."

"So you're going to join them?" Annabelle asked.

"No," he answered firmly.

"But that means..." Annabelle couldn't make herself finish the sentence. Her downward gaze shifted up to meet his face.

"Don't worry about me, Cat, I can handle myself." He reached over and mussed the top of her head. "I'm not going anywhere."

My breaths were hollow–like maybe breathing was just a reflex but there wasn't any air left inside my lungs. Rionach's pendant warmed above my heart. *You can stop them, you know,* it seemed to say. I reached up, running my thumb over the glossy surface. *You can make them obey...*

"You all right, Quinn?"

"Hmm?"

"You seem a little dazed," Blaire said, studying me.

"I just have a lot on my mind." I let go of the pendant, brushing my hands against my thighs.

"We should probably get back to the house before it gets dark," Bryna said. "You'll inform us the moment the enchantress sends you another vision."

She didn't phrase her words in the shape of a question, so I didn't feel the need to answer. Instead, I met her gaze and held it. I was glad the Trinity chose Blaire instead of Bryna. Her path of righteousness was utterly irritating.

We walked back to the house in silence, everyone retreating into their individual thoughts. Wren held my hand the whole way, eyes scanning the forest for any sign of trouble as he scented the air. He was always so focused on keeping me safe, but did he know that his safety meant so much more to me?

After Blaire and Bryna had gone their separate ways, I walked Annabelle to her parents' car that was parked beneath the big oak. The autumn air had chilled as the sun dipped below the horizon line, smelling of the rich mountain pines that surrounded us. The forest was shadowed now, tucked beneath the curtain of the indigo painted sky.

"Are you holding up okay?" Annabelle whispered. She'd opened the driver's side door, positioning herself between the seat and door as she looked up at me with big, childlike eyes. "I know you're worried about Wren. I mean, everything that's happening is unlike anything you've ever gone up against."

I sucked in a gulp of air, exhaling slowly. "I'm going to find a way to stop the Darkness, *and* Thornwood. I just wish I had more control over the situation."

You have all the power you need, White One...

"If anyone can figure it out, it'll be you. You always perform better under pressure for some sick and twisted reason." She tried to joke.

"Bryna doesn't seem to think so." I snorted.

"I wouldn't put too much stock in what she says. She's a good witch, don't get me wrong, but the Trinity didn't choose her as an heir."

I nodded, chewing on the inside of my lip. "You know you don't have to be a part of this, right Anna? It probably isn't safe for you to know–"

"I'm going to stop you right there," she said, holding up her hand. "You're my best friend, Quinn. You're closer to me than my own sister. Human or not, I'm in this fight with you, and that's something you can count on."

"Whatever you say, Watchtower." I grinned and wrapped my arms around her neck. The road ahead was dark and full of terrors, but we were the force of Light. I didn't know what was going to happen; I just knew I wasn't going to give up. "I'm going to get us through this mess, one way or another."

"I know you will," she said, "I know."

Chapter Ten
A Dream Within A Dream

It was after nine and Dad still wasn't home from his date. I stared out my bedroom window, gazing up at the silhouetted branches of the big oak tree in the front yard. In the soft glow of moonlight, I could just make out the delicate heart-shaped face of a barn owl. Her eyes gleamed like crystal starlight. The white feathers on her chest were speckled with small charcoal dots, and with the frosted moonlight shining on her feathers she looked softer than velvet. She ruffled her feathers then, shaking them out before settling back into the crook of the big branch.

"What are you looking at so intently?" Wren asked. I didn't hear him come in; his silent dexterity was something I'd never get used to, but I was getting better at sensing his presence. I could feel him now, like the warmth of the autumn sun at my back. Wren stood behind me, fingertips skating down the sides of my arms.

"There's a barn owl–just there." I pointed. She twisted her head to the side a small fraction, almost as if she'd heard me. She seemed to be gazing back at us through the glass, her diamond-like eyes staring at Wren. "She recognizes you."

"How do you know it's a *she*?" His voice was low and close to my ear.

"Intuition, I suppose."

Wren made a sound, something like a grumble as his arms circled my waist. "All the night creatures recognize each other," he said in a low tone.

"She's not afraid of you."

"She has no reason to be afraid; we are both hunters." His lips pressed into the side of my throat, then parted as teeth grazed against the delicate skin. A tremor passed through my lower abdomen, kindling the embers in my core. As his hand spread over my stomach, I felt the heat of his palm searing through the fabric of my shirt. I leaned back against his chest, tilting my head as I reached up to pull his mouth to mine. Every time our lips met, I was amazed to find it felt like the first.

Kissing him was like willingly losing every part of my soul and allowing him to possess my being instead. He broke through the tumultuous frenzy until all I could feel was his body pressed against mine; the granite edges beneath my fingers. I could feel the flames bubbling up inside; a chemical reaction threatening to ignite.

He slipped his fingertips beneath the hem of my shirt and slowly, teasingly, lifted the fabric above my head. My heart began to race, and I knew he could hear the urgent beats. He brushed my hair back like a curtain, his lips pressing into the middle of my spine right between my shoulder blades–and I froze.

I was sure my heart stopped beating all together; the fire between us blown out like a candle. He lifted his hands, gently tracing the parallel marks on either side of my spine. I winced, noting the sting of the fresh wounds. I wasn't sure what hurt more; the physical pain from sliding down that brick wall, or the mental torment I'd faced from allowing Hailey too much control over my mind.

"What happened, love?" His voice was too gentle; his thumb brushing over my shoulder blades, studying the wounds on my back.

Shame burned raw in my chest. I turned my back away from his gaze and reached for the shirt that he'd tossed to the bed but he was quicker than me. His hand folded over the top of mine, and when I tried to pull out from underneath his grip, he only tightened his hold.

"Quinn, stop," he said softly. I breathed in a ragged gulp of air and sat back on the mattress with him kneeling on the floor in front of me, resting his strong arms on either side of my thighs. "What happened?"

"It's nothing," I said in a small voice.

"That doesn't look like nothing." His amber eyes burned into mine.

"I wasn't going to tell you." I sighed. "Hailey cornered me in the bathroom after I met you in the hall today." I paused, watching the way the tendon in his jaw bulged as he clamped his teeth. "She said some things. I let them get to me and I shouldn't have. I just needed some air. I went out the back doors and leaned up against the wall and sort of slid down the brick. I didn't realize I'd hurt myself."

Wren's tawny eyes hardened and a shadow passed over his features. "What did she say to you?" His voice was a low growl that sent the hair on the back of my neck standing at attention.

"Wren…"

"What did she say to you, Quinn?"

"She said that you were meant to be with your own kind… that you would get tired of being careful with me and when you did, she would be waiting." There were a few other choice words she'd said that had stung, but he didn't need to know every little sordid detail.

A rush of air left his nostrils as his jaw cocked to the side. He'd dropped his gaze, hands slipping away from the mattress until I reached out and cupped the back of his hand with my palm. "I shouldn't have let her get to me. I know she was just trying to push my buttons."

"She had no right to speak to you that way," Wren said, gaze shifting back to my face.

"It doesn't mean anything…"

"It does if she caused you any kind of turmoil." Wren rocked back on his heels, moving his hand out from under mine only to cover my knee instead. "There is nothing in this life more important to me than you, do you understand that?" His eyes flickered between mine. There was so much force behind his gaze that I could only nod in response. "I'll talk to her. I'll make sure she knows not to come near you again."

"Wren, I'm okay. I appreciate you looking out for me, but I can handle Hailey." I forced myself to smile for his sake. "Besides, I honestly think that I was overly emotional because of this thing." I picked up the amulet, turning it over in my hand. "Moonstone increases and magnifies emotional energy."

Wren made a face. "Yeah, well, we already know how I feel about *that*." He was glaring at the pendant as if the spark behind his eyes alone could destroy it; if only the solution were that simple.

I dropped the pendant back in place and rested my hands on my thighs. "I am curious though… Is what Hailey said true–about you having to be careful so you don't hurt me?"

"That doesn't matter," he said, reaching out to stroke the length of my cheekbone with his knuckles.

"What would happen if you lost control?" I wondered aloud, swallowing hard before I lost my nerve. After all, this had been going in an entirely different direction before he'd found those scratches on my back, and I wanted nothing more than to get us back on track. I wanted him, and I wanted to be what he needed. I reached for the hem of his T-shirt, letting my fingers trail across his sides as I lifted the fabric away. His body was so perfect.

"I don't know," he grated out.

"I don't want you to hold back with me," I said. "I don't want you to suppress anything that comes natural to you."

"Quinn," he breathed my name against my lips and the heat surged across my skin. I heard the warning in his voice but I didn't care. I pulled his mouth to mine and wrapped my arms around his neck. "*Stop*, love," he said against my lips. He reached up and unlocked my arms from their hold on his neck. "I hear the truck."

I bolted upright and just like that, the magic of the spell was broken. I tucked myself beneath the quilt as I heard the garage door open.

"Quinn?" Dad called up the stairs.

I stayed silent and closed my eyes as Wren folded himself into the shadows, becoming one with the night creatures. I heard the steps creaking as Dad padded up the stairs and then paused in front of my bedroom door. He knocked softly, waited a beat, and then opened it just a small fraction to check on me. As the door closed and he moved on to his own room, I caught a faint, floral scent drifting through the air.

Josephine's perfume.

Wren climbed in beside me then, pulling me against his chest. He pressed his lips in between my shoulder blades and traced the shape of the marks on either side of my spine with his thumb. I reached up and stroked the moonstone at my throat, letting the warmth of it soak through my fingers.

I wondered what would have happened if Dad hadn't come in. Hailey's words were circulating in a sort of mindless desperation–waking a hunger I didn't know was there–a need to prove her wrong. I didn't want Wren to be careful with me. I ached for his power–needed to feel the force of it crushing down on my soul. *That was new*, I thought as I clung to the moonstone pendant.

"You're running out of time, Quinn." Her voice was like a cosmic explosion, like something not of this world or even this realm. I knew it was a dream because the air was full of color–big, bright, shapeless nebulas that pulsed against a black, glittering background. I saw glimpses of her face in the stars and knew she was beautiful. Her hair was a rich auburn that glistened among the starlight like spun silk. Even her dark eyes appeared almost red in color. It was impossible for me to identify her approximate age; her skin was like smooth porcelain, timeless in its youth.

"Who are you?" I asked.

"You'll know when you find me," she replied in that honeyed, heavenly voice of hers.

"Are you the enchantress?"

"Seek the sun, when day takes up the false cloak of night. You need to hurry White One. You're running out of time."

"Your insistence of speaking in riddles won't speed up the process," I said with a sardonic edge and rolled my eyes. I mean, what was it with all of the cryptic messages anyway? Frustration welled in my chest. *"We solved your puzzle–you just need to tell us where we're supposed to find you. I suppose a map is too much to ask for?"*

"Open the door Quinn!"

A great burst of power surged through the center of my chest and I sat up, clutching a hand to my heart as I gasped for air. The room was filled with the golden light of the early morning. It shimmered on the floorboards as wind rippled the curtains of my bedroom window. The cool air made me shiver and I frowned. I didn't remember opening the window last night. I dropped my hand and it crinkled the piece of paper I hadn't seen resting on the pillow beside me.

> **Good morning love,**
>
> You were sleeping so soundly that I didn't want to wake you. I know you haven't been able to get much rest as of late. I won't be gone long. I'm just going to gather some things at the cabin and then I'll pick you up before school.
>
> Your owl was still in the tree this morning; I think she's keeping close watch over you. Niall used to say that the Creator assigned an animal spirit guide to his believers to help them on their life journey. He always felt he had an affinity for the sky creatures. Owls are intuitive and intellectual. I suppose I should be grateful to share the privilege of protecting you with such a being, but I still like to think I'm the only guardian you need.
>
> **Yours eternally,**
> **Wren**

I couldn't help but smile. "Werewolves," I breathed, shaking my head. I traced the word 'eternally' with the tip of my index finger before folding the note and placing it in the top drawer of my nightstand. I pushed to my feet and padded over to the window, sweeping the curtain aside. My owl was still nestled in the branches, tilting her head as she watched me.

"Good morning," I told her. "You'll have to excuse me, but unlike my werewolf boyfriend, my blood is not liquid fire." I reached up and tugged the wooden frame down with a complaining screech. My barn owl seemed unfazed by the commotion and continued to watch me. I studied her a moment longer, entranced by her diamond-like eyes. I couldn't get over how much they reminded me of the starlit night sky–and in turn, my dream came rushing back at full speed.

The walls began to hum with an impatient energy. In my dream, the enchantress wanted me to open the hidden door. There had been a sense of urgency in her velvet tone as she told me I was running out of time. My gut was hollow and a lump seemed to have lodged in my throat. The incentive to open the door had grown so much stronger–willing me to give in.

I pulled a tank top on over my bra and opened my bedroom door, peeking out into the hall. "Dad?" I called.

He didn't answer. I glanced over my shoulder through the window and realized his truck was missing from the drive. Perhaps he'd gotten an early start to his morning–or maybe he had breakfast plans with Josephine. Either way I was alone now, and the energy in the walls was beckoning me forth.

I reached out, brushing the wall with my fingertips. A trail of blue sparks erupted beneath my touch. For once, I didn't feel fear grinding through my bones. Instead, I felt a sense of power and strength and need radiating through my limbs. I traced the pentagram on the wall, watching the bright blue embers burn there before fizzling out and disappearing into nothing.

"*Oscailte*," I commanded.

A brilliant display of blue flame crackled up the wall, sparking and sputtering until a white door emerged. Glowing golden bands twisted in spirals of Celtic knot-work against the frame and the Trinity symbol burned into the center. *This is it*, I thought. Every other path I'd taken had led me to a dead-end. It was up to me to stop the Darkness and protect Wren from the Thornwood pack. This was my last hope.

Yes, that's it, White One, the energy seemed to encourage. *You can save them all.*

Breath tight in my lungs, I reached for the golden doorknob. The moment my fingertips made contact, the moonstone around my throat decided to awaken. The talisman retaliated, scorching my skin with the force of a red-hot iron. My vision went white at the edges, teeth grinding as I wrenched the moonstone away from my flesh.

An impression of the amulet had formed between the curves of my breasts. The skin was red, bubbling with small blisters. A thin line creased my brow. The amulet, I realized, was trying to protect itself. It couldn't be destroyed by a spell written by the laws of nature, but the pendant must have *feared* whatever was behind that door.

The electric energy of the walls was still humming, building and beckoning. I lifted the chain over my head and held firmly to the thin antique threading as I twisted the doorknob and pushed.

At once, the humming stopped.

Shadow and light gave way to a spiral wooden staircase. I held my breath as I took that first tentative step; planks whining beneath my weight as I climbed up to the platform of the attic floor. The high ceiling sloped into wooden-paneled walls, and a large circular window let in a bright stream of light. *Weird*–I'd never noticed a window from the outside let alone known we even had an attic. *It's spelled, genius, of course you wouldn't see it from the outside.* Particles of dust drifted idly in the haze and filled my nose with the scent of something old–stagnant–like an archive of ancient newspapers.

I followed the light-stream to a small circular table that sat at the exact center of the room. It was a deep mahogany with ornate patterns that twisted the legs into the natural shape of tree roots. The table quite literally looked like it was growing out of the floorboards. In the middle of the table sat a leather-bound book, not entirely dissimilar to the grimoire of Blaire's ancestors. This too, was a deep emerald green and covered by intricate bands of silver and gold knot-work. Visibly raised in dimension, a triquetra symbol rested between opposite facing crescent moons.

I was sure my heart was beating loud enough to hear as I traced the patterns on the cover. The ridges were smooth and cool to the touch. My mother had left this here for me, and now that I was seeing it with my own two eyes, a sensation of calm strength washed through my being. I turned the cover and caught a faint scent of vanilla musk in the air as my eyes scanned the neat, cursive handwriting that belonged to my mom.

Dearest Daughter,

I believe I have some long overdue explaining ahead of me. If you're reading this now, it means that the prophecy of the Trinity has come to pass and your greatest powers have awoken. I know I should have told you what might become of your future, but I just wanted to keep you my little girl for as long as I could. If I know you like I believe I do, my choices in shielding you from the truth have hurt you deeply. Please understand that I would never intentionally cause you pain, but this was the only way I knew how to protect you. Speaking of the Darkness was dangerous. Whispers can travel to wicked ears, and I was afraid that the things I feared most could be willed into existence. Maybe it wasn't the right decision, but it was the decision I made nonetheless.

Your father and I knew we wanted to raise a family together, and there was nothing in the world I wanted more than to be a mother. Shortly after we married, I found out that I was unable to conceive. I was heartbroken and devastated. When the Earth Mother came to me and told me she could help, it was an offer I couldn't refuse. I knew from the beginning that there was a chance of the Trinity's reunion, but it was a risk your father and I were willing to take. Carrying the heir of Luiseach Callaghan was a privilege of the highest honor. The Earth Mother had given me the greatest blessing of all, and also the greatest responsibility.

When I chose to have you, I knew that I would spend my life trying to keep you safe. Rionach the Dark was just one of many threats you'd have to face carrying the burden of the White Witch. There were other creatures that would seek to destroy you simply for the power that you could come to possess. On your tenth birthday, the Earth Mother appeared to me in a dream. She told me about a young werewolf who had seen us celebrating in the forest, and that he had forged a connection with you. I suppose I always knew that you would find one another, but a cold fear began to squeeze my heart. Somehow I knew that was the first clue that the Trinity would be called – why else would the Earth Mother come to me?

A couple of years passed nearly in peace. I kept a watchful eye on the forest, wondering if perhaps I would ever see this werewolf of yours. I wanted to meet him, knowing that if I could just see his face and read his heart that I would know you would always be protected. You see, I had just found out about my illness, and I knew my time on Earth was coming to an end. I thought that if I knew you were always being looked after that I could leave this world in peace. I never did get a chance to meet him, but I met another being instead.

They called her Winter Fengári. She goes by many names but what her true name is, I will not speak. All you need to know is that she's a lunar goddess with an affinity for animals and I trust her with your life. It was she who helped me spell the attic. We made it so that you wouldn't find it until the exact time you were meant to. If Rionach's amulet has come into your possession, you and the Trinity are no longer safe. Remaining in Silver Mountain is no longer an option. I wish that I could explain, but you're going to have to take a leap of faith and trust me.

You need to find Winter and seek her refuge. Keep your eyes on the stars and trust your instincts. Let Orion show you the way. Please know that I believe in you. You have always been a strong, capable spirit and it has been my absolute privilege to watch you grow and turn into the beautiful young woman that you've become. You were my greatest achievement, Quinny, and it was an honor to be your mother. No matter what, I will always be with you.

So for now, I leave you with this book and the hope that it will help you find the answers you seek. Please remember that there must always be a balance between light and dark, for you cannot have one without the other. Take care, my daughter, and know that my love for you will never end. May we someday meet again.

Love, Mom

I fell to my knees as a wave of raw emotion ricocheted through my body. My fingertips tightened on the book's cover as a flood of hot tears spilled from my eyes and ran over the curve of my cheeks. I allowed myself this moment of weakness, clutching the book that still smelled of my mother's perfume against my heart.

Reading her words had awoken a sadness that had never really gone away. It stayed dormant, but the moment I saw her handwriting the familiar ache pulsed through my chest and clawed at my heart. I missed her so much–missed the way her nimble fingers would plait my hair in a perfect French braid. I missed her smile and the way her eyes would crinkle at the corners when she grinned. But mostly I missed her voice and the way she taught me about life with such love and kindness.

I wasn't sure how long I cried, but when the tears finally stopped–I could feel the sum of my age within the gravity of my limp bones. I pressed the heels of my hands into my raw eyes, rubbing until the dull ache was gone. I straightened, trembling fingers turning to the next page after my mother's letter.

Blank.

A thin line creased my brow as I turned the next page and found that it was also blank. I skimmed through the entire book, finding that every page after what my mother had written was completely empty. "So much for finding answers," I mumbled disdainfully and pulled myself to my feet. She'd left me with more riddles than I'd bargained for but strange enough, also some very substantial answers. She wouldn't have given the book to me unless I could figure out the encryptions on my own. There were clues in the text; I just needed to clear my head and focus.

I slipped Rionach's pendant back over my head and tucked the book under my arm as I headed for the stairs and spelled the hidden door behind me. Back in my room, my barn owl was still perched on the fat tree branch, just level with my bedroom window. *I'm not going anywhere* she seemed to say by tilting her heart-shaped face. There was something reassuring about her presence and I was comforted knowing she was keeping watch over me. My animal spirit guide, the night huntress.

Chapter Eleven
Hope Springs Eternal

The amulet had done more damage than I wanted to admit as I examined my skin in the bathroom mirror. The wound was tender to the touch; warm and coated in a nasty looking blister that had bubbled up over the burn. *Awakened power indeed.* I sighed and tugged on a long-sleeved shirt, adjusting the collar to make sure it covered my wound. I palmed the grimoire and tucked it into my bag before glancing at the digital clock. Wren would be here in less than thirty minutes to pick me up for school, but sitting idle was not one of my strong suits. My head was still reeling from the morning events, so I decided to make use of my time by heading outside to convene with the elements. I was not prepared, *however*, for what was waiting for me when I opened the front door.

Wren's mother was standing with her hand raised as if she were about to knock. I hated that I saw so many of Wren's beautiful features in this cruel woman's face. She dropped her hand, straightening the hem of her red top and smiled at me. "It's Quinn, isn't it?"

"What are you doing here?" I cut right to the point.

Her eyebrows flickered in brief surprise, but for her part, Gabriella maintained an easy smile. "Well, I was looking for my son," she paused, acting as though she were peering around my shoulder into the house. "Is he here with you?"

I snickered in disbelief. "I think you know the answer to that. You could smell him if he were." I was surprised at how level my voice sounded, even more surprised at the amount of animosity circulating through my veins at her very sight. "He doesn't want to see you."

Now it was her turn to sneer. I'd known she couldn't keep up that friendly act. "I take it you know all about what he is, then."

It wasn't a question so I didn't answer. Instead, in a bored, flat tone, I repeated, "What are you doing here Gabriella?"

"Despite what you may think you know about me, I *do* care about my son. I know about the Thornwood pack, and I know they're planning on taking control of the Silver Mountain territory." She was watching me carefully and I made sure to keep my expression neutral. "I came here to see you."

Okay, *that* did surprise me. "Why?"

"Because I know that my son thinks he loves you and men do stupid things when they're in love. I don't believe you fully understand what could happen to him if he stays with you." Gabriella took a step forward and my palm tightened on the door handle. "Wren's heart has always been his greatest weakness. He cares too much. He always tries to play the hero, and one of these days it's going to get him killed."

"It speaks volumes of your character that you see his benevolence as weakness," I said acidly. I stepped out onto the porch and let the screen slam against the frame behind me. Gabriella and I stood just about the same height, unwavering in our stance. "After what you did to him, you don't have a right to come here and say *anything* about what Wren should or shouldn't do with his life. His choices are his own."

"You're protective of him, that's good," she replied, nodding slowly. "It's a shame you're not a wolf. You'd make a good Were." Gabriella turned from me and sat down on the porch swing, staring with a blank expression across my yard. "I saved my son's life by abjuring him from our pack. When he challenged my mate for the Alpha Master position, my heart shattered." Her voice barely registered above a whisper. "Reese is a big man. Wren wouldn't have lasted longer than a minute. I did what I had to do to save him. I hope you can understand that."

She didn't turn to look at me. She dropped her gaze, staring down at her shoes instead. I wasn't buying the pity act. "You left Niall for Reese. Everyone says you were cheating on him with Remy. Now you stay married to a man that is an abusive monster."

She turned her cold gaze on me. "Don't pretend to know all the dirty little details of my life Quinn Callaghan. You don't know the half of it."

"I know that Wren had to watch his mother leave his father because she chose to run away with the new big bad wolf, and that she repeatedly abused him when he tried to save her from being a human punching bag."

"I've always done what I needed to survive," she spat. "I won't apologize for that. Leaving with Reese was the only way I could save Niall. When Remy died, Niall fell into a pathetic slump and could no longer lead our pack. I may not have loved him in a romantic sense anymore, but I didn't want him to die…" she paused. "But I do love my son and everything I've done was to protect him."

"Did you ever stop to think that maybe Wren never needed you to save him?" I lowered my tone, matching her venomous glower.

"That's where you're wrong," she said. "Wren uses his heart when he makes decisions and that will always end badly. Ryker is dangerous, and if Wren doesn't join the Thornwood pack, Ryker will have no choice but to kill him. I know my son is a proud young man and won't submit to anyone's authority. That's why I'm here. I'm asking you to save him, Quinn. I need you to break it off with him so he no longer has a reason to stay."

I took a step back, recoiling as though she'd physically slapped me; my reaction was that visceral. "I can't do that, Gabriella."

Her ruby lips curled into a smug sneer. "So you'd just let him die?"

"Of course not," I snapped. "I would never let anything happen to him."

Gabriella's gaze was a blank stare, and then her expression shifted into something like amusement as a burst of laughter exploded from her mouth. The sound cut along the edges of my conviction and I felt the fury of it rising in my blood. I stiffened, nails biting into the soft flesh of my palms as I squeezed my hands into fists.

"That's rich," Gabriella managed through her bitter laughter. "I hope you know how ridiculous it sounds coming from a mere human. I mean, you are aware that nothing can ever become of your romance right? He won't be able to escape his nature, believe me. Eventually he's going to want to belong to a pack, and eventually he's going to want children and those are all things that you can never give him."

Gabriella continued to point out all the ways that Wren and I were wrong for each other, but at some point my mind must have tuned her out. Her mouth moved in succession as hatred swirled in her eyes, but all I heard was the slow and steady rhythm of my heartbeat. She sounded like Hailey, and I was tired of people telling me I would never be enough for the one person I couldn't live without.

A shadow began to veil the surrounding forest, conjuring inky tendrils of black vapor from the earth. Smoky strands slithered across the forest floor like hungry vipers. Gabriella didn't notice the Darkness working its way into my yard, or see the way the clouds suddenly obscured the sunlight. An invisible touch, cold as ice, swept up my sides and pulled my shoulders back.

You can make them obey, the Darkness whispered. It was the look on Gabriella's face that made me realize I had raised my right hand and a ball of black and white electrical-charged vapor was swirling across my open palm. I held it there, letting her see the storm that was brewing from my rage.

"I. Am not. *Human,*" I hissed.

Gabriella's dark eyes filled with a mixture of wonder and fear. She swallowed hard, taking a step backward. A terrible realization washed over me then. I *liked* watching her skitter away from me. I liked knowing that I could cause her fear. Her dismay was fuel for the nebulous power building inside me. I closed my hand over the energy ball, distinguishing the flame.

I didn't hear the Pontiac pull into the lane. Wren was out of the car and on the porch before I could blink, shifting me behind him. Gabriella looked up into her son's face, blinking back a frown and raised her chin.

"What the hell are you doing here?" Wren growled.

"Quinn and I were just having a little chat," she replied, her tone was composed but slightly disoriented.

"What did you say to her?"

"It's okay, Wren." I reached for his wrist and his skin burned beneath my fingertips.

"No. You have no business coming here. If you have something to say, you'll say it to me, and you'll leave Quinn out of it." He stepped forward, towering over his mother. Gabriella didn't budge. Her eyes sparked with the colors of the noonday sun and she smiled.

"You wouldn't see me at the funeral and you wouldn't come to Nelly's. What other choice did I have?"

"You shouldn't have come here."

"I miss you, Wren. When I heard that Niall was killed I had to see you. It isn't safe here. It isn't safe for you to be without pack protection." She met my eyes and squared her shoulders. "Rogues killed Niall; you'll share the same fate if you don't submit to Ryker's authority. Thornwood is a smart choice, Wren." She reached out as though she meant to comfort him, but his hand caught her wrist and held her at bay.

She snickered. "You don't honestly believe that a *witch* can protect you?"

My gaze traveled up to the side of Wren's face, and I saw the artery in his neck jumping beneath taut skin. Tendons strained on the back of his hand, the muscles in his arms bunching. Gabriella stood still, glowing eyes fixated on her own wrist in his unforgiving grip.

Finally, she met his gaze. "Let go, *son.*"

He released her wrist and she cradled it against her chest, fingertips massaging the hurt. "What I do is no longer your concern." His icy timbre spiked the tiny hairs on the back of my neck. "You gave up that right when you abjured me from your pack. I may share your DNA, but that is all." His eyes, burning with summer lightning, flickered back and forth between hers. "Go back to Washington. You're not welcome here."

He turned from the porch, not once glancing over his shoulder. My heart was pounding, but I forced myself to meet her gaze. "There's a lot you don't know," I told her in a voice that barely pierced the sound waves. "I'm not going to lose him."

Gabriella flexed her hands at her sides, squaring her jaw. She didn't bother with a reply. I turned my back on her and climbed in the passenger's seat. We left her standing on the porch, her figure melting away as we backed out of the drive and pulled out onto the road. For a minute we said nothing. I watched Wren shift through the gears, the loud roar of the heavy engine a welcome sound as we wound through the mountainside.

"She asked me to leave you," I said after a while. I stroked the moonstone at my throat as the weight of the amulet seemed to shrink in on itself. I thought of the black vapor coiling out of the ground from the forest, slithering towards me with hunger. Was it possible that I'd conjured the Darkness in anger–or had I imagined the whole thing? The amulet lay dormant; a resting and insentient thing once more.

"She had no right to come to you," Wren replied, downshifting as we came around a bend. His left leg worked the clutch while his right hand pumped the gears in place. Wren glanced up at me beneath the veil of his eyelashes, the lingering effect of his lighting gaze turned on me.

"She believes she's protecting you."

Wren snorted. We were pulling into the school's lot now and Wren parked the Firebird where we had a view of the track.

"I'm not saying I agree with what she did, but, I think in her own sick and twisted perspective she believes she did what she had to do to keep you safe." I looked down at my bag, the corner of my mother's grimoire peeking out through the opening. My own mother had chosen to shield me from a future she believed was too dangerous for me to learn about. She thought she was doing the right thing, too. I no longer possessed a black-and-white perspective of right and wrong, but I did understand the actions behind those choices. They were hard choices, but they were made with good intentions, I was coming to realize.

I ran my thumb along the edge of the grimoire before pulling it to the surface. Wren was looking at me; whatever residual anger he'd been clinging to faded from his eyes. "I woke from a dream this morning that the enchantress sent me," I told him. "She told me I was running out of time and I needed to open the door to the hidden room." I glanced up at him then, gauging his expression. "My mother left this for me." I handed him the grimoire.

I watched as Wren's lips pursed as he ran his fingers over the insignia on the cover. "I told you that I would be there with you when you chose to open the door." His tone was hard, but I knew it was coming from a place of concern.

I waited a beat before replying, "I needed to do this on my own."

He looked up at me then, and I saw the question floating across his irises without him needing to speak. *What if something had happened to you?*

It was in that instant that I wondered if maybe Gabriella had been just a tiny bit right about him. Unlike her, I saw his kindness and his heart as strength, but I worried that he would willingly sacrifice himself to make sure that nothing ever happened to me. What was it that Blaire said about Conan? He'd been brave–almost to a fault, but he loved Luiseach for all of hers. There was honor in giving your life to protect someone you loved, but I didn't want him to be the hero. I wanted him to live.

And that responsibility rested on my shoulders. "Open it," I encouraged.

He did, and I caught another small wave of my mother's vanilla fragrance as Wren read the letter she'd left for me. I waited patiently, keeping my eyes positioned on his face, watching the way his dark eyelashes kissed the skin above his cheekbones whenever he blinked.

When he finished reading, he rested his hand on the page and turned to look at me. I saw both the rush and the absence of words building behind his troubled eyes. I understood the conflict better than he could imagine because it mirrored my own.

"It's empty after that," I said, scratching my eyebrow with my thumbnail, "at least to the naked eye. I think the rest of the pages are spelled."

"Have you told the others?"

"Not yet. I wanted to show you first." I leaned over the console and pointed out a couple of lines that caught my attention. "I think this is another clue about where to find the cabin."

"Let Orion show you the way," Wren read aloud. A frown creased his brow before he glanced my way. "Like the constellation?"

"That's my take on it." I shifted closer, angling my head so that a lock of hair slipped across my forehead, brushing the back of Wren's hand that was poised on the book. Wordlessly, he turned his palm, fingertips sliding through the ends of my hair as he studied the words and phrases my mother had used in the letter.

"Text Blaire," Wren said a moment later. "Have her meet us in the courtyard at lunch. She should see this."

"We don't have the same lunch period," I pointed out, glancing up at him.

A sly grin tugged at the corner of his mouth. "I think I can manage to cut class, Quinn." He closed the grimoire and held it out for me. As I reached for it, his index finger hooked the collar of my shirt and tugged it downward, exposing my cleavage and the gruesome blister on my chest. His jaw clenched. "How did this happen?"

"How did you know it was there?" I yanked my shirt collar back up, knotting my brows together in a grimace.

"I can smell it," he said. "It's from the amulet, isn't it?"

"Okay, that's rather disturbing." I stuffed the grimoire back into my bag.

Ignoring my comment he said, "What happened?"

"I'm not sure." I reached up, running my fingers through the knots in my hair. "It happened when I reached for the handle of the hidden room. The amulet just sort of zapped me like it didn't want me going in there or something. I think it's aware that whatever is in this book has the answers we need to destroy it."

His jaw clenched and unclenched. "You shouldn't be wearing that thing," he growled. "You should pass the amulet along to Blaire or Bryna. If it hurts you again–" he trailed off, shaking his head emphatically.

"You know I can't do that. I'm the one that's been entrusted to protect it." Wren sighed, but it sounded more like a low growl catching in the base of his throat. "It's going to be okay," I said to him. "I can feel it."

Annabelle and Shawn were standing by her locker when I walked up. She was laughing at something he said, and the smile on her face was bright enough to light up the entire hall. Since they'd started dating, Shawn was making more of an effort to dress up and comb his impossible hair that flopped across his forehead in an attempt to impress her. I'd never noticed before, but his cheeks dimpled when he smiled, and it made him all the more adorable.

"Good morning love-birds," I teased as I sidled up to my locker. Shawn pushed his glasses up the bridge of his nose in an attempt to cover up the color staining his cheeks.

"Hey Q, where's your other half?" Annabelle returned. The mischievous gleam in her eye did not go unnoticed by me. It was payback for my love-bird comment.

The title didn't embarrass me. It was one I was happy to own. "He's already in his homeroom." I twisted my combination and began switching out books.

"Have you decided what you're going to do for your constellation project?" Shawn asked.

"Yeah, actually," I said. "I think I'm going to focus on Orion." The bell rang then, signaling for homeroom.

"Not a bad choice," Shawn said. "Well, I guess I'll see you guys later." I waved and walked ahead of them, giving them a moment of alone-time since Shawn was still so shy about PDA in the school hallways. Once settled in homeroom, I pulled out one of my notebooks and flipped it open to a fresh, blank page and wrote: *Winter, a lunar goddess with an affinity for animals. Keep your eyes on the stars and trust your instincts. Let Orion show you the way. There must be a balance between Light and Dark, for you cannot have one without the other.*

The second bell rang, dismissing us for our first period classes. I gathered my things and met Annabelle in the doorway as we headed for our English class. "Okay, what gives?" She bumped my shoulder with hers.

"I'll explain everything at lunch. I'm assembling a meeting of sorts."

"You mean with the Trin–"

"–*Don't* say that word," I said in a rush. "It's not safe, but, yes."

"Sorry, I guess we need like a codename or something." She entered the English room in front of me, spinning on her heel to face me as she walked backward down the aisle. "Like The Justice League!" she shouted.

A small bubble of laughter escaped me. "I think that's already been taken."

"Oh, come on, it's kinda' perfect."

I sank down into my usual seat beside her. Wren entered a beat later and sat his books down on his desk before leaning down to give me a quick kiss on the forehead.

"Oh, barf! Get a room," Annabelle feigned gagging.

I couldn't help sneaking a glance to the seat in front of Annabelle where Courtney, Silver Mountain's cheer captain, shot me a look that was anything but cheerful. She'd been obsessing over Wren since the day he arrived in Silver Mountain. He'd chosen me instead of her, and the girl was holding a mean grudge against me–like what could I possibly have that she didn't?

"Interesting necklace Quinn," Courtney commented. "Did you get that from your great granny?" She'd said it innocently enough in that sweet, candy-coated voice of hers but I knew she hadn't meant it as a compliment.

"Haven't you heard, Courtney? Vintage is the new black," Annabelle retorted.

"What*ever.*" Courtney rolled her eyes and turned away.

I reached up, clutching the moonstone in an innate protective grip. For a minute, I felt that strange inky pull of Darkness like I had this morning. The weight registered around my neck as though that brief moment of anger triggered the stone's awakening. It was gone now, departing just as fast as it had arrived.

Miss Lane strode into the classroom and began talking about our next assignment. "Can anyone tell me who Prometheus is?" she asked, folding her hands together as she stood in front of her desk. Her eyes scanned the room until a smile lit up her face. "Yes Harper?"

"He's one of the mythological Greek Titan gods," Harper answered.

"That he is, but do you happen to know what he's most credited for?" The room was silent. Miss Lane waited a beat before continuing, "Prometheus was the god of fire and forethought and was said to have a very scientific oriented mind. Because of this, Zeus tasked Prometheus to create the mortal race of humans by molding them from clay. Prometheus was successful in his creation but he wasn't satisfied with the simplicity of human life. Though humans were made to worship the gods, Prometheus wanted to see mankind thrive. He took it upon himself to steal sacred fire from the heavens and gifted it to humankind. Angered by Prometheus' rebellious actions, Zeus decided to punish him for all eternity.

"As we recently learned from *Frankenstein*, intervening with mankind can also result in tragedy–in fact–Mary Shelley chose *The*

Modern Prometheus as a subtitle for her novel. Which brings me to my next question–does anyone know why Shelley chose this particular subtitle?"

In front of me, Wren raised his hand. Miss Lane nodded, giving him permission to speak. "Shelley is comparing Frankenstein to Prometheus."

Miss Lane nodded again. "Can you guess why?"

"Prometheus provided mankind with a tool that freed them from their dependence upon the gods," Wren answered thoughtfully. "When Frankenstein created his monster, he was taking immortality into his own hands and taking away God's will."

"That is absolutely correct," she praised Wren. "Now, we know that Frankenstein felt disgusted with himself immediately after the monster's awakening, and his feelings embody the eternal torture that Prometheus had to face. But the two are vastly different beings. Prometheus cared a great deal for mankind and chose to stand by them even though it angered the gods. It's unfortunate that we cannot say the same of Frankenstein.

"Prometheus was punished by being chained to a rock in which an eagle visited every day and ate from his liver. Since Prometheus was immortal, his wounds healed and he endured the repetitive suffering. In some versions of the story, it is said that Hercules came and killed the eagle and set Prometheus free, but Zeus was still angered and wanted mankind to suffer as well–thus, he created the maiden Pandora."

Miss Lane paced across the front of the room, pausing by the window as the morning sunlight caught the strands of her honey-colored hair. "Pandora was fashioned to life from the earth and blessed with attributes from the goddesses. Though warned by Prometheus, his brother, Epimetheus, accepted Pandora as a gift from Zeus. Upon their wedding, Zeus gave Pandora a jar in which she was told never to open but her mind became consumed with curiosity–"

"–I thought Pandora had a box?" someone asked.

"Modern mistranslation I'm afraid," Miss Lane explained. "The original text says that it was in fact a *pithos*, which means it was a storage jar. Eventually, Pandora gave in to her restless thoughts and lifted the lid from the jar, releasing the things that Prometheus had wanted to protect humankind from ever enduring–things that consisted of diseases and misery and evil. Horrified by what she'd done, Pandora slammed the lid back on the jar but it was too late–for all the contents, save for one small thing had been released.

"Does anyone know what that last content was?" Miss Lane asked.

"Hope," I blurted.

Miss Lane's eyes flashed to mine, and though I knew she wasn't pleased with my outburst, I could tell she was satisfied that I'd known the answer. "That's right, Miss Callaghan. Pandora lifted the lid once more and let hope out of the jar. Even though hell had been unleashed on earth, hope healed the wounds that evil had created. Even in the darkest of times, hope has always remained one of humanity's greatest strengths."

Chapter Twelve
Chaos Personified

Annabelle and I took our lunches to the courtyard and sat at a picnic table beneath the branches of a maple tree. The autumn canopy above was a sunburst of threaded vermilion and marigold color. A dozen or so students milled around the courtyard but they were far enough away that they wouldn't be eavesdropping on our conversation. I double-checked the perimeter, making sure Hailey was nowhere to be seen before I launched into the tale of what happened this morning.

When I finished, I pulled out the grimoire and passed it to Annabelle so she could have her turn reading my mother's letter. I watched as tears pooled in her eyes as she came to the end of the page. "Wow," she breathed, "this is really from your mom." She shook her head as if she couldn't believe it.

"It's incredible, right?"

"That's one word for it." She smiled and glanced up at me. "How are you processing all this?" She gestured to the book.

"Well, I ugly-cried for what felt like a million years before I was able to pull myself together." I laughed. "I'm just glad no one was there to witness it."

"Wow," she repeated breathlessly.

We sat there a moment, absorbing the comfort in the silence. I'd been so afraid to open that door and my apprehension had been for nothing. My last memories of my mother weren't corrupted; if anything, they were stronger now–more tangible. This grimoire was her way of holding on and giving me something to cling to. The book was my version of Pandora's jar; all that remained was hope.

"The others should be here soon, and then we can dig into these clues," I said, tapping the page of notes I'd scrawled in homeroom.

"What class does Wren have this period?"

"AP physics, I think," I said.

Annabelle raised her eyebrows. "He's like, ridiculously smart, isn't he?"

"Yeah but he won't brag about it because he doesn't like the attention."

Annabelle snorted. "I mean, he is aware that he's a walking billboard for attention–what with all his godlike appearances, right?"

"I know he's aware," I said. "I'm probably going to be chasing girls away from him with a broomstick for the rest of my life."

"Or energy-balls."

Already been there this morning, I thought–though his mother was an entirely different story. The side door of the school building opened up, and Wren slipped out into the noonday sun. He lifted his face to the wind, sampling the scents tangling in the breeze as he made his way to our picnic table. He slid in next to Annabelle, grabbed an apple from her lunch bag and bit into it before she could stop him.

"Hey, keep your paws off the edibles, Wolf Boy!" She swatted his bicep and made a reach for her fruit. "I'll stab you with my silver spoon."

Wren laughed, handing over the stolen goods.

"Well I don't want it now that you've poisoned it with your germs." She made a show of crossing her arms over her chest and shuddering from head to toe.

"Such a feisty little kitty," he teased her.

Penny's truck caught my peripheral as Blaire pulled into the senior lot. My mood soured when I spotted a familiar copper mane of tight curls and the head it was attached to climbing down from the passenger seat. I groaned, slinking down on the bench.

"The cavalry has arrived," Blaire called cheerfully, waving as she approached us.

"Could have done without the Wicked Witch of the West," I said under my breath. I straightened in my seat and held my shoulders back as the sister witches joined us. Blaire plopped down beside me, tucking a leg beneath her as Bryna sat on Annabelle's free side.

Annabelle mouthed the word 'help' from across the table, and I pinched my lips together to keep from smiling. Bryna was the first to speak. "Blaire tells me you've found a grimoire your mother left behind."

"I did indeed." I slid the grimoire towards the center of the table and reiterated the dream the enchantress sent me while the two of them took turns reading my mother's letter. When I finished my tale, Bryna's brows puckered in such a tight frown I thought her brain might explode and leak out of her ears.

"You should've informed us the moment you found it," Bryna chastised.

I rolled my eyes.

"Leave the girl alone," Blaire said to her sister. "She deserved a moment alone with her thoughts after having read that letter."

"Thank you," I said, reaching for the grimoire and handing it to Blaire. "Can you detect what kind of spell she used to keep the rest of the pages locked?"

Blaire waved her hand over the cover of the grimoire in a slow semicircular motion. "It's a bit difficult to identify the source of the magics. It's very old. I'd say we could try a tracing spell, but I have an odd sort of feeling what happened to the amulet would happen to the book."

"I hate to agree," Bryna admitted, pursing her lips.

"I started decoding some of the clues she left behind," I said, handing her the notebook. Bryna leaned across the table to get a better view as Blaire read what I had written.

"Keep your eyes on the stars and let Orion show you the way," Blaire repeated, running her finger along my scrawled handwriting. She looked up. "Where is the Orion constellation located in the night sky?"

"Well, for people who live in the Northern Hemisphere, the Orion constellation is located in the south-western sky during late autumn and all of winter," I explained. "If we take my vision into consideration, we know the enchantress wants us to go somewhere on the East Coast."

"So how the hell would Orion show you the way?" Annabelle frowned.

"That's what I don't know. Anyone else have an idea they'd like to pitch?" I waited for my friends to take a guess but no one seemed to know what that part of the riddle could mean. Blaire slid the grimoire to the space in front of her, running her fingers along the metal symbol on the cover.

"This seems to be cryptic depiction on the triple moon symbol. Traditionally, the trinity knot shouldn't be here, but I'm guessing it was made specifically for us."

"What's the triple moon symbol?" Annabelle asked.

"It's a goddess symbol, representing three phases of the moon." Blaire pointed to the outward facing crescent on the left and worked her way to the right as she said, "Maiden, Mother, and Crone. Some consider the symbol to represent a life cycle."

"The phase of a new moon symbolizes a new beginning. Combine that with the power of the eclipse and it represents rebirth," Bryna said. "The grimoire's symbol could have something to do with the eclipse itself."

Blaire waved her hand over the cover once more and said, "*Nochtann.*" She opened the cover, flipping through the pages. Still empty. "I've no idea." She shook her head, sliding the grimoire to me. "Perhaps Bryna and I should phone the Coven and ask if some of the

Wiccan elders know about the symbol. I suspect it has something to do with the grimoire's hidden contents."

"This is a good start, Quinn," Bryna said.

I almost fell off the bench with the small amount of praise she'd given me.

"Winter Fengári," Blaire repeated the name and glanced up at her sister. "Where have I heard that before?"

"It's the Greek word for 'moon' I believe," Bryna answered.

"Winter Moon," I said aloud, chewing my inner lip. "Maybe it's another code name for somethi–"

"–Keep your voice down," Wren cut me off. He'd lifted his chin in the air, smelling something in the wind that the rest of us couldn't detect.

"What is it?" I asked.

Courtney and Hailey pushed through the double-doors at the front of the courtyard, their arms linked together at the elbows. It was right about then that I heard a deep rumbling coming from around the bend. I looked up at the road as a group of bikers, clad in black leather jackets, slowed in front of the courtyard. Hailey lifted her manicured hand in a wave, pulling Courtney along as they hurried across the lawn to the parking lot. Beside me, Wren stiffened.

"Weres," Blaire said, rubbing the goosebumps that trailed her arms. I noticed that her ring was glowing aqua.

"Thornwood," I corrected. My stomach tightened as the group of five parked their bikes in the side lot. I picked Roy out of the bunch first. He was the only one with long hair; the wind had pulled a few strands loose from the ponytail fastened at the nape of his neck. I recognized a few of the others from the bar, but they'd remained in the shadows and hadn't introduced themselves.

"Friends of yours?" Blaire asked acerbically.

"I wouldn't call them friends. Pack your things away." He meant the grimoire; I didn't have to be told twice. I grabbed the notebook and the grimoire and stuffed them in my bag as the bikers, led by Hailey and Courtney, started making their way in our direction.

The back of their jackets were adorned with a large face of a wolf. Its jaws were parted in a menacing snarl, revealing sharp white teeth. Bloody roses covered in thorns formed the shape of parentheses on either side of the wolf's head. *Thornwood* was written in bold letters across the back of their shoulders, and below the wolf's head was the phrase: *honor thy brothers with blood.* I swallowed hard.

"Well, well, if it isn't Wren Whelan," the leader of their group said. He was shorter than the others but he was built like a tank. Bulky muscle jutted up from his shoulders, joining either side of his equally thick neck. He had short, spiky blond hair and eyes the mirror image of Hailey's. He smiled and offered his hand to Wren.

"Maddox," Wren said in greeting, shaking his hand. I remembered what Wren had told me about him–he was in Ryker's inner circle, and possibly the pack Beta. Hailey was his younger sister. "What brings you out this way?" Wren's tone was even and borderline unfriendly but Maddox didn't appear addled in the slightest.

Maddox draped a big arm around Hailey and pulled her into his side. "Just came to check on my little sister," he said. "I wanted to make sure she's playing nice with all the new kids." Maddox's cool water gaze leveled with mine.

"Stop it," Hailey said in a playful but annoyed sounding tone. "I haven't bitten anyone... *yet*."

Courtney laughed.

"Sorry I missed your father's memorial," Maddox said, shifting his eyes back to Wren. "I was away on business."

"I heard that you're still Ryker's errand boy," Wren commented in a detached sort of tone that made Maddox's expression falter.

"I'm his second." Maddox glowered, eyes darkening. Yep. Definitely the Beta.

"Oh, his second; well then I suppose I should congratulate you. It's good to see all the ass-kissing finally paid off."

Maddox sniggered, revealing a straight set of teeth. Wren had Maddox by a couple of inches in height, but Maddox's bulk was nothing to take in stride. Wren was already treading very dangerous waters, squaring off with the Beta–especially one that was besieged by his pack brothers–was not in his best interests. I reached out, wrapping my palm around Wren's wrist hoping that my touch would convey a reminder. Maddox saw this, and his eyes cut to me.

"You must be Quinn."

"That's right," I said, forcing myself to hold his gaze.

"Ryker told me all about you," he said in a tone that one might mistake for charm, but I heard the mocking nature in it. He pulled my free hand to his lips and brushed the back of my knuckles with a kiss that sent a shiver of disgust slithering down my spine. I pulled my hand free of his grasp and squared my shoulders as Wren bristled beside me.

"What do you want, Maddox?" Wren growled.

"Be nice to my brother, Wren, or you will be the first one I bite," Hailey said with a smirk. She slipped out from under Maddox's arm and grabbed Courtney by the elbow and started introducing her to the rest of the pack. I watched Courtney flirt with the guys, knowing that Hailey had pulled her away so Maddox could talk more freely with Wren.

"Ryker wants to know if you have an answer for him." Maddox leaned up against the trunk of the maple tree, crossing his arms over his chest.

"So he sent you and four others to what–drag the answer out of me if I didn't comply? He'll have his answer tomorrow," Wren said.

Maddox smiled even bigger. "We both know you've already made up your mind. We're just here to remind you of your fate should you choose to concede."

"Come on Summer Boy. You know what you need to do," Hailey added. "You know what would be *best* for you."

Rage flickered through my core. I took a step forward on instinct, but it was Blaire who wrapped a hand around my arm to hold me in place. My chest swelled with an icy heat, feeding the Darkness that was swelling in my amulet.

"Such fire," Maddox commented, staring at me. "I can see why you like her, Wren. But is she really worth dying–"

Behind me, I heard the school bell ringing, signaling that our lunch hour had ended, and thankfully, cutting off the rest of Maddox's words.

"Come on Hailey, I don't want to be late for the student council meeting," Courtney said, reaching for Hailey's free hand as the two skipped away.

"Since you're incessantly headstrong, Ryker told me to tell you that you have until sundown tomorrow night. Be at the bar, seven o'clock sharp with your answer." Maddox pushed himself away from the tree trunk and the others flanked to his side. As he started walking away, he called over his shoulder, "I hope she's worth it, Wren."

My teeth ground together as my fists clenched at my sides. Fury surged through my body like a bolt of lightning and the sky above seemed to darken. It revealed the veil of the in-between and shrouded my vision.

Teach them their place, the Darkness whispered against my ear. The rage that had been building inside me boiled over the surface, and my neck snapped sharply to the side. A big gust of wind swept out of the eastern woods and knocked all five of the heavy chrome-plated bikes over in the parking lot.

"What the hell?" The group took off running toward their fallen machines.

Blaire squeezed her nails into my arm until the pain registered. I blinked away from the scene and turned to face her coal-black gaze. "Quinn," she breathed, "did you do that?"

My lips parted, and air rushed through my lungs in a ragged gulp. "I-I don't know." Her eyes were swimming over mine, and I knew she was searching my aura for the Darkness that had already departed.

I looked back at the parking lot, watching as Maddox stood there– studying me. *Shit.* Could he tell that I was a witch now? Wren waited until the bikers had righted their heavy chrome machines and fired up their engines before he turned to me.

"It's that *thing* isn't it?" Wren pointed to the amulet around my neck–in which I immediately scooped up in my protective grip. "Tell them what it did to you this morning," Wren demanded.

"It's nothing," I said, blinking.

"Like hell it isn't." He reached for my shirt collar, ignoring the chain as his knuckles brushed against the silver and a strip of gray smoke snaked into the air from his burning flesh. He tugged my collar down and revealed what the amulet had done to my skin. My cheeks burned with chagrin as I pulled out of his grip.

"What happened, Quinn?" Annabelle's eyebrows laced together in concern.

"The amulet is protecting itself," Bryna said. "Did that happen when you unlocked the hidden door to the grimoire?"

"Yes," I admitted.

"She shouldn't be wearing it," Wren interjected with a sharp snap in his tone.

"It *chose* her," Bryna said. The two faced off, and I watched as the lightning current began to swirl in Wren's irises. The air was thick and pulsing with tension, but it was Blaire's gentle voice that broke through the disarray.

"There was something else the White Witch said to you in our vision quest," Blaire said. "After we'd linked ourselves, she said–"

"She said that only I had the power to walk the path of shadow and not turn from the Light," I finished for her. "She told me that you guys would try to help me, but I was the only one who could do it. She was talking about this." I held up the moonstone pendant. I had been denying it ever since the amulet came into my possession but I couldn't deny it any longer. All the dark whispers, shadows, and impulses were revealing their hidden truths about the amulet's awakened power.

"Hold on," Annabelle held up her hands, "you knew about this?"

"Well, I wasn't a hundred percent sure until now," I said, "but I had my suspicions. I can hear things sometimes, like little suggestions."

"It's trying to control you," Wren said. A mixture of worry and anger flashed across his beautiful features and his brows furrowed. The others were gawking at me as though I'd grown a pair of horns and matching pointed tail. Might as well hand me a pitchfork and call me Satan.

"Guys, I'm *okay*," I said, stressing the word. "It's not like the amulet can actually possess me or anything…" Everyone remained quiet just long enough for an icy fear to creep up from my gut. "Right?"

"We best not linger on taking that chance," Blaire said, squeezing my wrist. "Let's get this riddle solved so we can get this amulet destroyed."

"I second that motion," Annabelle replied.

"And there's one other thing that you really need to take care of, lass," Blaire said, looking solemn. "You need to talk to your dad. Too much has changed. I know you think you're protecting him by keeping him in the dark, but I think he needs to know what's going on–especially now that we need to leave."

My stomach clenched. "I know," I heard myself say.

Chapter Thirteen
Nyla

"You have got to be kidding me." Annabelle came to an abrupt halt at my side and the motion had her long ponytail swinging from side to side like angry windshield wipers. She jutted her hip out, staring at Hailey who was dressed in the tiniest pair of black shorts I'd ever seen and a low cut white tank. The tops of her breasts were spilling out of her sports bra like swollen water balloons. I know they say werewolves are territorial, but she was talking to Coach all flirty-like, and at that moment, I wanted nothing more than to pop those massive balloons of hers with a needle just to find out if they'd explode.

"New girl has some serious curves," Huck commented, bending to readjust his shoestring that had started to come undone. Jamie fell in after him, as the two were never very far apart. I watched him brush a lock of bronze hair out of his face, grinning like an utter moron.

"Hey, keep your eyes in your head, or else I'll tell Torrance you were checking out the trashy merchandise," I told Huck.

"She's not trashy," Jamie inserted on the defensive.

"What's the matter Q, you're not afraid she can run faster than you, are ya'?" Huck grabbed the end of my ponytail and gave it a little tug. I spun and cracked him in the bicep. "Ow," he muttered, rubbing his arm.

"No, I'm not afraid of that," I said haughtily.

"She's only here to get a rise out of Quinn," Annabelle said. "She has a serious thing for Wren."

"Of course she does." Jamie rolled his eyes as he pulled his leg back into a thigh stretch. "His presence is inconvenient for my game."

"*What* game?" Annabelle retorted.

Huck burst out in laughter and slapped a hand across Jamie's back. "Burn!"

"Screw off, man." Jamie shoved him hard in the chest but Huck just continued to laugh. "Plenty of ladies dig me."

Now it was my turn to snort. "Jamie, plenty of ladies would like you if you weren't so massively full of yourself," I said.

"And how is that any different from Wren?" He extended his arm out, gesturing to Wren who was warming up in a jog around the track. The afternoon sun was playing in his dark hair, catching the auburn strands in the light and coloring his skin a perfect shade of gold. I bit the corner of my lip, letting out a sigh. "See, you're swooning and he's not even doing anything." Jamie pointed out.

"That's the difference," Annabelle said. "Wren doesn't have to *try*."

"So you're saying I shouldn't do anything at all and ladies will just flock to me like moths to a flame?" He lifted an eyebrow.

"Nobody likes arrogance rubbed in their face," Annabelle said. "It's not an attractive trait."

"Huh." Jamie rested his hands on his hips as his eyebrows furrowed in what appeared to be contemplation. A slow smile spread across my face as I shook my head. Jamie really was clueless–cute–but clueless.

In front of us, Hailey flashed a bright smile at Coach before turning in our direction. "What are you looking at?" Her icy blue eyes narrowed in my direction.

"I think you made a wrong turn out of the locker room," Annabelle told her. "The Zombie Squad is that way." Annabelle pointed to the group of cheerleaders practicing on the grassy patch next to the bleachers.

"What makes you think I have any interest in joining a cheer squad?" She sneered, rolling to one of her hips.

"Oh I don't know, maybe because your new BFF is the cheer captain and the two of you seem to share equally wicked souls and a freakishly bizarre taste in toddler-sized clothing."

A bubble of surprised laughter escaped me. I cleared my throat and pressed my lips together in amusement.

"Well, at least I have something to show," Hailey reached up and cupped her breasts in a vulgar gesture which had the guys whistling.

"Did your parents actually sign for that half-priced boob job?"

I swore I saw a scarlet blaze flash across Hailey's irises. Clearly Annabelle had touched a raw spot. "Oh they're real all right, you nerdy, flat-chested chink." Hands on her hips, Hailey stepped toe to toe with Annabelle.

"I'm half Japanese, you racist slut." Annabelle inched closer. "If you're going to insult someone, the least you can do is hurl the right derogative."

I took a step towards Hailey, blood pressure spiking until I heard Wren's voice behind me. "Everything okay here?"

"Fine," Annabelle and Hailey said in unison.

"What are you doing here, Hails?" Wren asked, keeping his voice level. I couldn't help but notice he'd used a nickname for her and my stomach twisted.

"Joining the cross-country team, what's it look like?"

Wren snickered. "It's too late in the season for that."

"*Duh*, numbskull, I'm aware. Coach so kindly agreed to let me practice with the team in order to condition myself for track season. I even get to tag along to all the meets with you guys." She beamed a spurious smile. "You know, if Thornwood was big enough to have a cross-country team, I would have come in first. Every. Time."

"Quinny is our star," Huck surprised me by saying as he wrapped a solid arm around my shoulder. "Though I'm sure she'd welcome some competition."

"Perfect, what are we running today?" She pressed her lips into a tight smile.

I rolled my eyes. The world was in the midst of ending, and here I was staring down a werewolf bitch–completely ready to strangle the life from her lungs. Ugh–*priorities*. "Coach," I called, "what are we running today?"

"Sprint work, two hundred relay," he answered, waving his clipboard in the air.

"Perfect," I echoed Hailey and started for the track.

A few minutes later, I was standing on the second curve in the fourth lane with Hailey in the fifth lane beside me. Annabelle and Harper were on the starting line. I wasn't worried. In fact, I was in my element, and I knew that both Harper and Annabelle were equally matched in sprint-work. Annabelle would run her heart out to make sure that baton hit my hand before Harper reached Hailey. I bent forward, adjusting my heel in the starting block.

"Looks like that's a notch too short for the length of your legs," Hailey commented, reaching back to tighten the elastic band around her annoyingly perfect blonde ponytail.

My gaze narrowed. "I think I know what I'm doing."

"That's right," she breathed, "I forgot you were the *star.*"

"You are planning to make this a fair run, right?" I lifted my brows and shot her a pointed look. I didn't want to say anything about her werewolf abilities in front of the girls in the lanes beside us. "I'll know if you cheat."

"Cross my heart," she replied with fake sweetness, drawing a mini X over her chest. "I'll beat you fair and square, Quinn Callaghan."

"We'll see about that," I muttered under my breath.

We leaned forward, taking our stances in the starting blocks as Coach blew the first whistle, signaling for us to get ready. The familiar burn of adrenaline began pumping through my chest. I inhaled deeply, pooling air into my lungs and breathing in the crisp scents of autumn coalescing with the warm rubber turf.

"Jamie is pretty cute," Hailey said, nonchalantly examining her nails. No doubt she'd heard him talking about her. "Huck is pretty cute too, but I have no interest in guys who are already hung up on someone else."

I snorted. "That doesn't seem to stop you from going after Wren."

"I already told you, it's different with Wren. He *belongs* with me."

Coach blew the second whistle and the first leg of runners burst out of the starting blocks. I didn't even look behind me. I extended my right arm behind my back, palm facing up. I pushed Hailey's comment about Wren to the foreground of my mind, using it as fuel to burn on the track. Annabelle and I had this down to an exact science. I began counting the seconds as blood pulsed through my veins and arteries. The cool metal of the baton slapped down into my hand and a burst of adrenaline fanned through my chest. I squeezed the baton and shot out of the starting block as the boys cheered us on.

In that moment there was nothing but the roar of wind rushing against my face, and my breaths coming faster and faster as I pushed with everything I had against the track. The wind stung my eyes, pulling liquid from the corners. Everything in my peripheral was a blur. I was rounding the corner to the straightaway when for a fleeting instant I caught sight of Hailey's white-blonde hair glinting in the sunlight at my side.

"Go, Quinn, go!" I picked Wren's voice out among the combined shouts and cheers from our team and leaned forward into the straightaway. I ground my teeth together as the muscles in my whole body exploded with heat. *Leave everything you have on the track*, Coach would say. I became an atomic bomb, detonating into a sharp cry as I crossed the finish line one step in front of Hailey. I was running so hard that it took another thirty meters for me to slow my momentum. And when I did finally come to a halt, my gelatinous limbs gave out and I collapsed against Wren's chest. His arms circled my waist to help keep me upright.

"Take it easy, love." His breath was warm at my ear.

"Nice running, ladies!" Coach clapped and whistled along with the others. "That was a close race but Quinn still holds the reigning undefeated title!"

"Hell yes I do!" I shouted. The others began laughing, patting me on the arm in congratulations as Wren led me toward the bleachers.

Annabelle pulled me out of Wren's arms and gave me a sweaty hug. "You should have seen your face when you crossed the finish line. It was *so* unattractive." She laughed.

"Thanks." I giggled. "I'll take it if it means beating Hailey."

"Harper and I got to you guys at the same time–that was definitely all you," she said. "I never doubted you for a minute."

"Congratulations, Quinn. Way to kick some ass." Huck pulled me against his side and squeezed me just a little too tightly.

"What made you go all 'Team Quinn' all the sudden?" I asked him.

"I've always been all 'Team Quinn' and besides, I don't like bitchy girls. And that girl," he pointed to Hailey, who was currently slamming her baton into the box, "is seriously demented. Bottom line–you don't talk shit about my friends. I have zero tolerance for racial slandering."

"Aw, thanks Huck." Annabelle gave him a side hug.

"She might be hot, but that was a dick move," Jamie agreed with a shrug.

"She's more like a hot mess," Annabelle said.

The boys started walking toward the starting line for their race. I was still reeling from my win with smug satisfaction when a twinge rippled through my temples. It wasn't painful so much as it felt invasive–abrupt and forceful. My eyes flashed up to Wren's and his expression shifted, filling with apprehension. "Quinn?"

"Get me off the tra–"

White-hot pain exploded in my temples, forcing my eyelids to snap shut. *This isn't right,* I thought desperately, *it isn't supposed to hurt anymore and I didn't even touch any blood!* That was my last coherent thought before the rippling current of the ocean swirled around my ankles and ripped me below the surface of the waves. The water surged, altering the collage of images until the ocean spewed me from her watery depths and thrust me along the beach. It was there I sucked in my first gulp of air, and there that the wind billowed past me in visible strands of color.

Quinn, her voice sounded as if it were coming from a broken surround-sound speaker, crackling with static. *Stop fighting me–I'm trying to show you.*

"Show me what?" I asked, raising my arm above my brow to shield my eyes from the brilliant stream of light spooling with endless blue.

Your…future…stop…fighting. Her words were all jumbled and spaced apart as she struggled to get her message through. *Your…subconscious…turn it…off.*

"Tell me how?" I shouted, dropping to my knees. *Oh goddess please let my mind go blank.* I closed my eyes and tried to ignore the wind that was rushing past me and howling in my ears. *I surrender, I surrender.*

The roar of the wind began to slow. I concentrated on my breathing and focused on becoming one with the elements. *That's it, White One; you are smoke, you are Air.* The voice told me.

I felt my body dissolve then–broken down into tiny little particles that drifted about like dust in the sunshine. I was no more than an echo, or an afterthought of something left behind or forgotten. The world came back together piece by piece, and the first thing I saw was the neon sign flickering above Thornwood's Were bar. I heard the steady hum of electric buzzing from the transformer and spotted Sal mopping down the bar top with a stained rag. A group of men were playing pool while my spirit seemed to float above them, undetected. I had no control over my movements. I was vapor and fog–moving through the room like a cloud drifted in the sky. My spirit drifted over to the corner where two figures lingered in the shadows. Maddox was one of them, and he was talking to Ryker.

"Has Hailey made any progress with Wren?" Ryker asked Maddox. Ryker's left arm was folded across his chest while cradling his right–stroking the stubble on his chin in a contemplative manner.

"No. Using Hailey as bait was a good move on your part, but Wren is entirely too infatuated with that little brunette to be tempted. Hailey refocused her efforts on Quinn. She appears to be the weak link in that thick armor of his," Maddox replied. "I think if we focus our efforts on using her as leverage, we can convince Wren that this pack is his only option."

"What are you suggesting?"

"If Wren refuses the pack, I could convince Quinn that it's the only way to save his life. I know you don't want to kill him Ryker, but he's not going to submit willingly. Quinn is a smart girl; she's not going to let him sign his own death certificate. We're going to need her help."

Ryker considered this, continuing to stroke his chin. "Hailey says they're never apart. Finding a way to lure her away from Wren might be a problem." Ryker paused, "Also, there's still the question of *what* she is... She smells human, but she made it through the door so we know she has some Supernatural DNA."

"She's pretty enough to belong to the Fae," Maddox said grimly. Maddox explained his suspicions of what happened to their bikes when he and the others visited us at school. "She was standing with three others, so it could have been one of them, but, I'm willing to stake my next meal on her."

"You think she can perform psychokinesis?"

Maddox nodded. "That doesn't exactly narrow a Supernatural species down, but being able to move an object with one's mind is a specialty of witches and Fae born. Unfortunately for us, it's a common practice among Supernaturals so it's impossible to know for certain."

Ryker dropped his arms to his sides, pushing out from the shadows, he began to pace. "We need Silver Mountain. Rhea has foreseen what could happen if we don't take it." He heaved a great, frustrated sigh.

"So we use Quinn. If need be, we can threaten her life to force Wren's loyalty and take over Silver Mountain."

Ryker stopped pacing, turning to face Maddox and rising to his full height. The blacks of his eye seemed to glitter in the overhead lighting.

His body was resolute and unwavering in its stance, but I saw the disgust flashing across his dark eyes at Maddox's suggestion. "You see Maddox; that kind of thinking is what got Nyla and the others banished from this pack." Ryker's voice was ice-cold, so much that I felt the effect of it rippling through the Air that I had become. "I will not use a mortal soul to force another's compliance."

"I'm sorry, Ryker, I didn't mean–"

"I know," Ryker lifted his hand, gripping Maddox's shoulder firmly. "This fight is with our kind and our kind alone." He leveled his eyes with Maddox.

A loud bang erupted from behind. I spun in my fragmented state, catching a glimpse of a feminine figure standing in the doorway of the bar. In a flash, Ryker materialized in front of her, wrapped a hand around her slim neck and pinned her against the wall to his right. Her skull cracked into the plaster, and a horrible sickness washed through me–or at least it would have–if there was a physical me to wash through.

I recognized that face.

The fluorescent light above the pool table turned her wild mane of hair a dirty-dishwater brown. Her caramelized eyes were wide and full of fear as her fingers clawed at Ryker's hands around her throat. She ground her teeth, and I saw the white flash of her canines extending. "Amnesty," she choked out.

Ryker tightened his grip, baring his fangs just inches in front of her face. "You and your deviant companions were abjured from this pack, Nyla. I don't grant amnesty to those who serve the Darkness."

"It's about…_Quinn_," she croaked. Her skin was beginning to turn a sickly shade of eggplant. Ryker held her there on the wall for a heartbeat longer before allowing her feet to reconnect with the floor. He loosened his hand around her neck but jammed his fists into the wall on either side of her body, blocking her exit.

"Why should I believe anything you say?"

"Because… I'm trying to help you." She sucked in a gulp of air, struggling to retain a normal tone now that her vocal chords were shredded. "I wouldn't risk coming here otherwise. I know you've vowed to kill anyone who does."

Ryker snickered humorlessly. "Go on," he breathed.

"She's a witch," Nyla blurted.

"Damn it to hell." I heard Sal mutter from behind Ryker's shoulder.

"We can handle witches," Ryker replied in an indifferent tone. "In fact, they're known to be of use for the Supernatural realm. This bar is spelled by one."

"She's not just any witch," Nyla said, and absolute dread clenched my stomach into knots. "She's the White Witch incarnate."

The atmosphere iced over. Every soul in that room stopped breathing. Ryker's nostrils flared as he continued to stare hard into Nyla's caramel eyes. "How?" he enunciated the word slowly–*deadly*.

"The Dark Witch's spirit has been summoned by one who shares a bloodline with her," Nyla explained. "Her spiritual essence alone triggered the Trinity's awakening. Quinn is one of them, and so is Wren."

The muscle in Ryker's jaw worked over the bone and I watched the muscle in his forearm rippling with the Change. Patches of fur sprouted over his wrists, retracted and sprouted again on the sides of his neck. His eyes were churning with neon yellow color.

"You've sold yourself to Darkness, Nyla, what's in this for you? Why should we believe anything you say?" Maddox asked, stepping up from the shadows.

"I've turned from the path of shadow," she said, and Ryker snorted. "I was wrong, Ryker. I thought I wanted power, but I didn't realize the cost in which it would come."

He spun on his heel, his face so close to hers that it almost appeared intimate. "I used to admire your thirst for blood but you are truly toxic. The only reason you're here is because you've gotten yourself involved in a shit storm and now you need the pack's protection. I can't help you. If Darkness marked you for her own, then you're as good as dead." His heartless tone matched the cold depth of his eyes.

"We're all as good as dead if we don't do something to stop the Dark Witch from returning," she said, raising her voice. "She commands the power of an ancient artifact that can control us. She'll use her amulet to enslave us in our wolf skins and we'll never walk in our human forms again."

The bar erupted in anxious murmurs. The atmosphere shifted and I sensed the clammy tendrils of their fear tainting the air. Ryker's powerful voice rose above the masses. "How did you come by this information, Nyla?"

"Garrett was captured by the Trinity after the fight in the forest, they held him for questioning. It was Quinn who told them the true intentions of the Dark Mistress. I didn't want to believe it at first, but we've lost contact with the human guardian. It's my belief that the amulet has come into Quinn's possession," Nyla finished.

Ryker began pacing again. "This changes things," he said, more to himself than to the others. Nyla, still cowering against the wall, kept her eyes glued to Ryker's every move. "You risked a lot coming here tonight," he told her.

"I know," she said, "but there was no other choice. The power of the amulet affects us all."

"If what you say is true–"

"–It is true!" she interrupted. "You know the legend of our creation. We can't knowingly allow someone else to wield a weapon that can control us!"

"So what would you have me do?" Ryker growled.

"Capture Quinn and take the amulet from her! There's no power on earth that can destroy it, and I will not stand for the amulet to remain in the possession of a *witch*. Their existence is an abomination! If we have to kill her to take back control of the amulet, then I say she should die!"

The bar erupted in a mix of angry growls and cheers. Ryker slammed Nyla back into the wall–so hard that I was certain the plaster cracked. "Bite your tongue. You will not speak so freely in a pack that you are no longer part of. Your opinion bears no weight. Do I make myself clear?" Nyla spit a stream of blood onto the floor in response. Ryker grinned. "I hadn't meant for you to take my command so literal."

"What are you going to do with me?" she snarled.

"Maddox, Asher," Ryker called over his shoulder, the two men emerged at his side. "Take Nyla to the cells, I'll address the council before we decide her fate."

"You're nothing but a coward, Ryker Donavon." Nyla laughed bitterly as the two men hauled her–kicking and struggling–toward the back door. "You're an idiot if you don't go after Quinn. This fight affects us all!"

Ryker squared his shoulders and his irises began to swirl. I watched the breaths coming hard from his chest as anger rose within. Sal stood beside him, laying a gentle hand on his arm.

"I know you don't trust her," Sal said, "but she risked her life coming here tonight. She's scared Ryker, and I think she's right. We can't let anyone hold a weapon that could control us. We need to get that amulet."

"I know that Sal," Ryker said. "The question is how…"

Chapter Fourteen
Star Magic

Coming back to my body was like waking from a lucid dream. I was aware I was having a vision, but it was unlike any other I'd experienced. My spirit was scattered by Air, and I was waiting for the element to put all my pieces back together. I could feel them rearranging inside me– the fragments coming together like a foot being stuffed into a shoe that was just a size too small.

"If she's out much longer, I'm going to have to call the ambulance." That was my father's voice. He sounded frantic. I wanted to tell him I was fine, but my brain wouldn't send the signal to my mouth to speak.

"They won't be able to do anything, what happened to her was magic related. I can feel it," said Blaire.

"You're sure she didn't touch any... *blood?*"

"I'm positive," Wren said. "I was standing right beside her when it happened."

Oh good, I guess that meant Dad was aware that Wren knew I was a witch. One less thing I'd have to explain when I came to, I thought.

The fragments were settling now–tingling through my body so that I became aware of my limbs. Maybe if I could just will my foot to move...

"There!" Annabelle shouted, "She's moving."

Eesh–just how many people were in this room?

Pins and needles exploded over the surface of my skin and my whole body jerked back to life in unbelievable pain. I sucked in a sharp breath and my lungs ballooned like an inflated life vest. I coughed, trying to regulate my air intake while fumbling to push myself in an upright sitting position. The room was too bright. I felt like I was looking at the sun through a crystal prism.

"Slow it down there, Quinny," my dad was the first one to speak, but it was Wren's touch that registered. I could feel the absolute warmth of it soaking through my cold skin.

"Why is it so cold in here?" I shivered.

"Toss me that afghan there," Dad instructed. Wren sat down beside me a beat later, readjusting my body so that I was cradled against his side. He covered me with the blanket and began running his palm against my arm to generate friction. I suppose I should have been a little embarrassed to be curled up this closely with my boyfriend (though *boyfriend* was a loose term considering he was my soulmate) in front of my dad, but when I looked at Dad's face, all I saw was concern.

"You're too pale," I told him.

Annabelle laughed. "Someone should hand you a mirror." She reached over, smoothing a piece of hair out of my face.

"How are you feeling, lass?" Blaire asked.

I considered her question for a moment and then answered, "Like a pop can that someone shook up but never opened–or maybe like a sardine."

"That good, eh?"

"What happened," I asked, "back at the track after I blacked out I mean?"

"Wren scooped you up before you hit the ground," Annabelle explained. "We sort of had to fake an accident to cover up your blackout."

"How?" I frowned.

"Easy," Annabelle said, "fabrications are my specialty, after all. Blaire sent me an imaginary picture of her scraped knee and you saw my cellphone screen when I opened it. Everyone already knows blood makes you squeamish. Coach was worried of course, but he let Wren and I escort you to the nurse's office–AKA home so we could call in the cavalry."

"That's twice today," I croaked.

"You're welcome." Annabelle beamed.

"Thank you." I managed a small smile, but it hurt like hell. With my frozen body pressed against Wren, I began to thaw. The amount of heat he was generating was soothing, and at that moment I wanted nothing more than to curl up and take a nap. But then I saw the wad of bloody tissues piled up on the coffee table. I reached up, touching my nose. "Are those all from me?"

"Yeah." Annabelle pressed her lips into a thin line.

"How long was I out?"

"Just a little over an hour," Blaire said.

I pressed my hands against my face, and as I shut my eyes, the vision the enchantress sent me came rushing in at full force.

"Can you tell us what happened?" Blaire encouraged.

I blinked my eyes open, waiting until the fuzzy spots cleared from my vision while my dad's face settled into view. He looked tired–the worry lines creasing his forehead seemed deeper than usual. But there was something else there, too–a sort of warmth that had been missing from his eyes since Mom died. Seeing that old flame spark again gave me the strength I needed to finally tell my dad the truth.

"Dad," I said, and he reached for my hand, wrapping his warm, callused palm around mine. "I need to tell you something."

"Honey, I already know." His eyes filled with tears but he smiled through them.

"About the Trinity?" I asked tentatively.

His lips formed a tight line as he gave my hand a squeeze. "Vivian told me everything when the Earth Mother came to her. She told me that if the time ever came, you would find out on your own. Her hope was that you would come to us when it happened. When she died…" A tear escaped the corner of his eye. "I was afraid that if it happened, I wouldn't know how to help you."

"Lucky you've got all of us," Blaire added.

"We just wanted to protect you," Dad said.

"I know." I squeezed his hand reassuringly as my heart swelled behind my breastbone. I wouldn't tell him that I'd been angry with their decisions to keep me in the dark. The truth was ever since I found Mom's grimoire in the spelled attic, all of that turmoil and sorrow had faded away. There was no point in dredging up the past that would only serve to inflict pain. "When did you find out?" I asked him.

"I had my suspicions about Blaire when I discovered she was a witch," Dad admitted, "But everything clicked when I saw the three of you together."

"This is weird, isn't it?" I scrunched my features together.

"I've had a long time to prepare myself about how all this would make me feel," Dad said, reaching up to scratch his head, "but *weird* is an understatement."

I laughed and Wren squeezed my shoulder. "I'd apologize, but I know it wouldn't suffice."

"No apology is required," Dad said.

A thought occurred to me. "Dad, you don't remember Mom working with the enchantress to spell the hidden door to the attic do you? I found the book that she left for me."

"I sort of feel like maybe I did, but," he frowned, "it's like I can't remember anything. If I try, it's just really foggy."

Blaire waved her hand over my dad, reading things from his aura that I couldn't detect. "His memory has been tampered with," she said. "I can feel the traces of a lingering protection spell."

"It was probably the enchantress's doing," I said at the turn of an eye roll. "I'm starting to feel like everything is entirely on her terms."

"So about that vision," Blaire said, gently leading me back on track.

"Hey, where's Bryna?" I realized the room seemed quieter and less judgmental than usual.

"She's been trying to dig up research on the grimoire's symbol. I told her I was coming over to practice spell work with you and suggested she stay at the cabin. I'll catch her up to speed later," Blaire said.

"Right," I cleared my throat, "the enchantress led me to the Thornwood Were bar via spirit quest style. The vision started with Maddox and Ryker talking about Wren and how Hailey was being used as bait to get you to join their pack." I looked up at Wren. "Maddox wanted to use me in hopes of coercing your decision, but Ryker wouldn't allow it." I could feel the tension building in Wren's muscles beside me. "But then…" I froze, remembering the horrible truth of what happened after that, and an icy chill passed through my body.

"Go on." Blaire reached out, placing her hand on my knee. A fresh burst of air rushed through my lungs, filling me with warmth and smelling of lilacs in the spring. Somehow she'd known I needed the strength of her goddess given affinity to deliver the awful message that was making my stomach lurch.

In a voice that was barely audible I managed to say, "The woman who killed Niall was there. Her name is Nyla." I sensed Wren's penetrating gaze from the side, but I was glad he'd kept me tucked against his body because I didn't think I had the strength to look up into his eyes. His whole body had become an unyielding block of solid marble. I stayed silent until I was sure I felt him breathing again.

"You know who killed Niall?" came my dad's stunned reply.

"When we performed the spell that linked us as the Trinity, we were attacked by a group of rogue werewolves that had been working for the Dark Witch," Blaire explained. "One of them sacrificed Niall in the name of Rionach. It was a warning."

Dad blinked rapidly as he struggled to absorb this harsh piece of information. He staggered up from the chair he was sitting in and crossed his arms over his chest. "Attacked by werewolves? Quinn, why didn't you tell me about this?"

"I'm sorry Dad, but, I didn't know how... I wanted to keep you safe."

Dad's eyes expanded. "I'm the parent. It's my job to–" he stopped short, working his jaw as the little vein in his temple began to twitch. "You didn't go to the police?"

"We can't turn her in." I heard the harsh, low rumble emitting from Wren's chest. "Werewolves are subjected to the three phases of the full moon cycle; we have no choice but to Change. A werewolf can't go to human prison."

"Well, is there some sort of Supernatural justice system?" My dad lifted his hands. "There must be a way to make her answer for her crimes."

"Ryker told the others to take her to the cells–whatever that means," I said. "They were hauling her away and that was the last thing I saw before I woke up."

"Usually when something like this occurs, the punishments are left up to the Supernatural race it involves, but should they fail to serve appropriate justice, the Aurora Coven will step in if deemed necessary," Blaire said. That was news to me. I knew the Aurora Coven was top of the line as far as witches were concerned, but I had no idea they played a role in the rest of the Supernatural realm. I frowned at Blaire, wondering what else I didn't know about the esteemed coven. She turned to me and asked, "Do you think that's what the enchantress wanted you to see–that they were punishing her?" Blaire's eyebrows knitted together.

I shook my head. "There was more. Ryker knew about Nyla following the Darkness. He banished her and the others from the pack and swore to end their lives if they ever came back to Thornwood. She asked for amnesty and told him that she knew about us–about the Trinity. She said she was turning from the path of shadow, and that she believed the Dark Witch only wanted the amulet back so she could control the pack. And then she told them that I was carrying the amulet," I finished in a rush. "They want to take it from me."

"Ah, hell," Annabelle muttered.

"We're not going to let them have it," Blaire said with determination. "The vision the enchantress sent you is going to keep us one step ahead of the others."

Dad's face had gone ashen and he was staring through me like he'd seen a ghost. Blaire noticed; she laid her hand on his shoulder and used her affinity to help calm him. "If this is too much–" I started to say but Dad cut me off.

"No. I'd rather be in the know. I just don't like feeling so useless."

"You're not useless," I told him earnestly.

"But knowing that there isn't anything I can do to help–to protect you…" His gaze dropped from mine, fingers trembling.

Wren leaned up from the couch, making sure that I was covered with the blanket before placing a solid hand on my dad's shoulder. "Mr. Callaghan, let's take a walk." My dad blinked up at him, shrugged and then nodded. Wren held the front door for my dad, looked back at me for a brief moment and shot me a wink that under the circumstances should not have made my stomach flutter, but it did.

"He loves you," Blaire said, watching the two men through the window as they walked across the lawn.

"What do you think they're talking about?" I dared to ask.

"You, obviously," Annabelle said.

My intestines felt like spaghetti being wound through fork tines. I tried to ignore the sensation and tucked my legs beneath me to help trap in the warmth. "Nyla thinks they should kill me," I paused. "She told Ryker that there's nothing on earth that can destroy the amulet. They don't want a weapon that can control them resting in the hands of a witch."

"We can use this to our advantage," Blaire said. "We have a bargaining tool."

I was sure I was staring at her like she'd lost her mind. "You're not actually suggesting that we hand it over, are you?"

"Of course not! But maybe we can buy more time for Wren if we tell them we're going to the enchantress to have the amulet destroyed," she suggested.

"That's a horrible plan," Annabelle said. "No way should you guys even step foot in Thornwood if you think for a minute they might possibly try to kill you!"

"Someone is always trying to kill us," I replied, "what's new?"

"I mean what are you going to do if they try to attack you?"

Blaire and I exchanged knowing looks, and at the same time opened our palms with a flick of the wrist to summon our elemental energy-balls. Swirls of blue and opal vapor danced across our palms.

"Oh, yeah, sure, that'll knock out a whole pack of werewolves." Flabbergasted, Annabelle ran a hand through her hair.

"Ryker doesn't want to hurt me," I told her. "His pack won't outwardly disobey him. As long as I'm under his protection, we should be fine."

"How can you be so sure?"

"Because I saw another side to him—one that shows he actually has a moral compass. He's not as ruthless as the rest of the pack sees him. It's a mask he has to wear, but it's not his true nature." I felt the truth in the statement as I said it and knew this was one of the reasons the enchantress had showed me the vision.

"So what do you want to do, Quinn?" Blaire folded her palm over my ankle.

"Wren is supposed to give Ryker an answer tomorrow night about joining the pack. Maybe the three of us should go before the council. They know who we are now, we might as well own up to it. It will give us an opportunity to present our case."

"I still don't like it," Annabelle said.

"Neither do I, but, we don't really have another choice."

My owl was there–resting in the branches of the big willow tree. Her drooping branches concealed the gazebo like a beaded curtain, shielding it from the outside world. The tips of her branches dipped low over the creek bank and if the wind blew just right, sometimes the branches would caress the surface of the water. It was quiet there, save for the sound of water cutting across the rocks in the creek bed as it churned along the bend. The sun had just disappeared below the horizon line, leaving the cloudless sky shimmering in shades of amethyst. Sirius, the brightest star in the sky, was just beginning to shine.

I called upon the elements to replenish my body. The vision sent by the enchantress had taken a lot out of me and wearing the Dark Witch's amulet in place of my own didn't help matters. I missed my iolite stone and the strength it provided me when I had a vision. For now, the healing elements sufficed.

The owl above me ruffled her wings. I looked up from the grimoire and spotted Wren making his way to the gazebo. Twilight glossed his skin, shimmering as though he'd been fashioned from the moon. He ducked below the sweeping branches and my favorite, cavalier half smile pulled at one corner of his mouth.

"You found me," I said.

"I never lost you." He sat down on the worn wooden bench and drew me nearer. His lips pressed into the side of my temple as his arms circled my waist. "Are you feeling any better?"

"Yeah, a little." I ran my fingertips across the cover of the grimoire, tracing the crescent moons on either side of the triquetra symbol. "The elements are making me stronger."

"It's been a long day," he replied, as if that could somehow sum up the emotional rollercoaster we'd been on since dawn.

I let go of a sigh, pulled my knees to my chest, and leaned against him. "Is my dad okay?"

"He's been through a lot of heartbreak in his life, but he's stronger for it. He knows he has to accept that he can't protect you anymore, but

I assured him that I would never let anything happen to you." Wren shifted me in his arms, gently tilting my chin so that I was looking up into his golden eyes. "You know that, right?"

"I know it, and I'm not afraid."

"What if I am?" His eyes flickered back and forth between mine.

"Then you should know I'd never let anything happen to you, either." I grinned and nudged his ribs with my shoulder.

He rolled his eyes and dropped his hand from my chin. "That is absolutely not your job. You might be a super powerful sorcerous with kick-ass abilities, but you are *mine* to protect." He lifted his eyebrows, setting his jaw stubbornly.

A shiver passed through my lower abdomen at the way he'd emphasized that I was his. I leaned into him, pressing my mouth against the side of his throat, and his pulse jumped beneath my lips. He tilted my face to his, bringing his mouth down on mine. His kiss was a slow and steady burn that tangled with the scents of his skin, wrapping deliriously through my brain. He broke the kiss too soon, resting his forehead against mine, and traced my lower lip with his thumb.

"You know that I love you, right?"

"I know," I breathed. And even though I did know, my heart still raced and swelled at the notion of his declaration.

We held each other for a long while, hidden beneath the gazebo and the willow tree's canopy until the night sky stretched above us and filled with billions of silver stars. Above us in the tree, the barn owl cried out into the night. The echoing call startled me and I jumped against Wren's side. Quiet laughter rumbled in his chest.

"Wow," I said, "The epitome of Darkness is on my doorstep and an owl screeching in the tree causes me to jump. If that's not embarrassing, I don't know what is."

"She's just talking to you." Wren tipped his head back against the support beam and gazed up at her through the branches.

"What do you think she wants?"

"Probably to catch a mouse for dinner," he mused. I made a face. He chuckled and squeezed my shoulder. "Come on, we better get you inside."

"Yeah, okay," I agreed. I reached for my mother's grimoire that was resting next to me when I noticed something was different. My brows laced together and I pulled the book onto my lap. "Wren, look," I pointed to the cover, "the crescent moons are facing inward now."

"What?" He tilted the book in his direction.

"They weren't like this before, they were facing out." I sat up straight, pinching one of the moons between my thumb and index finger to try and get it to move but the thing wouldn't budge.

"I think you might just be sleep deprived."

"Wren, I'm telling you, it wasn't like this before!" As if to prove my belief, the triquetra symbol in the middle of the moons began to glow gold. The crescents began glowing with the light of the silver moon, and I gasped. "Oh my goddess!"

"Open it," Wren suggested.

My stomach fluttered as I flipped the cover, turning the first page past my mother's letter and then saw something that at first I couldn't comprehend. Elegant script leapt from the page, gleaming in luminous metallic silver. "It's star spelled," I said in awe. "Blaire said it was spelled by Old Magic–star magic is about as old as it gets." I ran my fingers over the beautiful lettering. "There's no way my mother could have done this," I said. "It's got to be the enchantress."

"It's incredible," Wren said.

An emblem of an ornate silver bow and arrow decorated the top of the page. It emitted lunar light, like it was made from the heavens. When I touched it, sparks of blue danced beneath my fingertips on the page. "It's just like the attic door," I breathed. Beneath the bow and arrow, I read the script aloud.

By lunar light she follows
The stars shall guide her way
Beneath the moonlit meadow
Behold: a night within a day

When I finished reading the poem, a little gold arrow lit up in the bottom right-hand corner of the page. I didn't hesitate. I flipped the page, and a metallic map glistened across the surface of the page.

"It's the coastline," Wren said. The map itself wasn't very large, but I recognized a few pinpoints the enchantress had marked along the jagged coastline. "It's probably about a five and a half-hour trip. We can make this in a day."

I turned the next page, expecting to find detailed instructions or at least any indication of *where* on the coastline she might be but the pages that followed were blank. "Damn," I muttered, and then the page lit up again in neat, cursive writing.

All will be revealed in time.

"Damn," I muttered again. Wren laughed and kissed the side of my head.

"This is a good thing," he reminded me. "We know the book is star spelled, and we know there's a plan. For now, that's going to have to be good enough."

"When did you become the optimistic one?" I lifted an eyebrow.

"I'm optimistic," he said, jabbing his thumbs into his chest. Now I laughed. Wren was a lot of things, but 'naturally optimistic' wasn't one of them. He worried too much for one thing, but I knew that was because he was constantly thinking one step ahead. It was that natural wolf instinct–the need to hunt and protect and claim freedom. He was confident and strong and caring–all attributes that carried over from our previous lives. He was a warrior, and he was mine.

"Come on, Optimistic Man," I said, lacing my fingers through his. "We have good news to share with the others."

Chapter Fifteen
Letting Go

The smell of hazelnut coffee woke me the next morning. Dad had the 'good stuff' out, which meant that he was feeling pretty rough. I rolled over, tossing back the covers as I tore myself away from the comfort of the mattress. Wren was still asleep, lying on his back with his head tilted to the side on his pillow. He slept with one arm above his head; his fingers nimbly curled into his palm. I studied the way the morning light encased his body; watched the way his chest rose and fell with each steady breath.

He'd had nightmares in his sleep. I'd woken several times throughout the night from his tossing and turning, growling in a way that was more animal than human. I wondered if it was still images of his father's death that plagued his dreams, or if it was the unknown darkness, we still had to face. Tonight was the night Ryker expected a decision, and my heart skipped a couple of beats just thinking of what was to come. I reached out, brushing the lock of hair back from his forehead. He stirred, blinking up at me with midsummer night eyes.

"Sorry," I whispered, "I didn't mean to wake you."

"Don't apologize," he said, reaching for my hand. "How'd you sleep?"

"Better," I said. "I'm going to go talk to my dad. He put on hazelnut coffee." I pressed my mouth together in a tight line.

"I take it that's not a good thing?"

"Let's just say the last time he had it out was after my mom passed."

Wren pulled my hand to his lips, pressing his mouth against my fingers. "Do you want me to leave?"

I knew he was only asking because he'd be able to hear everything that we talked about. I shook my head. "I want you to stay."

"Okay." He kissed my hand again, rolling to his side.

I smiled a small smile before heading for the door. I padded down the steps and spotted my dad through the sliding door, sitting on one of the lawn chairs on the deck. The steam from his coffee cup was rising and rolling through the air. I poured myself a cup and took it outside to join him.

He looked up at me, forcing his mouth into the shape of a smile. The shadow of a sleepless night underscored his swollen eyes, matching the disheveled case of bed-head. His dark locks curled above his brow which somehow managed to be endearing. "Hey Quinny, I didn't wake you did I?"

"No, I was awake," I lied. The crisp morning air rose gooseflesh on the back of my arms, so I tucked my legs beneath me as I sat, and curled my fingers around the ceramic mug for warmth. "How long have you been up?"

"Oh, not long."

I nodded, letting the sound of the wind rustling through the leaves distract me. Golden leaves shook loose from surrounding branches and tumbled across the pale frosted grass. "So, I didn't get to ask you what you and Wren were talking about last night," I prompted.

"It was a man-to-man conversation," Dad said. He was looking at his coffee cup, but the corner of his mouth quirked. "He promised me that he would never let anything happen to you. He's a good kid–a good *man*," he corrected.

"I'm glad you approve," I said.

"This is all just going to take a while for me to… adjust, but, I want you to know that I'm okay. You don't need to worry about me." He looked up at me then, meeting my eyes. "I know that I can't help you, and I know you have to save the world so to speak. It's hard for me to look at you and not see my little girl; I'll always want to protect you. But," he drew a breath, "I also see the woman that you are becoming. You remind me so much of your mother, and I see her strength in you. I know that she's watching over you." He smiled. It didn't quite reach his eyes but there was a soft, warm glow there.

I reached out, cupping the back of his hand and squeezing. "I know this can't be easy for you, but it means a lot to have your trust," I told him. "If I could protect you from this burden, I would."

"That's not your job, Quinny." He turned his hand over and squeezed mine instead. Tears welled in my eyes, and I wondered if he knew just how much I loved him. "So," he said a moment later, "Wren filled me in on what's been going on in the world of Supernaturals. He says you'll have to leave to find this... enchantress... person."

I nodded. "We have to find her before the solar eclipse."

"Are you sure you can trust her?"

"I'm not really sure of anything," I admitted. "I believe that she's on our side. Mom wouldn't have let her help spell the attic and hide the grimoire if she wasn't. I think she's our only hope against the Darkness."

Dad nodded. "This is the hard part... letting you go."

"I know," I said, voice steady and soft. "I was made for this, Dad. I'm not afraid."

"That's because you're just like your mother. Nothing ever scared her, either." He chuckled then, remembering.

I let the silence settle around us for a small while, but then I remembered something that had nothing to do with the supernatural... "How was your date with Josephine?"

Dad blinked and cleared his throat. "It was great," he admitted.

"So I can assume that she'll be on the Thanksgiving guest list this year." I grinned, bumping his shoulder with mine. I purposely steered the conversation to something that didn't involve magic. It was important that he gripped hold of this human reality and didn't linger on thoughts of things he couldn't control.

"Well, that's still a little way off, don't you think?" Dad shot me a suspicious glance. But I could see the eagerness in it too.

"Nah," I said, "I think it gives us something *normal* to look forward to. We can invite the whole gang–make it a big event."

"A werewolf, a couple of witches, and a few humans–I'm not so sure that's exactly a normal Thanksgiving."

"It's normal for us." I laughed.

Dad titled his head to the side and raised both of his eyebrows. "I suppose you're right about that." He grinned.

"I love you, Dad, always."

"I love you, too." He tipped his mug to his lips, finishing the last gulp of his hazelnut coffee, and then the sun crested the horizon line.

"No way," Wren said. I watched his hands tighten over the steering wheel until his knuckles turned white; his jaw set sternly.

"*Yes* way," I persisted stubbornly. Wren steered the Firebird around the curve just a little too fast, and I gripped the edges of my seat. I broke the news of my plans to go before the Thornwood council on our drive to school, and needless to say, the conversation was going just as I imagined it would: Wren protesting, and me not backing down until I got my way.

"They know what you are now," Wren continued. "The whole pack is going to be on high alert, there's no way I'm going to let you walk in there and present yourself before the council. That's like leading an animal to slaughter."

"Oh, and I suppose you thought *I* was just going to let *you* go alone?" I snickered. "You're delusional Wren Whelan. The fact of the matter is we're both stubborn to a fault and neither of us wants to let the other walk into a situation where a possible threat is lurking. Blaire and I think this is an opportune time to go before the council as the Trinity, and work on forming some kind of an alliance."

The corner of Wren's mouth twitched. "An alliance?" We pulled into the senior lot and parked the Firebird next to Huck's beat-up hand-me-down Ford truck. Wren lifted his customary eyebrow and leaned back in the seat, his long fingers tense on his knee. "You think forming an alliance with the Thornwood pack is an option?" His tone indicated he thought otherwise.

"I think," I said, reaching across the console to cover his hand with mine, "that we need to *try*." I peered up at him through my eyelashes, raising my eyebrows. "What happened to Mr. Optimistic from last night?"

"He's trying to keep you safe," Wren breathed. "As usual, you're making it difficult."

"You love me for it."

Wren's expression softened then. The sunlight caught the coin at his throat, and I reached over, running my thumb across its surface in the little V that split his shirt collar. His hand folded over mine. He was looking into my eyes with such intensity it was hard not to feel the burn from it. He had that way about him. I felt it that night in the woods when he let me watch him Change from man to wolf; his bold, unapologetic gaze making me feel stripped raw to the bone. He was looking at me that way now, and I felt myself coming undone.

A pair of hands smacked into the window over his shoulder and I vaulted out of my skin, clutching a hand over my heart. A slow smile spread over Wren's lips as he turned to roll down his window. Huck, Jamie, and Torrance were standing there laughing. "You should have seen your face," Torrance said, pointing at me.

"You almost gave me a heart attack!"

"Careful Tor, you know she's fragile," Huck said. "Are you recovered from yesterday's incident?"

"I can't believe you passed out from looking at a bloody picture," Jamie added.

"I'm fine, thank you," I retorted.

"I guess we know that you'll never be in the medical profession," Torrance said. "I'm sorry you blacked out though."

"I take it the whole school knows?"

"It is a small town," Jamie said, shrugging. "Silver Mountain's star runner passing out over seeing a bloody picture is unfortunately the only exciting thing that's happened since..." he trailed off, having realized what he almost said. I narrowed my eyes at him and Huck slapped him upside the back of the head.

"Do you ever think before you speak?" Huck shook his head.

"It's okay," Wren said. He clicked out of his seatbelt, and the three of our friends stepped away from his door so he could climb out of the car. I joined them on the sidewalk as we headed for the school's entrance.

"Has there been any progress in the case?" Torrance asked softly.

Wren shook his head. "The police are grasping at straws. They don't have a clue what they're looking for." *And hopefully it stays that way*, I thought.

"I'm sorry," Torrance said, placing her hand on his arm as we walked. "I'm sure they'll find out what happened soon."

Jamie snorted. "Not with shit-for-brains Officer Stevenson leading the investigation. He thinks a badge and a uniform makes him tough, but the rest of us remember him crying on the football field when he got his knee blown out during the big rival game against the Cougars his senior year. You remember that?" Jamie nudged Huck in the shoulder. "That was our freshman year, right?"

"Jamie that's ancient history," Torrance said, scolding him with one of her disapproving looks. "Besides, the sheriff is the one in charge, not Carl."

"My dad is a city council member," Huck said. "I heard they're thinking of bringing in outside help if Stevenson can't pull something together soon."

"Outside help?" I repeated.

"Yeah," Huck said, "from one of the bigger departments. Stevenson's not going to like anyone else taking charge on his turf, though. It's bad enough being a cop in a small town–can you imagine the beating his ego is going to take?"

"What's his ego got to do with anything?" Torrance asked.

"Because if he can't solve this case on his own, it goes to show that he's not cut out for the job. Silver Mountain's law enforcement is a joke."

My stomach tightened into knots. Now I understood why Stevenson showed up the day of Niall's funeral asking all those questions about Remy's case. He was digging around, trying to uncover old skeletons in Niall's closet because he didn't want one of the bigger departments getting involved.

We'd been banking on Niall's murder case going cold. But I wondered, for a split second, what would happen if they brought in outside help... Was there a chance we might have missed something in the woods? Blaire had cast a spell that destroyed the knife–disintegrated it into millions of miniscule pieces that were now part of the Little Silver Creek. There was nothing that would lead the police back to us–nothing that would ever explain what had happened in the forest.

Then there was another part of me that wondered how many innocent lives had been taken because they'd been in the wrong place at the wrong time–victims by happenstance and Supernatural conflict. It occurred to me that I hadn't given much thought to the man that Niall had killed all those years ago in order to protect his pack. Clyde Sheridan's life was taken from him–what had he been forced to leave behind? Did he have a family? Were there kids somewhere out there that had grown up without a father? Nausea raked my gut. Rionach's moonstone pendant began to heat, the weight expanding beneath my shirt.

You would take someone's life to save the ones you love, the voice of Darkness whispered to me. *Don't fool yourself into thinking you're a protector of the innocent, White One. You live in the gray. You're no force of Light.*

I doubled over, wrapping my arms around my stomach as we entered the lobby. Wren stopped walking and slid his arm across my shoulders and pulled me against his side. "Are you okay?" His eyebrows furrowed.

The others were staring at me with similar concerned expressions. "Must have been something I ate," I said, straightening. The pain had departed just as fast as it had struck. "I'm okay."

"Get some water," Torrance said as the first bell rang.

"I will," I told her. Torrance nodded and then took off with Huck and Jamie in the opposite direction.

"What happened?"

"I just had a weird pain in my stomach. I'm fine now," I assured him. I stood up on the tips of my toes and kissed him before turning for the door of my homeroom. He watched me go, and I was sure he stayed there even after I was out of view. I could still sense the weight of the amulet beneath my shirt, humming and swelling with an ancient power. I balled my hands into fists to keep them from shaking; I wondered–not for the first time–if I was stronger than the Darkness I was carrying.

Sweat trickled down the back of my neck, chasing the hollow of my spine as I ran through the forest. Today was distance day, and my muscles were bunching as I climbed over an uneven hummock. We ran a familiar trail that traced through the National Park nowhere near the Hollow, but every shadow caught in my peripheral became an unknown danger. Gnarled branches took on the living shape of a human being, half hidden and crouching in the brush. The crunch of dried leaves under shoes drowned out any other source of sound.

There was a creek bed three miles in, its rocky embankment constructed of smooth stones and exposed roots from nearby trees. We stopped there to take a break and stretch our muscles. It had been almost a month since the team had been permitted to run in the woods, but the wardens had deemed this area clear from dangerous wildlife activity. Team spirit was at an unusual high, and several of the members took advantage of the warm autumn temperature and waded out into the creek to splash around while we waited for the whole group to arrive.

Wren had arrived first, crouched on top of a boulder and lifted his face to the wind. I ambled up beside him, leaning against the cool stone while my chest heaved. "Anything out there?"

"Dead squirrel about a half-mile that way." He pointed in a general eastward direction, quirking his lips in a mischievous smile.

I shot him a pointed look.

He jumped down from the boulder, landing soundlessly on the balls of his feet and flipped the hair out of his face. "Relax, Quinn." His palms rolled over my shoulders. "The rogues won't come near a large group of humans. They wouldn't risk exposure."

I remembered the wild gleam in Nyla's eyes as she gave the order for the others to attack us when we'd linked ourselves as the Trinity. She was their ring-leader, and she was currently being held in the cells of Thornwood–whatever that meant. Had the others given up the chase after Nyla turned herself in, I wondered?

Wren studied me a minute more, brows puckering as though I was a riddle in need of solving. "You love running in the woods," he said. "What's wrong?"

"I don't know." I shook my head. "I just feel like my whole world has changed and I can't look at anything the same. Sometimes I wonder if I ever will again." I let my gaze fall from his lightning scrutiny and looked out at our teammates splashing around in the creek instead. "I lied to you this morning," I said in a low tone. "About what happened in the lobby." Clyde Sheridan's death had been sitting heavy on my heart since this morning, and a storm of conflicting emotions had been brewing through my soul since the Darkness spoke to me.

Wren's hands dropped away from my shoulders. I heard the sharp intake of air through his nose, and watched as he leaned against the boulder, waiting for me to continue.

"The Darkness whispered to me again," I admitted with some reluctance. "It said that I wasn't all good–that I would kill an innocent to save someone I love." I drew a breath and prepared myself to meet his gaze. "I'm not so sure that's far from the truth."

Wren was quiet for a moment. A thin line creased his brow, hooding his tawny eyes. "Why didn't you tell me?"

"Because I was thinking about your father…" I let my voice trail off. "I realized that I'd never stopped to think about the man he killed–about the life that he didn't get to live and it made me question what he'd been forced to leave behind."

Wren swallowed; the skin pulled tight through the column of his neck. Wren turned his gaze toward the creek, speaking in a quiet tone, "Niall chose to sacrifice one for the good of his people. Maybe there was a better way, but that *was* pack law. It consumed him from the inside out. He could never forgive himself for what he did. That's the thing about free will. We have to live with the consequences of our actions."

"If I did that… If I had to kill someone–"

"It would be justified," Wren interrupted.

"Would it?" I wasn't so sure…

Wren met my gaze and held it for some time before he spoke. "We all have our Darkness, Quinn," he spoke softly. "Not a single one of us is all good. The Darkness will use your greatest fears and weaknesses against you, but you have to *choose* not to become the monster."

The autumn wind swept dark hair across his forehead, and I swore there was a light in his eyes that hadn't been there a moment before. The burden aged him beyond his eighteen years, and I glimpsed the man he was destined to become. It took all my self-control not to close that small distance between us and wrap him up in an embrace that I prayed conveyed the things I couldn't bring myself to say.

The moment was ruined when Jamie walked by and tugged on the end of my ponytail. "Lover's quarrel?" he quipped.

"Seriously though, the look you two are giving one another could freeze a lake," Huck added.

"Or set it on fire," Annabelle said. Leave it to my best friend to be exceptionally intuitive.

"We're fine." I recovered with a forced smile. "Is everyone here?"

"By my headcount, yes," Jamie said.

"Then we better count again." Annabelle grinned and shot him a wink. "God, my thighs are burning. It's been way too long since we've done a distance run through the woods."

"Yeah, and we still have about three more miles to go." Huck pulled his arm in a shoulder stretch. "Wren, you up for a little competition? Last one back to the parking lot buys dinner."

A slow smile tugged Wren's full mouth upwards.

"Trust me Huck," Annabelle said, "you do *not* want to foot that bill."

"That implies you think I'm going to lose," he retorted.

"There are no implications needed," Annabelle said. "I know you're going to lose."

Wren laughed and mussed the top of her hair. "I appreciate your vote of confidence, *Cat.* When I win, I'll buy you one of those fry boats you like so much."

"With extra cheese?" Her eyes widened expectantly.

"You got it."

"Deal." She clapped her hands and rubbed her palms together. "Runners!" she called. "On your mark..."

Chapter Sixteen
The Council

Huck lost the race by a total of four seconds, though I suspected Wren had intentionally taken it easy on him. Torrance and Shawn met up with us at Jo's after practice, and Huck, in good nature, bought Wren's meal. As promised, Annabelle was gifted with a large boat of cheesy fries, and the seven of us crammed into the back corner and devoured an early dinner. About halfway through, my phone started ringing and I dug through my bag to find it. Blaire's name flashed across the screen. "I'll be right back," I said, sliding out of the booth. "It's Blaire."

"Tell her I love her," Jamie called after me as I wove through the maze of tables.

"In your dreams, Jamie." I laughed and shook my head as I answered the phone. "Hey Blaire, what's up?" I was at the front of the diner now, pushing out through the doors.

"Have you a minute to talk?" she sounded anxious.

"I'm outside the diner. No one is listening."

"The Aurora Coven just phoned in and said they've spotted Penny. She's fled to Ireland as we'd expected."

I drew a breath, leaning against the warm brick of the building as I scratched my eyebrow. "Has anyone tried to talk to her yet?"

"Not yet. They've assigned an emissary spy to track her movements."

"A *what?*"

"They're an elite team of Supernaturals with special abilities in tracking. Most members are made up of werewolves and vampires," Blaire explained. "They're loyal to the Coven."

I blew out a breath of air as my brows hitched clear into my hairline. She'd said they were loyal to the Coven, but what I heard was something different. If there were other races of Supernaturals working for the Coven–that meant the Aurora Coven had more secrets than I realized. "You're more than just a world-class coven made up of witches, aren't you?"

Blaire let the static linger on the phone line.

"Blaire..." I pressed. "What aren't you telling me?"

"Nothing important," she said after a pause. "I just wanted you to know their aim is to capture her and bring her in for questioning."

"Good. I look forward to learning what reasons she has for trying to unleash hell on earth, and how she went about doing it."

"As am I," Blaire said.

"You okay?"

"I'll feel a great deal better once we get this meeting over with at Thornwood. Goddess knows we need a win, even if it is a small one."

"I wanted to be wrong about her too," I said regrettably. I turned my head to the side, peeking in through the window at our group of friends laughing and smiling. I'd wanted to be wrong about so many things, if only to keep the ones I love safe. "I'll see you soon, Blaire."

"Soon," she agreed.

"Where are you going?" I asked Wren. He'd just driven past the main parking lot of the Were bar and was turning down a narrow side street. The alley was cracked and dimpled and full of potholes that looked big enough to swallow a black bear. The Pontiac dipped low over a bump, and I smacked my elbow into the side of the door. I rubbed at the sore bone, grimacing.

"Sorry," he said, taking note of my pain. "Roy's family owns this convenience shop, if we park around back with the employees, no one will know we're here."

"We should have taken the truck," Blaire added. "It's a little less conspicuous than your Firebird–as if you don't already stick out enough. Driving around a classic muscle car with a gold bird on the hood," she muttered under her breath while shaking her head. "What is this anyway–an eighties model?"

Wren smirked, glancing back at her in the rearview mirror. "Seventy-nine." He parked the Pontiac in a diagonal space next to a beat-up Ford in front of the brick building. The foundation was crumbling at the base and weeds sprouted through the cracks. When I climbed out of the car, all I could hear was the old air conditioning unit rattling like loose change in a tin can.

Wren led the way down the dark alley with Blaire and I close on his heels. I watched him sampling the air; his keen eyes taking a full sweep of the shadows as we headed for the Were bar. What had Ryker called it–Club Canis Lupus? The Thornwood werewolves were a lot of things, but subtle wasn't one of them.

Sal opened the back door when we reached the platform. Her cropped hair was pulled back into a sloppy ponytail with flyaway strands framing her face. She crossed her arms, leaning against the doorframe as her gaze raked over us. "Ryker was only expecting Wren," she said hesitantly, like maybe she couldn't quite figure out what do about the three of us–maybe she was wondering if there was anything she *could* do.

Instinct had me reaching for the amulet. Sal followed my movement with her eyes, and I watched her shrink back into the doorframe. "He sees all of us or none," I replied coolly.

The corner of Sal's mouth rose into small sneer. "Follow me," she instructed. She stepped away from the doorframe and allowed us to step up into the small hallway. I heard rock music playing from the overhead speakers and knew we must have been near the pool tables.

She jerked her head toward the right, signaling us to move along. At the end of the hall, she knocked on a wooden door that had deep claw marks scratched into the surface of the wood. She noticed me gawking. "They don't always come willingly." Sal grinned and pushed open the door.

I don't know what I'd been expecting, but a neat office wasn't on the list. The walls were the color of snow, clean, and free of posters or tack marks. A simple black desk was pushed up against the wall with an expensive looking office chair. I narrowed my eyes, studying the tidy stack of papers and binders sitting on the desk in their individual organizers. The Thornwood pack emblem of the wolf's head and bloody roses made up the screensaver on the monitor.

"Ryker will be right with you," Sal said, closing the office door behind her. The three of us exchanged wary glances.

"Can you feel that?" Blaire said a beat later.

The office was too quiet–too clean and ordinary. I realized that it was *meant* to look that way. I sensed it in the air, the cool hum of energy pulsing through the invisible particles of the atmosphere. "It's spelled," I said.

"It feels like Old Magic," Blaire said. She was waving her palm through the air, seeing things I couldn't. "I can't really get a good read on the witch who spelled it." She squared her shoulders, extended her arms with her palms facing up and said, "*Nochtann.*"

The very air in the room rippled, and white paint melted down the walls–reminding me of the famous Dali painting, *Persistence of Memory.* The paint washed away to reveal plain, cracked cement beneath. The desk was still there with its organized office supplies, but the room smelled foul, like the stale air of a basement. Wren stiffened, and I looked over my shoulder to see that another door had appeared within the cement wall. This one was deadlocked by a heavy iron bolt.

"I'm impressed." Ryker's deep voice echoed behind us. He'd literally materialized from the wall and he wasn't alone. He was standing next to a girl with copper skin. She looked to be about fifteen with deep, sapphire eyes and choppy jaw-length chocolate hair. She was staring right through me, those sapphire eyes searching some deeper part of my soul. Ryker leaned against the wall, crossing his bulky arms over his chest. "I should have known a member of the revered Trinity would be able to sense a spelled room."

"You know who we are," Blaire said, lifting her chin. "Don't suppose you'd like to share how you came by that information?"

"A little bird told me," Ryker said, pushing away from the wall. "I have to admit… we were hoping to speak to the three of you but I didn't expect it would be tonight." His gaze cut to me and lingered on the moonstone pendant hanging from my neck. "We have a lot to discuss."

"We wish to make an appeal before the council." I curled my fingers into fists at my side to keep from reaching for the amulet.

If Ryker was surprised to hear this declaration, his placid expression wasn't any indication. He simply turned his face to the side, looking to the young witch. She laid a slender hand on his bicep and said, "I'll assemble the others."

Ryker nodded and the young witch vanished from sight. "We have someone who might be of interest to you," Ryker said to Wren. He waved us forward as he unlatched the heavy bolted door. At once, the scent of rot and must wafted up the staircase in a wave of cooler air. "Watch your footing, the planks are steep and uneven."

The muscle in Wren's jaw bulged as he clenched his teeth. He started down the steps, taking the lead in front of Blaire and me. When we reached the bottom, the smell only worsened. The hall was lined by several rows of silver bars that stretched from the floor to the ceilings–cellblocks, I realized. By my count, there was a total of eight–four per side. The narrow passage was lit by old gas lamps that were fastened into the walls. I swallowed hard, training my eyes on a shadowed figure slumped over in the last row.

Her stringy hair hung lank in her face, dirt and dried blood streaking her bare arms. Nyla looked up as we approached, and the flames reflecting in her caramel eyes revealed her fear. When I looked at her, I only saw the blade at Niall's throat gleaming in the moonlight. I blinked as my memory replayed the image of Nyla slicing open his neck and hyper-focused on the scarlet curtain that pooled from his throat. My stomach tightened with boiling sickness and resentment.

"Death is coming for you, Stone Keeper!" Nyla shouted from her prison cell. "The Dark One is coming after all of you–no one is safe!" She lunged forward in the blink of an eye, wrapping her hands around the bars. I startled, stumbling back into the solid wall of Wren's chest as Nyla screamed. Her cry coalesced with the sound of burning flesh as wisps of smoke lifted from her skin. She let go and grit her teeth against the pain. "Let me out, Ryker!" She fell to her knees and began to sob. "No one is safe. No one."

"What the hell happened to her?"

"Prolonged exposure to pure-grade silver messes with our brain," Ryker explained. "The scent alone is enough to trigger a psychological breakdown."

Wren was staring at her; his yellow irises swirling as canine teeth poked the soft flesh of his lower lip. I felt his breaths coming quicker against my spine.

"What are you going to do with her?" Wren asked.

"Your questions will be answered soon enough." He ushered us away from Nyla's prison cell. The hall forked at the end and Ryker pushed through a set of double-sided doors to our right. The room was dimly lit; the walls were wooden paneled and a long table stretched through its center, holding a total of twelve chairs. I spotted Maddox and Sal– and also, to my surprise–Hailey. I didn't recognize the fourth, an older man with a thick head of silver hair and drooping dark eyes.

"Sit," Ryker instructed, pointing to the seats in front of the others. He glided to the head of the table and eased his muscled body into the chair with grace. I swallowed over the lump that had risen in my throat, forcing myself into the chair opposite the older man. Sal and Hailey took the chairs in the middle, leaving Maddox to Ryker's right-hand side.

The council greeted us in a formal manner. "The Thornwood council wishes to recognize the Trinity and welcome them to our table," the old man spoke. His voice was calm, but it rang with authority–rough with years of experience and hardship. "My name is Thomas Donovan, Elder and former Alpha Master of the Thornwood Pack. I believe you've already been acquainted with the others." His gaze swept around the table before settling on me. "The original purpose of this meeting was to speak with Wren about his fealty to the pack, but it seems we've other important matters to discuss." His dark eyes lingered on the amulet. "It's been brought to our attention that Rionach the Dark's amulet has fallen into the Trinity's possession. We understand that the Dark Witch held imminent rule over the binding of werewolves in their animal skins with the stone alone. According to legend, it's also my understanding that such a talisman cannot be destroyed. While it remains in existence, the Thornwood pack cannot allow it to rest in the hands of a witch."

A warm fire spread through my veins and filled my core, mixing with equal parts of ice–two natures–one belonging to me, the other manipulating my mind. I had to fight against one to gain control over the other, but I desperately wanted to wield that ice as my own. "You want the amulet." My voice was filled with a calm strength I didn't recognize as my own.

Although I hadn't phrased the statement as a question, Thomas nodded. "If that stone is able to control my kind, you must understand we cannot let it fall in the hands of the Dark Witch–or *any* witch that knows how to use it."

"And you believe that you have the power to keep the amulet safe should the Dark Witch return?" Blaire's dark ringlets spilled below her shoulders, bouncing as she spoke. "The Trinity was made to stop the Darkness–*we're* the rightful Keepers of the Light."

I held up my hand. "It's okay Blaire." I felt warmth pooling inside me now and knew what to say as though someone else were guiding my words. "If you understand the amulet's origin, you also know the

Dark Witch cannot return to full power or physical form without it...What if I told you the amulet *could* be destroyed?" I offered as bait.

I watched as Ryker clenched and unclenched his jaw, flexing his hand into the shape of a fist. "We would need proof," he answered.

"We intend to have the amulet destroyed. It's like Blaire said–the very reason behind the Trinity's existence is to stop the Dark Witch from ever returning to power. We're the balance between Light and Dark," I said. "The Trinity doesn't want to control werewolves, we believe in free will as the Mother goddess originally bestowed, and as the White Witch granted to the enslaved wolves of the Ossory line."

"She's telling the truth," the young witch spoke up. She'd been so quiet I'd forgotten she was there. She stepped forward from the shadows, standing just behind Ryker's right shoulder. "The White One wants to destroy the amulet, but the amulet wishes to control her."

My head snapped in the young witch's direction. "How do you know this?" Blaire asked, craning her neck toward the young witch.

"I have an Earth affinity," the young witch said. "Things that have been made of the Earth speak to me."

"Who are you?" Blaire narrowed her eyes.

"I am called Rhea," she replied.

I knew that name... I'd heard Ryker speak it to Maddox when the enchantress sent me on the vision quest. Blaire opened her mouth like she wanted to say something, thought better of it, and clamped her jaw shut. Rhea smiled. It wasn't a cruel smile, but there was something very *knowing* about it. Like perhaps she was in on a secret the rest of us weren't privy to. I'd have to keep my eye on her, I thought.

"So what's it going to take to destroy the amulet?" Ryker ventured, "Returning it to the fires of Mount Doom?"

A bubble of laughter escaped my throat. Wren raised his trademark eyebrow at me. "What?" I said, "A Mordor reference is kind of fitting."

"More to the point," Blaire said, turning her attention back to the council members, "The Trinity's business with the amulet is a private matter. The Aurora Coven is already involved, so you're just going to have to trust that we'll get the job done."

Ryker snorted. "I'm not letting that thing–" he pointed to the amulet around my neck "–out of my sight."

The amulet was growing warm and heavy as if it were swelling with ancient power. "I'm sorry, but you don't have a choice."

"I'm not leaving the fate of my kind in the hands of a witch no matter what your intentions are. I don't care if you are the White Witch incarnate or God himself." Ryker pounded his fist against the table, but it was Wren's low warning growl that caused the hair on the back of my neck to prickle. He'd turned to Ryker, the cold heat of an unspoken threat filling his moon-colored eyes.

My gaze cut to Thomas as his fingers curled against the table's surface. He looked at me with eyes that had seen too much, and they were weary with the burden of great knowledge, and desperately eager for something I couldn't name.

It was Rhea who broke the silence, laying a hand on Ryker's shoulder as she addressed the council. "Perhaps," she began, "Ryker should accompany the Trinity on their journey to see the amulet destroyed."

A protest was taking shape on my lips, but I looked to the others before speaking. The eagerness in Thomas's eyes sparked anew as the council members took Rhea's suggestion into quiet consideration. I saw their mental gears turning. Maddox, however, was looking at me– watching me with a mixture of fear and apprehension.

"The Trinity does not trust Thornwood," Rhea continued, "I believe this would be a wise move, Ryker. In times of darkness, the forces of Light should work together. Prove to the White One that she did not grant the wolves freedom for nothing. As it stands, she also has the power to take that freedom away." When Rhea spoke that way, she looked and sounded years older than her appearance let on. It was apparent that her role in the council was important–whatever it may be.

"Rhea makes a considerable point," Thomas said. "It's clear that both parties have no love for one another. Perhaps this is an opportunity to bridge a gap between the Supernatural races and begin building trust."

Blaire snickered. "We're not the ones who need to earn it."

Power continued to swell inside me and I felt brave–more than I had in a long time. I wasn't sure if it was my own power growing, or power the Mother goddess was breathing into me from somewhere in the firmament above. It felt strong–pure. "The Trinity will agree to Ryker accompanying us on one condition."

"Name your price," Rhea said.

"The Thornwood pack must agree to grant Wren permanent amnesty. I know he's here today in part to answer to Ryker's request to join the pack, but, Wren belongs to the Trinity–*not* Thornwood." The room fell silent. Hailey glared up at me, a sneer curling her lip. "You speak of bridging a gap and building trust… let this be the first step," I added bravely.

It was Thomas who spoke first. "It's against our law for a lone wolf to venture in a claimed territory without having allegiance to an Alpha Master as I'm sure you're aware… However, perhaps it would be conceivable for the pack to make an exception and recognize the Trinity as a separate entity. You would of course, make yourselves known to our community and declare that Ryker is Thornwood's rightful Alpha."

I glanced over at Wren and Blaire–they nodded in agreement. "Deal," I said.

"I'll consider your oath binding," Rhea said.

"Then it's done," Thomas said. "Ryker shall accompany and assist the Trinity on their mission to destroy the amulet. From this moment forward, Thornwood and the Trinity are allied by the forces of Light."

I wanted to address my views of Thornwood encroaching on Silver Mountain territory but I knew in my gut that was a discussion best saved for another time. A weight had lifted from my shoulders–Wren was a free agent, belonging only to himself–and to me, always to me. For now, this one victory would have to be enough.

"Maddox, you'll fulfill the role of Alpha Master in my absence, serving alongside the council's authority," Ryker told him.

Maddox nodded. "When do you leave?"

"Tomorrow, just before sunset," I said. Since my grimoire was spelled by star magic, I had a feeling the majority of our travels would take place under the cloak of nightfall. Blaire and I thought it best to leave early since we still didn't know the exact location of where we were going. We wanted plenty of time to get there and meet the enchantress before the solar eclipse. "You'll want to pack for the weekend, and bring outdoor provisions," I told him.

"Now, for our last matter of business," Thomas spoke. "We'd like to address the heinous crimes committed by Nyla Coburn. Miss Coburn has been abjured from the Thornwood pack and has confessed to the murder of Niall Whelan after claiming former allegiance to the Dark Witch. Pack law states that a crime committed against a recognized member, or one in alliance with the pack, has the right to sentence the accused or take vengeance into his own hands."

I sat motionless and rigid in my chair, stealing a glance at Wren from the corner of my eye. He leaned forward, propping his elbows on the burnished surface of the table. "You're leaving Nyla's punishment to me?"

"You have the right to take revenge for the crimes she committed against your father," Thomas said. "That is and has always been pack law." When Wren didn't give an immediate answer, Thomas spoke, enunciating every word slowly, "The traditional punishment for a crime such as this is death."

"Death would be a kindness. She should suffer for what she's done," Wren said. I watched the tendons and muscles in his arms begin to bulge. Patches of course black hair sprouted across his forearms. I reached over, squeezing the back of his hand with my palm. When he looked at me I felt his pain. The force behind it was so overwhelming I had to force myself to keep gazing into his midsummer night eyes– willing him to hold on just a bit longer.

Even in his darkness, Wren was stronger than me. Nyla deserved to die for what she'd done, but Wren was choosing to not become the monster.

"Life behind bars–this is your sentence?" Thomas spoke.

Wren gave one firm nod of his head.

"So mote it be," Rhea said.

I couldn't be sure, but in the dim light of the room, I thought I saw her sapphire eyes sparkling.

Chapter Seventeen
Astrologically Challenged

The wind rustled through the branches, sending a spray of dark gold
and red leaves swirling across the backdrop of the midnight-blue sky.
They flitted downward, catching a thermal wave of our campfire and
rose in a sort of dance with the embers before settling to the ground. I
leaned forward, brushing a few stragglers off the grimoire's cover.
Somewhere above the thick layer of clouds, the silver stars were
shining; I just hoped it wouldn't be long before the clouds parted and
the symbols on the cover would rearrange and grant us access to the
star spelled pages.

Beside me, Annabelle plucked a blade of grass and twirled it
between her thumb and forefinger. Her cheeks puffed as she sighed and
let the blade float down to join the others in the small pile she'd created.
She looked at her watch and rolled her neck from side to side.

"Would you please stop fidgeting?" I reached over and laid a hand
on her ankle, apprehending her joints from shaking.

"I'm sorry," she said. "I have an hour before I'm supposed to be home.
My parents still think I'm studying with Shawn at the library. No offense
Q, but I'm starting to second guess your book's willingness to comply
with the night sky."

"Trust me, if I could manipulate the weather I would." I shot the
clouds above us a scowl for good measure.

Across the fire, Bryna snickered and crossed her arms. I felt my jaw slide out of place as I fixed her with a glower instead of a snarky reply. After returning from Thornwood, the three of us had filled Bryna in on what happened during the council meeting. She'd waited until we were finished recapping the events before placing her hands on her hips, rearing up for what I guessed was a verbal lashing. I'd been right.

"Have you gone mad? Inviting another werewolf to join you on a quest to destroy an amulet that can't be destroyed?" She narrowed her glacial eyes in my direction. "What were you thinking?"

"You weren't there Bryna, Quinn didn't have another option," Blaire told her.

"She's risked everything," Bryna spat, pointing an accusing finger in my face. "Involving another race of Supernatural in a task that was given to the Trinity alone is unthinkable and unheard of. You can't trust them."

"Werewolves and vampires work for the Coven," I pointed out, thanks to Blaire informing me of their elite Supernatural spy team. "It's not unheard of."

"That's not the same thing!" Her alabaster cheeks heated to reveal strawberry-red splotches. Any brighter and fire alarms might start ringing. "The enchantress might not help us now."

"Why? Because I tried to form an alliance with a werewolf pack to stop the Dark Witch from returning to power?" I shot her a disbelieving look. "News flash Bryna—we all want the same thing."

"Well we'll just see about that, won't we?" She snatched my grimoire off the counter and marched right out the back door and across the lawn to the small fire pit in Wren's backyard. My vision turned red around the edges as I chased after her, ripping the grimoire out of her grabby little hands.

"Don't you *ever* touch this without my permission," I snarled. My face was inches from hers, and I was seconds away from snapping her pretty little neck. I might have, had I not been clutching the grimoire to my chest. Blood rushed to the surface of my skin, warming my face and rang in my eardrums. The amulet warmed at my throat, swelling and thrumming with power.

Wren, who'd been in the shower, appeared behind me and the weight of his palms registered against my arms. I felt the beat of his heart thudding against my spine and I forced myself to focus on the realness of that, letting it conquer the boiling rage that had taken over. I turned away from Bryna. Blaire was a half-step behind Wren, her forehead wrinkled in worry.

"I'm fine," I told them.

"We'll wait to see if your theory holds true," Bryna said. She called on Fire and sent a ball of flame leaping into the fire pit. There were only a couple of logs and dead leaves, but they caught in an instant. In that moment, I forgot all about my irritation and gazed into the flames.

"How did you do that without getting mental whiplash?"

"What?" She frowned.

"Personal gain," I said, pointing at the fire pit.

"I'm not abusing the element," she said, drawing her eyebrows together even deeper. "Fire is of nature, and it's being used to keep us warm. Honestly." She shook her head and brushed by. "I'm going inside to fetch a blanket while we wait."

I rolled my eyes, letting my gaze settle on Blaire. Her hands were tucked in her back pockets; I watched her draw a breath and sigh. She didn't have to tell me what she was thinking. I saw the sadness and worry clouding her dark eyes, but it was Bryna's end remark (*honestly*) that made me feel about two inches tall. It was the tone in which she'd said it–like how could I possibly be the chosen descendant of Luiseach, the exalted White Witch, if I didn't even know how to properly invoke the elements? It didn't take a genius to deduce the plain fact that she had little to no faith in my ability to get the job done.

Now, I gave the sky a hopeful look, praying that my instincts had been right with the decisions I'd made during the council meeting. Taking Ryker along would be an inconvenience, but we needed Thornwood on our side. The pack was a necessary tool in defeating the

Darkness, and I was going to do whatever it took to make sure that Wren remained free from their law.

A dark shadow cut through the tree line. The sliver arc of the moon above shone just bright enough through the clouds to halo Wren in her glow. I wondered if the Great Moon gave a piece of her lunar light to all the night creatures, covering them with an essence of immortality. Wren made his way to the fire, strategically placing a couple of the logs in the pit before dumping the extra pieces in a heap beside it. He unknowingly stepped on Anna's grass house, crushing it beneath his boot before lowering himself to the blanket beside me and reclined on his forearms. Annabelle shot him a look before brushing the grass clippings into the base of the fire and crossed her arms.

With his face lifted to the night sky, Wren pointed at a bright object shimmering between the thinning clouds. "That's Venus, right?"

"That's a planet?" Annabelle furrowed her brows. "I didn't know you could see planets from Earth."

"Well, you can't see all of them, but Venus is the closest planet to Earth," I said. "Thanks to its thick clouds reflecting most of the sun's light back into space, it's also the brightest planet in our solar system."

"I should've paid more attention in science," Annabelle said.

"You can learn a lot about magic from the night sky," Blaire added. "A witch's power is born of nature, but the planets have a great deal to do with the elements we have an affinity for. You, for example," Blaire turned to face me, "have an affinity for Fire, which means you were either born an Aries, Leo, or Sagittarius."

I nodded. "I'm a November baby."

"So you're a Sagittarius," she said, "which doesn't surprise me. Your ruling planet is Jupiter."

"Why doesn't that surprise you?" I narrowed my eyes.

"In short, a person born in Sagittarius values freedom; they're often very honest individuals and impatient–almost to a fault. They're passionate and curious, and they will do anything to achieve the goals they've set."

"That doesn't sound anything like you," Wren teased. I craned my neck back to shoot him a look which he only met with a smile.

"What about you, Wolf Boy?" Annabelle asked. "What's your sign?"

"I'll wager he's a Scorpio," Blaire guessed.

"How could you tell?" He lifted his trademark eyebrow.

"Scorpio's are natural born leaders, brave, resourceful, determined. They're passionate and also extremely stubborn," Blaire said. "They are also said to be the most mysterious of all the astrological signs, and loyal to a select few."

Annabelle burst out in laughter.

"The moon is also a participating ruler," Blaire added.

"Definitely doesn't sound anything like *you*," I teased him back.

"I know I'm not magical," Annabelle air-quoted the word, "but I've always felt like I clicked with my sign. I'm a Pisces."

"I had a feeling you were," Blaire said. "That's why I had you stand in for Water when we cast the spell in the forest. Pisces are selfless, and always willing to help others. They're wise and artistic."

"Yep, that's me." She beamed. "What about you, Blaire?"

"She's a Taurus," Bryna said, piping up for the first time since our little altercation. "Closely allied with the Earth, Taurus born are the most balanced of all the signs. They're patient, sensible, dependable, and trustworthy." Bryna picked a clump of grass from the ground and tossed it into the fire. "Probably why the Trinity chose her, after all."

No one spoke. We just listened to the sound of the fire snapping and popping the wood in the pit. I slipped my gaze in Blaire's direction. Her raptor-like eyes were fixed on her sister. After what felt like a lifetime, Blaire finally spoke, "Capricorn's are also allied with the Earth, and those born unto the sign are known to be well disciplined and independent. While a Capricorn has the ability to be a great leader, often times their weaknesses get in the way. They're always expecting the worst and have a knack for being patronizing and unforgiving. That, Bryna, is why the Trinity didn't choose you." Blaire bolted upright and stomped off toward the cabin in a huff.

"Whoa," Annabelle mumbled.

I looked over at Bryna. Her arms were crossed over her chest, eyes downcast toward the embers burning at the bottom of the fire pit. Her lion's mane of curls trailed down her back, half tucked behind her ears to reveal the sharp set of her jaw. She had conviction–I'd give her that. I wondered though, if that hard outer shell of hers was more for show.

"I should go check on her." I motioned toward the cabin with my thumb. "Keep an eye on my book?" I looked over at Annabelle and then back to Wren. They nodded.

I followed the arc of the indigo sky and hugged my arms on my trek back to the cabin to chase away the night's chill. Blaire held it together better than most, but even the strong-willed had a breaking point. I let myself in through the back door and found her struggling with a corkscrew opener and a bottle of wine.

"Hey," I said, letting my presence be known.

"If you've come to make me apologize you can forget it. I'm up to ninety with her bloody shenanigans."

"Translation?" I grinned.

"Sorry," she said, giving up on the bottle and placing it–along with the opener–down on the counter. "Bryna's always meant well enough, but she can be an awful pain in the arse when she feels like it. I should have said something earlier when she pulled that stunt with your grimoire. I'm sorry."

"Blaire," I reached out, placing my hand on her shoulder, "you don't need to apologize for anything. I came to see if *you* were okay."

Blaire nodded. "She's older than me, our Bryna. Not by a year, but, I've no doubt she thinks that entitles her a bit."

"I think it's pretty safe to say that she's not my most favorite person in the world, but, there is a part of me–however small that part may be– that can sympathize with where she must be coming from." I paused, dragging my fingernail across the cool surface of the countertop. "I know you two were very close growing up in Ireland. She's always had you in her corner and things are changing now. You're part of something so much bigger. Maybe she's acting this way because she's scared of losing you."

Blaire braced her hip against the counter. "I hadn't thought of that."

"Annabelle was scared, too. I recognize the signs."

"Still… It doesn't excuse the way she's been treating you."

"I can handle myself," I said, and felt Rionach's amulet warming in objection. I ignored the pull, clearing my throat. "And, for what it's worth, I'm glad the Trinity chose you, Blaire. I couldn't do this without you."

"Me too." She grinned. "Despite what Bryna said earlier, I hope you know that Wren and I back the calls you made during the council meeting. You did the right thing, forging a new alliance. It was the decision a leader would have made."

"Thank you," I told her earnestly. "I sort of needed to hear that."

"Yeah and you sort of need to trust your instincts a little more, too." She winked. "Well, we should get back. The clouds are thinning out. The grimoire should open any time now." She nudged my shoulder and we headed back to the campfire.

"Anything?" I asked once we'd returned.

"Not a thi–*oh* look!" Annabelle pointed to the grimoire and the symbols began to glow.

I watched as the crescent moons spun to face inward, almost as if they were cupping the trinity knot in a gentle embrace. I knelt on the blanket, spinning the cover to face me while the others huddled around. I tried not to gloat as I opened the grimoire and saw the same poem and the bow and arrow symbols lighting up in metallic silver on the second page.

Over my shoulder, Blaire read aloud, "By lunar light she follows, the stars shall guide her way. Beneath the moonlit meadow, behold: a night within a day." When she finished the incantation, the little golden arrow appeared at the bottom right-hand corner. I flipped the page, allowing them to see the map of the coastline. Bryna got up from her spot opposite the fire, and when she looked at the book her eyes expanded. I was above saying it out loud, but that didn't mean I wasn't thinking it in my head. *I told you so.*

"That's it?" She reached for the book–presumably to turn the page, when a spark of blue and gold erupted from the page and she yanked her hand back like it had zapped her. "Ouch!" She gave her hand a little shake.

"I told you not to touch it," I said. She scowled.

"Wait a minute," Annabelle said, craning her neck. "I think I recognize this." She pointed to a piece of land that jutted out in the shape of a crooked C, half on land, half in the water. "This is near the abandoned Firefly Light Station on the peninsula."

"Oh, you're right," I said, picturing the small white building at the end of a long pier with its red tin roof and black storm shutters. Annabelle and I had spent our spring break vacation with her family there three summers ago. It was a marsh lighthouse, placed in a small harbor on the sound side of the ocean. The C curve stretched up the inlet, curving before meeting the deep ocean on the other side. Miles and miles of maritime forest lay in between. "Annabelle, you're brilliant!"

"I'm aware," she said, grinning.

"It's still not an exact location," Bryna pointed out. "The enchantress could be anywhere on the coastline."

"But it's still our best lead," Wren said.

"Well, as exciting as this is, I better get home," Annabelle said, brushing invisible debris from her pant legs as she stood. "Some of us still have a curfew."

"I'll walk you out." I linked my arm with her elbow and the glow of the campfire faded behind us; the night air cooling my cheeks.

"So, you're leaving tomorrow?"

"Yep, just before sunset."

"How are you feeling?" Annabelle turned on her heel to face me once we'd reached the driver's side of her parents' car.

"A little nervous, but strong," I said.

"No, that's not what I meant. I know you're ready to take on the Darkness, I just meant—how are you doing with the amulet?"

"Oh, that." I glanced over my shoulder, watching as the others were making the trek back to the house. I saw the way the moonlight was playing against Wren's skin and knew that he would be listening in even if he wasn't trying. The truth was I could feel two halves of myself– almost an even split right down the middle now. I was still in control, but I could sense the balance of Light and Dark–fire and ice spreading through my veins.

"It's getting harder isn't it?" Annabelle asked when I didn't respond.

"I can handle it."

"That's not what I asked. I can see it draining you. I know you have to be tired." She reached out, squeezing my arm. "I just don't want you to get too brave. You're not in this alone; it's okay to ask for help."

The amulet was listening and it began to grow heavy. It seemed to be resonating in time with the beat of my heart. *You could make them all obey*, the Darkness seemed to whisper. I closed my eyes, clutching the moonstone at my throat. The surface was like cool liquid beneath my thumb; a sea of endless energy swelling within it.

"Quinn?" I looked up, meeting her dark eyes. "Are you hearing me?"

"I'm hearing you." I forced my lips into the shape of a smile. "I'm fine Annabelle. I appreciate your concern, but you don't need to worry about me. I just need you to stay safe."

"I'll be safe," she said.

"You're still carrying the talisman I gave you for protection, right?"

"Yes." She rolled her eyes.

"I gave one to my dad, but, it would mean a lot to me if you could just keep an eye on him while we're away."

"You know I will. Just like I know you asked him to keep an eye on me, too."

I grinned and pulled her in for a hug. I smelled the lingering scent of her shampoo and it reminded me how familiar everything about her was to me. I still remembered the first day we met in our Kindergarten classroom, when Mrs. Gunther sat us in alphabetical order. She'd been wearing a Hello Kitty headband and a matching pink dress. Our friendship was easy and instant. The thing about Annabelle was that she'd never pretended to be anything different than who she was. Maybe that's what drew me to her. The world I lived in could be altered; changed, manipulated by magical events. Nothing in my life was constant, so I clung to the one person who was.

So when the Darkness tried to strip the Light away from me; I would remember why I was fighting in the first place. For people like Annabelle–and my dad, whose light was too bright to extinguish. I'd keep pushing myself for them.

"Take care of you," I said, releasing her from my grip.

"I will," she said, slipping behind the wheel. I backed away from her car, giving her enough room to maneuver into reverse, and then she was pulling out of the drive. I stayed there a while longer, becoming a shadow in the night. A small sound rattled in the branches above me, and I looked up to see the barn owl stretching her wings. She looked down on me with her star-filled gaze, and some of the weight pooling in my chest began to lift. I was comforted to find that she was following me.

Strong arms circled my waist then. I jumped, but only just a little as laughter vibrated in Wren's chest at my spine.

"You know," I said, "this whole predator thing is hardly fair."

"Still so jumpy," he murmured, bending to press a kiss to the back of my neck. "Blaire and Bryna are having a heart-to-heart. Since I can hear everything they're saying to one another, I thought I'd better give them a little space."

"Is it not going well?" I turned to face him, looping my arms around his neck.

"I'd say their relationship is on the mend. Not that it's any of our business." He grinned. "That was some display between you and Bryna earlier."

"She shouldn't have taken my book."

"No, she shouldn't have," he agreed, "but if I hadn't shown up, what would you have done?"

I let my arms drop to my sides and blinked up at him. "What do you mean?"

"I'm not a stranger to rage, Quinn. I know what it looks like. You were seconds away from snapping."

"Then why are you asking?" I crossed my arms.

"Because," he said, "I'm worried about you being in control." He tapped my chest, his index finger resting on the moonstone that was tucked beneath my shirt.

Saliva clung to the sides of my throat, making it hard to swallow. "You won't let me lose control." I looked up into his eyes as I said this, knowing that he'd understand what I didn't have to explain. I saw the pain behind his eyes as his face shone in the moonlight. All of those bone-sharp edges of his features softening as he reached out, gently cradling my face in his palms.

"I promise," he said solemnly.

Chapter Eighteen
Primordial Ghosts

The next day, I met Annabelle in the locker room after classes had ended and changed into my cross-country gear. Hailey slipped in while I was tying my shoe. I caught her eye for a brief second before she turned for her locker. I waited for a snarky comment, even prepped for it by squaring my shoulders. She dialed the combination and tugged her lock free before lifting her face to look at me again. "I want to come with you guys on your little hero mission," she said.

My features rearranged themselves into a look that conveyed a range of emotions that started and ended with shock. What the expressions in the middle were–I couldn't say. "That wasn't part of the deal," I managed.

"What I can't figure out is how someone with so little brain power is even a part of a functioning council?" Annabelle said.

"Jesus, Quinn, is there anything you *don't* share with your little sidekick?" Hailey sneered. "Not that it's any of your business, but Maddox pulled some strings and they let me join early–not because of my lack of brain power, but because I proved my worth to the pack."

"Yeah, as the Alpha Slut," Annabelle retorted.

Hailey slammed her locker shut and took a step towards Annabelle, her irises glowing with rage and a touch of the Change. I stepped between them, holding out my arm. "Knock it off guys. Seriously."

"Whatever. Just keep her away from me before I lose more than my temper."

"But then I'd lose more than mine, and neither of us wants that, do we?" I reached down, stroking the pendant at my throat. Hailey followed my hand, jaw clenching as she nodded.

For a minute I just stared at her, wondering what it was about her that made Wren decide to ever give her the time of day–other than the obvious visual aesthetics. Maybe that was enough for a teen boy. There were just so many layers to Wren; it was hard for me to imagine him ever being that shallow.

"Give me one good reason why I should even consider your request," I said.

"Because," she said, "The Thornwood pack is my home. I don't want me or anyone else I care about to have their will just stripped from them."

And there it was, I thought–a vulnerable truth. "Hailey, since the moment I met you, you've made it clear that you intend to make my life a living hell. I don't trust you," I said. The little altercation we'd had in the ladies' room just a few days ago flashed to the front of my mind. It ranked second next to the cruelty she'd shown Annabelle on the track.

"I know," she said. "You don't have to. But you can trust the fact that I have my pack's best interests at heart."

"The council agreed to send Ryker," I told her, "the decision is out of my hands. You'll have to take it up with him."

"That's funny." She snickered. "He told me to take it up with you."

I stared at her for a long moment before saying, "The car only fits five people." It was lame as far as excuses go, but it was the truth.

"Ryker and I will drive separately." She shrugged.

"Quinn, you can't honestly be considering this," Annabelle said, frowning.

"This better not be some pathetic attempt to go after Wren, Hailey, because I swear to the goddess–"

"–It's not, okay?" she interrupted. "I know about the legend. I know you two are freakishly bound to one another. Whatever. I'm going because I care about my pack, and if you're going up against evil forces, then you need all the Supernatural muscle you can get, right?"

I stared into her baby-blue eyes as I chewed on the inside of my lip. "Does Maddox know you want to do this?"

"I don't answer to my brother." She grabbed her bag from the bench and side-stepped around me. "Ryker and I will see you tonight." She exited the locker room then, leaving Annabelle and I staring after her.

"Can she do that?" Annabelle asked.

"As much as I don't want her there, I think it will help Ryker trust us. Like she said, we need all of the Supernatural muscle we can get."

"You've been dealt a shitty hand my friend… now you're stuck with Bryna *and* Hailey." Annabelle made a face.

"I heard that," Hailey called, her voice echoing down the hall as Annabelle and I started for the back doors.

"Damn werewolf super-hearing," Annabelle muttered. "Have you talked to Coach about Saturday yet? He's going to be pissed when he finds out his star runners won't be at the race. I mean, there's only three weeks left until State Championships."

"I know, Anna, but, Championships don't exactly rank high on the list of priority right now." We'd started across the lawn, our feet shuffling through the fallen leaves. It wasn't until I reached the back of the stadium that I even saw the red and blue streaks of light glinting on the pavement. I looked up, spotting the police cruiser parked next to the gate at the side of the track. Coach was standing on one side, and Officer Stevenson was on the other. Coach had his hands anchored on his hips, a clipboard pressed to his side as he and Officer Stevenson exchanged words.

"What's he doing here?" Annabelle asked.

I didn't answer. Instead, I scanned the group of our friends who were huddled together on the track, stretching. Wren was looking in my direction, his expression unreadable. "Come on," I said, tugging on her sleeve.

Jamie was the first to speak when we entered the circle. "I can't believe you two are ditching us this weekend." He shook his head. "Three weeks until Championship, we *need* you."

"I know, Jamie, I'm sorry, but it's the only time we could get an appointment with the coach in Wilmington," I lied. We'd told our friends that the cross-country recruiters out of WU had seen our last race and requested an interview. (This, at least, wasn't a lie, but we actually hadn't set up a time to meet with them.) As far as our friends were concerned, our "appointment" was Saturday.

"I thought you'd already been accepted to SMU?" Huck added.

"I have," I said, "but Wren and I want to go to the same college. We're just exploring our options. I mean, who knows what could happen."

"Yeah, but, we're a team," Jamie said. He was looking at me now—his features crumpling into disappointment. I wished I could tell him that what we were doing was in fact bigger than the team, but Jamie's world was right here—in the right *now*. I could never make him understand something I couldn't begin to explain—that I was fighting to save that world of his.

I pressed my lips together. "I'm sorry, Jamie. You and Huck have this in the bag though. You won't even know we're gone."

Jamie snorted. "Whatever man."

Wren hadn't taken his eyes off Coach and Officer Stevenson. When they finished talking, it was impossible to decipher Coach's expression as his eyes were shaded behind his favorite pair of mirrored sunglasses. He shook the clipboard and scanned our faces before calling on Huck and Annabelle. As he explained our running assignment for the day, I slid my gaze over to Wren. His shoulders were pulled back, hands rolled into fists. The veins in his arms were pronounced, but his tendons and muscles weren't twitching which meant we weren't in danger of the wolf emerging.

"What was that about?" I whispered.

"Wolves," Wren said. I blinked up at him, waiting for him to explain. "They found nine deer carcasses in the Hollow where my dad was murdered. Their stomachs were torn open by teeth and claws, blood and entrails all over the place. Stevenson was telling Coach to keep us out of the woods again. They suspect foul play."

"It wasn't *us* if that's what you're thinking," Hailey said. "Thornwood hasn't stepped paw in the National Park, and we wouldn't do something like that."

The back of my throat tightened. The skin covering my vertebrae tingled, like someone was standing behind me in shadow.

"Quinn?"

"The Hollow is sacred ground," I said. "One of five places in the world that houses a chasm of raw energy–power that is neither good nor bad but can be manipulated to go either way." I heard myself repeating the information Blaire shared with us a few weeks before. "Nine is a specific number. It's not random."

"What are you saying?" Hailey asked.

"It was a blood sacrifice," I said, "an offering."

"For what?" Wren narrowed his eyes.

"I really don't want to be right about this, but, I think it's intended for the nine circles of hell." I swallowed hard. "A gift for the Lord of Darkness."

"But who would do something like that and why?" Hailey asked.

"Someone who favors Darkness." I glanced up at Wren. "We need to find out if the rogue werewolves are responsible. I'd hoped that with Penny being gone and Nyla being locked up that they would just move on, but I guess that was too much to hope for."

"We can head up there after practice and I can try to track their scents. If it's any of the rogues, I'll know."

"I can go with you," Hailey volunteered. "If it is the rogues, Ryker will want to know about it too."

"This will be the closest we've gotten to finding them since that night," I said.

"Text Blaire and have her meet us there," Wren said. "If they're still using any magic, she should be able to detect the source."

"Let's hope you're right."

Wren pulled the Firebird into an abandoned access road that backed up to the National Forest. The last time I'd been here, Blaire and I were dragging Garrett's unconscious body out of the woods so we could take him back to the Magic Shoppe and question him about Penny. That hadn't been one of my finer moments, and my gut lurched at the memory.

"Blaire's just a few minutes behind us," I said as I climbed out of the car and pocketed my cellphone. Hailey had pulled in after us, driving a white Honda. By the time she was climbing out of the car, Blaire was pulling in and Bryna was riding along with her.

I drew a breath and sighed.

"I could tie her to a tree if you want." Wren snickered behind my shoulder.

"Don't tempt me."

"All right, let's get a move on," Blaire said, slinging a pack over her shoulder. "We don't have much time before we have to get on the road."

The five of us started heading in the direction of the Hollow; the two Weres leading the way with their superior sense of smell. White cloud plumes shifted above me, revealing the azure arc of the sky. Somewhere in between, the naked boughs of the surrounding trees stretched up toward the sunlight as if they were trying to keep us away–limbs pointing us in another direction. The deeper we walked into the forest, the heavier the amulet around my neck seemed to grow.

Up ahead, I spotted the broken yellow caution tape the police had used to seal off the area of Niall's murder investigation and my stomach dropped. Wren's jaw clenched, the tendons in his neck protruding as he lifted his face to sample the wind.

I smelled it before I saw it; death and blood, the foul stench that cloaked the earth in front of us. The smell hit me with the force of a tidal wave, raking through my stomach as it juggled the leftover contents of my lunch. I swallowed hard, fighting down the bile. There should have been flies. The forest should have been swarming with them, humming with the buzz of their wings. Instead, an eerie silence greeted us. I took a few more steps, and then their bodies came into view. The deer were almost lined in a perfect circle around the big boulder that jutted forth from the earth. Their bodies were bloated, stomachs savagely torn open with bits of flesh and entrails strewn across the russet pine needles. There was so much blood, pools of thick dark liquid, stretching and soaking into the earth.

"I guess we know why the police are suspecting foul play," Wren said. "This looks like the work of some satanic cult."

"It's not far off, I'm afraid," Blaire said. She was in the center of the Nexus with her arms raised high, her eyes closed as she sifted through the energy in the atmosphere. I was aware that Bryna was somewhere to my left. I couldn't see her, but I heard her retching. My own stomach heaved, but I couldn't tear my eyes away from the deer. I kept staring at their wide eyes–the depthless black pits that seemed to go on forever, and yet, nowhere at all.

"It was a massacre." Hailey was frowning at the carcasses.

I wondered if they'd seen it coming. I tried to imagine the werewolves stalking their prey and taking them down. Their necks were broken–bent back in unnatural angles. They'd died before the wolves had sliced into their bellies and spilled their life's blood into the earth. Their immobile eyes gazed back at me. Cold. Haunted. Tortured.

Wren's hands were on my shoulders. It took me a moment to realize that he had stepped in front of me, obscuring my view of the carcasses. My ears were ringing, a high-pitched sound that seemed so far off, I wondered if it was only in my head. He'd been trying to get my attention. I saw his mouth moving, the shape of my name forming on his full lips as his eyes glowed with the colors of a lightning storm.

"Quinn." He squeezed my shoulders and I blinked up, this time registering.

"I'm fine," I heard myself say.

"Are you?" his tone was doubtful.

The amulet warmed at my throat, pulsing with Dark power. It was feeding off the sacrificial death, swelling and aching for more. My fingers twisted around the pendant, squeezing as my eyes lulled back in my head. The last thing I saw was the sky; crimson and gold leaves blurring above me as my body drifted away. It wasn't until the cooler air hit my face that I realized Wren was carrying me; the scents of the crisp forest clearing the smell of rot and death from my mind.

Wren eased me down in a bed of dried leaves. I leaned forward, letting my head droop between my knees while Wren's hand found the small of my back. I could feel the heel of his hand on one side, the tips of his fingers stretching to the other; my spine against his palm. I shifted my weight against the side of his body and let myself breathe in the familiar smell of his skin–the pine that always seemed to be clinging to his clothes and the strands of his hair.

"I'm sorry," I breathed.

"Don't apologize," he told me. "What happened back there?"

"I could feel the Darkness. The amulet was feeding from it." I pinched the milky jewel between my fingers and dropped it beneath the collar of my shirt. "I'm okay now."

A thin line creased Wren's brow, and the corners of his mouth pulled tight. His yellow eyes were boring holes of disbelief into my face.

"What did you pick up on back there?"

"There were a lot of smells to sift through, including the officers and a team of forensics, but I picked up on the scent signatures that match with the wolves we fought against the night we became the Trinity," he told me. "Garrett surprisingly wasn't one of them."

"No, but the rest are our rogues," Hailey said, appearing beside me. "I sent a text to Ryker to let him know they're still in the area."

"Can you track them?"

"That depends–"

"The protection spell they've been under has worn off," Blaire said. She and Bryna were sloshing through the blanket of dried leaves just a few yards away.

"How is that possible?" I frowned.

"Unless magic is being reinforced, all spells will eventually come to an end," Bryna said. "I'm going to assume it's because the link between Penny and Nyla has been severed. Whatever magic they were using must not hold while the two are so far away."

"Someone must still be helping them," I stated. "Not necessarily a witch, but someone who knows enough to tip the scales of Light and Dark."

"Ryker is putting Maddox in charge of a team to track the Weres. They'll start searching tonight before the scent trail runs cold." Hailey waved her phone before pocketing it.

"Good."

Blaire plopped down beside me, propping her forearms against her knees as she gazed off in the distance before turning to face me. "What did you feel back there?"

"Dark power," I said, "very old and very strong. It was almost..."

"Otherworldly?" she guessed.

"Yes."

"They used an offering incantation."

"What's that?" Hailey asked.

"Nine deaths to offer thee, nine deaths be true. Nine times I've walked the shadows, nine souls I give to you," she said. "There's only one purpose an incantation like that can serve, and it's to awaken the Lord of the Underworld."

"A sacrifice like that would have to be performed at each of the world's five Nexus points in order to awaken him," Bryna added. "I'll alert the Aurora Coven and make sure they send word to the guardians. We don't want a repeat of this happening elsewhere."

"What would happen if they succeed in awakening him?" I heard myself say.

"Well," Blaire said, mashing her lips together. "It depends on their motive, but it most certainly wouldn't be good."

"Evil forces teaming up–when has that ever been a good thing?" I snickered.

"Maddox is our best tracker," Hailey said. "He'll find them."

"Just make sure he doesn't do anything rash–like killing them before we've had a chance to question them."

"I can't promise they won't be damaged, but they'll be able to talk."

Wren's chin snapped up, nostrils flaring. "We've got company. I would have smelled them sooner, but the wind isn't blowing in our favor. It's Officer Stevenson and someone else–her scent was here earlier. They're about four hundred meters to the north of us."

"Shit," I breathed. "Can we get away?"

"Not all of us." He rose to his feet and offered me a hand up. "Hailey, can you guide Blaire and Bryna out of here? Quinn and I will distract them."

"Sure thing." She sampled the air and tilted her head to the left. "This way." Reluctantly, Blaire and Bryna followed her away from the crime scene.

Wren twined his fingers through mine, pressing our palms together as we started down the hill. I didn't like the idea of purposely crossing paths, but it was the only way to make sure the others got away. A spark of silver flashed through the trees–sunlight, gleaming off Officer Stevenson's badge. There was a woman with him, dressed in a pair of black slacks with a button-down shirt tucked into the waistband. She wore a matching blazer and let her pale locks trail over her shoulders.

"Forensics," Wren said under his breath.

Officer Stevenson had spotted us, his right hand moving to the gun holstered on his hip. "Hey," Stevenson called out. "What are you two doing out here?"

"Walking," Wren retorted as we stopped just a few feet short of them. I almost laughed. Stevenson squared his shoulders, jaw tightening. His eyes were hidden behind a pair of mirrored sunglasses, but I imagined the cold look in them was present just the same.

Stevenson snickered. "Your tone isn't cute, son. I'd watch it if I were you."

The corner of Wren's mouth twitched. "Forgive me, Officer. I meant no offense. I'd very much appreciate if you would take your hand off your gun though. We're not a threat."

Stevenson cocked his jaw, anchoring his hands on his hips. "Are you two alone out here?" Stevenson made a show of checking the woods around him like he expected someone to pop out from behind a tree.

"We are."

"Huh." Stevenson clucked his tongue. "Couldn't help but notice your Firebird was parked in an abandoned access road on State property. There were two others there as well."

"We noticed that," Wren said, glancing down at me. "We didn't see a no-trespassing sign at the entrance so we assumed it was all right to park there."

"Yeah, Officer, we do it all the time with cross-country," I added in a practiced honeyed tone. "One of our regular trails is out this way. We're not in trouble are we?"

At first, Stevenson didn't know how to reply. "I'd prefer you park in an actual lot from now on. Those access roads were abandoned for a reason."

"Right. We're really sorry. It won't happen again." I forced my lips into the shape of a smile. "So, um, is everything okay? I mean, we never see the department outside of, *well*, the department." I glanced between Stevenson and the blonde woman. She'd been quiet, muddy-brown eyes fixated on Wren.

"Have you found anything new regarding my father's murder case?" Wren asked.

"You're the Whelan boy?" the woman spoke with a note of surprise in her tone. "I'm Alison Johnson, head of the forensics department. I'm working on your father's case."

Wren reached forward to shake the woman's hand. "It's nice to meet you, I'm Wren and this is my girlfriend, Quinn Callaghan."

"Pleasure to meet you both," Alison said, greeting me next. She smoothed a manicured hand over the back of her head before straightening the hem of her blazer. "Unfortunately, we don't have any new leads at this time, but Officer Stevenson agreed to accompany me back to the crime scene to comb it over–just in case we overlooked something."

"It's been weeks," Wren said. "Taking the weather elements into consideration, I can't imagine what you'd be hoping to find."

He was baiting her, I was sure, but for whatever reason the officers were content to keep their true intentions a secret. As far as they knew, we hadn't been to the crime scene to see the deer carcasses spread out in a circle, making it look like a cult sacrifice. Perhaps this woman was trying to find evidence to link the two incidents, considering Niall had been murdered in the exact spot of the sacrifice.

"You make a good point Mr. Whelan," Alison told him. "But what I'm looking for won't be affected by the weather. I'll be in touch if we find something," she said dismissively.

"We still haven't cleared the area to the general public so make sure you and your friends stay out until the investigation is over," Stevenson warned.

"What makes you think I have any desire to visit the spot where my father was murdered?" Wren replied. "I just want the person responsible brought to justice."

"Have faith, Mr. Whelan. Our team is doing everything we can," Alison said. She nodded once and she and Stevenson began walking towards the crime scene.

Wren and I stood there a moment before continuing on our own path. "They're not planning to release the second incident to the media," I said.

"No. There's no need to induce further panic at this point, not until they find anything useful. They'll have that site wiped clean before the end of the day." Wren pursed his mouth. "That could pose a problem for Maddox and his trackers. Certain chemicals make it really hard for werewolves to find scent trails."

"So what do we do?"

"Pray to the gods that the humans don't mess this up for us." Wren sighed. "Come on; let's get back to the others so we can get a message to Maddox before it's too late." Wren squeezed my hand reassuringly as we picked up the pace.

Chapter Nineteen
"The Ties That Bind"

I tossed my backpack in Wren's trunk and closed the heavy lid. Blaire walked out onto the porch, dressed in a pair of black jeans, hiking boots, and a green and black flannel with the cuffs rolled up her forearms. Her long black hair cascaded over her shoulders, tangling with the silver and emerald trinity pendant she kept around her neck. "Any sign of our traveling companions?" she asked, tucking her hands in her back pockets as she stood beside me.

"Not yet." I gave a halfhearted glance down the gravel lane, half hoping they'd changed their minds and decided not to show up. After Wren and I had reached the access road, we'd caught the others up to speed with what happened in the forest. Hailey skipped out right away to get back to Thornwood, and I wondered if maybe she and Ryker had elected to stay behind to help Maddox and the tracking team.

"Well, all our loose ends are knotted up here," Blaire said, glancing at the cabin. "Bryna is finishing placing the wards, and Wren is–"

"–Right here," he said, appearing from around the side of the house with a backpack slung over his shoulder. Blaire jumped, clutching a hand to her heart.

"Now you know how I feel," I told her.

"Warn a person before you've scared them half to death," Blaire said. "You're an awful right pox you know that?"

"No, but, I'm gathering it's an insult." He grinned.

Blaire rolled her eyes. "Make yourself useful and open the boot, I've bags to dump in." She gestured towards the trunk.

Wren lifted the trunk and offered to take Blaire's gear before dropping his own bag in. The sound of gravel crunching caught our attention, and we all looked down the lane as Ryker and Hailey pulled up in a large white GMC Denali. Ryker pulled the truck up beside Wren's Firebird, put it in park but left it running while he slid down from the driver's seat. He parked his sunglasses on top of his head, walking over to shake Wren's hand. Hailey stayed in the passenger's seat.

"You're taking the Trans Am?" Ryker asked, eyeing Wren's car.

"She made it all the way from Washington, I think she can handle a couple hour's drive to the coast," Wren said.

"I've got plenty of room in the truck if you guys would rather ride with me."

"No thanks," Blaire said. "The Firebird is more than adequate."

I raised my eyebrows. Blaire must have really had it out for werewolves, considering the comments she'd made yesterday about Wren's car being too conspicuous. Not that I was protesting. I didn't want to ride with Ryker and Hailey, either.

Bryna came out of the cabin then and gave the big werewolf a thorough once over with her glacial eyes. He introduced himself and reached for her hand. She hesitated before taking it. "Tough crowd," Ryker commented.

"We're not here to entertain you," Bryna said. "This isn't a game. We've work to do and I don't want you standing in the way of it."

I watched the corner of Ryker's mouth slide into a mischievous grin. He glanced at me. "Well then, White One, where are we going?"

"Uh, here," I said, stepping forward. I fished a folded map out of the back pocket of my jeans and handed him the coordinates to the Firefly Light Station. "This is where we start."

"What do you mean *start*?"

Hailey opened up the passenger's side door of the truck and slid out, her boots crunching on the gravel as she landed.

This was the part I had been dreading trying to explain. "We don't have an exact location," I began. "My grimoire is spelled by star magic, and the enchantress who spelled it has only been revealing a few pieces of information at a time and only under starlight."

Ryker's dark eyes seemed to harden as Hailey crossed her arms over her chest. "Who is this enchantress you speak of?"

"Someone who is trying to help us destroy the amulet, and that's all you really need to know."

Hailey's eyes narrowed. "You don't actually know, do you?"

"She'd better," Ryker said. "I'm not going on some wild goose chase—not when I have rogue werewolves to track down and question about the little stunt they pulled in the forest with those deer."

"By all means, you're welcome to stay behind," Bryna told them.

"Look," Wren said, squaring his shoulders, "I want to track those Weres down just as much as you, but right now our goal is destroying the amulet. Far as I'm concerned, that's our first priority."

Ryker bristled. Hailey reached out and placed her hand on his forearm. "Rhea wouldn't have sent us on some bullshit mission to accompany them if she didn't think it wasn't worth the trouble. Wren's right. We need to focus on the amulet. Maddox can candle the rogues."

Ryker's gaze shifted to Blaire and then turned back to Wren with a clenched jaw. "Fine. We'll meet you at the light station." He turned towards his truck then, and Hailey climbed up in the cab beside him.

"Can you guys please make more of an effort to be friendly with one another?" I said. "This isn't easy for any of us, but we have to work together or else this isn't going to work at all." I was looking at Bryna as I said it.

She nodded and climbed in the backseat with Blaire as Wren and I slid into the front with him at the wheel. I hooked my phone up to the charger and used it to plug in the directions to the Firefly Light Station. It was a five-hour drive to the coastline, and with twilight settling over the forest, I knew it wouldn't be long before the stars lit up the sky. As Wren pulled the Pontiac out onto the road, I pulled my grimoire out of my bag and ran my fingers over the symbol on the cover, waiting.

☾

"Anything?" Blaire asked a couple hours later. Night had fallen, blanketing the sky in shadow. The clouds above were too thick to let the starlight shine through, but I remained hopeful that the symbol would light up any moment to give us our next clue.

"Nothing."

Blaire leaned forward, wrapping her arms around the headrest so she could hear me above the noise of the engine and the road that stretched beneath the Firebird's tires. When she touched my shoulder, a fresh floral scent filled my nostrils, and strength burrowed itself where uncertainty had been. I glanced over my shoulder, pressing my lips into a small smile.

"How old were you when your empath powers manifested?"

"Oh, not ten, if I recall."

"That's young."

"Keep in mind Bryna and I were practicing as soon as we could talk. The women in our coven encouraged it and helped us hone our powers."

I twisted in my seat so I could see her better. The glow of the dashboard glossed her pale face, lighting up the whites of her eyes. Freckles dotted her cheekbones, but you really had to be looking to notice them. Blaire's features stood prominent on her face; large, bird-of-prey-like eyes and a slender slope of a nose positioned above full lips. Her face was striking—so much that I didn't take note of the little things—like her freckles, or the small scar at the corner of her left eye.

"I wish I would have embraced my ancestry more after my mother died," I admitted. "My mother and I practiced, but, nothing like what you described growing up. I think she was always afraid that the wrong someone might see. And after she died, I didn't much feel like practicing."

"We can't change the past; we can only learn from it and hope to do better in the future."

"Everyone says that." I gave her a small smile.

"That's because it's true."

Wren flipped his turn signal, slowing as we approached a gas station in the middle of nowhere. We'd been out of the mountains for about an hour now, and the terrain was flattening out into something unfamiliar. Wren pulled up to the pumps, down shifting the gears as he put the car in park and turned off the engine. "You guys want anything?" He glanced over his shoulder before letting his gaze rest on me.

"I could really use a coffee," I said.

"Make that two," Blaire said.

"Should I get one for Bryna for when she wakes up?"

Blaire looked over her shoulder at her sleeping sister. Bryna's arms were crossed over her chest, her head tipped into a pillow that was propped up against the window. "She only drinks coffee in the wee hours of the morning," Blaire said. "Thank you for offering, though."

Wren nodded, and I watched as he slid out of the car and slipped his wallet from his back pocket, sliding his bank card through the machine at the pump.

"He hasn't got a job does he?" Blaire frowned.

"No," I said. "He worked for a construction crew his last summer in Washington though. He says he has some money saved up from that, but I doubt it's very much–even with Niall's inheritance."

"Niall left him everything?"

I nodded, and then my nod turned into a frown. I waited until Wren walked into the gas station before asking, "Um, Blaire, I wouldn't normally ask, but, I was wondering if you've gotten a good read on his aura as of late?"

"You mean with how he's coping?"

"Yeah. He says he's fine, but I know he's still having nightmares."

"He's hurting," Blaire answered after a while, "but it's not debilitating pain. He misses Niall, wishes he could have saved him. But you already knew that."

I nodded again. "I probably shouldn't have asked."

"He's more worried about you and what the amulet is doing to you. Of course, you don't have to be an empath to figure that out."

I drew in a shaky breath, exhaling slowly. "It comes in waves," I said after a moment. "The Darkness, that is." I looked up at Blaire. "There are moments when I feel strong and capable and in control, and… others when I don't." I glanced away from her eyes and gazed out the window, watching as Wren picked his way through the aisles, grabbing this and that on his way to the counter. "I'm not just scared for me," I said, "but for all of us–for everyone counting on me to know what it is I'm supposed to do to stop this thing." I thought about my dad, and Annabelle, and all our friends we'd left in the dark because it wasn't safe to involve them. What would happen to them if I failed?

"We're going to get through this," Blaire told me. "No one expects you to have all the answers, Quinn. The White Witch chose you as her heir–remember that when doubt rears its ugly head."

"Or when Bryna gives me that look–you know the one."

Blaire chuckled. "I've been on the receiving end of that look all my life, but, Bryna means well. The world's all Light and Dark for her, she doesn't understand the in between. Never has."

I lifted my eyebrows. "Well it must be nice to feel so sure about something, regardless." A white blur attracted my attention and I turned my head to see Ryker pulling up to the pump in front of us. Hailey was climbing down from the cab before he'd even cut the engine. She was heading for the gas station where Wren was depositing all our goods on the countertop and waiting for the clerk. She bumped her shoulder into his on her way to the ladies' room. He turned his head, but his facial expression remained neutral.

"*Werewolves,*" Blaire said under her breath, watching Ryker trail in after them.

"That's right," I said, recalling the fact that she'd once dated one. "You owe me the rest of your story by the way."

"There's not much to tell."

"Don't lie to me, Blaire. You have a talisman ring that lights up, alerting you to their presence–correct me if I'm wrong, but most Supernaturals don't carry those unless they have a reason. You told us that your family was sworn to protect the wolves of the Ossory bloodline and that you dated one…"

"Have you finished drawing your conclusions?"

"Hardly," I teased. "Come on, Blaire. You started the werewolf one-oh-one crash course when you helped me get ready for the bar the other night; you obviously know more about them than I do. What was his name–the guy you dated?"

"Griffin Fáelad," Bryna replied. I turned my head in her direction along with Blaire. Evidently she'd woken up and had been listening awhile. "Blaire was seventeen, and Griffin a year older. He was to be the next Alpha Master. I told her it was a bad idea to entertain the romance, but she wouldn't listen. She thought he'd still be with her when his title took effect, but an alpha Were *must* take a female Were as his mate if he wants an heir."

From the corner of my eye, I caught Blaire grinding her jaw.

"He was a bloody awful gobshite if you ask me," Bryna continued. "Dropped her the moment he became Alpha Master."

"That's quite enough, Bryna, thank you," Blaire said, tucking a strand of hair behind her right ear.

"I'm sorry Blaire, I didn't–"

"No, it's all right," she said, cutting me off. "I was a fool for thinking I'd be an exception. Weres are loyal to their pack above all. Now you understand why I said witches and werewolves don't mix, unless of course they're the heirs of Luiseach and Conan. Excuse me," she said, lightly pushing against the back of my seat. "I think I'll go use the jacks."

"Oh, sure," I said, hopping out of the car so she could slide out from behind the seat.

Wren backed out of the door with his arms full, a bag of chips hanging from his teeth as Blaire strolled in past him. He looked at her, and then looked back at me, eyes narrowing. I pivoted on my foot, taking a step toward the gas station and stopped. What could I say to her now that would make what she'd gone through okay? Nothing. The answer was nothing.

I turned back towards the car, peering in the backseat at Bryna instead. "Do you enjoy pissing people off all the time?" I asked her.

"It needed to be said," Bryna told me. "Weres don't make for good company. She needed to be reminded, and it would do you just as well to remember. We can't trust them. Betrayal is in their nature."

"Right," I replied, tongue snapping on the 'T'. Wren was at the car now, depositing the coffee carrying case on the hood as he pulled the bag of potato chips from his teeth.

"What happened to Blaire?"

"Upset stomach," Bryna said, "she'll be fine after she visits the bathroom."

I closed the car door with a little more force than necessary, tuning out the sound of Bryna's voice. Wren lifted his signature eyebrow, lips puckering. "Okay, what did I miss?"

"What would you say if I told you I wanted to ride with Ryker and Hailey the rest of the way?"

"You want my honest reaction?"

I gestured for him to proceed.

"Initially, I'd say hell no. Secondly, after I calmed down, I'd want to know what was so bad to make you want to abandon ship and hang out with people you like even less than Bryna." He cracked a glimmer of a smile.

"Short version–I just found out that Blaire's ex-boyfriend was a werewolf that dumped her when he became Alpha Master, and Bryna is on her high horse about how we can't trust werewolves because betrayal is in their blood, or whatever." I waved a hand through the air.

"Oh."

"Yeah. *Oh*." I reached up, pinching the bridge of my nose as I squeezed my eyes shut. Wren pulled me into his arms then, his chin resting on the top of my head. I breathed in the scent of his shirt, relaxing and feeling guilty for having him to cling to when things got rough and Blaire had no one.

Damn you, Bryna.

"Blaire never said anything to you before?"

"No." I shook my head. "She's kept her personal life fairly private."

"Ignore Bryna," Wren said, fingertips skating over the corner of my jaw. "She'll either come around or she won't. Not our problem."

"Except for the fact that she's with us, so she is in fact our problem."

"Bryna's issues stem from a sense of entitlement, that doesn't have anything to do with you. Don't let her get under your skin." Wren's hands slid down my back, gripping my waist as he pressed a tender kiss to my cheekbone, just below my eye.

"Get a room," Hailey scoffed, shooting us a look before climbing back up into the cab of Ryker's truck. Ryker was behind her, smirking. Blaire strolled out of the gas station, crossing her arms over her chest to fight the chill of the night air. Ryker watched her. Something in his expression changed. Softened, perhaps.

Wren pulled one of the coffees from the holder and handed it to her. "Two sugars, one cream, right?"

Blaire's eyes lifted to his face, a genuine smile tugging at her mouth. "Thank you," she said, "it was kind of you to remember."

"I've got a roll of Duct tape in the trunk, you can use it to silence your sister if you want," Wren added with a wry grin.

"Wren!" I smacked him in the shoulder, but Blaire and I were both laughing.

"I'll keep that in mind." Blaire took a sip of her coffee, reaching for the door handle. I stepped out of the way, letting her slide back in.

"Two sugars, two creams," Wren said, handing me a coffee cup. "You can't say I'm not attentive."

I grinned at him. "You're a werewolf–nothing gets by you."

"Hey, I pay attention to your needs." He pretended to be offended. "Leave my abilities out of it."

"Uh huh," I said, slipping into the car. "Let's get a move on, Wolf Boy; we still have a world to save."

We reached the Firefly Light Station just a little after midnight. The parking lot was deserted–save for a lone silver car that was parked beneath a lamppost and looked as though it had been dumped there in the eighties and forgotten about. After giving it a thorough inspection and determining it was safe, Wren took off to do a perimeter check and Ryker followed. Two werewolf noses were better than one, and the rest of us waited in the parking lot for them to return.

I heard the calm water of the river inlet lapping against the dock and smelled the rich scent of salt in the night air. The light station, though no longer monitored, sat at the end of the dock about forty meters out into the marsh. The beacon on top of the structure rotated, flashing at odd intervals. I stretched my cramped muscles, and propped my grimoire on the back of the Pontiac, casting hopeful glances up at the night sky that was still obscured by thick clouds.

"Did you know that lighthouses all have flashing patterns that distinguishes them to mariners coming in from sea," Blaire said beside me. "For example, this one appears to be on a twenty second interval, flashing only three seconds before repeating itself. That tells the mariner what lighthouse they're approaching."

"I didn't know that," I said, glancing up at her.

"When I was a small girl, I wanted to be a lighthouse keeper." She grinned. "My mother brought me to one every year for my birthday. Fastnet Lighthouse is my favorite. It was built on the southernmost point of Ireland on an isolated rock that juts up from the sea. *An Charraig Aonair*," she said. "The lonely rock."

Blaire was smiling distantly as she stood gazing out at the Firefly Light Station. The wind pulled her hair back from her face, the strands blending with the onyx sky. As I stood there looking at her, I realized that I had only known her for a few short weeks and Blaire had offered very little of herself. Granted, we'd been surrounded by chaos that trumped the whole 'getting to know one another' thing, but because of our Trinity bond–I felt like Blaire's identity was also a part of me. I knew her, on some deeper plane, like the way my soul had just recognized Wren and I had this overwhelming sensation of... *well*, of home. I knew I belonged with him, just like I knew Blaire was linked to me in sisterhood.

Maybe I was so caught up in my own troubles to realize that we were deeply linked, and if I tried, I could feel her presence. Right now, for example, I sensed her loneliness, and knew she was hurting. Her aura put out a calm haze, like the color blue, and I felt her ache as if it were my own.

"Holy shit," I said, staring at her.

"What's the matter?" She frowned.

"I can read you," I said, reaching out and latching on to her arm. I clutched my chest where the ache resonated. Blaire's lips parted, her frown slipping into a question.

"Of course you can," Bryna said. "It's part of the Trinity bond. You have to be concentrating on the person and then you can invade their personal thoughts."

"I can't *read* her thoughts," I retorted. "I can just feel them."

Blaire's eyes widened. "Try Wren," she instructed.

"Okay." I nodded once, closing my eyes and pictured Wren. I drew his face in my mind, concentrating on the specifics until I felt a sort of warmth spread through my limbs. I smelled the earth, the deep scents of the marsh and the traces of other smells–human smells, like hairspray and deodorant. My heart was racing, senses in overdrive. I felt his instincts kicking in: protect, defend, claim. They were strong instincts–very animalistic. I snapped out of it, opening my eyes. "He's prowling," I said.

"You've barely just begun to tap into the Trinity's potential," Bryna said. "It was said that the Original Trinity operated as one unit–that's how they were so successful in the Battle of the Dark Ages. They could sense what the other needed without words ever being exchanged."

"That sounds bat shit crazy," Hailey said, joining us at the back of Wren's car. "I couldn't stand knowing someone else was invading my head."

"You wouldn't care if it helped save your life," Bryna insisted.

Hailey sniggered. "Weres can take care of themselves. We don't need *saving*."

"I'll remember that next time you're in a bind," Bryna said.

I rolled my eyes. I'd had enough of the bickering to last a lifetime. Hailey looked at me. "Any word from your 'mysterious' enchantress?" she air quoted and pivoted to her hip. "It's kind of inconvenient that we have, oh–" she lifted her wrist, taking a peek at her watch "–less than forty-eight hours until the eclipse and still no clue where we're supposed to meet this chick." She crossed her arms, eyebrows disappearing into her platinum hairline.

"We made it to the coast," I said. "According to my vision, we just need to find the little cottage somewhere due east of here."

Hailey snorted. "Through all that?" She pointed to the marshland that mixed with the maritime forests on the other side of the river. "You do realize that this isn't your forest, Quinn. Maritime forests are teaming with a whole crazy ecosystem of lizards, poisonous snakes, alligators, mountain lions and even bears."

My eyes widened. "Silver Mountain has all the things you mentioned… well, except for alligators."

"My point is you *know* Silver Mountain. You don't know this forest."

"If you're scared Hailey, you don't have to go."

She sneered down the bridge of her nose. "You forget I have an advantage. I'm not scared. I was just… concerned," she said the word like it caused her pain, "about those of us who don't come naturally equipped with night vision."

Blaire invoked Spirit, and the element responded by pushing out a soft, indigo light that radiated from her body and turned her into a human lantern. "Seeing in the dark won't be a problem for us either."

"Hmph," Hailey responded.

Up ahead, Ryker and Wren were returning from the woods. I spotted their eyes, glowing with a touch of the Change, before I spotted their bodies.

"There's a narrow path that winds around the river for about a half mile before we have to make our own path," Ryker said. "We can start our trek tonight, choose somewhere less public to rest and then pick up again in the daylight." He nodded at me. "Anything from the book?"

"No," I said, "too much cloud cover."

If Ryker was doubtful of my grimoire, he veiled it behind a stoic expression. "Then I guess we have no choice but to trust your vision. You can take the lead, Hailey and I will bring up the rear."

I nodded.

It took us less than five minutes to gear up, call on Spirit to help guide us, and then we were heading off through the trees. Even in the dark I could tell that we were close to the river. The ground was soft, a mix of sand and dirt and roots that made up the embankment. Wren took the lead with me a half step behind him, Blaire and Bryna trailing close behind. I concentrated on mimicking Wren's steps, ducking here and there to avoid low-hanging branches. The path was easy enough to navigate until it ended and the marsh grasses grew thicker. Since the stars refused to shine, I had to trust Wren's instincts, along with the Spirit element to guide us in an eastward direction. There were thick snarled vines hidden in the underbrush that latched onto my ankles and pulled at the heels of my boots. The werewolves seemed completely at ease in the environment, navigating the terrain as though they'd lived here all their life.

I stumbled over a root, and Wren reached back to steady me. His eyes were glowing with the Change. "You okay?"

"Yeah. Thanks."

He didn't let go of my arm, just looped his hand around mine and helped guide me as we walked. We walked for what seemed like miles in silence, and I watched as Wren lifted his face to the wind, nostrils flaring as he sampled the air. The ground was hardening beneath my feet and I couldn't hear the river anymore. I couldn't hear much of anything, actually. I glanced over my shoulder to make sure the others were still close behind. We moved uphill; dogwoods and sugar maples towered over us, shielding us beneath what was left of their canopy. Dried leaves crunched beneath my feet.

"Oh, gross," Blaire muttered from behind.

"What happened?"

"I think I just accidently squashed a spider against my face."

I smiled. "You're right. That is gross."

Wren slowed, sampling the air again and then glanced towards the back of the pack as Ryker brought up the rear.

"This is a good place to stop for the night," Wren said when Ryker approached. "We're a good four miles in and not encroaching on any claimed animal territories. I picked up a scent of a bobcat about a mile back, but he didn't like the smell of us so he'll stay away."

"Hailey and I caught that, too. I'll scout another mile of the perimeter and double back to make sure we didn't pick up a tail." He dropped his pack at the base of a dogwood and pulled the T-shirt he was wearing over his head. I meant to look away, but I was momentarily stunned by the amount of defined muscle that had been hiding under his shirt. He looked like an NFL linebacker–like he could crush a human skull with minimal effort and not even break a sweat doing it. I swallowed hard.

Blaire had dropped her pack next to mine and was unrolling her sleeping bag, mumbling under her breath, "*Werewolves.*" Ryker heard this, of course, and grinned as he kicked out of his boots and shoved his jeans down past his hips.

"I swear to the goddess, if you drop your boxers in front of me I will hit you so hard with a knockout spell you won't walk right for days," I told him, covering my eyes with my hands.

Ryker laughed and stepped behind a tree, hopefully concealing the rest of his body as he brought on the wolf Change.

It didn't take long for Ryker to shed his human form, but my stomach lurched at the awful sound of bone and sinew popping and realigning into a wolf's anatomy. Ryker strode out from behind the tree, showing off his massive frame and dark coat. Where Wren was solid black when he Changed, Ryker's muzzle, flanks, and elbows were marked by lighter colored fur. His deep-yellow eyes shone in the darkness, gazing briefly at Blaire before he took off without a sound through the maritime terrain.

Wren rolled his sleeping bag out next to mine, and from the light of Spirit's glow, I saw the muscles twisting and bunching beneath his forearms. "Are you okay?" I asked him, placing my palm on his arm.

"It's the Change," Hailey said. "When one of us shifts, we all feel the pull."

I looked up to see that her eyes were lucid, glowing translucent-yellow. Her canine teeth were extended, the tendons in her neck rippling. Rionach's amulet began to heat and swell–feeding off the power of the werewolves' Change. I reached up, wrapping my hand around the stone and squeezed.

You can make them obey...

I shivered, turning my neck to the side as I fought off a different kind of calling. I was beginning to understand the amulet's power source was derived from magic that could either threaten it, or magic that could feed it–and in doing so, awakened an otherwise sleeping talisman. I knew a part of Rionach's essence of spirit remained trapped inside, amplifying the pull of energy. The amulet wanted me to use it as Rionach once had, but I had no desire to lord power or control over another living being. I ran my thumb over the glossy surface, willing it to silence.

"I roam the night in my animal skin, shedding one half of who I've been. And as the moonlight frees my imprisoned soul, it's here among the beasts that I find my home," Hailey said, peeling off her jacket.

"That's beautiful," I said.

Her eyes expanded. "Marion Wayne wrote it. She was a werewolf of course, but also a famous poet in the sixties."

"I wouldn't exactly call her famous," Bryna said.

Hailey rolled her eyes and kicked out of her boots. "I'm going to help Ryker scout. If you need something, just cry wolf." She laughed as she slipped behind the same tree Ryker used to Change and tossed her clothing to the side. A few minutes later, Hailey emerged from behind the tree in her wolf form. She was stunning of course, much to my dismay. Her fur was a lustrous white with the tips of her guard coat a light tawny-brown. She darted into the thicket, and I noticed Wren glancing in her direction before examining the food contents in his pack.

"I'm going to gather wood for a fire," Bryna said, rising. She strode off through the trees, keeping in close enough range so that we could still see her Spirit glow.

"If you want to run with them…" I trailed off, hoping Wren wouldn't make me finish my sentence. I didn't want to be possessive or jealous, but there was a part of me that hated that I could never share the wolf Change with him–at least, not the way that Hailey and Ryker could. Wren had belonged to a pack for most of his life, and he told me that running with the pack was a natural instinct. I saw how much he needed it–and even more–how much he wanted it.

"I'm not being sexist, but I really don't want to leave you here without–"

"If you say the word 'protection' I swear to the goddess I'll hit you so hard with a knockout spell you won't walk right for days," Blaire said mockingly with a wry grin.

Wren chuckled. "A lot of swearing going around tonight."

"*Guys.* Ryker was going to drop his boxers in front of everyone. What was I supposed to do? Forgive me, but, Wren is the only naked werewolf I want to look at." I glanced up at him, grinning.

"Doesn't mean the rest of us wouldn't have enjoyed the show." Blaire laughed, and I felt some of the sadness she had been clinging to evaporate in the air between us. I chuckled along with her.

"Oh, so you think he's handsome do you?" I teased her.

"He is that," she said, "but he's also a werewolf, and therefor strictly off limits. Trust me, I've learned all the lessons I've cared to when it comes to Weres." She sat down on her sleeping bag, bending to untie her boot laces. "You two should take a walk though. I'll stay and help Bryna with the fire. I'm knackered anyway."

I looked over at Wren. His muscles were still twitching. He needed the Change, but I knew he didn't want to leave me. "You sure?" I asked Blaire.

"Positive," she said. "Go on now, enjoy the night while you still can."

Chapter Twenty
Hide and Seek

We headed west, the opposite direction from the others. Wren held on to my hand, guiding me through the unfamiliar forest as we started downhill. "I smelled a creek on our way in," he said. "We shouldn't be too far from it."

"Oh, how romantic," I teased.

"I know it isn't ideal, but, I'll take all the stolen moments I can get if it means I can have you all to myself." He squeezed my hand and I felt my lips shift into an involuntary smile.

Maybe I should feel guilty for sneaking away like this, but we were in fact living on 'stolen moments' and for all I knew, this could be one of the last. I didn't know what would happen when we found the enchantress, but I couldn't allow myself to hyper-focus on the fear of the unknown or I'd drive myself insane.

Clinging to Wren was my link to sanity. Maybe we'd never have a shot at a normal life because of what we were, but these stolen moments–even in the midst of the chaos–made it worth it.

We walked on for a while longer, until I estimated we were about a half mile away from the others (far enough so we'd have some privacy, but close enough to come running if anything should go awry.) I heard the low gurgle of running water now, cutting over rocks in the creek bed. The ground dipped over a small hill and I could just make out the shape of shrubbery silhouetted against the water's edge. Some of the smells were more familiar here–closer to home and the forest that I left behind. Wren pulled me close, backing me up against the trunk of a dogwood and leaned down to press his lips to mine. I closed my eyes. He smelled like the forest and that delicious scent made me dizzy. I had to reach up and loop my arms around his neck to steady my balance. A small fire was building in my core, working its way up and knotting in my chest. He gently tugged on my lower lip with his teeth, a low growl caught in the back of his throat. That only added fuel to the fire.

My hands dove under the hem of his T-shirt, fingertips trailing over the hard contours of his abdomen. He hoisted me up so that I had to hook my legs around his waist. His teeth grazed the skin at my neck, lips pressing into my throat. I tipped my head back, opening my eyes and discovered a pair of bright orbs staring back at me from overhead. My breath caught and I startled.

Wren looked up. "Just an owl," he murmured, pressing another kiss to my jaw. But there was something oddly familiar about those jewel-like eyes, and the way they seemed to hold a map of the galaxy within them.

"It's the owl from my house," I said.

"Impossible." His hands drifted beneath the hem of my shirt, heat spreading through my lower back.

"Wren, I'm telling you. I got a good look at her eyes. This is the same owl." As if startled by my declaration, the barn owl spread her tawny wings and took flight, disappearing into the cloak of the midnight sky.

Wren stared after her, and then sighed, lowering me back to the forest floor. He kept his hands on my waist, but I could tell some of the fire had burned out because I'd allowed myself to get distracted–when really–he was the only thing I wanted to be distracted by. "I'm sorry," I said. "Guess I kind of killed the mood." I reached up, running my fingers through the silken strands of his hair. "It couldn't have been her, right? My brain is just scrambled... Forgive me?"

"That depends," he said.

"On?"

"How easily I can unscramble your brain." The corner of his mouth twitched, pulling into my favorite half smile.

I giggled. "I thought we were coming out here because you wanted to Change?" I countered, taking a few steps backwards. "I saw your muscles twitching. I know you need to burn off some energy." A few more steps separated us.

"I can think of other ways I'd rather burn off energy." His even tone lowered an octave, dripping with a tantalizing lure.

"So can I." I took a few more steps backwards.

His signature eyebrow rocketed up. "What game are you playing, Quinn?"

"I was thinking a nice round of hide and seek might be fun."

"Now?" He shot me a look.

"Well yeah, but, there's stakes involved."

"This should be entertaining… I'm listening."

My hand brushed the trunk of an ash tree the size of a fire pole so I took hold, spinning myself around like a kid on the playground. "You have to Change," I said, "and you have to give me a two minute head-start, otherwise the game won't be fair. You'll have a total of eight minutes to find me, and then I'll let you claim your prize." I grinned at him, spinning again around the tree.

"Eight minutes is considerably generous… You should at least make it challenging."

Truthfully, I had no idea how generous the time frame I'd given him was. I knew he was fast, and I knew his super-senses would kick into high gear in wolf form, but I had no idea just *how* fast he could find me. "Six minutes?" I guessed.

Wren shook his head. "Lower."

"Four minutes?"

"Come on, Quinn… now you're just insulting me."

Now it was my turn to raise an eyebrow. "You're feeling pretty confident about yourself, aren't you?" He grinned. "Tell me then–how fast can you get to me?"

"I can cover a mile in less than six minutes in my human form, as a wolf... that's a joke. With a two minute head-start, I can find you in less than a minute."

"All right then. You have forty-five seconds."

Wren was still grinning as he kicked out of his boots and pulled his shirt above his head. I bit my lip. Even without the moonlight, his skin seemed to shimmer in the darkness. He reached for his belt buckle, shimming out of his jeans. "You better get going," he said, "your two minutes start now."

As much as I wanted to stay for the show, my competitive nature kicked in and I took off, tearing through the forest. I glanced down at my watch, staying close to the creek bed in hopes that the sound of the running water would mask my footsteps. Spirit's glow helped me navigate through the darkness, pushing out a soft light as I jumped over fallen logs and roots that were jutting out from the embankment. The stream narrowed, and I spotted a stone that looked big enough for me to launch myself to the other side of the bank. Maybe the river would throw my scent. I took a running jump, shoes sliding as they hit the opposite side of the bank. I reached out and caught myself on a root and used it to propel myself up and over the other side. The smell of raw earth and dirt filled my nose. Another glance at my watch told me I only had a minute to go.

I zigzagged, doubling back in a circle before choosing a narrow path that led to a thick patch of underbrush, and beyond that, a patch of loblolly pines. The trunks were long and narrow, shooting over a hundred feet in the air. They weren't like the pines in my forest, but I knew the ground would be soft there, and the needle-coating would mask the sound of my footsteps.

I dashed through the first row, skidding to a halt when I saw that one had recently fallen and the trunk was thick enough to hide behind.

I climbed over the top, lowering myself in a crouch as I glanced down at my watch with only nine seconds to spare. I took a deep breath and concentrated on slowing my breathing.

The countdown began.

I wondered if I could use the Trinity bond to see into Wren's mind like I had before in the parking lot. I closed my eyes, picturing him in wolf form and concentrated. It didn't take long before my head filled with intense warmth. I sensed his joy, felt it swell in my chest as he tore through the forest with the ground beneath his paws. He savored the feeling of being in his wolf form. I imaged this was probably as close as I'd ever get to sharing the experience with him, and through the bond-link, I felt just how powerful it could be. I sensed the freedom and the excitement that pulsed through his veins. The thrill of the rush shifted into a feeling of satisfaction and a sense of victory.

He was getting close.

I opened my eyes, stealing a glance at my watch as the light-up face reached the twenty-second-mark. I looked around, searching for any sign of him as I strained to pick up the sounds of his footsteps. Without the glow of Spirit, my eyesight was useless. I picked up a faint sound to my left, turned my head in that direction and was tackled from the opposite side. Even though I knew he was coming, I still jumped and ended up falling to my side with Wren hovering over me.

"*Ooph*," I let out a sound as my body collided with the ground and Wren towered over me, warm nose nuzzling my face. "Gross," I teased, pushing at his massive chest. I called on Spirit, accepting the warmth of the indigo glow as Wren's body came into view. "Thirty-four seconds," I said, "not bad, Wolf Boy."

He grumbled, nudging my face with his muzzle. I pulled myself upright, sliding my fingers through his dense coat and felt the heat radiating from his body. When I stood, the top of his head reached my ribs in height. I didn't have to bend to pet him. Which–I suppose in the grand scheme of things was kind of weird. But what else were you supposed to do when your boyfriend could turn himself into a massive wolf? Not many humans got the opportunity to be that up-close and personal with the species so I was taking full advantage. Besides, the shift from man to wolf was one of the most beautiful forms of magic I had ever seen.

"Did I at least manage to throw you off my scent at the river?"

He let out a gruff, managing to shake his head.

"Damn."

He snorted, and I thought maybe that was the equivalent of a laugh. He took a few steps away from me and stretched his long limbs, shaking out his coat. He lifted his muzzle to the wind, nostrils flaring as he sampled the scents drifting in the breeze. He must have decided everything was fine out there because his body began to tremble, and I knew he was Changing back. I backed up a little more to give him room and watched as he morphed back to his human form. Bones snapped and shifted, repositioning as the hair on his body retracted and left a man standing in place of where a wolf had been.

His lean-muscled body was glossed with a light sheen of sweat, his hair matted against his forehead. I loved seeing him this way–loved the way he looked at me. I saw desire and confidence in his eyes, and a need that only I could satisfy. I stepped into his arms as his mouth came down on mine; the heat of his lips sent out sparks that awakened every nerve ending in my body. Tendrils of fire began rising in my belly, but when he kissed me like that, I didn't care if I set the whole forest ablaze.

"You're mine," Wren said, nibbling my ear.

And the world went up in flame.

I woke to the sound of birds chirping high up in the trees. I blinked a couple of times, straining, until I realized that I could see the boughs of the branches above me. It was light out. I sat up so fast my ears started ringing. The forest was hazy, covered in a smoky predawn fog that hugged the tops of the surrounding pines and dogwoods. I looked at my watch and the little green numbers flashing across the screen told me that it was nearly six in the morning. "*Oh my goddess,*" I breathed.

Wren shifted, nudging me back into the curve of his body where the warmth of his skin was more comforting than any blanket I'd ever used. It took me a minute to realize where we were. I smelled smoke from the campfire, and remembered we'd gone back to the campsite after–well, *after*–and slipped into a shared sleeping bag while the others remained asleep. At least, I think they were asleep. Hailey and Ryker had pulled their sleeping bags on the opposite side of the campfire, keeping a good five feet from one another and at least ten or fifteen from the rest of the group. Wren had pulled our sleeping bags about that far just so we wouldn't disturb the others. He'd unzipped his, spreading it out as a makeshift mattress and used mine as a blanket to cover us–even though with his body heat, we didn't need it.

His hand drifted below the hem of my shirt, spanning over my stomach as his thumb swept over my ribs. My stomach fluttered, and the images of last night came rushing back with vivid detail. My heart sped up as Wren pressed his lips to the back of my neck, sweeping the curtain of my hair to the side.

I didn't mean for it to, but the nearly burned out flames of the campfire sprung back to life, billowing with a rush of heat.

"What the–" Bryna sat up sleepily, squinting at the flames.

Wren chuckled.

"There'll be none of that or I'll dunk you in the cold river," Blaire said.

"I'm going to die now," I mumbled, covering my face with my hand.

"*Why* are we talking at six o'clock in the morning," Hailey grumbled.

"Because one of us is playing with her element," Blaire said with a chuckle.

"Huh. Is that what we're calling it now?" Wren's tone was filled with amusement.

"Please stop. Now," I begged, rolling so I could burrow my head into Wren's chest. I closed my eyes and tried to concentrate on anything aside from the way his body felt pressed against mine. I couldn't though, because I still smelled the forest on his skin, and felt the beat of his heart against my cheek.

There was shuffling across from the campfire, and I glanced over my shoulder to see that Ryker was climbing out of his sleeping bag. He'd slept in his boxers and nothing more. He shimmied into his jeans, fastening the belt buckle. "We're all awake now," he said, "might as well get a move on."

Hailey growled, flung out of her sleeping bag, snatched up her pack and started marching in the direction of the creek. "I'm going to wash up."

Blaire was the next to roll out of her sleeping bag. She'd slept in her jeans and a camisole and sat down on a log to pull her boots on. Ryker was pretending not to watch her as he slipped his shirt on over his head, straightening the hem. Behind me, Wren kissed my shoulder and then slipped out of the bag. The coolness of the morning air hit me then, sending a wave of goosebumps down my arms.

"I take it nothing has changed since last night–no mysterious messages from the enchantress or visions you'd like to share with the rest of us?" Ryker asked me.

"Sorry to disappoint you," I replied, "but no."

"We'll keep heading east then," he said, "unless you have a different suggestion?"

I didn't. I looked up at the tops of the trees, shrouded in inky fog and wondered if today would be yet another that was covered by clouds. The solar eclipse was set to begin at eight fifty-two on Sunday morning, which meant we needed to get to the cottage and find the enchantress before nightfall. Coordinates were obviously too much to ask for, so I closed my eyes and concentrated on the vision. I recalled tall slender pines at the edge of the forest, and then a small rocky cliff area that provided shelter for the cabin.

"East is good," I said, climbing out of the sleeping bag. Blaire tossed me a protein bar, which I ate while I packed up my things. We took turns washing up at the creek, brushing teeth and applying deodorant before starting on our journey through the forest. Bryna, I noticed, was particularly quiet this morning. She'd only barked a few commands about making sure we didn't spit our toothpaste into the stream 'lest we contaminate nature' and 'make sure you don't leave any garbage behind.' Hailey rolled her eyes at that one, but chose not to exercise a snarky reply.

We walked for about two miles before the trees began to thin out and the ground flattened into an overgrown field of slender wheat-colored grasses. The clouds obscured the sunlight for most of the morning, but the fog eventually tapered off and revealed and even more ominous sight to the west. Dark clouds were gathering, and it looked as if a storm might be heading our way. Wren lifted his face to the air, nostrils flaring. "Rain?" I asked.

He nodded. "Storm's still a few miles off, but, we might want to think about finding shelter soon."

"Great," Hailey muttered. "Are you sure this enchantress even wants us to find her?"

"I highly doubt she's responsible for the weather," I said.

"I just feel like if this is such a time-sensitive operation that she'd be, I dunno, intervening to make sure we didn't screw up."

Bryna chuckled. "Why is it that werewolves are always so impatient? The enchantress will be found when she wants us to find her and not a moment sooner."

"Why is it that witches are a just bunch of pretend know-it-alls that rely on relics and prophecies to get anything done?" Hailey countered. "Can you actually think for yourselves, or do you just always do what the Good Books tell you? It's really no wonder that your kind was almost wiped out at the stakes."

I choked on a laugh, wishing Annabelle was here to witness the verbal battle of the Supernatural divas.

"You know that witches weren't the only ones burned at the stakes in the sixteen hundreds–werewolves were captured and tortured too."

I shook my head, trying my best to ignore the bickering that continued behind me. I wondered how witches had gone from the once proverbial heroes that freed the werewolves from the rule of the Dark Witch in the Dark Ages, to the feared villains of the twenty-first century. What happened to the alliances and mutual respect for one another? Were we not fighting for the same team–working towards a mutual goal? The werewolf as we know it today wouldn't even exist without the kindness and love of Luiseach. Had it not been for her then–

Pain snapped through my temples, blotting out my vision. I winced, squeezing my eyes shut as an aurora of light filled my mind with vibrant bursts of color. *There must be a balance between Light and Dark, for you cannot have one without the other.* The voice of the White One lifted and filled my mind. *Let Orion show you the way...*

I doubled over, coming to as my knees barely brushed the ground before Wren caught me. "Whoa, are you all right?"

"Fine, just–" I trailed off, looking up as a barn owl swooped down from a nearby tree and soared across the field to our left. I narrowed my eyes, staring after it as it disappeared through the opposite side of the tree line. "We need to go that way." I pointed to the spot where the owl had flown.

"Are you sure?" Ryker asked. "That's south."

"I'm sure," I said, "just trust me."

"Did you have a vision?" Blaire asked, eyebrows furrowing.

"We're supposed to follow the owl." The amulet swelled and heated. The line in the grimoire about keeping my eyes to the stars and letting Orion show me the way had nothing to do with the actual night sky at all...

The owl I saw in the tree last night was in fact the same owl that I had seen at home. I recognized its eyes because they looked like diamonds, shining like a map of the whole galaxy with starlight twinkling in its irises.

Orion was a codename.

Bryna was frowning, crossing her arms as she studied me. "I suppose we didn't take that part of your vision into consideration. I thought the owl had been a metaphorical guide, not a physical one."

Thunder rolled in the distance.

"All right, let's start heading south and find some shelter before this storm hits," Ryker said. "I'll run ahead and make sure we're not walking into a trap. No offense Quinn, but I'd rather be on the safe side."

"That's actually not a bad idea. You'll get there faster if you travel in your wolf form, maybe you can scout out shelter for the rest of us."

"I'll go," Wren said. "I move faster."

Hailey snorted, but Ryker didn't protest. He simply said, "Two sets of eyes are better than one." He took off his pack and handed it to Hailey and began undressing. "I suggest if there's anything you don't want to see, you turn around."

Wren did the same.

Blaire and Bryna walked ahead while Hailey and I stayed behind to gather clothing articles and carry the extra packs while the guys Changed into their wolf forms. And no, I wasn't exactly ecstatic about having Hailey there to bear witness to my soulmate's naked body, but Weres were anything but shy when it came time to strip out of their clothing. And, if I was being honest with myself, I gathered it was probably nothing she hadn't seen before...

Still, I stood in front of him, watching as he brought on the wolf Change. His bones popped and snapped, and I had to work at keeping my expression neutral while I listened to the gut-wrenching sounds of his body shifting forms. Patches of black fur sprouted across his chest, traveling down his abdomen as his chest arched toward the sky. His face twisted in agony; his mouth and nose extending into a muzzle as his ears shifted high on his head. In less than two minutes he dropped to all fours and began sprinting toward the opposite side of the tree line with Ryker trailing after him.

I glanced at Hailey. Her irises were enlarged and swirling–canine teeth exposed and extended over her lips. She looked at me and a shiver crawled down my spine. It wasn't fear that caused it, but something akin to it–primal, even.

"Shall we?" She tipped her head, gesturing toward the others. We started walking. Blaire and Bryna were at least a hundred meters in front of us, but they were in eyesight so we didn't try to catch up. Not on account of me wanting to spend any time with Hailey, believe me. I just wanted to keep her separated from Bryna for as long as possible. The less bickering, the more tolerable this trip would be.

"I was wondering," I said after a while, "how old do you have to be before you're on the council?"

Hailey shot me a look that said *why are you even speaking to me?* She waited a beat before replying, "Eighteen is the youngest, but, the council is chosen at the Alpha Master's discretion. He can appoint or kick off anyone he chooses."

"Except for the Elders?"

"In order to kick off an Elder, the whole council has to vote unanimously, but that rarely happens. Thornwood has always had a strong Alpha Master and the pack respects its leaders–even when they become Elders."

I nodded.

"Why do you want to know?"

"Just curious." I shrugged. "I mean, you have to be pretty important to the pack if you're on the council, right?"

Hailey stopped walking. "What are you getting at Quinn?"

"You're really defensive, you know that? I'm just trying to make conversation." I started walking again and decided I didn't really care if she followed.

She caught up. "Why? I haven't exactly been chummy towards you or your friends. You said so yourself."

I couldn't disagree with that, but chose not to bite. Instead, I opted for a different route. "Yeah but you were just looking out for your pack, right?"

Hailey stayed quiet for a moment. "If you want the truth, Wren was the first boy I ever really liked. When Ryker told me that he was back in Silver Mountain and explained what he wanted me to do, I wasn't just doing it for the pack. I was doing it because I thought I might really get him back. I had no problem taking him away from you, Quinn, so if you're looking for an apology you're not going to get one."

I sniggered. "I'm not looking for an apology. Just as long as you drop the whole act of pursuing him, we'll call it square."

"I might not understand the Trinity bond, but I'm not an idiot. I know I can't come between you so there's no point in trying. He's yours– you win, or whatever."

"Good," I said, reaching up to tuck a lock hair behind my ear. "What about Ryker?"

"What about him?"

"I just thought that with you on the council that maybe you were trying to work your way up to being–"

Hailey snorted, cutting me off. "Ryker is sexy as hell, don't get me wrong but, I'm not into him like that, and he's definitely not into me. As much as the idea of being Alpha female appeals to me, I couldn't cross that line."

I fought the urge to chuff out a laugh. Maybe it wasn't a straight line, but the girl had some form of moral compass after all. "What line is that?"

"Look, Ryker has been looking out for Maddox and me since we were little. He's like an older brother to both of us. Not that it's any of your business, but Ryker and Nyla were supposed to be together."

Now I frowned. "I didn't realize they were ever a couple."

"They grew up together. Both their families were pretty tight-knit and had hoped that the two would lead the pack together when they came of age. Everything was leading up to that when Ryker found out

Nyla had been listening to the voices of Darkness. He was heartbroken, but he had no choice but to banish her and those who were following her."

"Do you mean they were listening to Penny?"

"Is that the wannabe witch that's related to sisters Yin and Yang up there?" She nodded towards Blaire and Bryna. From appearance to personality, they were total opposites, no doubt about that—like fire and ice; night and day.

I nodded. "Penny was using her lineage to summon Rionach's spirit. We assumed that's how she convinced the rogues to join her in getting the amulet." I reached up, squeezing the pendant at my throat.

"We don't know how any of it started. We just know what Rhea told us. That's how Ryker found out about Nyla's betrayal in the first place. Rhea foresaw Nyla and the rogues working with Penny to try and bring the Dark Witch back."

I stopped walking, reaching out to catch her arm so she would face me. My eyebrows shot up to my hairline. "Who exactly is Rhea?"

Hailey's lips parted, features contorting when she realized that I really didn't know. "She's the daughter of your Earth Mother, Gaia. She's a prophetess, Quinn. I thought you guys knew... She's a goddess incarnate."

Chapter Twenty-One
Signs from the Otherworld

The guys managed to find a makeshift cave where we could ride out the storm. 'Cave' was a relative term considering it was more like an outcropping of a small cliff. It slanted at just the right angle to keep the rain from pelting us. The patch of loblolly pines to our left helped, too. The six of us hugged tightly against the back of the rock wall, watching the rain coming down in steady sheets. Only Blaire was pacing, lost in thought over the information I'd made Hailey repeat once we were all together.

Hailey and I had caught up with the others at the edge of the forest, and Wren popped through the tree line–still in wolf form–to show us what he and Ryker had found for shelter. When we got there, Ryker was just shifting back. It was at a distance, but I still saw more than I bargained for, and made Wren follow me to the other side of the cave for his Change. I handed him his boxers first, and let him slip into his jeans before saying, "We need to talk."

"If it's about modesty, you might as well save it," he teased, the corner of his mouth pulling into my favorite half smile.

"It's about Rhea," I said. He frowned, following me back into the cave where Hailey reiterated her story.

"You should have told us about her," Blaire said, shooting a serious look at Ryker. She paced in front of him, toying with the trinity pendant around her neck. "It's bad enough you lied about the rogue werewolves being ex-members of your pack–and now this?"

"I didn't think it was relevant information," Ryker said. There was usually a bite to Ryker's tone when he addressed us, but I noticed it was gone now. "Look, I'm not saying mistakes weren't made, but I thought we both wanted the same thing–to stop Rionach from returning to power."

"That we do," she agreed, "but if Rhea had any knowledge on Penny, it would have been nice to know."

"I don't know why you're surprised to find that a werewolf would withhold information," Bryna said, a visible pout lining her lips. "I told you they're not to be trusted."

"We didn't withhold anything," Ryker snapped. "We didn't even know this Penny person was of any relation to you or how involved she was with the rogues. Rhea didn't foresee the Trinity's awakening. She might be a prophetess, but she doesn't know everything before it happens. You should understand that better than most."

"It's not like Rhea sees things in wholes," Hailey added. "She doesn't get a complete background check on someone when the goddess gives her a vision."

Blaire crossed her arms, tilting her head to gaze at the cave ceiling in silence. "Have you heard anything more from the Coven's emissary spies?" I asked her.

"Not yet," she told me. "They made it clear their intentions were to gather information on Penny's movements before bringing her in for questioning. It's standard procedure."

"What about you," I asked Ryker, "has Maddox checked in with any updates on tracking the rogues?"

"He said the forensic team had already cleared the area before he and the other trackers got there. It made it difficult to pick up a good trail, but they found it and followed it out of town. They tracked them across the border to Tennessee and lost their scent when it started to rain. They're still searching."

"Was that last night?" I asked. Ryker nodded. "This must be the same storm cell."

"The rogues probably realized they picked up a tail," Wren said. He leaned forward, propping his arms on his knees. "They'll stay close to rivers and streams, making it hard for Maddox and his team to pick up their scent."

"He knows that." Ryker pushed up from his spot on the ground and walked over to the opening of the cave, leaning against the wall. The backlight from the rain illuminated the two-day dark stubble on his face and showcased the brackets around his mouth. The hollows of his eyes were underscored in shadow, allowing me to see the fine lines pulling at their corners as he gazed into the falling rain.

His mask was slipping, allowing me to glimpse a piece of the man underneath all that armor. He was so much more than tooth and claw; more than spiteful words and hard leadership. With the pale light gleaming against his ebony irises, it was easy to see just how much he cared. Somewhere, deep within me, I knew this mission was more than just a pack thing. Ryker was doing what he had to do to protect his pack, but also to protect the world. I saw the pain and sadness weighing on his shoulders; the regret that the rogues we were hunting for were former members of his pack. He blamed himself for their betrayal–even if he wouldn't say it out loud; I saw it, plain as day.

"Nothing has been easy for us so far, but if anything, we've proved we have determination. This is still our world, and there is still good left in it–even in the midst of darkness. It doesn't matter if Light and Dark are out of balance, so long as there is always a force fighting to keep it in order," I paused, turning to look at my group of comrades. "*We* are that force."

The cave settled in silence. I listened to the rain falling outside, matching the racing rhythm of my heartbeat. Blood circulated through my veins with awakened power and I knew this mission would only come to fruition if we believed in the Light. It was so hard to keep fighting when Darkness was trying just as hard to spread its poison, but

I'd made a promise to those I loved and vowed to protect that I'd never give up.

☾

The rain relented at about three in the afternoon, and the rich scents of the earth tangled in my nostrils. I inhaled deeply, letting those fumes invigorate my senses. We started our trek through the forest, heading south as I kept my eyes on the branches of the surrounding trees, hoping to spot my owl.

We came to a steep gully that was now filled with a torrent of muddy running water. It wasn't deep, but I doubted any of us wanted to make the trek in wet boots so we'd have to find some way over it. The dead leaves and vegetation made the ground extra slippery, so I picked a spot about twenty meters down where a tree had fallen over the ledge. The branches and roots would provide something to hang onto while we climbed down. It was partially dry rotted, but it looked stable enough to hold our weight so long as we went down one at a time. Wren was the first over the ledge; he used one of the branches to swing down and landed on the rocky bank with barely a sound. "Show off," I muttered.

He grinned, perched himself on some branches near the bottom and reached up to help me down. I lowered myself over the edge, finding nooks in the dead trunk to place my feet while I climbed out to the middle. He eased me down from there and repeated the process for Bryna. Ryker had already slid down the muddy slope, skipping the aid of the tree all together, and Hailey followed suit. Blaire stepped up to the ledge, peering over with apprehension. "What's wrong?" I asked.

"I don't much care for heights," she said, staring over the edge of the gully. It was at least a fifteen or sixteen foot drop to the bottom.

"You would have made an awful lighthouse keeper," I teased.

"Why do you think I became a witch instead?" She tried to joke, but her tone lacked the easygoing buoyancy to land the same effect.

"Just step out on that ledge right there," Wren pointed, "and I'll help you down the rest of the way." He climbed up on the tree trunk, bracing himself on a limb as he extended his arms. She hesitated, tentatively stepping out onto the roots that were sticking out of the embankment. She leaned forward, reaching for Wren when her foot slipped out from under her.

"Blaire!" Bryna shouted her name as she went down fast and hard, knee cracking into the trunk as she toppled sideways. My breath hitched as she caught herself at the last second, dangling from a small branch. Bits of dead bark crumbled from the limb and pinged off the rubble below. Her backpack shifted to the right–anchoring her in place.

"Hold on!" Wren was up the tree before any of us could blink, pulling her back onto the trunk. "Let go of your pack," he told her. Ryker was standing beneath her, ready to catch her if she fell.

"I can't!"

"Yes you can. I've got your waist and I'm not going to let you fall."

She squeezed her eyes shut, moving her arm as the pack tumbled across her shoulders. She let it drop. Ryker caught it, quickly depositing it to the ground as he moved into position underneath her.

The branches started to crack.

"Oh, *goddess*," she panted, arms trembling.

"Let go of that limb, Blaire," Wren told her. His low tone was delivered with a gentle demand. "I've got you, but you have to let go."

"Wren, I can't," she sobbed. Her features twisted in fear and she still had her eyes closed. The branch she was clutching began to crack.

"Come on Blaire, you can do this," I told her. "Use the Earth element to ground you."

"Wren, you're going to have to let her go or that tree is going to bring the both of you down," Ryker said. "I'll catch her."

Wren let out a slew of curses.

"Okay, okay," Blaire said in a panicky rush. She opened her eyes, turned her head so she could see Wren on the trunk right behind her.

"You've got this, Blaire. It's not that far. Just give me your hand."

She reached for him, fingertips stretching–

The branch snapped.

A spray of dried bark and debris rained down as Blaire's body was propelled over the side. Wren dove forward, reaching for her wrist as Ryker caught her, diving to the ground in a tuck and roll as the tree came crashing down on top of them.

I was sure I screamed.

Wren's body was a blur of motion; his name ripped from my vocal cords as I launched myself forward, waving my hand in front of me as if I could somehow will the tree to move. And it did. The tree lifted and slammed into the side of the bank, wood snapped and splintered, spraying debris through the air.

Blaire was folded up in Ryker's protective embrace, tucked against the side of his body. Wren was on his stomach, propped up on his forearms, and everyone was looking at me. *Gawking*–was actually a more accurate description.

"Holy shit." Hailey chuffed.

Bryna flung herself to Blaire's side, pushing her hair back from her face as she inspected her for injury. "Oh, goddess, Blaire–are you all right?"

"Fine," she said breathily, shifting as Ryker loosened his hold on her. "Quinn, did you–" she trailed off, staring at what was left of the tree some twenty-odd feet away from us, smashed in the side of the bank.

"I think so," I said, gazing down at my unmarred palms.

"The White Witch was telekinetic," Bryna said. "It doesn't surprise me you've been gifted with the power. After what happened with the motorcycles back at your school, I had a feeling that you'd begin to manifest the power."

Ryker was helping Blaire to her feet now, and she stumbled against his chest, wincing in pain. His big hands moved to the small of her back to help steady her. My eyebrows lifted. Ryker's dark eyes seemed to soften in concern. Maybe I was imagining things, but, I thought I saw a spark.

Wren was dusting off his shirt as I caught his wrist, turning his forearm to see that the skin running parallel with his elbow was bleeding. "You're hurt," I said, leading him over to where I'd dropped my pack.

"It's just a scratch," he said.

"That's more than a scratch." A dark pool of blood was dripping from the three-inch gouge, snaking down his forearm and spreading like forks in a river. I took out my water bottle and uncapped the lid.

"Don't waste your water," Wren said, wrapping his hand around mine. "You know I'll heal fast anyway."

"There are plenty of streams out here, I can always refill if I run out." I peeled his fingers back from the water bottle and twisted his arm so I could clean the cut. As the water poured over his wound, I saw just how deep it actually was. If he were human, he'd need stitches. "You must have landed on a sharp rock or something," I said.

"I've had worse." He grinned, and I knew he was thinking back to the fight that almost killed him a few weeks ago when he was helping me rescue a fellow classmate from the rogue pack of werewolves in the forest. That was the first night I heard the voice of Darkness–the first night I heard the legend of how the werewolves came to be. It was strange how it seemed as though a lifetime had passed since then. So much had changed and altered the course of my life forever.

I pulled a T-shirt from my pack and ripped it down the middle, using it as a makeshift bandage for his arm. I tied it off gingerly, running my fingertips across the strong contours of his arm. "That should hold until it heals."

"Thank you," he said, catching my chin.

I smiled at him and then went to check on Blaire. There was a hole in her jeans at the knee, and already a swollen knot had formed and was turning purple. The skin was scraped, but nothing worse than a rug burn. "On a scale from one to ten, how's your pain level?"

"It's about a five," she said. "It's uncomfortable, but nothing I can't manage."

"You better not be lying."

"I wouldn't dare," she said. "You might toss me off the side of a cliff with your telekinetic powers."

I snickered. "I'm sorry about all that."

"We had to cross somehow," Blaire said. "It wasn't your fault."

"Climbing out might be tricky. We can walk down here along the bank awhile, see if it flattens out somewhere." I looked up at Ryker, noticing that there was a cut running through his dark brow. Blood was dripping down the side of his face. "Is it deep?" I asked, nodding towards the cut.

He reached up as if just noticing it for the first time. "No, head wounds always bleed more but it isn't deep."

"You and Ryker should hang back with Blaire and I'll lead us out of this mess," Wren said. A glower passed over Ryker's features, simmering in his dark eyes. Apparently it didn't matter if Wren was part of his pack or not–Weres (namely alpha Weres) did not like taking direction from another guy. Even if said direction gave you an excuse to hang back with the girl you were so obviously crushing on...

"I can walk with my sister," Bryna insisted, jaw setting as she shot a look of mistrust in Ryker's direction.

"I'm fine, Bryna. Why don't you keep a lookout for that owl, yeah?"

Bryna pressed her lips into a tight line, straightened the straps of her pack and marched forward.

Ryker picked up Blaire's pack, hoisting it up over his arm. "Thanks," Blaire said with a grateful nod. I slipped my arm under her shoulder as we started across the bank. "I just need to get my blood flowing again, and then I'll be right as rain."

I pressed my lips into a smile, knowing better than to coddle her. When I concentrated, I could feel her chagrin–she hated that this had happened to her and that she'd shown fear. She was used to being the kind of person that swooped in and handled everyone else's troubles, not the one that created them.

Wren found a spot about a half mile up where we could climb out of the gully. The dirt wall there was maybe six-feet high, and there were roots sticking out of the ground that would help propel us up and over. Blaire sighed when we reached it. Wren was already at the top, helping pull Bryna up.

"You want me to carry you?" Ryker asked.

Blaire turned her sharp gaze on him. "Thanks for the offer, but I'm not yet dead." She hobbled up to the embankment and offered her hand to Wren. He locked on to her wrist and pulled her out of the gully as if she weighed no more than a sack of apples.

"You know," I said to Ryker in a low tone, "she's not swayed on looks alone. If you like her, you're really going to have to work at it. She's not fond of werewolves."

Ryker chuckled dryly. "Thanks for the tip."

"Anytime." I grinned and walked up to the embankment to let Wren pull me out. "How's that arm?"

"Fine," he replied. "Stop worrying about me."

"No chance of that."

"Owl!" Hailey shouted, pointing toward a large live oak in front of us. Its hulking branches were draped in light green Spanish moss, and the owl was nestled on a branch about ten feet up. He was staring down at us with those peculiar diamond-like eyes. It blinked, ruffling its soft tawny feathers.

"Looks like we're still going in the right direction," Bryna said.

The owl took flight, stretching its graceful wings as it swooped through the trees. We adjusted our course and continued following along. To my surprise, Hailey asked a question about the food in Ireland, and both Blaire and Bryna began sharing stories about their favorite recipes and the best places to eat overseas. The talk of hot, hearty meals was making my stomach grumble. We'd packed basic things that would keep up our strength and not weigh our backpacks down. But after dining on granola bars, nuts, and dried fruit for breakfast, lunch, and dinner, one started to miss the idea of a greasy slice of cheesy pizza.

"I could go for a huge helping of fish and chips right now," Hailey said, echoing my thoughts. "And whatever that boxty stuff is sounds pretty good, too."

"We could always Change into our wolf forms and hunt down a couple of rabbits," Ryker suggested.

I made a face. "I'm not *that* hungry."

"Rabbit is delicious–especially raw," Hailey informed me.

"Bunnies are too cute to eat."

"Oh please," Hailey said in a condescending tone, "you better not be one of those crazy animal-rights activists that don't agree with people hunting."

"I didn't say that, I just–"

Someone laughed. It was a laugh that had me slowing my pace and looking through the trees. It sounded like child's laughter–light and musical.

"–Did you hear that?"

"Hear what?"

"Someone was laughing." I stopped walking, straining my eyes to see through the branches up ahead. "It sounded like a little kid."

Blaire frowned beside me. "Mountain lions and bobcats sound like human children when they scream; maybe you heard a forest cat?"

"I didn't hear anything," Wren said–which meant that I was probably hearing things in my head because werewolves had super-hearing abilities, and if they hadn't heard anything, I was definitely losing my mind.

I was just about to declare my insanity when I heard it again. This time it was behind me. I spun around, catching a glimpse of something satin–moss-green fabric shimmering in the light before disappearing behind a tree. I moved towards it but Wren caught a fistful of the back of my shirt, stopping me.

"You didn't see–"

"No, and you're certainly not going to go exploring things the rest of us can't see *or* hear." He shot me a knowing look.

"The Earth element is strong here," Blaire said, "I can feel it. Not quite like the Nexus, but something as equally charged."

I started forward again but Wren pulled me back. "Would you let me go?" I spun on him, working his fingers from my shirttail.

"It's not sinister," Blaire told him, hoping that would help rein in his defensive instincts. The guy had a protective streak a mile wide, which was nice for some things, but with others, unquestionably irritating.

His jaw tightened, and he let go of my shirt with reluctance as I started for the patch of sunlight where I'd seen the silky green thing disappear. Wren was right behind me of course, so close that I could feel his breath on the back of my neck. I turned around the trunk and heard more giggling coming from my left. I whipped around in that direction, catching a flash of something–skin, maybe?

The giggling lifted; tangling around my head like it was coming from every direction in the forest. Another flash. Definitely an arm–slender, like it belonged to a female. I jogged to catch up, but when I circled the tree, there was nothing but a small, patch of pale pink flowers growing out of the moss.

"Eastern Springbeauty," I said, bending to pluck one of the buds. I twirled the delicate star-shaped flower between my thumb and index finger. "These only bloom from March to May around here," I said. "My mother taught me about them when I was a girl. She had a plant book she kept around for potions and things."

Blaire took the flower, studying it as her eyebrows knitted together in concentration. She glanced up at Bryna. "Perhaps we've got ourselves a woodland nymph."

"A *What*?"

"You can hear laughter the rest of us can't," Blaire began to explain. "Nymphs are said to be minor Greek deities who inhabit forests and rule over nature. They're a carefree spirited bunch, playful and beautiful."

"Greek deity," I repeated. "In the letter, my mother said the enchantress went by the name of Winter Fengári, and we know 'Fengári' is Greek for moon…" I paused to wet my lips. "I wonder if this is another clue about who the enchantress is."

"Woodland nymphs are mythological beings," Bryna informed us. "We've no proof of their existence."

Blaire held up the spring flower. "It's October, Bryna. Have you an explanation for this?" She didn't of course.

I chewed the inside of my lip, glancing up to see that Wren was watching me, his amber eyes poised on my face. This was a clue–I knew it in my gut. "Let's keep moving," I said, "we need to get to the cottage before nightfall."

Chapter Twenty-Two
The Cottage by the Sea

The scent of sea salt was thick in the air. I lost track of how long we'd been walking, but I knew the sun was sinking low in the Western Hemisphere, leaving paintbrush strokes of rose and gold through the sky. The ground was sloping again, growing softer as we approached the beach. A mixture of excitement and fear swelled in my chest as I looked ahead and saw a stretch of dark blue through the break in the trees.

Wren caught my wrist, his palm warm against my skin. He stepped in front of me, half crouching as we approached the end of the tree line. His face lifted to the air, decoding all the surrounding scents. That first gust of wind coming in from the open sea washed through me. The light from the golden sun danced across the surf, the whitecaps turning to burnished glitter before crashing against the shoreline. I gazed out into the deep blue as the sound of the waves filled my ears.

Wren shifted, sticking close to the tree line as his predatory gaze scanned the beach. I followed along, heart beating fast when I saw the arc of the ocean stretching out into the shape of a C where the open ocean met the sound. The water was calm there, still moving towards the shoreline but in tiny ripples. The beach tapered off and the coastline became more jagged, dotted by large rocky boulders that formed the ocean's break line. It was there beneath the twisting branches of an old knobby oak that the cottage sat–nestled against the back end of the forest and the shore.

Wren bristled, coming to an unexpected stop in front of me. I smacked into his spine and let out a grumble as I righted myself. "What is it?" I whispered.

"I don't smell anything."

"That's good, right?"

"No, I mean, there's no one here." He nodded toward the cottage. It was a small, two-story building that at some point had been painted but years of neglect and coastal storms had taken its toll. The roof slouched, its wooden beams yawning as though we'd woken it from a restless sleep.

The barn owl swooped down from the forest, flapping its wings as it descended and perched itself on the roof. "This is the right place," I said.

"We should scout the perimeter," Wren said as Ryker approached. "I'll circle the cottage if you and Hailey want to make a sweep of the woods."

The muscle in Ryker's jaw flexed over the bone. He turned those unforgiving ebony eyes on me and nodded. Wren was already undressing.

Hailey was the first to Change, clearing a large boulder in her wolf form as she leapt into the forest with Ryker trailing close behind. Wren crept along the boulders, circling the back of the cottage before disappearing around its side.

"They are magnificent in their animal skins," Blaire said, coming to stand beside me. She'd pulled on a jacket from her backpack, but it wasn't until I saw her that I even felt the chill in the sea air.

"How's your knee?"

"Bruised, but I suspect I'll live." She winked.

Wren appeared around the corner, tipping his head toward the cottage and motioning for us to come inside. We followed.

A stagnant scent of decaying wood and salty air filled my nostrils when we entered the cottage. It mixed with forgotten embers of a fire that had long ago burned out. Soot and ash blackened the floorboards in front of the hearth. The wooden mantel was bare, save for an empty glass jar that had frosted over from dust and salt damage. I circled the fireplace, finding a stairwell that led to a narrow hall on the top floor. The cramped quarters contained only two sets of doors. With a little effort I managed to wriggle the doors open to reveal two threadbare bedrooms. The bedframes were made from brass posts; each still contained a mattress and a long-forgotten faded quilt. "This place is a ghost town," I muttered under my breath as Wren shoved against the bedroom door with his muzzle. He nudged the small of my back, gesturing for me to head to the living room area. I eased myself down the steps and found Blaire and Bryna talking in low voices. They stopped when they saw us.

"There you are," Blaire said, working her lips into a smile.

"I was exploring upstairs. There are only two bedrooms."

"There's a bathroom down here but of course, no running water," Bryna said.

"It doesn't appear anyone has been here in quite some time," Blaire said. Beside me, Wren chuffed in agreement. He turned his head toward the doorway, left ear shifting like an antenna. Hailey strolled in, still in her wolf form.

"I take it the woods are clear?"

She nodded. Ryker's massive frame took up most of the doorway. He stayed on the porch though, looking at the cottage as if he feared it might collapse if he entered. The sea breeze drifted through the strands of his coat, and he lifted his muzzle to the wind, nostrils flaring.

"I know this doesn't look promising right now, but, this is where we're supposed to be. I can feel it." Some of the tension that I had been carrying around since we started our trek through the coastal wilderness had settled. It wasn't gone, necessarily, it was just resting. The whole atmosphere seemed to be lying dormant—like a thing in between. It was hard to describe the exact meaning, but it felt similar to the way the amulet would awaken now and then, trying to get me to use it, or hurt me when it tried to protect itself. The power was neither here nor there–past or present–just *existing*. I pinched the moonstone between my thumb and forefinger, stroking the glossy surface; sleeping now.

"Let's get settled then," Blaire suggested. "Dusk will be here before we know it. We can gather some wood and get a fire going before it gets too cold."

Ryker barked, and I about rocketed clean out of my skin. I clutched a fistful of my shirt above my heart and shot Ryker a serious look. Wren grumbled beside me, and I imagined that was the wolf version of telling Ryker off. He turned from the doorway and started towards the ocean. Wren and Hailey followed. "Where the heck do they think they're going?" I asked.

Blaire and I exchanged a look and then decided to follow them to the shore. Ryker was wading into the surf, water up to his elbows. Hailey trudged in after him, but Wren looked back over his shoulder, finding me before following suit.

"They're bloody mad, that water's not ten degrees," Bryna said.

"Celsius," Blaire said, gauging my confused expression.

"Oh, right," I said. "That might be unpleasant for us but they probably don't even feel the cold."

The wolves swam out deeper as if to prove my point. They spread out from one another, staying equal distance apart before turning back to face the shoreline. At first, I thought they might have just been enjoying a nice dip in the ocean, but then I realized they were using strategy–*hunting* strategy. The water towards the shoreline began to ripple at the surface. The tide was low, revealing long stretches of sandbars that crested above the waterline. They were herding fish to those areas, hoping to trap them in the shallows. Several seconds passed before I caught sight of fins breaking the surf as the wolves chased them up onto the shore.

"Looks like Hailey will be getting those fish and chips after all," I said, shaking my head in disbelief.

"Let's just hope one of them packed a knife," Blaire said.

"Why? You don't like your fish covered in scales?" I teased. "I find the texture to provide a satisfying crunch."

Blaire chuckled. "Right, well, I think I saw a rusty old bucket back at the cottage to hold your scaly fish, I'll be right back."

Bryna had already left, searching the tree line for broken branches and twigs to use for firewood. I climbed up on one of the boulders, letting the sea breeze tangle through the long strands of my hair while I watched the show. Wren was the first to catch a fish. It was decent sized with russet-colored scales. He trotted out of the ocean practically wagging his tail. Blaire returned with the rusted pail and Wren dropped his fish in with a clunk. I noticed puncture wounds in its head and knew the kill had been quick and effortless, delivered by his razor sharp canines.

"This whole outdoor survival thing is a breeze," I joked.

"You say that now, but another day without running water will have us all aching for a hot bath," Blaire said.

Ryker was the next out of the water with an equally impressive fish. He dropped it into the bucket and then started back towards the shallows as Hailey came trotting out with a fish bigger than the other two. The fish flopped between her smiling jaws before she crushed its skull between her teeth.

We had a total of six fish within the next fifteen minutes, and Bryna had gotten a fire started on the beach–shielded from the wind by the boulders. The Weres had disappeared momentarily to shift back to their human forms and returned a few beats later fully clothed.

Wren exited the cottage in a pair of jeans and a long-sleeved black shirt that hugged his chiseled frame. His ocean damp hair swept across his forehead, and when he leaned down to kiss me, I smelled the salt on his skin. I'd wanted to see him standing next to the ocean, and in the fading light of day, the view did not disappoint. He climbed up on my boulder, sitting behind me as he pulled me to his chest.

"Hello you," I said, reaching up to touch the side of his face. "That was some nice fishing you did out there."

He chuckled lightly, the deep sound vibrating through his chest. "Hailey will never let us live down the fact that she caught the biggest fish."

"Yeah, and I think she ate it raw." I made a face.

"Sushi isn't half as bad as scales," Blaire said, looking up from her spot by the campfire. She'd fashioned a makeshift spit over the fire while Ryker skinned the fish. They worked together side by side in near-perfect coordination. I wasn't about to point that out, seeing as how the pair were refraining from all forms of verbal communication. In my opinion, actions spoke far louder than words.

"Sushi refers to the seaweed wrap, and it usually comes with rice and little strips of avocado and cucumber," I said.

Hailey laughed. "Sounds like someone is dreaming of a California roll."

When the fish were done cooking, we sat around the campfire and divvied up the goods. Wren pulled out the bag of potato chips that he'd bought from the gas station and joked that we now had an official fish and chips meal. The group laughed at that, taking a few chips as the bag got passed around the campfire. Considering our current circumstance, the food wasn't half bad.

We talked—not about our impending responsibilities, but about ordinary things that normal human teenagers got to converse about. Ryker was the exception; he stayed quiet, but he watched Blaire, entirely absorbed in her stories about Ireland and all the trouble she and Bryna had gotten into as girls. Even Hailey was being pleasant.

Before the meeting with the council, I had seen Thornwood as the enemy, but now... something was changing. I saw those enemy lines shrinking, knowing deep down that they were never the bad guys. They were dangerous, yes, but Ryker was a good leader with his pack's best interests at heart. Rhea had been right for suggesting a forge in our alliance; the truth was that we needed each other.

The sun had slipped below the horizon line, disappearing behind the forest. We were miles away from civilization, and across the sound I could scarcely see pinpricks of twinkling lights, an indication that life existed somewhere out there.

"What are you thinking about?" Wren asked as he reached up to sweep the curtain of my wind-blown hair back from my face.

"The cottage and how it got here–who it belonged to, and why it's been abandoned. Just seems strange that it's out here in the middle of no-man's-land."

"It was built in the twenties," Ryker said from across the fire. "It was a safehouse for rum runners hiding from the law."

"How do you know?"

"There's a storage cellar on the side of the cottage, it's filled with old whiskey crates," he replied.

"Is there still whiskey down there?" Hailey asked.

"Some," Ryker said.

"Thanks for holding out," Hailey said sardonically, pulling herself to her feet.

"Where do you think you're going?"

"To drink whiskey from the age of prohibition," she replied, heading for the side of the cottage.

"The legal drinking age is twenty-one Hailey Reynolds, and you are neither legal nor twenty-one."

"Bite me, Ryker. We're in the middle of nowhere and it's not like anyone is missing it," she called over her shoulder.

Ryker's jaw fixed, muscle flexing as firelight danced across his ebony eyes. He shook his head but said nothing.

"We need her sharp," Bryna told him. "We don't know when the enchantress will arrive and the last thing we need is to be looking after a fluthered werewolf."

Ryker turned his sharp gaze on Bryna. "If you think you can stop her, be my guest." He rose to his feet, straightening the hem of his jacket. "I'm going to gather more firewood. It's going to get cold tonight."

"I'll go with you," I blurted. The whole camp shot me a questioning look, but I ignored them. I squeezed Wren's hand before sliding down from the boulder. "I'll be fine," I said in a lower tone. His jaw tightened as his brows furrowed, but he managed a stiff nod before I let go of his hand.

Ryker's expression remained neutral, but I could see the curiosity behind his eyes as I joined him on the other side of the fire. He tilted his head, gesturing towards the tree line. I walked beside him in silence. The sound of the ocean's waves crashing against the shoreline filled my ears as we walked until even that became a muffled whisper. I called on Spirit, using the indigo glow to light my way.

"They can't hear you now," Ryker said, finally breaking the silence. I met his gaze, slightly charged with a touch of the Change. "That is why you wanted to come with me, right?"

I reached up to tuck a lock of hair behind my ear. "I wouldn't ask you anything I couldn't say in front of Wren."

"So what do you want?" His tone was cut and dry, but not disrespectful or snappy.

"I want to talk to you about our alliance, and about Rhea. There was a reason she wanted us to work together, and I believe it's because the forces of Light have been divided for too long. Supernaturals stick to their own races and don't really integrate. We're going to have to change that if we have a chance at destroying the Darkness."

"I'm listening," Ryker replied.

"I've been thinking about your plan to move the pack to Silver Mountain. When we make it back from all this, I want to know what your intentions are."

Ryker snickered. "It's a shame you're not a wolf–bossy as you are."

My lower lip twitched. "I'm choosing to take that as a compliment."

"It was meant as one." He tucked his hands in the pockets of his leather jacket and leaned his massive frame against the trunk of a tree.

"Rhea has been pushing a move on Thornwood for the last year but my father was very firm on his opposition because of the alliance with Niall. I may not have agreed with it, but I did respect it."

"Why does Rhea want your pack to move?"

"Well," Ryker began, "when some of the pack broke from my lead and chose to follow Nyla, Rhea saw a shift between Light and Dark. She knew about the Nexus in Silver Mountain and knew that other Supernaturals would be drawn to that area. She wanted us there to help protect it." He lowered his gaze, eyebrows lifting.

"Too bad you didn't start from that angle when you propositioned Wren..."

"Like that would have made a difference." He sniggered, bent over at the waist and picked up a broken piece of a branch. "I was hoping if we had his allegiance, it would make the transition into Silver Mountain easier."

"So you threatened to take his life if he didn't join," I paused, folding my arms over my chest. "I guess I sort of fail to see how that's rolling out the welcome mat."

Ryker's lips spread into a slow smile.

"Oh wait, let me guess... That's just a werewolf thing. I mean, you have to show your status, make sure dominance is established.

"Bossy *and* intuitive."

I rolled my eyes. "Look. Silver Mountain has been home to me all my life. I don't–" I corrected myself, "–I *didn't* trust you. I'm not saying I'm ready to roll out the welcome mat either, but, I think this trip has shown me a lot about the kind of being you are... Ultimately I think we want the same things. I may not be a werewolf, but I understand what it means to be a leader that people depend on. I know how important it is for you to have the respect of your pack and still have that dominance established. Tell your pack whatever you want about moving territories, but understand this... Silver Mountain is *mine*. If you're going to live there, I'll have rules I expect you and your pack to follow."

Ryker's eyes glowed with the Change, his canines exposed from his smile. I held my ground as the amulet began to pulse and swell like the ebb and flow of the ocean's tide. The power was awakening, humming with electricity. *That's right, White One, make them all obey...* I fought like crazy not to reach up and touch it. It wanted me to use the power to force my will over the werewolves, but I wouldn't–no matter how strong the pull was corrupting that desire. When Ryker didn't say anything, I continued, "We both know I have the power to make this decision for you," I paused, "but out of respect for your position, I chose to have this conversation with you *alone*. The rest of the pack never has to know that these conditions came from me."

"And what are they?" His tone was a low growl.

"Your werewolf identities can never be made known to the humans. There can't be any wolf sightings in town–especially with the forest wardens on high alert for the rogue pack. Until things settle down, I would recommend keeping your Changes limited to nightfall. No hunting in the Nexus. Any major decisions the council makes should be brought to the Trinity for the sake of respect. And, I know it's going to be extremely hard for you, but, you're going to need to try and blend in. And no trashy Were bars."

Ryker barked out a laugh. "And what of the decisions the Trinity makes... Are you planning on sharing those with the council–for the sake of respect?"

"I'm planning on running them by you," I said. "If you choose to take them to the council, that's your business."

"I like you, Quinn Callaghan, you've got nerve."

"So, I take that to mean you're in agreement with my terms?"

He stared at me long and hard before nodding. "Silver Mountain is yours." He stepped forward, extending his hand. I took it, feeling his palm crush around mine.

"So mote it be."

"So mote it be," he echoed.

Chapter Twenty-Three
A Thing in Between

Ryker and I finished collecting firewood and began making the trek back to our campsite. In the distance, I spotted Hailey tipping a bottle to her lips, the glow of firelight refracting from the glass. Ryker growled under his breath.

"Can I ask you a question?"

"Be my guest," Ryker replied with a plastic smile.

"For someone in your position, you let her get away with a lot…" I observed. "What's their story–Maddox and Hailey's I mean."

Ryker's jaw flexed before he answered. "Their parents were killed by werewolves. They were hunting inside the territory of another established pack on the night of a full moon and the Alpha Master intervened. He killed their father first, and their mother died trying to defend her mate. Maddox was ten and Hailey was only eight."

I dropped my gaze from his face, tightening my arms around the bundle I was carrying.

"I know what you must be thinking," Ryker said, studying me from the side. "But there are rules that must be followed, Quinn. We make no exceptions. It's just our nature–the way of the beast."

I clenched my jaw, nodding once. "I'm not a werewolf," I said, touching the moonstone at my throat, "but I know what it's like to be governed by something you can't control. I get that you're not entirely human, but sometimes I overlook the animal."

Ryker shifted his bundle. "When Rebecca and John died, Thomas brought Hailey and Maddox to live with us. They had no other family. I go easy on her because she's still angry at the world for taking her parents away from her. I go easy on her because I never want her to question her place in my pack–in my family."

I looked up at him then, watching as the mask peeled away and he showed me a glimpse of the man that was not at all a beast, but entirely human.

At the campfire, Hailey stumbled and dropped the bottle of whiskey onto the sand. She giggled, sweeping the curtain of blonde hair back from her face. "I'm going to get her up to bed," Ryker said. "We'll talk later, White Witch."

I drew a breath and sighed, choosing to head for the cabin. Blaire was coming down the stairs when I entered through the door. "Hey," she said, "back with the kindling I see."

I dumped the load of wood into the hearth and brushed bits of bark and dried leaves from my clothing. "Bryna already go to bed?" I asked.

"She did," Blaire told me, joining me in front of the fireplace. "I'd love to know what you and Ryker talked about on your little adventure."

Just then, Ryker shuffled through the doorway with a very intoxicated-looking blonde werewolf in his arms. Hailey rolled her head to his chest, murmuring something inaudible as he stepped into the living quarters. "Can she have one of the bedrooms?"

"Second door on the right," Blaire said, thumbing towards the staircase. "Bryna is in the other."

Ryker nodded and carried Hailey up the stairs. Blaire shot me a questioning look.

"It's kind of a long story," I said, "can I tell you tomorrow?"

"Of course." She pressed her lips into a smile. "Let's get this fire going, shall we? I'll summon Water in case the chimney is clogged and we end up smoking ourselves out."

I chuckled as I called on Fire. "You ready?"

"Ready," she replied.

"*Solas*," I commanded, and the flame from my palm leapt into the hearth, igniting the dried leaves and branches we'd collected.

"Well done, you." Blaire grinned. She sat down beside me, pulling her knees to her chest as her arms wrapped around them.

I watched the hypnotic dance of the gypsy flames licking at the branches in the hearth. It had been a long couple of days, and exhaustion was taking root. I heard footsteps shuffling on the floor above us and knew Ryker was getting Hailey tucked into bed.

"You should get some rest," Blaire said. "There's no sense in everyone staying up when we've agreed to take watches."

"Then what's your excuse?" I raised my eyebrows. "Ryker agreed to take the first-watch and Wren has second."

She shot me a look. "Trusting a Were not to fall asleep on the job," she scoffed.

"Oh come on Blaire, Ryker isn't so bad."

"You've spent less than forty-eight hours with the man and you've decided he's all good, yeah?"

"No. I just think there's a lot more to him than what meets the eye." I shrugged. "He has to present himself in a certain way for his pack, but I think that's just one of the many faces he has to wear."

Blaire huffed, brushing a strand of hair back from her forehead. "Or maybe he's worn the different faces for so long he doesn't know who he really is."

"I don't think that's true, Blaire." There was more to Ryker than I'd first gathered. Blaire would see that too whenever she opened her heart enough to learn that not all werewolves were going to treat her as Griffin had. "Stay awake if you want, but Ryker won't let us down. I'm going to find Wren and check the grimoire one more time before bed."

"If you need me I'll be here," Blaire said, reaching for her pack to roll out her sleeping bag in front of the hearth.

The moon wasn't visible in the night sky, but millions of stars lit up the midnight canvas, twinkling above the ocean like miniature homing beacons. I found Wren sitting on top of one of the boulders facing the ocean, the wind blowing through his hair. The night was glowing on his skin, just as it always had, never failing to make my heart skip a beat. There was really no point trying to sneak up on a werewolf but I practiced walking quietly anyway. The wind was coming in from the sea, playing to my advantage. I crouched, preparing to spring on his back, but as I lunged he twisted and caught me. He laughed and hauled me into the small space in front of him, wrapping his arms around my waist.

"Silly girl," he whispered against my ear, "when will you ever learn there's no such thing as sneaking up on a werewolf?"

"It's still fun to try," I said.

"So, are you planning to tell me what was so important that you had to talk to Ryker *alone*?" His tone had stiffened a little.

I winced. I knew he wouldn't have liked me going off with him. I sucked in a deep breath before explaining my reasons. I told him about our alliance moving forward when we returned to Silver Mountain and told him about the terms I'd given Ryker. When I finished, Wren seemed to relax. "It's not that I didn't want you to be there, I just didn't want Ryker to feel threatened."

"And you think my presence causes that?" Wren lifted his trademark eyebrow.

"Think about it," I said, "you belong to the Trinity, which sort of makes you the Alpha of all Alphas, right? That's bound to be intimidating."

Wren considered this, running his thumb along the sharp edge of his jaw. "I just wish you'd told me about it before you went off with him."

"Well I hadn't exactly planned the whole thing out," I admitted. "The opportunity presented itself and I acted. You know I do better with spur-of-the-moment decisions. It's having all the time in between to think and wonder that causes me to panic."

Wren chuckled. "Yes, I've learned that about you."

"I am sorry though, if I caused you to worry."

"The day I stop worrying about you is the day the world stops spinning on its axis." He tightened his arms around me, delivering a kiss to the curve of my cheekbone.

"I love you, Wren."

He caught my chin, tilting my face to his and lowered his mouth to mine. His thumb swept along my jaw when the kiss ended, and he tipped his forehead to rest on mine. "You are my whole world," he whispered.

I swept my hand across my mother's letter, knees tucked to my chest. Wren was lying beside me on his back, face tilted toward the heavens. A flutter of movement drew my attention to the cottage where 'Orion' was perched on the roof; the owl's watchful eyes scanning its surroundings in silence. The cottage had been quiet for a while now–the fire before me had died down to a low flicker, the embers glowing in the cracks of the branches like molten lava. The glow held my gaze with its entrancing pulse; beating like a heart. My own heartbeat seemed to match its rhythm, but despite the steadiness, mine would not rest.

"You should be sleeping," Wren said, his voice waking the darkness.

"Can't sleep."

"You haven't tried."

I closed the grimoire, stretching out my legs as I turned to look at him. "There's still so much we don't know," I confessed. "What if this is all for nothing–what if the eclipse comes and the enchantress doesn't show?"

Slowly, Wren rolled his fingers into his palm as a thoughtful expression rearranged his features. He rose up on his elbow, leveling his face with mine. "She'll show."

"How can you be so sure?"

"Because I have faith in you," he answered as his fingers tapped the grimoire's cover. "Look at what we've faced, Quinn–look at what we lost." He paused as his eyebrows twisted above his eyes and I knew he was thinking of his father. "I refuse to believe this has all been for nothing." His tone was adamant.

A dull ache thrummed in my chest as I reached out to cover the back of Wren's hand with my palm. Like so much else, I wished I could take on his pain so he wouldn't have to bear it alone. He tipped his forehead to mine, closing the space with things he didn't have to say. The meaning of his silence was understood–all he had to do was look at me and I would know...

"Hope I'm not interrupting anything."

Wren's hand stiffened beneath mine as I made out the shape of Ryker's frame in the darkness. He stepped into the fading light, his skin still shadowed in blue. "Coming to switch me for second-watch?" Wren guessed.

"That's the plan," Ryker said, hooking his thumbs through his belt loops. "At least, that *was* the plan before I found something I think you both might want to take a look at."

A frown creased my forehead. "I should get Blaire."

Ryker was shaking his head. "No. It isn't far. I think you'll want to bring your grimoire."

I waited a beat, gauging his calm expression before agreeing. "Okay." I palmed the grimoire, hugging it to my chest as the cool air slipped through the cotton fabric of my clothes and caressed my skin. I shivered. Wren wrapped his arm around my shoulders as we began our trek into the forest. I called on Spirit to light my way, and the element responded by pushing out its familiar indigo hue.

We walked for about ten minutes before the ground seemed to level out and the trees thinned. It was hard to distinguish, but I thought we were approaching a meadow. The grasses were longer and softer, and I saw some kind of faint, blinking neon glow. I stopped walking, squinting my eyes. "Are those–?"

"Fireflies," Wren answered, confirming my suspicions.

"But it's–"

"October, I know," Ryker interrupted.

"I *can* finish my own sentences you know," I snapped.

"Sorry." Wren squeezed my hand.

"This looks familiar... I think the enchantress showed me a glimpse of this place in the first vision she sent me." I tilted my head, studying the fireflies.

"Try to catch one," Ryker said.

I looked up at Wren and he nodded. I stepped out into the clearing, walking until I'd reached the middle. The fireflies were twinkling all around me, lighting up the meadow with intermittent bursts of neon light. I waited until one was within arm's reach before reaching out and cupping it in my palm. Or at least–that's what *should* have happened. The firefly passed through my hand as if it were no more than a hologram. My lips parted, eyebrows furrowing as I swiped through another. "What the heck?"

"I was hoping you might have a supernatural answer," Ryker said, nodding towards the grimoire that I was still hugging to my side.

"Oh. Right." I sat down, crossing my legs and spread the grimoire out on my lap. I waited until the starlight unlocked the cover, and then opened the book, scanning through the star spelled pages. There was nothing new after the map. I took my hand and waved it over the book and said, "*Nochtann.*" I'd seen Blaire do it before and had little faith anything would happen, but the pages began to glitter. An aurora of bright light burst through the binding. Squinting, I watched as beautiful, golden script bled onto the pages. The letters trickled down the page, filtering through the parchment like spilled watercolor until I could make out the words. It was a spell, I realized, running my fingers across the title: *To Awaken the Ancient Sleeping Ones.*

As the sun sleeps the moon rises to shine
unbroken, be the ties that bind.
Winter's Moon will come at last
behold, the future is the present and the past.

"What's it say?" Wren crouched behind me, peering over my shoulder.

I twisted the book so he could read the inscription. "It's an incantation to awaken the ancient sleeping ones." I frowned at the page. I looked up, watching the peculiar dance of the fireflies, wondering how it was possible that they were just existing in suspension as if they were neither here nor there. *The future is the present and the past,* I recalled. That was the last line of the incantation. "It's a thing in between," I mumbled.

"What?"

"The fireflies. We can see them, but, I think they exist in a different realm. That's why we can't touch them." I jumped up so fast I nearly fell over. Wren steadied me. "I think the incantation is meant to bring the enchantress to us during the eclipse. That's why she's not here right now. She doesn't exist on this plane!"

"My life was so much simpler before I met you," Ryker said, shaking his head.

"I could say the same about you," I retorted. "I need to talk to Blaire. She'll want to see this." I lifted the book.

Ryker volunteered to wake Blaire when we got back to the cottage. Wren and I waited on the decrepit porch; the boards sagging beneath our combined weight. Inside, I heard rustling, and then soft murmurs as Blaire returned to the land of the waking.

"What the devil? *Get off me!*" she shouted, and then a burst of blueish-white light exploded from the opened cottage door and a loud crash had both Wren and I bolting inside.

Blaire was standing in front of the fireplace with energy-balls circling her palms and Ryker was rolling to his knees across the room, laughter shaking his chest. He wiped the corner of his lip, spitting blood onto the floorboards.

"What the hell, Blaire?"

"*Me*?!" She flattened a hand over her chest, eyes bulging from their sockets in total disbelief. "What would you do if you woke to find a hulking giant hovering over top you? He's lucky I only hit him with a knockout spell."

"Seriously Ryker?" I narrowed my eyes at him as he pulled himself to his feet.

"I wasn't *hovering*," he insisted, "I was trying to wake her without scaring her." He snickered, rubbing his jaw.

Blaire snorted. Hailey and Bryna came thumping down the staircase, both dazed and disoriented. "Do you people value sleep like, *at all*?" Hailey snarled.

"Sorry," Blaire said, "you can go back to bed. Nothing happened."

"Well I'm up now." Hailey sauntered across the living room and plopped down on an old couch; a cloud of dust billowed from the cushions. Bryna lowered herself to the arm gracefully. "What's going on that couldn't wait until–oh, I don't know–sunrise? It's always something with you people." Hailey reached up, massaging her temples.

"You're the one that asked to come," I reminded her.

"Yeah, because I didn't trust you guys to get the job done and I wanted to make sure my pack wasn't getting screwed in the deal."

I glanced at Ryker. His jaw worked forward in a glower that he cut right at Hailey. The growl vibrating from his chest was low, but it managed to raise the hair on the back of my neck, and reminded Hailey of her place.

Ryker explained what he found while scouting the woods, and then I jumped in for the grand finale. When I finished, the room sat motionless. After what seemed like a lifetime of silence, Blaire finally spoke. "That is concerning. I've never heard of an incantation like that before." She turned her face towards her sister.

"Waking ancient beings isn't a practice the Aurora Coven would indulge," Bryna added. "Ancient sleeping ones might imply that the beings are primordial. That's dangerous territory."

"I don't think the incantation is meant to wake a bunch of primordial beings," I said thoughtfully. "I think we're supposed to use the enchantress's name to wake her specifically. That's why we've been given all the different clues. She doesn't exist in our world—we have to summon her."

Hailey snorted. "Right, because the clues have been so entirely helpful thus far. *Do* you know her name, Quinn?"

I narrowed my eyes, but I had no reply.

"Well I'm going back to bed. Try to keep the cryptology lesson down to a whisper." Hailey rose to her feet, tossed her platinum hair over her shoulder and marched up the staircase. I heard her mumbling under her breath about the mission being nothing but a wild goose chase.

I sighed, pressing the heels of my hands into my eye sockets. "We at least have to try the incantation," I said in a tone that sounded defeated. "When the eclipse begins, I'm reading the spell."

Blaire reached over, palm squeezing my shoulder. "You should try and get some rest, lass. We need everyone to be as fresh as possible for the eclipse." She turned to Wren. "Are you still good for second watch?"

Wren nodded.

Ryker ambled to the couch and lowered himself to the cushions. His body was so big it took up the entire space, his legs splayed over the arm Bryna wasn't perched on. Blaire chuffed out a laugh and blinked up at me with her arm extended in his direction.

"I'm sorry, did you want the couch? I can make room…"

Blaire stared blankly into his face before retorting, "That's charming but I think I'll pass."

Ryker grinned, his straight teeth glowing in the firelight. He propped an arm under his head and settled into the cushions. Blaire's face screwed up into a perfect grimace. I saw the frustration plain as day, but there was something else there, too. He tried her patience–

ruffled those elegant raven feathers of hers. But it was clear to me that he was making her *feel* something.

"We'll be outside if you need us," I said.

"Fine, I'm going upstairs." She grabbed Bryna's elbow and wrenched her up from the arm of the couch. "Next time you need me, don't send the wolf."

"Duly noted."

Wren's left eyebrow was hitched up to his hairline. He looked at me, started to open his mouth, but I grabbed him by the arm and hauled him out onto the beach before he could say what he was thinking.

"Okay," I glanced at my watch, "we have approximately four hours until the eclipse starts. You should probably–" he peeled off his shirt, tossing it to a boulder beside me, "–do that," I finished, clamping down on my lower lip.

He grinned and began working on the removal of his belt.

"Where will you go?"

"Never far," he replied as if sensing my unease. Gently, Wren framed my face in his palms and pressed a kiss to the center of my forehead.

"Be careful," I told him, covering his hands with mine, "and come back to me."

"I promise," he said, moonlight stirred in his eyes as he brought on the Change.

Morning light pierced through my eyelids until the brightness woke me. I sat up in a daze, head spinning from the onslaught of irretrievable dreams. Wren was curled around me, still in wolf form. His golden eyes were focused on me. The wind sweeping in from the sea was playing through the strands of his onyx coat, ruffling the scruff at his throat. He whimpered, nuzzling my face in concern. "I'm fine," I told him. "I must have fallen asleep."

He pressed his face against the side of mine and leaned into me. His long limbs straightened out in front of us, and I reached for his paw that was larger than the palm of my hand. His coat was both soft and course beneath my fingertips. I slipped my fingers through the fur at his neck and pulled him even closer. The grimoire lay to our right, sunlight glinting off the arcs of the crescent moons. Wren lowered his head, resting on his paws. "You're probably exhausted."

He grunted a protest.

I glanced at my watch. "We still have close to an hour before the eclipse starts; I can stand watch if you want to catch some Z's." Another grunt. His head lifted, face turning towards the cottage. "Someone awake?" I guessed.

Blaire walked onto the porch then, arms folded over her chest, bracing against the cool morning breeze. She spotted us and I waved.

"Hey," I said, "couldn't sleep?"

"I got enough." She shrugged it off and rubbed at her arms. "It's a bit cold out here."

"I barely feel it, what with all the heat Wren puts out."

He grumbled and gave the wolf equivalent of an eye roll. Blaire chuckled and climbed up on the rock beside me. "I miss the sea," she said with a look of nostalgia in her eye. She gazed out at the inky blue of the vast ocean. "The water is colder in Ireland, but the views from the Cliffs of Moher are breathtaking."

"I can imagine."

"You'd like Ireland. The lands are pulsing with ancient power. It's like being in the Nexus no matter where you are–always surrounded by the elements. It's the ideal place to be a witch."

"We'll have to visit," I said. "I'd like to see it and learn more about my heritage. Plus, it would be great to meet the faces behind the mysterious Aurora Coven."

"They would like that." Blaire smiled.

Something occurred to me then, and the thought soured the emptiness in my gut. "After this is all over… Will you go back–permanently, I mean?" I turned my face to hers.

"I hadn't much thought about it." Blaire drew her knees to her chest and wrapped her arms around them. "We'll always be the Trinity; nothing will happen to our bond. But, my life exists within the Coven and their need of me, too."

I nodded and traced a crack in the boulder with the tip of my index finger. "It's your home," I said. "I understand your need to protect it."

"Just as Silver Mountain is yours." She bumped her shoulder into mine. "We'll always have each other, but we'll always have greater responsibilities that may separate us for a time being. That's how it goes for those who bear the honor of following the Light."

"Ryker will be disappointed," I teased her. "I think he's quite taken with you."

She snorted, lifting her face to the wind. "You know how I feel about werewolves–namely ones that are called Alpha Master."

"He's not Griffin. I don't think he cares about the whole heir thing since he's carrying a serious torch for you."

"Well that may be, but I haven't decided whether or not I want children of my own."

"*Oh*," I said, puckering my lips.

Blaire laughed. "No matter–we've a world to save before all that. Come on. Let's wake the others and get ourselves to that enchanted firefly meadow of yours." She tugged on my sleeve and slipped down from the rock. "Based off your vision and the first incantation in the grimoire, that's probably where we ought to be when the eclipse takes place."

"I'm right behind you."

Chapter Twenty-Four
Awakening a Goddess

I wasn't afraid.

Fear was too simple a term for the restless energy humming through my veins. The tension gripping every fiber of my being was like static, tingling with acute awareness. The amulet around my neck pulsed with awakened energy, swelling and feeding from my anxiety. Wren placed a hand on the small of my back; the feather-light pressure a reassurance.

"This is the place," Ryker said as we stepped into the meadow's clearing. The fireflies were still hanging in suspension, existing in a space that wasn't part of this world.

Blaire reached out to catch one, her palm swiping neatly through its tiny body. "Strange," she breathed in a tone laced with fascination and curiosity. "Quite remarkable, really."

"If by remarkable you mean creepy as hell, then yes," Hailey said, "I tend to agree." She crossed her arms over her chest and tilted her face towards the sun. "So what's the plan *Your Esteemed Highness*?" Her gaze cut to me.

Ignoring her tone, I replied, "We wait for the eclipse to move into alignment and then I read the incantation." I swallowed, forcing my nerves to the pit of my stomach.

"Place the grimoire in the sunlight," Bryna suggested. "You should be able to watch the eclipse move across the symbols as it would in the sky."

I did as she said, holding the book so the sunlight gleamed off the metal. As the moon above began to slide into position, the first crescent began to glow on the cover. My breath hitched as I looked up and caught Blaire's gaze. She stepped to the left of me, fingertips tracing the arc of the crescent. "Try to unlock the page with the spell."

I opened the grimoire. "*Nochtann,*" I commanded, waving my hand across the page. Light crackled through the spine and the golden words of the incantation bled through the parchment. *This is it,* I thought as my heart slammed against my ribs. Every wall that we'd climbed–every dark road that we'd crossed to get here would soon be validated. My eyes found Wren's, and he was looking at me with such conviction that I borrowed the strength from him and blinked down at the page.

Blaire's shoulder brushed mine as she helped to steady the book. "Together?" she said, pressing her mouth into a thin line.

"Together," I agreed. The corners of the grimoire bit into the tips of my fingers as we read aloud, "*As the sun sleeps the moon rises to shine. Unbroken, be the ties that bind. Winter's Moon will come at last. Behold, the future is the present and the past.*" My vision sparked white around the edges as a blazing light erupted from the grimoire. An explosion of heat scoured my skin where the amulet rested. I cried out, dropping the grimoire as I clawed at the necklace with rigid fingers, attempting to wrench the stone from my chest. Liquid fire flooded my veins, burning and scorching me from the inside out. My eyes snapped shut, knees buckling.

"*Quinn!*" Wren's voice penetrated through the excruciating torture. I felt his hands tighten on my shoulders as I hit the ground, but his touch only heightened the burn. The fire had spread to my throat–too hot now to scream.

You know who I am, White One, call out my name.

"The enchantress isn't here." I picked out the strain in Hailey's voice. "The sun is almost in full eclipse now. What do we do?"

"Quinn, can you hear me?" That was Blaire.

"What's happening to her?" Wren's tone was gravel, raw with anguish and rage. His hands were still on my shoulders–his arm, moving under my back as if to support my weight. I couldn't see anything. The fire had blinded me–it was burning me alive and they couldn't see it happening because it was on the inside. I couldn't move my limbs or my mouth to make them understand that I was dying. My muscles were melting; veins and sinew all turning to mush and waste inside my body.

Call my name and make it stop. Tether us together, White One.

"What's happening to her eyes?"

"What the hell *is* that?"

"They're... *stars.*"

Like the map of the galaxy glowing in the eyes of the owl. The owl called Orion–clues–all clues. *They called her Winter,* my mother had written. *She goes by many names but what her true name is, I will not speak. She's a lunar goddess with an affinity for animals.* Lunar goddess–affinity for animals–all clues, I thought. *Let Orion show you the way.* In my mind, I saw the little golden bow and arrow light up on the page of the grimoire.

You know who I am. Call my name and this will all be over.

"Artemis!" I choked out.

Was this what dying felt like?

There was no blinding bright light at the end of the tunnel, or a familiar voice calling out to welcome me to the Great Beyond. I couldn't see anything in the veil of endless black. The pain was gone–in fact, I couldn't feel anything. Not just physically, but, also emotionally. I was contentedly numb.

You can't stay here, a voice said. There was a cosmic ring to its tone. Where was it coming from, and how could I make it go away? Didn't she understand that I was dying? There was nothing left for me back in the world in which I'd left.

Not true, she said, as if she could read my mind. *How could you forget?* Her face appeared before me, indescribably beautiful and radiant. Her features were framed by thick auburn hair that seemed to be floating in the air around her; the silken strands catching light as they drifted along. She bent before me, pressing her rosebud lips to the space between my eyes, and my fragmented mind was restored.

The ache in my chest expanded as Wren's beautiful face filled my mind's eye. He was my whole world. I needed him. That ache crumpled and expanded, squeezing my heart until all I could do was choke on the sobs that had risen in my throat. There were other faces now–faces from my childhood that smiled at me. I saw my parents, Annabelle, Torrance, Huck and Jamie and knew that I had to keep fighting for their sake. Blaire's face came into view, and a fresh pang of grief tightened in my chest. I couldn't leave them yet. I needed to get back to them–back to Wren.

Dúisigh, the voice commanded.

I opened my eyes and bolted upright, sucking in a sharp lungful of air. I coughed, head pounding. Strong arms smashed my frame against a solid chest. My face folded into the curve of a neck, and the scent of the forest and sea burned my nostrils. Wren's hands were rough against my face, brushing the hair back from my eyes. When I was finally able to look up at him, his large golden eyes were glossed over, a mix of tribulation and relief contorting his eyebrows.

"I thought I lost you. I thought you were–" his rough voice broke on the words. His thumb stroked my cheekbone, warm lips pressing to my brow.

It took most of my effort but I reached up, catching the side of his face in my palm. "I'm sorry," I managed. He caught my hand, squeezing it.

"Oh, thank goddess," Blaire breathed behind him.

"W-what happened?" I blinked against the dim lighting I now realized was haloed behind his head. I saw that our group had gathered around, but their faces were in blurs. I tried to sit up, but the motion caused pain to spike through my chest. I winced.

"Take it easy love, you're hurt."

"She'll be all right," said a feminine voice. I twisted my head to the side, trying to peer up at the face it belonged to. She was more beautiful than humanly possible, with skin so flawless even her age was impossible to determine. She looked just as she had in my dream–long, dark-auburn hair cascaded down the middle of her back with eyes that matched in color. I studied the braided leather cuffs on her arms–arm guards for archery–and the dainty silver jewelry she wore looked as though it had been fashioned from the moon. The pendant around her neck depicted a downward facing crescent moon with three arrows piercing the center.

"Artemis," I breathed. "You're here."

"Not for long, I'm afraid. I'm sorry it has to be like this, but it was the only conceivable way I could come to you. It's forbidden for gods and goddesses to interfere with mankind, but the power of the eclipse is keeping me shielded from their watchful eye."

A frown creased my brow. "How did you know we would need you?"

Artemis smiled, and the silver moonlight glossed her lower lip. "That is quite a long tale, so I shall try to explain the short version." She paused, drawing a breath. "I was born unto the Titan god Zeus and Titaness Leto. Since the beginning of time, I've always loved nature and all her divine creatures. I vowed to be a protector of nature and women, to be a Light Bringer, and to always watch after those who still seek my aid–"

"You're a Light Bringer?" I interrupted.

"She is *thee* Light Bringer," Bryna said in a voice of awe.

Artemis cast a glance my way, and her russet eyes glittered like the stars. "When the Dark Witch rose to power, it was I who called for the creation of the White Witch. Luiseach was a daughter of my desire to restore balance between Light and Dark. I breathed life into her, but it was she who established the Trinity. I've always been watching your bloodline, Quinn. That's how I knew your mother would need my help protecting you."

I swallowed over a lump that had begun to rise in my throat. "You created Luiseach?"

Artemis nodded. "The Light Bringers needed a champion to bring an end to the Darkness. Since I could not physically enter the human world, I called upon nature to fashion a maiden from the earth and breathe life into her. She was to be Pandora's incarnate–a human version of the goddess herself with the purest of white Light. After all, there must always be balance between Light and Dark."

"If you can't physically enter the human world, how is it that you are here right now?" Ryker asked the goddess.

"It's the eclipse," Blaire answered. "We're being held in suspension between the realms."

"We are, my daughter, yes." Artemis turned her lovely smile towards Blaire. "The stars are in planetary alignment with this exact spot but only for a few short moments. I wish I had more time to spend with each of you, but this is all the time I have to offer. The Trinity has a very dangerous journey ahead of them. More dangerous than any that's ever been." The goddess reached out, her fingertips brushing against my arm.

"That's why we came to you. We were hoping you could help us find a way to destroy the Dark Witch's amulet." I reached up, fingertips brushing over the stone and the fresh wound it had left on my chest.

"We were told that nothing on earth could cause its destruction," Blaire added. "That's why the Aurora Coven has been guarding it for generations."

Artemis nodded, touching the moonstone with her index finger and the jewel began to glow. "The Lord of the Underworld began to whisper to Rionach's bloodline," she said. "The Dark Lord thrives on death and chaos, and must remain trapped in the nine circles, for if he is freed, the world as you know it will end. That's why he wants to wake her. Rionach is the only being that's ever come closest to bringing an end to your world."

"The sacrifices in the Hollow…"

"They failed," Artemis said. Her starlit gaze rested on Wren. "Your father's death was a sacrifice for the Light. His blood was given in protection to the hallowed ground because I knew the beings you call rogues would try to poison the Nexus. I am truly sorry for your loss, Wren, but your father died a warrior to our cause. He understood what was required of him, and his sacrifice has atoned for his past sins. Please take comfort that he is in peace in the realm of the Otherworld, and you will meet him again one day." Artemis clasped Wren's shoulder, and my eyes burned hot with tears.

"You're the one who sent me the vision before he died," I said, dropping my gaze from her face. Silent tears began streaming from the corners of my eyes. "I thought I was supposed to save him. I thought it was my fault he died."

"No, daughter." Artemis's voice rang with such tenderness the sound nearly broke what was left of my resolve. "I only meant to show you that it had to be done."

"So how do we stop the Dark Witch?" Wren spoke evenly. "How do I guarantee that my father's sacrifice wasn't for nothing?"

A shadow passed behind Artemis's eyes before she spoke. "The Trinity is young, and though there is great power within you, you still have much to learn. In the months to come, there will be a rise in Darkness. The forces of Light must unify and take a stand against the corruption." Artemis paused, looking around at each of our faces. "The unity of Light *must* start here. Before it's over, you will have to summon the Dark Witch and vanquish her before the amulet can be destroyed."

"You want us to bring her back?" I heard myself say. My heart picked up pace, frantically beating against its feeble cage of bones. That wasn't the answer I'd been expecting. Wren's hand worked up the side of my arm, fingertips squeezing into my shoulder.

"How?" Blaire asked.

"With help," Artemis answered. "The world has awakened a young necromancer not far from here. She's new and doesn't understand the rare and potential power of her gifts. You're going to need her on your side, for it was her blood that Nyla stole to give to the human woman of Rionach's bloodline. It is how the summoning must take place."

"The summoning?" I raised my eyebrows.

"Your bloodline can awaken Rionach's spirit," Artemis said to Blaire, "but the ritual to bring her body back requires the blood of a necromancer, spilled onto her amulet as an offering to bind her to her bones."

I shivered; the tiny hairs on the back of my neck crawling upwards.

"The Aurora Coven has a necromancer," Bryna said. "What need have we of this girl?"

Artemis smiled, but the light didn't quite reach her eyes. "Her blood is the key to vanquishing the Dark Witch and destroying the amulet for good."

"How do we find her?" I asked.

"Her name is Emery Green. I wish I could share more, but I've risked enough of fate as it is. I hope you understand that this is all I can leave you with." Artemis looked up at the sky behind me, at the fireflies twinkling in suspension. The moon was slipping past the surface of the sun, sliding out of alignment with the eclipse. "Rionach will meet her end in the place where it all began. To vanquish her, you must go to Ireland. Unite the Ossory clans."

"When?" I asked.

The light was already shifting; the sunlight bleeding through the clouds above.

"I'm afraid I'm out of time." Artemis stood and turned her face towards the sky. "Be brave, my sons and daughters. You will know when the time is right."

The world split in two, blinding us all with brilliant strands of shimmering light. I shielded my face with my arm, squeezing my eyes shut until Wren's arm slid across my shoulders and I felt his breath against the side of my face.

"She's gone," he said.

For a moment, I didn't know what to say. Artemis had departed before all our questions could be answered, and yet, she had answered so many in such a short amount of time... With a trembling hand, I reached for the amulet, gripping the moonstone between my thumb and forefinger. I looked around at each face before me, chest rising and falling in a steady rhythm. I lifted my chin as the weight of all that had happened settled on my shoulders. The burden was heavy, but I didn't have to bear it alone.

"It starts with us," I said. "If we want to see a change in our world, we have to *be* that change. Artemis said the forces of Light *must* come together in unity. The road ahead isn't going to be easy, but I need to know now... if we're in this, we're in this together. So if anyone wants out, now's your chance to say."

"I'm in," Wren spoke immediately.

"I'm in, too," Blaire echoed. Bryna followed suit.

Ryker worked his jaw, shifting his gaze towards Hailey; her face a mirror image. After a short clip, Ryker spoke, "This goes way beyond the initial concern of the pack," Ryker bit out, "*however*, if we don't join this fight, I fear there might not be a life waiting for us when it's all said and done. I think we can tolerate putting up with a few other Supernatural races if it means we're saving the world."

"As far as I'm concerned, we entered the big fight when we agreed to accompany you on this little adventure," Hailey said. "No chance I'm backing out now."

I nodded slowly. "I was hoping you'd say that."

"This is what we were made for," Blaire added, reaching for my hand, "this is our legacy... our calling."

The power of the White Witch soared inside me, filling me with strength. Something had changed when Artemis pulled me back from the deep–awakening something ancient within my blood. What it was, I couldn't yet say, but I knew this much… I wasn't afraid.

I held out my hands, reaching for Wren and Blaire beside me, until everyone in our group had linked their hands together. "So mote it be," I said, binding us once more in a mission to save the world from Darkness.

Epilogue

October had come and gone and November had taken its place, spreading through Silver Mountain in such a gentle, quiet manner that I couldn't help but wonder if it was something akin to an eerie calm before the storm. I tried not to think about that too much and scanned the computer for the hundredth time, typing in variations of keywords and phrases to try and find the one thing we'd been futilely searching for since our return from the coastline.

Wren entered my bedroom, carrying a ceramic plate with a single vanilla cupcake complete with colorful sprinkles and a birthday candle poking out from its center. A smile crawled across my face as I spun in my chair. "What is that?" I asked, shaking my head.

"This?" Wren pointed to the cupcake and furrowed his brows. "Well, it's a delicious dessert people sometimes eat in celebration of noteworthy events. For example, weddings, baby showers, graduations and birthdays are just a few of the things people tend to celebrate." He grinned wryly.

"But it's not really my birthday yet." I narrowed my eyes at him.

"It will be in a few short minutes," Wren said, gesturing to the little clock in the right-hand corner of the computer screen. "I just wanted to be the first to wish you a happy birthday." He sat the plate down on the desk beside me, perching on the edge of my wooden trunk at the foot of the bed.

I swiveled the chair in his direction. "Have I told you that you're the sweetest, most wonderful boyfriend a girl could ever hope for?"

"Not lately." He grinned. "Do me a favor though and don't go spreading that around. I have a reputation to uphold." I snorted and rolled my eyes. He might 'look' like a bad-boy, but his heart was anything but. "So," he said, "any luck tracking down our necromancer?"

I sighed, blowing out a breath that ruffled the hair across my forehead. "I keep searching for Emery Green but there are hundreds in the database. Artemis said she was new and young, so I've narrowed down my search to girls between the ages of ten and thirty."

"And you've searched the North Carolina coastline?"

I nodded. "What if she doesn't have social media?"

"We'll find her." Wren sounded more confident than I felt. He stood up from the trunk and bent forward to kiss me. "Happy birthday, Quinn. Make a wish."

The corners of my mouth lifted as I drew a breath, staring at the flickering candle flame. I made the only wish I could think of: *Please, help me find Emery.* I blew out the candle, and Wren lightly traced the slope of my cheekbone before glancing up at my window.

"Your dad's home."

"Mm, late date night with Josephine," I commented. "I'll have to get after him for breaking curfew."

Wren chuckled. "I better go offer him a cupcake before you ream him. I'll be right back." Wren winked and headed for the stairs.

A sigh left my lips as I turned back towards the computer, fingertips hovering over the keys. Artemis had told us the girl lived not far from where we had been on the coastline... I'd tried searching the major cities through the coast and came up with a whole lot of dead ends. But there was a smaller town–somewhere on the coast that my mom had once mentioned to me a long time ago. She'd known a couple of witches that lived there. I chewed on the corner of my lip as I typed Emery's name back into the search bar, and next to it: Casper North Carolina. I hit enter.

A news article caught my attention. *Local area teen dies after sailboat capsized in a pop-up coastal storm.* I clicked on the link, scanning through the article and read the names of the teenagers involved in the accident. My breath caught in my lungs when I saw her name—typed in bold font. She'd survived along with three others, losing the life of one of her friends.

I pressed the heel of my hand into my chest as I read the article more thoroughly, eyes glued to the screen. I didn't even hear Wren enter my room and jumped when he laid his hand on my shoulder.

"Take it easy," Wren said, peering over my shoulder.

"Wren," I breathed, "I think I found her."

About the Author

Brittany Elise is from a small town in rural Ohio and resides there today. She graduated college with a degree in photography, and later became a canine obedience instructor. During the day, Brittany manages an FBO at a local hometown airport and services aircraft. Writing has always been her greatest passion. She enjoys the outdoors and exploring new places in an endless quest to keep that artistic inspiration burning.

Note from the Author

Word-of-mouth is crucial for any author to succeed. If you enjoyed *The Calling of the Trinity* please leave a review online—anywhere you are able. Even if it's just a sentence or two. It would make all the difference and would be very much appreciated.

Thanks!
Brittany

Thank you so much for reading one of **Brittany Elise's** novels.
If you enjoyed our book, please check out the beginning of the series
for your next great read!

Awakening the Trinity by Brittany Jones

Silver Mountain is more than just a small rustic town tucked within the evergreen
pine forest. It's a supernatural hotspot–a nexus of raw energy hidden within the forest.
In the seventeenth-century, an all-powerful witch called Rionach the Dark ruled the
Celtic nations with an army of enslaved werewolves. In order to restore balance
between Light and Dark, the Trinity of Light was summoned to vanquish the Dark
Witch and end the Battle of the Dark Ages. Seventeen-year-old Quinn Callaghan lives
in the small, rustic town of Silver Mountain. Its location may be rural, but it is home
to an ancient pine forest that surrounds a supernatural hotspot–a nexus of raw and
powerful energy. When a charismatic witch from Ireland, and a mysterious guy with a
secret of his own are drawn to the area, Quinn finds out that she inherited her rare
abilities from a revered ancestor. Could it be that she shares a bloodline with the
Original Trinity? Nearly 300 years later, the Darkness is returning to Silver Mountain,
and the Trinity must stop it.